...author

"Ridgway's w— ...ose Control

"This sexy page-turner [is] a ... Ridgway's latest humor-drenched series."
—*Library Journal* on *Take My Breath Away*

"Emotional and powerful...everything a romance reader could hope for."
—*Publishers Weekly* (starred review) on *Bungalow Nights*

"Kick off your shoes and escape to endless summer. This is romance at its best."
—Emily March, *New York Times* bestselling author of *Nightingale Way*, on *Bungalow Nights*

"Sexy and addictive—Ridgway will keep you up all night!"
—*New York Times* bestselling author Susan Andersen on *Beach House No. 9*

"A great work of smart, escapist reading."
—*Booklist* on *Beach House No. 9*

"Sexy, sassy, funny, and cool, this effervescent sizzler nicely launches Ridgway's new series and is a perfect pick-me-up for a summer's day."
—*Library Journal* on *Crush on You*

"Pure romance, delightfully warm and funny."
—*New York Times* bestselling author Jennifer Crusie

"Christie Ridgway writes with the perfect combination of humor and heart. This funny, sexy story is as fresh and breezy as its Southern California setting. An irresistible read!"
—*New York Times* bestselling author Susan Wiggs on *How to Knit a Wild Bikini*

CHRISTIE RIDGWAY

can't fight this feeling

HQN™

HQN™

ISBN-13: 978-0-373-78003-7

Can't Fight This Feeling

In memory of my mother, who fostered my love
of books, fashion and family.
I love you forever, Mom.

Dear Reader,

Welcome back to Blue Arrow Lake, where the mountains stand guard over pine trees, deep lakes and the hardy souls who live there year-round. Brett Walker, the oldest of the Walker clan, works hard in his landscaping business and to keep his heart safe after more than one emotional upheaval. But there's a woman who threatens his equilibrium, and he's not sure how to fight off the temptation of her.

Angelica Rodriguez led a privileged life…but now it's shattered. She's looking to build something new for herself and is deeply attached to this beautiful mountain enclave. But it includes Brett Walker, who she's crushed on for months…and who seemed to disapprove of her on sight. Circumstances force them together, though, and she begins to hope that she can soften this granite man.

Trusting another person with your secrets and your happiness is never easy, as these two find. There are rewards to the risk and both Brett and Angelica have so much to offer each other. He needs her sunny smiles; she needs his unwavering strength. As always, it's a pleasure to tell the story of a couple finding each other and finding a way to get past their fears. Ready for me to take you on a sexy, emotional ride? Come on board, relax and let the events unfold. Destination…romance!

Christie

Autumn carries more gold in its pocket than all the other seasons.

—Jim Bishop

CHAPTER ONE

WHEN BRETT WALKER caught sight of the flashing lights in his rearview mirror, his heart gave a quick jolt and he wondered why he was being pulled over. His DMV tags were for the correct year. He was up-to-date on his bills. The license for his landscaping business was current, too. As he pulled to the side of one of the narrow lanes in the wealthy enclave of Blue Arrow Lake in the Southern California mountains, he thought perhaps one of his three younger sisters might have called the sheriff's department to execute a welfare check. Poppy was the most likely choice. But Shay might have done it, too.

It wasn't that he was avoiding his two youngest sisters exactly, but they were so damn starry-eyed over the men in their lives. While all four Walker siblings were pretty hardheaded, only his other sister, Mackenzie—Mac—had the same hard soul as he. All the smiles and sighs and grins and kisses a person had to witness when hanging around Poppy and Ryan and Shay and Jace rubbed said soul raw.

So he'd been pacing himself on the Walker fests.

Brett unrolled his window as a man wearing a tan uniform strolled up to the driver's side. Placing both hands on the wheel—this wasn't his first rodeo—he glanced up. "Don." Even a law-abiding citizen felt a spurt of relief at recognizing a longtime friend. "What is it, a broken taillight?"

"Naw, nothing like that." He hitched up the belt bristling with equipment. "I saw you go by and thought I'd take the opportunity to have a little chat."

Brett remembered another "chat" he'd been forced to have with a law enforcement officer. His gut curdled at the memory. The result had been a two-day stay in the lockup. "You're making me anxious here, Don," he said. "I'm shaking in my boots."

The other man snorted. "You're wearing your usual granite face. How's the family?"

He meant Brett's sisters, since his mother and father had been gone for years. "Poppy and Shay are both engaged now."

"I heard that. Flatlanders?"

It was what the mountain people called those who came from "down the hill" to visit their peaks and pines at 5,000 feet and beyond. Those who usually resided by the beaches and in the cities of SoCal could hardly believe it when they climbed into their cars and took a two-hour drive to discover a place with four actual, authentic seasons. Lakes for summer play. Snow for winter games. The spring and fall were quieter, but no less beautiful to residents like the Walkers who lived here full-time and had done so for one hundred fifty years.

The full-timers had to share with those flatlanders, though. The resort mountain communities of the area had palatial homes near ski runs and expansive mansions on the banks of private lakes. Wealthy people came up on weekends to their alpine retreats, which gave rise to businesses that provided for the visitors' needs and tastes:

gourmet grocers and house-cleaning services, organic restaurants and landscape-maintenance companies.

"Yep, flatlanders," Brett told the other man.

"Rich?"

Brett shrugged. "Eye of the beholder, right?" Money didn't impress the Walkers. The opposite, really, and he'd been inclined to dislike Ryan and Jace on that principle alone. But the men his sisters had chosen had proved themselves, which hadn't always been the case.

Shay had been the product of a brief affair between their mother and a wealthy visitor when his parents' marriage had hit a rough patch and his father had temporarily decamped to South America. But Dell Walker had ultimately returned and treated Shay as his own for the rest of his life—her bio dad had never shown his face again.

Poppy had become a single mom when her son's rich-but-shallow father had run back to Beverly Hills.

Brett had been screwed in his own way by the mon-eyed. He'd earned the chip on his shoulder.

"Business good?" Don asked now.

"Sure." This time of year, he was still mowing and trimming, but soon enough he'd be planting bulbs for spring and protecting flower beds and shrubbery from the coming harsher weather. "We'll see what happens in winter." Then he switched to snow removal. If there wasn't any white stuff to shovel or plow, he'd be in for a dry spell.

"But you're still out and about the area every day, right?"

Brett's eyes narrowed. Don wasn't just shooting the breeze. "Yeah…" He drew out the word, uneasy again.

Don cleared his throat. "I don't like to sound an alarm…"

Except that's exactly what he was doing. "Spit it out."

"Looks like we have a string of burglaries," he said, frowning.

"Here?" Brett glanced around. This particular community was gated, and besides the patrolling sheriffs, residents could let a security service know their schedule and request daily checks.

"Here, there, across the lake, on the mountain ridge. There isn't a real pattern we've detected, other than break-ins and missing valuables. You and I both know there are ways to get to these homes that bypass the gates and kiosks."

"Yeah." Brett ran a hand over his short hair. Thieves could come by boat or zip around on dirt bikes and avoid the paved roads. "We had trouble with kids in our cabins during the summer."

"I thought of that," Don said. "Any trouble since?"

"No. I'm living out there now." Four miles off the mountain highway was a tract of Walker land that had once been a successful, though small, ski resort. After a wildfire came through and destroyed nearly everything, it had been left to nature. Then, last spring, Poppy had decided she wanted to refurbish the dozen cabins that remained standing. Despite the initial objections from the rest of the siblings, they were making progress. Slow progress, but progress all the same. "We think the fire in one of the bungalows was set by local kids. This seem the same? Locals?"

"They'd know how not to get caught."

Unless they were naive enough to let themselves be used, Brett thought. But he shook it off because he wasn't eighteen any longer and at the mercy of a lying little rich girl and her daddy who thought his spoiled darling could do no wrong.

"Keep your eyes open, will you, Brett?" Don said. "Since you're cruising around all day, you might catch sight of something or someone that will help us crack this."

"Will do."

With a wave, Don returned to his car and Brett continued on with his day. But uneasiness continued to dog him. If people suspected area kids were the culprits, it wasn't a large leap to any local being blamed. If the owners of the vacation homes began distrusting the help they hired, it could impact the bottom line of people like Brett with his landscaping business. His sister Mac, too, who operated a cleaning service.

This wasn't good.

His schedule full, Brett's day didn't finish until he was nearly out of daylight. Muscles aching, he pushed the lawn mower up the ramp into his truck's bed. Then he settled into the driver's seat and grabbed some water, practically hosing it down his parched throat. He'd brooded over the burglaries while he worked at a handful of properties. The usual mowing and clipping, but he'd also raked up mountains of fallen leaves. The pinecones had seemed to have it in for him. Two of the prickly buggers had fallen directly on his head.

He wanted a cold beer, a long shower and a hot meal.

Since he'd have to make yet another stop to purchase two out of the three, his lousy mood was only amplified as he started off in the direction of the highway.

It was quiet in the neighborhood. Nothing unusual for a midweek autumn day. But, remembering Don's words, he paid more attention than he normally would. That's why he slowed and gave a piercing once-over of the Rodriguez place.

"Liar," he muttered to himself.

The piercing once-over was all about the damn woman he wanted to *be* all over—Angelica Rodriguez.

He sighed. She was so exactly not the type for him. She'd spent the summer at the house that now looked empty of life. Her mother was an infamous supermodel, now divorced from Angelica's father, a hedge-fund manager with a Midas touch. Brett didn't think the young woman did anything but dream up ways to torture him. When he arrived to work on the grounds, she'd come outside wearing radiant smiles and little sundresses.

She was evil like that.

Not to mention how she tempted him in other ways. Freshly made lemonade. Oatmeal and raisin cookies— his favorite. He didn't know how she'd discovered that fact, but he wouldn't put it past her to use Daddy's money to purchase a background check of him.

All summer he'd been completely, uncomfortably, maddeningly aware she'd had an itch to go slumming. With him.

But looking at the huge villa-style house on the lake, dark except for a couple of dim security lights mounted on the outside, he guessed she'd gone home…or at least to some other Rodriguez-owned domicile. In Bel-Air, maybe. Malibu. For all he knew, Paris.

Thank God. He'd been losing his will to hold out against her. Would any man blame him? She had liquid brown eyes, a wealth of silky, espresso-dark hair, a body…

Don't think about her body.

She'd once told him she'd modeled for a time in childhood to early teens, until she'd gotten too "fat." Translation: long legs, beautiful features.

And breasts.

Bountiful, distracting, unforgettable breasts.

Brett closed his eyes, and he could still see them, damn it. Beneath a tank top. Under a loose-fitting shift. Once he'd seen her in a bikini.

That day, he'd been afraid he'd lose his eyesight. Because not only had he garnered a glance at her front, but she'd turned around and he'd spied her luscious butt in bathing-suit bottoms.

Yeah, that kind of "fat."

It should be against the law.

Blowing out a breath, he opened his eyes to take a final look at the place before moving on. He could see it clearly enough through the iron bars of the wide double gate. Now that she was gone, he was going to forget all about her.

A tiny light moved behind a window.

Brett rubbed his eyes with his thumb and forefinger. Was he seeing things? Blinking hard, he surveyed the place once more. The light was gone—

No, there it winked on again.

A prickly sensation skittered down his spine.

Putting his truck in Reverse, he slowly backed up the street and parked twenty-five yards away. There was more iron fencing at the sides of the property and it didn't prevent him from seeing that light moving again, a firefly behind the glass and the briefest outline of a familiar figure. The hair on the back of his neck rose. All his nerve endings were awake now, and the weariness from the day's endeavors were replaced with something else—curiosity, anticipation, maybe some dangerous combination of the two.

Trying to be as quiet as possible, he climbed out of the truck.

He didn't bother pulling out his cell phone. This wasn't a police matter. It was something else—the someone skulking about the inside of that mammoth house was none other than its mistress.

Don't think of the word mistress.

His instincts were certain it was her because, since first seeing her, his body reacted in just this way when she was anywhere in his proximity. His skin would twitch, his scalp would tingle and he'd turn around and Angelica Rodriguez would be there in one of her witchy outfits—jeans, a pair of hiking shorts, a voluminous beach cover-up, it didn't matter what she wore—and he'd have to steel his spine to be as hard as that other part of him was becoming.

No, I don't want lemonade. Or a cookie. Or to spend endless nights in bed with you.

"Liar," he muttered again. He'd wanted it all.

But she was doing something shady, he could feel that, too, and so he made his way around the side of the house; his aim, that moving light. There was no fencing between the house and its lake access and soon he was prowling toward that window.

Then he was right outside it. In the minuscule glow of the penlight she had in her hand, he could make out parts of her as she moved about the den. The dark pools of her eyes. The elegant line of her small nose. The dip above her bowed upper lip. Without a hesitation, he rapped on the glass.

Jumping, she shrieked. He could see the sharp sound

of surprise on her startled face, which jerked his way, feel the vibration of it in his fingers, which were pressed flat on the pane.

She trained the light on him. He smiled at her. Toothily, he supposed, because she came toward the window at a wary pace until there was only a couple of inches between them.

And yet they were still worlds apart.

"Hey, baby," he said. "Why don't you let me in?"

ANGELICA RODRIGUEZ STARED through the glass into the early evening darkness and cursed fate.

She'd been doing a lot of that lately, as the very foundation of her life had cracked and then fallen away in the past few days. Some cheery—and at times annoying—inner voice kept reminding her to see this situation as an opportunity, but it sure didn't feel that way when the man who had disliked her at first sight was now staring her down.

The man who, from first sight, she'd liked entirely too much.

"Let me in," he said again.

Um, no. It didn't seem wise to be too close to him when all her defenses were in this rocky state. So she smiled and waved both hands in a gesture that was supposed to communicate that she didn't need him around or that she couldn't exactly hear him or perhaps she was just too busy for a chat…anything that would get him moving along so she could sneak out of the house where she wasn't supposed to be in the first place.

She turned away from the window to scoop up the papers she'd left on the desk and he rapped again.

Like a demand.

Holding on to her cool, she glanced over her shoulder. There he was, thirtyish, muscled and a bit threatening-looking, even though in the darkness she could only see his bulk and not those very fascinating scars on his face. One slashed through his brow to his hairline. Another crossed the bridge of his nose.

Angelica had never found the courage to ask him about them.

He jerked his thumb in the direction of the back door that led to the lake-view terrace. "Open up."

The sounds of the words were not hampered by the glass, but she sure as heck wasn't going to obey! Past June she would have opened up to him. She'd wanted to, and she'd been rebuffed enough times that it embarrassed her to count them. It had been amazing to her, how drawn she'd been to him then. For a woman who had a lousy history with the opposite sex—lousy enough that she was relatively inexperienced when it came to them—she was surprised to find Brett Walker brought out a different side of her.

The idea of kissing him had consumed her instead of making her cringe. The sensation of his arms around her was something she'd wanted, not wanted to run away from.

Now she didn't have time for fantasy. She had a real life she needed to build for herself.

His mouth moved again, four syllables that she thought he might never have said aloud before. "Angelica—"

Twisting away from the sound, from him, she moved forward at the same time…and tripped over a trash can beside the desk. That sick sense of falling lasted only milliseconds. Then her palms slammed to the hardwood, preserving her nose from a flattening. The penlight she'd held rolled away, dashing light on the floor and base-boards.

Adrenaline was still shooting through her system when she heard him knocking on the window again. Ignoring it, she got to her knees and breathed, trying to slow her heartbeat. She shook out her hands.

Cursed fate. Her own clumsiness.

The knobs on the back door rattled. She glanced through the den's open doorway, past the kitchen to the terrace. He was standing out there now, looking even bigger than before. More menacing. Impatient.

His fist pounded on the glass and it sounded so loud she worried the noise of it might carry across the lake and alert the sheriff's department or the private security force. On a sigh, she clambered to her feet and approached the French doors.

She turned the lock and inched one open, prepared to tell him to go away.

He pushed, forcing himself inside.

In retreat, her feet tripped again, and she thought she might go down once more. Brett Walker grabbed her by the elbow to steady her. "Are you all right?"

She wrenched her arm away. "I'm fine." Deciding offense was the best defense, she scowled at him. "What are you doing here?"

"I saw your flashlight moving around and decided to investigate. Power out?"

"No—" she started, but it was too late. He'd flipped on the closest switch. She squinted as the overhead lighting blazed on. "Please turn that off. The glare gives me a headache," she lied.

He instantly turned it off, surprising her. "Sorry," he

said, his voice going softer. "Do you get migraines? My mother did. I know it's hell."

Guilt stabbed. "Um…well." She couldn't think of what else to say as her brain became occupied with the notion that handsome, sexy, manly man Brett Walker had a *mother*. It seemed as if he should have been carved from a giant redwood. Hewn from a granite mountain outcropping. Fallen from the sky like a meteor to dazzle humanity.

Of course, she'd met his sister Shay—beautiful—but to think of Brett with a parent meant he'd once been a boy. It boggled the mind.

Her eyes had grown accustomed to the dimness again and she saw one corner of his full mouth hitch in a sort-of semblance of a smile. "Cat got your tongue?"

"I'm having a hard time picturing you as someone's little kid."

"I was a typical one. Too loud, hated taking baths, relished teasing my younger sisters."

It was the most conversation he'd ever had with her. She resisted the urge to hold the words close to her chest. The time for being thrilled over a tête-à-tête with Brett Walker was gone. More important matters should be occupying her mind.

The next thing she knew, he had hold of one of her forearms. "What?" she said, instinct causing her to try tugging free.

His clasp was gentle but firm. "Checking for damage. You went down hard. Not uncommon to sprain a finger that way. Break your wrist."

He was running a warm, callous hand over her, from fingertips to wrist in a calming gesture. Inside she was quivering. On the outside, she kept still as he moved each finger individually, then rotated her wrist. "Hurt anywhere?"

She shook her head. He let that arm go, only to take up the other one. His thumb stroked the tender inside of her wrist, where the veins seemed to be scrambling like every clear thought in her head. She was pure sensation: hot skin, thrumming pulse, a heartbeat loud in her ears.

The edge of his thumb traced the outside of hers, then probed the triangle of flesh between it and her forefinger. "Tender?"

She shook her head. That was him, his ministrations so gentle they made her ache.

"Sensitive?"

This time she nodded, because his touch made her so aware of the difference between the two of them. He was hard male; she was soft female. He could be the port she needed in the current storm that was her life. One move would put her against him, and she could cling to all that muscled strength. Lean on him to hold her up.

But men had only disappointed her before, and remembering that, she snapped back to reality and stepped away.

Brett's eyes narrowed, which reminded her again that he didn't even like her. "You could have a snuff-box injury—scaphoid fracture—if you're in pain there."

"I'm fine," she said again. "Really."

He studied her face. "What's going on?"

My father has been arrested for fraud. Our family properties have been confiscated and all his accounts have been frozen. Before being taken into custody, my dad siphoned off all my personal monies saved from my time modeling and from my trust, and he put them who knows where or used them for who knows what. I have

*no place to live, no money to live on, and I broke into
my former home so I could collect some things beyond
the clothes on my back.*

"My father's putting this place up for sale," she said,
lying again.

Brett's gaze ran around the gourmet kitchen, where
copper pans hung from a rack and spices were lined up
on a shelf. He looked at the couches and chairs in the
adjacent family room. "With all this stuff inside?"

"Uh-huh. Will add to the value as a very famous interior designer picked out everything from the paint colors to the window coverings to the custom furnishings."

His mouth curled. "I just bet."

It wasn't as if she'd expected him to be impressed.
"Anyway, there was a mix-up and I didn't get a chance
to pack my suitcases or retrieve my passport from the
safe in the den."

"That *is* a headache," he said, though she wasn't sure
he accepted that as a logical explanation for why she was
skulking around.

She smiled anyway. "So…I'm just going to make a
quick trip upstairs and dump a few things in a bag. The
rest I'll get another day." Without taking her eyes off
him, she moved backward, heading in the direction of
the stairs. "See you around."

He prowled toward her. "I'll go with you."

"No!" She swallowed, modulating her voice. "No, no.
You don't need to do that." While months ago she might
have swooned at the idea of having him in her bedroom,
now wasn't the time to have him in there, distracting her.

"I've seen women's underwear before," he said.

Of course he had. "Not *my* underwear." Curses! That
had come out a little…throaty. Flirtatious even.

One of his brows winged up. "I'll close my eyes when you go through that particular drawer."

She'd reached the bottom of the staircase and put one hand on the newel. "This is completely unnecessary—"

"It's completely necessary. There have been burglaries in the area. I don't feel right leaving you here alone."

"You didn't worry about me being alone all summer," she retorted, then felt her cheeks go hot. That sounded like a complaint from a silly woman with an even sillier crush. "Never mind," she muttered, and turned to stomp up the stairs. Arguing would only prolong this whole embarrassing encounter.

Still trying to do her business without attracting the attention of anyone who knew she shouldn't be in the house, she only allowed herself to turn on the closet light. If Brett wondered about that and why she pulled the curtains across her windows first, he didn't say a word. Instead, he just stood in the middle of her rug, hands in his pockets, while she hurriedly packed two suitcases and gathered up her toiletries from the bathroom and put them in a smaller bag.

The only noise he made was when she tried to stack all three pieces of luggage in preparation for wheeling them out the door. "You can't take them down the stairs that way," he said. One went under his arm, the other he gripped in his right hand, the third he took up in his left. "This all?"

"Yes." She gritted her teeth and tried sounding gracious. "Thanks." For months she'd wanted a bit of his attention and now it was coming at the lowest point of her life when she couldn't even enjoy it.

Maybe because *he* didn't seem to be enjoying it.
Great.

They made it outside and she locked up after setting the alarm. The key went into her pocket instead of its hiding place behind the mailbox. She'd return it later.

Brett didn't comment as he followed her to her car, which she'd parked down the road. If he asked why she'd avoided the driveway…

She hadn't a clue. Trying to think up some excuse only gave her the beginnings of that headache she'd laid claim to earlier.

He must have seen it. Because after placing her things in the trunk of her car, he studied her face with a new intensity. "Cool compress on your forehead. Pain relievers," he said. "Rest."

"Yeah."

"You have someone to take care of you?"

No. I realize now I never have. "Sure."

"Okay." Still, he hesitated. "You're certain everything's okay? There's nothing I should know about?"

He'd never wanted to know anything about her. "Yes."

"Good." He touched one fingertip to her cheek. "Because if I find out differently, there'll be hell to pay."

CHAPTER TWO

At Blue Arrow Lake's Hallett Hardware, Angelica stood at the rear, stocking lightbulbs, her tension unwinding with every minute she arranged the cardboard boxes on the shelves. Working at her part-time job was one of the few things that made her feel at peace these days. She'd taken the job before the financial disaster as a lark to help out her friend Glory Hallett when the other woman had lost an employee.

There was something soothing about unpacking cartons. The task was defined. It had purpose. A customer would come in, needing a 40-watt candelabra bulb, and she'd know exactly where to direct them. Better, she could convince them that the more expensive energy-efficient halogen bulb would be the best choice. Yes, more expensive in the short-term, but in the long run a smarter selection for both economic and environmental reasons.

She supposed some people would laugh themselves sick at the idea of Angelica Rodriguez—she of fancy boarding schools and an expensive women's college—enjoying work at a hardware store, but it was the first time she'd ever actually earned a paycheck.

Well, there was the modeling she'd done as a youngster, which had paid ridiculously well, but those gigs had been arranged by her mother, and she'd been so self-conscious as she grew older that when she turned twelve the photographer's assistant had started giving her mojitos before a shoot. The hangovers had been hell, so she'd started packing on the pounds until she'd lost her shot at a modeling career.

Turned out she never grew tall enough anyway.

The smell of rum and doughnuts still made her nauseous, though.

"What's that face for?"

Angelica swung around to see Glory coming down the aisle.

"What did that indoor floodlight ever do to you?"

Angelica smiled at her friend. They were opposites in practically everything. While she was tallish—though not tall enough for worldwide fame and European runways—Glory was petite. Angelica's long, brunette hair and dark eyes were nothing like Glory's short blond feathers and big blues. Until now, Angelica had led a fairly useless life, while Glory had been working at the family hardware store since she was old enough to push a broom and weigh a brown paper bag of nails. They'd struck up a conversation when she'd come browsing at the store one rainy spring weekend and just…clicked. Upon her return for her summer stay, she'd revisited the store and over one coffee and then a lunch, a friendship had fully formed. "The bulb is innocent. I was just mulling over my life."

Glory frowned. "What's happened now?"

"Nothing new."

"Did you get your clothes?"

Angelica nodded. "Last night." She decided against mentioning her run-in with Brett Walker. Glory didn't know about that silly crush she'd suffered, and there was no reason to tell her now. Away from the house where he landscaped on a weekly basis—she had no idea whether the authorities would have him continue the service—she'd likely never see him again.

Because if I find out differently, there'll be hell to pay.

It had been a macho-man parting shot, that's all. He wouldn't care enough to find out any more about her or her situation. His complete disinterest all summer had made that abundantly clear.

"I wish you'd come live with me," Glory said.

"No, no. You have that adorable one-bedroom cottage that is perfect for you…but not you *and* me. I've got that room at the Bluebird. They have reasonable weekly rental rates."

If you had more money coming in.

She didn't say that, but perhaps Glory could read minds. "I wish I could offer you more hours," she said.

"Please." Angelica touched her friend's arm. "I'm grateful for what I have. I'm here in the mountains, far from the limelight of the financial press."

"They'll be looking for you, you think?"

"Probably. Yes. I was warned about it by the lawyers, anyway." There was precedent for the families of fraudsters being hounded. *Daddy, how could you?* she thought now. Reporters—and those he'd swindled—would want to know the answer to that question, too, and she didn't have one. At his insistence, after college she'd gone back to their home in LA, where she'd been a hostess for his business soirees for a couple of years. But as time went on, he'd become increasingly reclusive.

He'd never shared the why of that or the what for. The man had never made it a secret that he'd wanted a boy and that her gender was a great disappointment to him.

Though she'd excused it as a cultural and generational thing, they'd never been close.

He'd been her dad, though. And she'd been dutiful, always seeking his approval, she saw now, instead of her own brand of happiness.

Glory picked out another package from the carton and stared down at it. "No word from your mom, either?"

"Not one. Likely traveling around Europe or Asia with Hubby Number Four." Angelica watched her friend frown, knowing that she'd find this baffling, too. While Glory was an only child like Angelica, her parents were still married to each other and lived in relative contentment in their beloved mountains.

Which were becoming beloved to Angelica, as well. "I'm happy to be here," she told Glory again. "It's going to be okay for me." As soon as she managed to build a new life.

"I—" But what her friend was about to say was interrupted by the sound of the bell on the door. "We'll talk later," she said, and headed toward the front of the store.

Angelica hoped not. Hashing and rehashing the particulars of her sucky current situation would only pierce the bubble of peace she'd found in Hallett's. During her shift, she wanted the most difficult thing she tackled to be the box of misplaced goods that required reshelving.

In the distance, she heard Glory greeting the customer. "Good morning," she said, in her friendly, I-know-you voice. "How's it going, Brett?"

Angelica froze. Brett? Brett *Walker*? The deep-voiced response told her that it was indeed him. Why? Shouldn't he be somewhere with his truck, working? She took a peek at the slice of front window she could see, and the sun was still shining. Perfect weather for him to be out on the job, away from here. Away from her.

Because, darn it, she couldn't seem to keep her feet rooted to the floor. Instead, they were creeping closer to him, her traitorous eyes wanting to get a glimpse of him. Shielding herself behind a rotating display of work gloves, she peered through the leather-and-fabric fingers.

Did he have to be so ruggedly good-looking? In the height of summer, he'd worn long shorts and work boots. A T-shirt that he'd often take off as he pushed the mower, allowing her to see the muscles in his back flexing. His arms were roped with muscle and more than once she'd stood at a window, hidden behind a curtain kind of like how she was hiding now, just to watch his pumped biceps and flexing forearms.

Those were covered now. Today a plaid shirt was buttoned over his torso and a worn pair of jeans encased his long legs. Hugged his most excellent butt. He ran a hand over his hair as he talked to Glory, a gesture she'd seen him make a dozen times. It always made her curious, that habitual movement, because his hair was shorn short enough that it never appeared disordered. The stuff was brown, but tipped in gold, highlights that a woman would pay a mint for in a salon, but that only needed his constant exposure to the sun.

Then there were those intriguing scars that only served to make him more sexy. More male.

Still ogling, Angelica tuned into what Glory was now saying. "That's right. I know those clippers are in from the sharpener's. They're in the back room somewhere. Hold on a second and I'll find them."

Angelica had to bite her lip to stop from volunteering for the task. Not only could she put her hands on them immediately—she'd designated a space in the storeroom for items delivered from the man who did the work— but Glory was hopeless when let loose in that area. She moved perfectly ordered items around, reshuffled organized paperwork and generally made a mess.

As Brett waited, the bell sounded again, signifying another customer.

Argh! Usually, with Glory occupied elsewhere, she'd be hurrying forward to help the person. But that would give her away to Brett, and she really wasn't up to a second confrontation with him in two days.

She was too busy to deal with her ridiculous response to him.

He murmured something, greeting the newcomer, she supposed. A local, she guessed, since the hardware store was hardly the midweek hot spot for the town's wealthy visitors. Drumming her fingers on the skirt of the sturdy, butcher-style apron she wore over her clothes, she wondered how long she could let the latest customer go without service.

Already, her conscience was pinching at her. Then it got worse. "Where's Angel?" an elderly man enquired.

"Angel?" Brett repeated. "You mean Glory?"

He'd make that assumption, Angelica thought, because he didn't know the name that Mr. Bowman used for her. *C'mon, Glory.* She sent out vibes toward the back room. *Get out here with Brett's tool!*

With him safely on his way, she could help the customer asking for her.

"No," Mr. Bowman said. "Angel. That dark-haired girl who works here. She's my color muse."

The dear, Angelica thought. One of her favorite parts of the job was keeping the display of paint chips organized. She loved playing with the colors and imagining them on walls, on furniture, covering the trim outside a house. Mr. Bowman had found her there one day and she'd helped him pick choices to freshen the interior of his home.

"Bob…" Brett cleared his throat. "I really don't think there's any Angel—"

"Of course there is. This is one of the days she works." His voice rose. "Angel? Angel!"

The jig's up, girl, she told herself, squaring her shoulders. "I'm here, Mr. Bowman. Do you want to meet in the paint section?"

"Certainly," the old man called back.

Angelica let out a breath. Maybe, while she was busy with Mr. Bowman, Brett would collect his tool and carry on his day. They'd never have to come face-to-face.

She gave all her attention to the older gentleman, who loved the shade they'd picked for his office and now wanted something to brighten the kitchen. They picked several tagboard swatches that he would bring home for his wife's ultimate approval. Before he went on his way, she kissed his cheek and he beamed at her. Then he wandered toward the front door.

Angelica, breathing easy, turned in the direction of the lightbulb shelves. Her face almost mashed into Brett's plaid shirt as he came around a corner. She skittered back.

His gaze ran over her, from her jeans and low-heeled boots, to the apron covering her long-sleeved tee. She'd written her name in block letters on the beige twill in blue permanent marker. It was situated in the vicinity of her collarbone, so there was no reason for her brea to respond as if he was staring at them. She crossed her arms over her chest.

"You actually work here."

"I'm helping out."

"That's your name on the apron, *Angel*. Some of it, anyway."

"Angelica wouldn't fit."

"Huh." He was still staring at her. "I guess I now have a new appreciation of having a short name."

"Even better for you, two of the five letters in yours are the same."

His brows rose. "Yeah. Made it so even a mountain yokel like me could learn to write it."

She glared at him. "I didn't say that."

"No, you didn't." There was a speculative light in his gray eyes. Against his tanned face, they looked almost like clear water. "What are you doing working here, Angelica?"

"I don't know what you mean." She loved the store and the hours she spent here gave her more job satisfaction, she suspected, than any career in high finance ever could.

"It's not your kind of place." He glanced around, his gaze roaming over the bins of nails and the spools of chain in various gauges. "A woman like you…"

The word *spoiled* went unspoken. So did *good-for-nothing*. One time she'd overheard him talking to his sister, and he'd referred to Angelica as a useless piece of fluff. Out loud.

She should despise him.

"Don't you know…" she started sweetly. "Oh, but you wouldn't, so let me explain. Some of us, you know, we *elite*, we have a program."

"Oh, yeah?" His eyes narrowed and now he crossed his arms over his chest. "What kind of program?"

"Kind of like…like scouting."

He barked out a laugh. "Yeah, how's that work exactly?"

"We earn badges for doing things the common folk do."

"Badges." He sneered the word. And though of course he couldn't possibly believe her, she continued in a haughty tone.

"Yes. Badges. For learning to boil water. Or helping out an elderly man. Or earning a paycheck for an honest day's work."

And with that she swept off. It wasn't a flounce. Only a rich, spoiled girl would do that, and the woman who was now Angelica Rodriguez was so far from that, it wasn't even funny.

THE PROPRIETORS OF THE Bluebird Motel had decided to close for the season early. The small rooms weren't properly winterized, so it had always been open for the fair-weather seasons only. Despite that, Angelica had thought she might have a few more weeks in room 4. Now they told her she could have her spot with the reasonable rates for just a few more days. The owners wanted to get to their second home in Phoenix as soon as possible.

Which meant Angelica needed a new place to live and another job to pay for it. Other rentals in the mountains were more expensive.

The village of Blue Arrow Lake was composed of fancy boutiques and lovely restaurants, but she'd struck out finding work in any of them. It was an in-between time. Not the summer when people came up to play in the sunshine and not the winter when they came for the snow. Still, as she walked to her car parked on a side street, the buttery color of the fall sunshine was buoying. The air smelled clean with just a touch of nuttiness from the drying leaves and grasses. The cool nip to the air was bracing.

As if to reward her rising mood, she saw a help-wanted sign posted in the window of a small building. Over the door was another that read Maids by Mac.

While she didn't have retail experience and had never worked in a restaurant, she'd gone ahead and asked about jobs anyway. It seemed she might have a better shot at a business that was actually advertising for workers. And perhaps cleaning wasn't something that required a wealth of prior professional experience.

Of course working as a maid might not be a coveted career choice, but Angelica was desperate enough to squelch any hesitation and hurry for the door. The knob turned and it swung soundlessly, allowing her to enter a small office space. Behind a counter was a desk with a computer and phone. A filing cabinet sat in one corner. A half-open closet door revealed shelves neatly stocked with cleaning supplies. No one was in the space, but another door was open at the rear that revealed a tiny court-yard. There she saw the back of a woman as well as a bistro table on which two coffees were set. The woman was talking to someone, but Angelica could only see a pair of long legs in jeans from where she stood.

Unsure whether to call out or just wait to be noticed, Angelica hesitated. The slender woman had hair as dark as her own, though shoulder length. She was dressed in jeans, boots and a thin, slouchy sweater in pale blue.

"You seem more grouchy than usual," the woman was telling the other person in the courtyard. "What's up?"

The human attached to the legs—a man—grunted in reply.

Maybe the woman sensed Angelica then because she suddenly looked around. "Oh!" She had eyes the same icy blue as her sweater. "There's someone here. Just a minute," she called out. Then to the grouchy man, "Don't go anywhere, honey."

And it was a familiar voice that responded. "Not moving. I have to make some calls." Brett Walker's voice.

Brett Walker *here*! Several days had passed since their contact in the hardware store and she wasn't thrilled to run into him again. But Angelica couldn't exactly retreat, now that the woman was coming toward her, wearing a welcoming expression.

Wait, Angelica thought, her stomach starting to jitter. The brunette had called Brett "honey," and he wasn't the kind of man to whom you threw out casual endearments. Could it be…was it possible… Might this woman be Brett's *wife*?

She felt a flush climb up her throat. What if all this time she'd been mooning over a married man? Maybe every night he'd gone home to this pretty woman with her warm smile and arresting eyes and laughed about Angelica's obvious crush.

"Can I help you?"

Her gaze shifted to the woman's left ring finger. No wedding band. She knew Brett didn't wear one either, but if these two worked with their hands it was conceivable they left their rings at home. She should have pumped Glory for information on the landscaper. Oh, why hadn't she pumped Glory?

"Miss?" the woman prompted again, her smile fading to a puzzled expression.

Embarrassment coursed through Angelica once more. She had to think up some excuse! With Brett—unmarried or not—nearby, she didn't want to beg for a job application. It would be mortifying for him to find out she was nearly broke. He didn't have a high opinion of her as it was, so she didn't want to add the term *wastrel* to the list of labels he applied to her.

Her gaze jumped around the room and landed on a plaque hanging on the wall. She gestured toward it. "I'm visiting the local businesses that are part of the Mountain Historical Society," she said, improvising like mad. Though she actually *was* a volunteer for the group, so it wasn't such a stretch, she decided. "I wanted to thank you in person for your past support and give you a report on the overwhelming success of our recent auction."

The woman came closer. "Say it again?"

Angelica realized she'd been almost whispering. Hoping like heck that Brett was preoccupied with his phone calls, she cleared her throat and drifted nearer the counter. "The Mountain Historical Society auction we held at the end of the summer. I was part of the committee that put it on."

"Oh." The other woman blinked. "Are you from around here? I thought I knew just about everyone."

"I'm a relative newcomer." She stuck out her hand—what else could she do? "Angelica Rodriguez."

"Mackenzie Walker." Her grasp was firm. "But everybody calls me Mac."

Mac *Walker.* "Nice to meet you."

"So how'd you get involved with the historical society?" Her assessing gaze took in Angelica's black jeans, black boots and the black-and-white sweater she was wearing that had white chiffon cuffs and a matching chiffon underlay that peeked out below the hemline. "It's not something I'd guess a newcomer would join."

Glancing toward the courtyard, Angelica saw the legs hadn't moved and she could hear Brett murmuring, presumably into his phone. "It was my friend Glory Hallett," she said. "She knew I had some experience putting together fund-raisers and she invited me to serve on the committee with her."

"Now Glory I know," Mac said. "And I remember hearing about the big party that accompanied the auction—at one of the fancy mountain lodges, right? I think my sister and her fiancé attended."

"It was a wonderful event at the Aspen & Oak Lodge. Dinner, dancing and then the silent auction. We had many beautiful and valuable things to offer, thanks to Walter Elliott. When he passed away, he left the historical society the contents of his mountain home."

At the mention of the name, Mac stiffened. "That's right. Walter Elliott," she repeated.

"It was quite the success," Angelica said brightly. "We hope to have an annual fund-raiser from now on. Maybe next summer you and your husband—"

"What are you doing here?" Brett said, strolling into the office. His gaze was trained on Angelica's face. He didn't look pleased to see her.

Mac glanced over at him. "This is An—"

"I know who she is."

The other woman's brows rose. She looked from Brett to Angelica and back again. "You two are acquainted," she said, in a speculative tone.

Angelica felt herself flushing again. "Uh, hardly. Not

even a little bit, really. I've seen him around once or twice."

"Not even a little bit?" Mac repeated.

Maybe the other woman was the jealous type who would scratch her eyes out for merely looking at her husband. If Brett was married to her, Angelica was sure she'd probably find herself very possessive. "I should be going," she said, taking a step back.

"Not so soon," Mac replied, a smile tipping up the corners of her mouth. "We're just getting friendly."

Angelica fanned herself. "Is it a little warm in here or is it just me?"

"I think it's just you," Mac said, with a light in her eyes that Angelica didn't trust. "I'm perfectly comfortable. How about you, Brett?"

He was still staring at Angelica as if she was something he'd brought in on the bottom of his shoe. "I'm always comfortable."

"Well. Um." Angelica wished the floor would open up and swallow her. "I was just popping by to give you that update."

"What update?" he asked.

Mac's expression looked way too innocent. "On the historical society fund-raiser. Angelica had a hand in it. Remember the one that Poppy and Ryan attended about a month ago?"

"I don't listen to half the things she prattles on about," he said.

Mac rolled her eyes in Angelica's direction. "Men! And then they wonder why they have so much trouble with us. If only they'd pay attention every once in a while."

Rather than speaking, Angelica responded with a tentative smile. With that pair of crystalline eyes on her, it was hard to think.

"I rarely have trouble with women," Brett said.

"Because they're often much too accommodating," Mac retorted. She directed her attention back to Angelica. "Are you married? Have a boyfriend?"

"No. I'm, um, on my own right now."

"Isn't that fascinating? Brett's on his own right now, too." She shot the man a look. "Or has that changed?"

When he didn't answer, Angelica gestured between the two on the other side of the counter. "Oh. I thought maybe you two might be married."

Mac let out a loud hoot. "No, thank you. He's my brother."

It wasn't relief or anything like it that sluiced through her, Angelica told herself. Or if it was, it was only because it would have been humiliating to have spent so much time fantasizing about a guy who was already spoken for. "I met your sister once, then. Shay?"

"Sure." Mac glanced over at Brett. "So our brother introduced you?"

"Angelica introduced herself," Brett said. "And if I recall correctly, she thought Shay might be my girlfriend."

"Hmm." Mac tucked her thumbs in the front pockets of her jeans. "You seem very interested in my brother's relationship status," she murmured.

Angelica barely registered the other woman's remark, as the memory of that particular meeting ran through her mind again. "You told her I was a useless piece of fluff," she said to Brett. It had hurt then. It still hurt.

He winced. "You heard that?"

"Never mind," Angelica muttered. "I've got to go." The universe, clearly, had its back still turned to her. "It was nice to meet you," she said, nodding to Mac. Then she headed for the door.

"Wait," Brett began, but she was already out the door.

When it shut behind her, she began jogging, even though the heels of her boots wobbled on the uneven sidewalk. No matter, she needed to put distance between herself and the man who always made her feel awkward and uncertain—not to mention hot and hyperaware of every inch of skin.

"Hey!"

She'd only made it half a block from Mac's business so, pretending she didn't hear Brett's voice, she moved faster.

Then a hard hand closed around her elbow. She skidded to a stop. Rounding on him, she yanked her arm from his hold. "What now?" she demanded, glaring at him through narrowed eyes.

He stepped back, then he smiled.

It was devastating. He'd never smiled at her, but there it was, a slice of white teeth and attractive lines around the corners of his beautiful eyes. How she despised herself for being so susceptible to him. She slammed her hands on her hips. "Well?"

"You're pretty cute when enraged." His smile widened when she made a low, furious sound in her throat and he held up his palms. "You can retract your claws, kitten. I'm not here to steal your catnip."

Still, he stole her breath. And if she wasn't careful, he might steal something else. "What are you following me for?" she demanded.

"To deliver an apology."

"Did your sister put you up to this?"

"No." He shook his head. "It's all my own idea, okay?

That was a lousy thing I said to Shay. I was probably in a crappy mood and just mouthed off."

"*Probably* in a crappy mood?"

"Okay, I'm sure I was in a crappy mood. You seem to bring out the worst in me."

"I am devastated to hear that," she said, her tone sarcastic.

He winced again. "Angelica—"

"Never mind." She pretended to wipe a slate clean. "Apology accepted."

"Thank you." He continued to watch her. "So."

"So." She refused to twitch. Then she couldn't stand the silence a second longer. "Well… Have a nice life."

One of his eyebrows rose, the one with the intriguing scar.

"We'll likely never see each other again," she explained.

"It's a small town," he said, rubbing his palm over his hair in that habitual gesture.

She shrugged. "Just in case, then."

There was a long moment of silence. "Just in case then," he finally agreed. "Be happy."

It would only take a job, some place to live and a way to forget all about him. "I intend to," she said, and hoped that intention was enough to make it so because luck hadn't been on her side lately.

CHAPTER THREE

BRETT RESISTED THE urge to watch Angelica walk off and instead turned to his truck, parked just a few feet away. Apology made, apology accepted and that should be enough to put her from his mind forever.

The breeze picked up as he fumbled with his keys. Autumn was doing its thing in the mountains. Warm sun, cool air, both energizing, and he should be looking forward to a day of vigorous outdoor work. Instead, he felt as if a weight was tugging him down.

We'll likely never see each other again.

It had nothing to do with that.

The door unlocked, he jerked it open. The tall pile of paperwork he'd forgotten he'd set on the driver's seat when he had exited the car began to slide off the cracked vinyl. He lunged for it, just as a rough, rogue gust caught at the sheets and sent them swirling. They flew about in the air, some behind the truck, some above the truck, some somersaulting like tumbleweeds along the asphalt in every direction as the wind blew.

He swore out loud and tried corralling the mass by stomping on the sheets near his feet and trapping others against his body. No way was he going to collect them all, he thought on a groan, snatching another that flew past his head. This was going to be a bookkeeping disaster.

Then, he glimpsed a figure in the periphery of his vision. He turned his head to see Angelica dashing about the scene, gathering up the errant documents. He allowed himself one second—okay, two—to admire her upturned ass when she bent over, then he continued on with his own search and seizure.

Several minutes later, the crisis seemed to have passed. When he turned in a 360, he couldn't see any more fleeing papers. Angelica came toward him, her hair messy and her cheeks flushed, a mass of invoices and handwritten notes clasped against her chest. "I think we might have gotten them all."

His own arms were full. "A good portion, anyway." With his toe, he pushed on the lever that folded the driver's seat forward and then stowed what he held on the narrow rear seat. Turning to Angelica, he said, "Let me take those."

"I've got it." She shuffled forward. "You stand behind me and block the wind while I set them down."

He pivoted and she half turned to sidestep into the narrow space he created between his body and the truck. The wind picked up again, tossing her hair so it slid across his face in a silky caress. It smelled amazing and he instinctively moved closer, blocking the breeze and also blocking her in.

She set down her stack, then moved back, her behind meeting his groin. At the contact, she froze.

He told himself not to bury his face in her hair. He told himself not to slide an arm around her waist and pull her closer.

So he didn't do either of those things.

But he also didn't step away. Which meant that when she spun around, they were face-to-face. Chest to chest. If he bent his head, they'd be mouth to mouth.

They stared at each other and all he could think about was how damn beautiful she was. It was the face of a heartbreaker, with fine-grained, golden-tinted skin and large eyes framed by sooty lashes. The lush mouth was maddening.

Tempting.

She put her hand over his heart, attempting to push him back.

The thrust didn't rock him. He covered her fingers with his, then frowned at how chilled they were. "You're cold."

"A little," she admitted. This time, when she shoved at him, he retreated, though he still had her hand.

"Let me buy you a hot chocolate," he said. Her cool skin, that killer face… It compelled him to offer her warmth. Sweetness.

She hesitated.

Her reluctance twisted something inside him. Did she consider him not good enough for her? He let go her hand. "You can still have a nice life," he muttered. "Just after the damn drink."

Then he ground his back teeth, instantly regretting his harsh tone. Why the hell was he like this around her? She put up his hackles. Made him feel prickly and irritable.

He was never the most genial of fellows, but he was actually considered by some women to be charming. No charm for her, though. No wonder she didn't want to spend another minute around him.

"Never mind," he said, making to climb into the truck. "Sorry."

This time it was she who grabbed his elbow. "I'd like that. The hot chocolate."

He blew out his breath, waiting a long moment to see

if she'd change her mind. When she continued to stand there, he shut the vehicle's door and pointed toward the corner. "Oscar's Coffee."

Inside the small shop were picnic tables painted a soft yellow. Brett directed her to one as he went to retrieve the beverages. He said yes to whipped cream and dark chocolate shavings without asking her.

Her gaze brightened when he put the oversize ceramic mug with its peak of fluffy stuff in front of her. "Yay. You got me the extras."

"I don't believe for a second you're one of those women who denies herself. I've smelled the cookies you bake."

She eyed his beverage, which was exactly the same as hers. "And here I expected you to order a cup of dark and bitter brew for yourself."

"I like my sweets, too."

"But not my cookies."

He refused to squirm on the bench. For months every instinct had warned him against getting "cookies" close. Those instincts were still clamoring at him even now, but she must have entranced him with those warm, melted-chocolate eyes.

Her hands surrounding the cup, she delicately sipped her drink. Then she set it down and licked at the cream on the top of her lip.

He told himself the little action didn't make him hard, but that was a lie. Clearing his throat, he attempted to think of something else. "Fund-raisers, huh?"

She glanced up.

"You told Mac about the one for the historical society."

"Oh. Right." Lifting her cup, she delicately blew on the liquid surface she'd revealed with her last sip.

Her pursed lips didn't do anything to ease his tight muscles. "You learn how to do that in school?" he asked.

"Plan fund-raisers?" At his nod, she shook her head. "I was actually an international finance major in college. I had the mistaken idea that studying the subject might win my father's approval and that he'd then bring me into his business."

Somewhere along the line, Brett had learned her father was a well-known and wildly successful hedge-fund manager, whatever the hell that was. "But he dashed your hopes?"

"All for the best," she said, waving a hand and directing her gaze back to her drink. "I'm not suited for that kind of risk, and it turns out I like to keep myself busy with more tangible activities."

"I have a degree in landscape architecture," he heard himself say. "But I can't stand being cooped up in an office for so much of the day, sitting at a desk. So I don't design landscapes as much as put my hands on them."

She looked up, her eyes widening. "Oh."

His voice turned dry. "Not quite the uneducated country bumpkin you thought, huh, uptown girl?"

Her brows slammed together. "It wasn't that. I was surprised you managed to share three sentences about yourself."

God, there he went again. If he could manage it, he'd kick his own ass. "I—"

"And that we might actually have something in common."

That shut him up. All he'd been doing since the moment he'd caught sight of her the very first time was telling himself they were opposites in every—wrong—way. He'd used that thought as a wedge, a shield, an impenetrable wall that prevented him from eating her cookies, from asking her out to dinner and from doing what he really, ultimately wanted—taking her into his bed.

He rubbed his hand over his hair, aware she was studying him. Suppressing the urge to touch his scars, he wondered what she thought of them. What she'd think if she knew that he liked them as a reminder of important lessons learned.

"So…" she said now, a thread of amusement in her voice. "That's quite a filing system you have."

Glancing up, he enjoyed the way her small smile curved her lips. "You'd think six years in the army would have drilled organization into my marrow, but the minute I got out, I went back to sloppy paperwork."

"You were in the service?"

"Tenth Army Mountain Division."

"Mountain," she said. "That must have significance."

"It was formed during World War II for warfare in the Alps. The civilian ski patrol was used for recruiting purposes, and they found soldiers on the slopes and in ski clubs all over the States. Those same soldiers developed skiing as a vacation industry after the war."

"I didn't know that."

"Now you do." He sipped at his chocolate. "Our grandfathers came back and laid out the ski runs and designed the lifts and operated the ski schools that this area became known for. So when mountain kids join up, the Tenth is tradition."

"Where were you stationed?"

"Fort Drum, New York. But I spent time in Florida

and a year in Afghanistan." Just saying the word brought the whop-whop sound of choppers into his head, the taste of red dust to his tongue, the pungent scent and the oily feel of blood onto his skin. Pushing it from his mind, he rubbed his hand over his hair and switched subjects. "When my time was up, I was ready to come home."

"No career as a military man for you?"

He shook his head. "I wanted to get away for a while, save some money. But my life is here in my mountains with my family. So I started my business, thus giving birth to my really lousy filing system."

"You can get help for that, you know."

"Yeah. And I'll have to hire someone and a crew eventually, after I sweat out a bit more of my restlessness and start soliciting design work. Maybe next year."

"Until then, paper chaos."

He shrugged. "I had a part-timer working in my office at the end of the summer. But then high school started and she's much too busy for me now."

At her raised brow, he added a little more. "Kid's a whiz with just about everything. She's my sister Shay's stepdaughter-to-be."

"Your sister's getting married?"

"Two out of the three of them. Both Shay and Poppy."

She opened her mouth, but he pointed at it before she could get a word out. "Don't ask me a damn thing about the weddings. I make it my job not to absorb a word they say about them."

"You don't approve?"

"The men they're marrying, Ryan and Jace, are great. It's the constant chatter about dresses, rehearsals and seating arrangements that make me want to bash my brains in with a shovel."

"Something else we have in common. I'm not a big fan of weddings, either."

Okay, now *she* surprised him.

"Don't look so shocked. Not every woman dreams of that big day. Between them, my parents have been married seven times. For all but the first, of course, I've been standing by in something itchy or ugly, pretending I believe they'll have a happy-ever-after."

"Seven divorces then?"

"Six. My mother's still married to her current, though I doubt they'll last." She gave a little shrug.

The small, indifferent gesture felt like a punch to the gut. For some reason he'd assumed she was like his little sister Poppy, who walked through life with stars in her eyes. She wore her open heart and her belief in happy endings right there on her sleeve.

But Angelica had a more jaded view and it wasn't sitting well with him. Just as he'd felt compelled to chase away her chilled hands with hot chocolate, now he wanted to gather her up and soothe those old hurts he sensed.

It was a damn dangerous urge, because going soft for a woman was a sure way to get himself crushed.

Had that T-shirt.

Brett looked down at the table. Their cups were drained, meaning it was time to move on and move her out of his life. He hitched back his chair and she immediately took the hint and rose from her own. He stood, too, and they were close enough that if he had all the time in the world he could count each one of her luxurious lashes.

We'll likely never see each other again.

With that in mind, maybe he could kiss her.

His hand drifted toward her. He snagged an errant lock of hair with his forefinger and brushed it away from her cheek. Her color heightened and he saw her fight a shiver—and lose.

Hell. He closed his eyes a moment, willing himself to keep still. But her visceral response to his touch only made him want more…more access to her hair, her skin, her body. More opportunities to watch her react to his hands on her, his mouth on hers…

Opening his eyes, he saw she was staring at his shirt buttons, hard. Her fingers were curled into fists and as he watched, she swallowed. "Time to go," she said.

Neither of them moved. That weight was back, anchoring him to the floor, slowing his heartbeat to a funeral dirge. "Yeah."

"Yeah." She edged back, now far enough away that it would take effort to claim that kiss he shouldn't be thinking of. *Smart girl.*

He cleared his throat. "That ghastly pile of paperwork is waiting for me."

She glanced up. Their gazes caught. "You know, maybe I could…" Her voice trailed off.

The sentence didn't need to be finished for him to understand the half-spoken offer. And why she'd stopped herself. Unless they went separate ways, their certain collision wouldn't end pretty. *Yes, a very smart girl.*

"No," he said. "You're not suited for that kind of risk, either."

Brett might as well have been saying those words about himself.

ANGELICA WALKED WITH Glory from the parking lot to the headquarters, and museum, of the Mountain Historical Society. It was a stucco bungalow seated among tall pines and partnered by the blacktop parking area made bumpy by roots that had caused deep ruts and sudden swells. "I'm afraid I'm not going to be very much fun this evening," she warned her friend. "I should have stayed home."

The darkness was barely alleviated by a lone dim light on a tall pole, but she didn't need to see Glory's face to know the other woman sympathized. "Another call from the lawyers?"

"Yes. Any day now, they say, the word will get out." While she had nothing to do with her father's perfidy, she still felt terrible about it. And, to be honest, felt terrible for herself. Terribly alone. She sighed.

Glory linked arms with her. "It's good for you to do something besides mope. You need more work and making contacts is the right way to find it. You'll get better acquainted with people and then who knows what might come up?"

Though the auction wrap-up meeting was open to the general membership, Angelica didn't expect many besides the committee members would bother to attend. It looked as though she was right. When she gazed about the conference table, the only one there who hadn't been directly involved was Vaughn Elliott—whose grandfather had donated his mountain home's contents to the group.

They'd made over a million dollars from the silent sales.

Angelica stared as the committee chair, Ruth Nagel, made the announcement. The older woman could hardly contain her excitement. "I think Piney is our good luck charm!"

They all glanced through the open doorway to the lobby, where a seven-foot stuffed bear loomed over the welcome desk. It had been part of the Elliott estate, but they'd unanimously decided to keep it as the society's mascot of sorts.

"Maybe we should be grateful to Angelica, too," Glory put in. "It was she who curated the items, providing context and provenance whenever possible."

Ruth beamed and toasted her with her foam cup of terrible coffee. "Thank you, Angelica."

She waved the gratitude away, though she did appreciate it. Glory had cajoled her onto the committee early in their friendship and she'd enjoyed the work she'd put in. It had been interesting to catalog the historical items, everything from exquisite furniture to antique sets of golf clubs to a beautiful world globe inlaid with abalone shell.

"Maybe we should contact the buyers and get them to write up testimonials we can put in next year's program," Vaughn Elliott said. About thirty, he was tall and golden-haired and maybe with a trust fund or something because Angelica didn't get the impression he worked for a living. "I'd be happy to take that on if you'd give me the list of names."

"Can't do it," Ruth said. "That's confidential info… something the lawyers insisted upon. Anyway, next year we won't be having an auction—just a big black-tie event. This was a once-in-a-lifetime opportunity."

Vaughn nodded, seeming satisfied. "I'm sure my grandfather, wherever he is, is thrilled by the value of his gift."

There was little more to cover. Each of them made promises to write up their thoughts and ideas for improvements for the coming year's committee. "Though we would love all of you to continue," Ruth said. When several people murmured an assent, her gaze zeroed in on Angelica. "Please say you'll be helping again."

She hedged. "I'm not sure of my long-term plans." But under the circumstances staying in the mountains would suit her best. She had familiarity, a friend or two, and it would keep her hidden away from the financial media. "But right now I'm still able to work my weekly shifts." The tasks weren't rigorous, but helping with the database and creating packets for new members was a good way to keep busy.

Short minutes later, the meeting adjourned. Vaughn walked her and Glory to their cars. "I still think the members would like to hear from the auction winners," he said, sounding a bit peeved. "Ruth is too worried about keeping that list sacrosanct. Any way you can get your hands on it?"

"Nope," Glory answered, digging through her purse. "I think only the executive board or maybe just the president has access."

Angelica didn't say that she, actually, did know the password to all the files and thus had access. When updating the member roster, she'd noticed the other list was in the same directory.

Vaughn wandered off to his own car, a pricey SUV that looked like an overmuscled panther. Angelica frowned at her little convertible, wondering if she could trade it for something more practical for winter in the mountains and if doing so would require any cash outlay.

"Ready?" Glory said. "We agreed on Mr. Frank's, right?"

"That was your idea. I told you I wasn't sure."

"C'mon," Glory cajoled. "It's ladies' night. The drinks are really cheap."

"I don't know. In my mood I might get sloppy drunk and make a fool of myself."

"No, you won't." Glory snatched Angelica's purse from her hand and fished out her keys, too. "Because you have a higher purpose."

"What's that?" She eyed her friend. "Tonight, getting sloppy drunk might *be* the higher purpose."

Glory grabbed Angelica's hand and slapped her keys into her palm. "What did I already tell you? Once you get more acquainted with people, who knows what might come up?"

Angelica had to admit it was at least some kind of plan. She had a life to form for herself. Hunkering down in her room at the Bluebird with its clunky television and four available channels was no way to network. So, on a sigh, she turned to her car and, once behind the wheel, followed Glory to the restaurant they'd agreed upon, just outside of the village of Blue Arrow Lake.

"This is a locals' hangout," Glory said as they approached the door of Mr. Frank's. "Red vinyl booths, bar straight out of the 1950s. No blenders on the premises… so you have to take your hard booze on the rocks or not at all. No trendy cocktail orders. Got it?"

Angelica held open the heavily carved door for her friend. "I'll resist my urge to ask for a mango-kale daiquiri."

"Still," Glory said, taking her by the arm to lead her toward the dimly lit but clearly crowded lounge, "it's very popular on ladies' night. Everybody will be here… We'll make sure you meet at least some of them."

They found stools on the short end of the L-shaped bar. A heavyset man in white shirtsleeves and a red vest slapped napkin squares in front of them. He glared at

Glory. "I remember what you asked for last time and the answer is still no. I won't make anything with the ridiculous name of—of—" His face turned red and he broke off. "You're getting a beer."

She winked at Angelica and leaned close to whisper. "I invent names of drinks just to embarrass him—last time it was 'climax on a cloud.' He's an old friend of my dad's."

"You?" the bartender growled at Angelica.

She folded her hands on the bar like a perfect student. "Chardonnay, please."

He shot her a glance of approval before going about fulfilling their orders. "You new around here?" he asked, placing the generous pour in front of her.

Glory spoke before she could. "This is my friend Angelica Rodriguez. She's seeking work, if you hear of anyone who needs help. She's part-time at the store and I can give her a glowing recommendation."

He ran an assessing gaze over Angelica. "Has a flat-lander look about her."

Angelica bit her lip. She knew the word was synonymous with *other* to the people who lived full-time in the mountains.

"Yep," Glory said, waving a hand. "But she's up the hill now and wants to stay that way."

Angelica busied herself with her wine as an excuse not to watch the man's reaction. Too much was at stake.

"I'll keep that in mind," the bartender said, and she glanced up. He winked at her. "I can pass the word."

"Thank you." Angelica decided she'd leave him a huge tip, no matter the slim state of her wallet. "I appreciate your kindness."

He double tapped the bar with the flat of his hand and

then turned to obey the summons of another customer. Glory glanced around the crowd, not bothering to pretend she wasn't checking out the clientele. "Like I said, it's popular here on ladies' night."

Angelica made a more surreptitious examination. There was warm laughter and a convivial, community feel with people grouped mostly in threes and fives and sixes. Because of that, a couple huddled close in a cozy booth caught her eye. The man was turned from her so she only saw his expertly cut black hair and wide shoulders. All his attention was focused on the slender blonde beside him who was obviously in full-on flirt. A little smile playing on her lips, she was gazing up at him through her lashes.

The big diamond engagement ring on her left finger flashed in the light from the candle on their table. A sudden pang of envy made Angelica rub at the spot over her heart. She hadn't lied to Brett. Weddings didn't make her go spontaneously squishy. Still, looking at those two, so wrapped up in each other…it was lovely. So lovely she felt the sting of tears in her eyes.

Quickly, she looked away, embarrassed by the effect they had on her. Loneliness was to blame, she decided. Uncertainty. The fact that her foundation had swept away from beneath her feet.

"Ugh," Glory said, turning from her perusal of the bar to hunch around her beer.

"What?"

"My dad's here." She grabbed Angelica's elbow. "Don't look! He'll see us and come over."

Angelica laughed because she liked Glory's dad. He was solid and friendly and had never cheated a soul—

you knew it by looking at him. "What's the matter? Does he know you stayed out past curfew last night?"

"I wish," Glory grumbled. Her lack of a love life was the subject of much lamenting. "There's nobody to get naughty with. By the time I was twenty, I'd dated every decent boy in the area. And every smart girl around here knows to keep her distance from flatlanders."

"Glory, you didn't stay away from me," Angelica pointed out.

"I know. We just hit it off from the first. But it's also different because you're another woman."

"Still—"

"We've had this argument before," her friend said, cutting in. "It comes down to this. Unless a man lives permanently in the mountains, I'm not risking heart-break by even giving him the time of day. I'm this generation's face of Hallett Hardware, which means I'll be behind the register until the day I give the keys to *my* son or daughter. No sense falling for some dude whose life is a long distance away."

Angelica sighed, but could hardly blame her friend for her practical outlook. When her dad had retired, only-child Glory had been given the reins to the store. It was expected she would hold them until she passed them on.

If Angelica had a place like this where she belonged, among people she'd known all her life, who watched out for her and who'd have her back no matter what—well, she'd be careful not to jeopardize that either by falling for the wrong person.

That kind of stability was what she wanted. What she'd always wanted. Close family. Trustworthy friends. A place where she could sink her roots deep.

Glancing over her shoulder, she cast another look at the happy couple. Some people had it easy. They found their partner and their place without effort. Those two had probably recognized each other by matching glows and then gracefully—and gratefully—given in to the inevitable.

Her body seized as a familiar figure strode up to the couple's table.

Brett Walker interrupted the pair's intimate conversation without hesitation. He lightly cuffed the back of the man's head and when he shifted, leaned around the other guy to buss the blonde on the cheek. She bounced on her seat and pointed at a free space on the curved banquette.

When he slipped onto the cushion, Angelica told herself to look away. But her gaze refused to budge because he was actually smiling at the woman, a real smile, a free smile, that looked relaxed and warm. Everything he wasn't in Angelica's presence.

Then the blonde made a gesture toward the bar and it was clear what would happen next. Brett would make his way there to pick up a drink and he'd see Angelica and...

She didn't know what would happen. She only knew she had to get away before he caught sight of her.

Murmuring something about the ladies' room to Glory, she slid off her stool and scurried in what she hoped was the right direction. A doorway led her to a darkened hall that didn't lead to restrooms, but instead a solid door with a sign that read Emergency Exit Only. Alarm Will Sound When Opened.

She approached it anyway, with some vague idea of hiding in the shadows there until...sometime when she felt it was safe enough to return to the bar.

Behind her back, a man called her name. "Angelica?"

Her eyes closed. Of course Brett had seen her escape. "Um…yeah?"

The rug muffled his footsteps, but she sensed his approach. The hairs on the back of her neck jumped to attention. "Are you all right?" he asked.

"Can't a woman have a little alone time?" she snapped out, without turning toward him.

She didn't need to see him to sense the rising of one of his eyebrows. "Hiding by the back door?"

With a shrug, she tried to indicate nonchalance instead of idiocy.

"Are you afraid of me?" he asked, his voice low.

"Of course not!" She glanced over her shoulder to see him rub his palm over his hair, his expression frustrated. "Why'd you follow me?"

"I—"

"Never mind. I'm leaving." But she did nothing more than turn to face him.

"What are you doing here, anyway? This doesn't seem your kind of place."

She was supposed to be networking, she remembered. Making contacts in hopes of finding another job. Because she was without family, without a home, without more than a few dollars to her name.

Suddenly, it was too much. Overwhelmed by her situation, overstimulated by the presence of the man she'd been attracted to for months, she felt another upwelling of those useless tears. Angry at her herself, she dashed them away with the edge of her hand.

"Angelica." Then he was close. Closer than when they'd been saying goodbye at the coffee place the other day. Closer than ever before. She felt his breath on her temple and his body heat made her own skin prickle.

His fingers gripped her chin to tilt her face to his. Then he groaned, the sound frustrated. Resigned.

"This is a bad idea," he murmured.

And before she could agree, because having his hands on her was *terrible*, he kissed her.

His lips were hard, his tongue insistent. She opened for him—there seemed no alternative—and he swept inside in the same way he swept away all her sensible thoughts. Her fingers clutched his biceps and they swelled under her touch.

His head tilted, and the kiss went deeper. Her tongue slid along his, and they both shuddered. He crowded her until she stepped back, her shoulder blades to the wall. That didn't stop him, he just kept pressing into her and instead of being nervous of his big, masculine frame surrounding her smaller one, she only felt... turned on.

And, strangely safe.

One arm curled around his neck and she tilted her hips, the jut of his sex against her belly. His hands clutched at her hair and he pushed into her, harder, and then...

He tore his mouth from hers. Stepped back.

"Bad idea," he muttered again, and was gone.

Angelica sagged against the wall, struggling to bring her breathing under control. Her fingers shook when she brought them to her lips, which felt both bruised and scorched.

A hysterical giggle tried to climb up her throat. She thought of what she and Brett had done. What Glory had said.

Once you get more acquainted with people, who knows what might come up?

A little one-on-one with Brett Walker was probably not what her friend had in mind.

CHAPTER FOUR

NURSING HER BEER, Glory Hallett kept her attention on her glass and her back to the rest of the crowd at Mr. Frank's. Angelica had just left after returning from the ladies' room, looking wide-eyed and unsettled, as if a ghost had goosed her in the back hall.

Her father was a bastard for taking his daughter's money—not just her trust fund, but money that she had earned and invested from her modeling days—and for putting her into this position. Glory might have her beefs with her own dad, but he wasn't a criminal. She peeked over her shoulder to see him in a far corner at a table with his cronies. Even though he was an exemplary citizen, she didn't want to engage with him tonight. A girl should get to enjoy a beer without having her pops come over to talk shop, which was exactly what he'd do if he spotted her.

Maybe she, like Angelica, should head for home. Another ladies' night at Mr. Frank's felt suddenly flat. If she hung around much longer, surely Hank Hallett would notice her presence and come out of his very tenuous retirement to decide it was time to once again intrude on the course the business's new management had set.

"This seat taken?" a deep voice asked.

"No," she answered, not distracted from the morose turn of her thoughts. Sighing, she decided leaving was the best option she had. She could spend the rest of the evening debating whether to join an online dating service—not for the first time—knowing from the outset nothing would come of registering even if she did. She already knew every eligible man living in the local mountain resort communities. Outside the area...well, given that she'd never be leaving it because of her ties to the store, finding a man with a life down the hill would be a big waste of time and only bring the potential for heartbreak.

"Great," the newcomer answered.

His low-toned voice niggled at her, and her gaze flicked to the right. When she saw a rangy body climb onto the stool, she took a longer look. Her heart jumped in her chest. "Oh. You."

His eyes cut to her. They were dark, to match his dark, shaggy hair. She refused to wiggle on her seat, despite the fact it seemed he was having trouble placing her. Embarrassing! *She* remembered *his* face.

His glance dropped down to her chest. She wore a button-up Henley over a tank top and, yes, she was revealing a bit of cleavage. After working in a hardware store sixty hours a week, on occasion she did like to remind people she was a woman. But maybe she should feel a little insulted by his ogling.

His eyes lifted to hers. "You're...Glory. I remember your name's written on the apron you wear at work."

Yay! All was forgiven! She smiled at him. "Hello, stranger." Holding out her hand, she introduced herself. "Glory Hallett, of Hallett Hardware."

His handshake was manly and brief. "Kyle Scott, of..."

She mentally cursed herself for her introduction. Did

it sound like bragging? When he'd come in for some Spackle, rollers and paintbrushes, he'd been wearing threadbare jeans with a T-shirt that was probably as old as he was. It wasn't easy making a living in the mountains. With housing and groceries and gas at resort prices, those who did certain jobs—say house painting or general handyman tasks—didn't have an easy time of it. But she came from mountain pioneer stock and knew well that all work was honorable.

"Kyle Scott of Evergreen and Piano Keys," she finished for him, naming two popular paint colors.

He blinked, clearly astonished.

Glory grinned at him. "I work in a hardware store. We sell cans of that stuff. I recognized those splashes on your clothes."

He looked chagrined. "I have to admit I bought that paint over at Murphy's," he said, mentioning one of their competitors in the bigger town on the north side of the mountain. "I didn't know about Hallett's at the time."

"Well, now you do."

He smiled, slow. "Now I do."

Glory swallowed the last of her beer. Then she signaled to the bartender, Murray. "Can I buy you a beer?" she asked the new guy, signaling for two without waiting for his answer.

At his silence, she glanced over, hoping she hadn't stepped on his ego. "It's ladies' night," she said. "I get a break on the price."

"Oh. Well, then." A strange expression crossed his face. "I appreciate it."

Upon arrival of their drinks, she tapped her full glass to his. "What should we drink to?"

"New friends?" he suggested.

Warmth curled like a kitten in her belly. "You in these parts for a while, stranger?" It was just a beer, she reminded herself. No need to get worked up about his permanent address.

"Kyle," he repeated. "I hope to be here for some time, yes. We'll see how it goes."

He hoped to be here for some time! It was good, though, that he appeared to understand that earning enough to pay mountain prices wouldn't be easy. "I can put your name and number in our files," she offered. "And we have a bulletin board near the front of the store where you can post a flyer. Customers often ask if we know of workers who do general home maintenance. That's your gig, right?"

"You'd do that for me?"

"Sure." She shrugged, pretending it was a casual proposal. Something she'd do for anyone she happened upon in Mr. Frank's. But the truth was, she had a sudden stake in his ability to make a mountain living. There was something about the man and his dark, intense eyes that caused her heart to race. Her whole body felt as if it was coming alive.

If he could afford to stay in the area…

She slid another quick look at his handsome face. There was a sudden change in the air, too. A first-day-of-school feeling. A first-day-of-the-rest-of-your-life feeling that sensitized the surface of her skin and made the oxygen she sucked in seem even thinner than normal.

No way was she going to ignore it.

Turning toward the new guy, she placed her elbow on the bar. "So…tell me about yourself. You really want to put down roots in the mountains?"

His gaze shifted from her to his beer and he hesitated.

Too long. Mortified heat crawled up her neck. "Um, sorry," she mumbled, and turned back to her own drink. "I'll shut up now and let you enjoy your evening in peace." *Stupid*, she thought. *Stupid, stupid.* He was probably married or gay or simply not interested in her in any way. Just because *she'd* been instantly attracted…

She remembered the day he'd walked into the store. The bell over the door had rung with its usual cheery sound, and she'd looked up from dusting the boxes of wooden matches that her dad insisted they stock but nobody ever put in their basket. The stranger had looked a little lost and a lot hot and she'd smiled to herself as she approached and asked if he needed help. There was something about a man and any kind of shopping task— even when it was hardware stuff. They always roamed the floor with an air of bafflement, as if the entire process confounded them.

Whether a woman was browsing or knew exactly what she wanted, she walked through a store with the confidence of a general on a battlefield.

He'd asked to be pointed toward the painting supplies and then he'd strolled off in the direction she'd indicated, leaving her to admire the set of his shoulders and those long legs. But she'd dismissed him from her mind immediately after he'd made his purchases, however. Because mooning over a visitor wasn't a practical thing to do.

Yet now that she'd run into him at mostly locals Mr. Frank's and he said he was hoping to remain in the area…well, that seemed promising.

Not if he wasn't interested, however.

The proprietor of a locally owned and operated hardware store had to be nothing but practical. So even if he wanted to be more than temporary to the mountains, if the spark wasn't mutual, she wasn't going to waste a moment worrying about it.

"Glory."

"Hmm?" She chirped it, faking happy and unconcerned. Her gaze stayed stubbornly glued on the TV above the bar. The coverage of an early snow in Wisconsin was fascinating.

"I've forgotten the steps," he said.

"Mmm." She made a mental note to check on her order of snow shovels. You never wanted to be deeply discounting surplus in April, but you'd better have plenty in stock between New Year's and Valentine's Day.

Kyle released a sigh. "So it's no wonder I've already stumbled on them. Give me another chance?"

She shook herself and shot him a quick look. "What?"

His expression was sheepish. "Is there a way to tell a woman you're rusty when it comes to bar pickups?"

Rearing back, she felt another hot flush overtake her. "I wasn't trying to pick you up!" It was sort of a lie, but still.

"Hell," he muttered, slapping his palm to his forehead. "I did it again."

"Did what?" she asked, narrowing her eyes.

"I…work a lot. Don't get out much."

Which sounded like Glory. "So…?"

"So, it was more like *I* was trying to pick *you* up."

Her eyes rounded. "You really *are* rusty. You're not supposed to admit the pickup intention right out loud like that."

He laughed.

She liked the sound of it. "Though to be truthful, I'm not into that kind of thing anyway." Yes, she'd wanted to talk to him, feel out the boundaries of the attraction she felt for him, but a pickup implied sex and she didn't jump into anyone's bed.

He grimaced, and as if he could read her mind, he said, "Yeah. I bet it sounded like I was after sex, huh?"

"Um…it did."

His hand slapped his forehead again. "I'm terrible at this, see?"

He was too good-looking to be "terrible." She figured he'd had plenty of opportunities to know women in every way possible.

"You're looking skeptical," he said.

"It could be just a good line," she told him honestly and lowered her voice to a manly tone. "'I'm inexperienced and utterly harmless despite my good looks and fabulous smile.'"

His mouth curved upward.

Yep, fabulous smile, Glory thought.

"I didn't say I was 'inexperienced.'" Mischief sparked in his eyes. "Just out of practice."

Smiling herself, she shook her head. "Looks like the rhythm is coming right back to you."

Their gazes met and she had to suppress a little shiver. Truly, she hadn't felt this sense of something-good-about-to-happen since she was twelve and found she was assigned to a seat beside Harper Adrian, the cutest boy in the seventh grade.

Of course, Harper had cheated off her the entire year and written a nasty note about her on the bathroom wall the last day of school.

She sighed.

Frowning, Kyle redirected his gaze to his beer as if he had his own heavy thoughts. "I like it here," he said. "I like working with my hands and I like that it's…simpler. Not like down the mountain."

"I like that you like it here," Glory said, smiling. "But it's down the hill."

He glanced over at her.

"You've got to use the proper locals' lingo if you intend to become one. We call it down the hill."

"Locals' lingo…" He drained the remainder of his beer. "About that—"

A meaty hand clapped on her shoulder. "Glory girl! I didn't see you come in."

She stifled her groan and half turned. "Dad. Having fun?"

"Sure. But I'm glad I caught you. I think we need to have a little chat."

"Oh, gee, Dad. I'm just about to…" What? Make another move on the total stranger? Or leave the bar and lose out on learning any more about him?

"This won't take long." The stool on her other side was unfortunately empty and her father slid onto it.

Glory peeked at Kyle and saw him stifle a yawn. Then he stood and withdrew some bills, leaving a nice tip for the bartender.

She was losing out on him, anyway. Her dad started yammering in her ear as Kyle sent her a smile and then tapped two fingers to his forehead in a silent goodbye. In return, she pinkie waved, saying farewell, most likely, to the most interesting thing that had come her way in months. Possibly years.

"About that bin of pumpkins…" Her father droned on. "I think they do better at the back of the store, where we've always kept them, not out on the sidewalk where you have to drag them in before closing every night."

Hank Hallett didn't like change. Glory supposed she shouldn't be looking for anything in her life to alter either, not when she'd already predicted this very serious discussion regarding pumpkin placement.

She snuck a look over her shoulder in the direction of Kyle Scott's exit. His hand was on the door. As he pushed it open, he glanced back. Their gazes tangled once again.

And Glory felt a new rush of hope, despite how impractical and nonsensical it might be. She sighed. Likely nothing would ever come of it.

As THE BROTHER OF three younger sisters, Brett had a keen appreciation of male companionship. It was why he enjoyed the little ritual he'd established with his brothers-in-law-to-be. A couple of times a week, they met for morning coffee and he always looked forward to it.

It was a no-stress way to start the day, hanging with the two men who didn't expect any more from him than the occasional comment on the news playing on the TV hanging in the corner. Brett was no less relaxed now, even though it was the first time he'd been in Oscar's Coffee since buying Angelica hot chocolate.

He'd banished her from his thoughts.

That he dreamed of her, well, he wasn't going to beat himself up for that. A man didn't have control over his sleeping self. But in his waking hours he had disciplined his mind not to linger on her big brown eyes, silky hair, bountiful breasts. He didn't think about the way her long lashes swept the pink-edged apples of her cheeks.

Her small hand, cool in his.

"What's got that expression on your face?" Ryan Hamilton asked. "Do you need a muffin or something? The breakfast burritos are good."

Brett glanced over. "Huh?"

"You look hungry, man."

Guilt poked at him. Made him grouchy. *Small hand, cool in his.* Yeesh. "I don't know what you're talking about," he muttered, wanting to soak his head in cold water. *She's supposed to be banished from your thoughts!*

A server approached, their coffees on a tray. She slid them onto the table, plucked their number from the silver holder, then sent Brett a bright smile. "Long time no see, honey."

Blinking, he noticed it was Danielle Shore. "You're working here now?"

She nodded, her blond hair swirling around her shoulders. "Just one shift a week. Not getting enough hours at the boutique."

A tough time of year for the full-timers. Autumn and spring were the slow seasons in the mountains. "I hope you can stay busy, Danielle."

Tucking the tray under her arm, she edged nearer, close enough to nudge his thigh with her knee. "I can think of things we can do to fill my spare time."

He considered her obvious proposition. They'd dated for a few months a couple of years before. But it had faded and they'd gone their separate ways. But Danielle's good looks hadn't diminished in the least. She was California-mountain-girl pretty, with that blond hair, those blue eyes and the dash of cute freckles over her nose. A round two might not be a bad idea.

Some vigorous sex might be just what he needed.

He opened his mouth to suggest a dinner later that week.

But then the image of dark-haired, dark-eyed Angelica popped into his thoughts. Her mouth pursed like a kiss as she blew on the surface of her hot chocolate in this very establishment.

Their actual kiss.

It had been a very bad idea. He'd said so…out loud. But that hadn't stopped him from reaching for her. From taking her mouth, certain and sure, as she wound an arm around his neck and pressed eagerly against his body.

It was her hair that had finally stopped him. He'd buried his hands in the silky strands and the fragrant stuff had seemed alive, winding around his fingers as if it could bind him to her.

Keep him tied up until he was helpless against her and what she could do to him.

Crush him. Suck the life from him. Break him into a million little pieces.

He'd been hurt like that once before, but he sensed that the havoc that beautiful, spoiled princess Angelica could wreak would be so much worse.

With a little smile for Danielle, he patted the pocket that contained his phone. "Maybe so," he said, keeping his tone neutral. His interest in a date with her had evaporated. "I have your number."

She sashayed away in tight jeans and a little T-shirt, but Brett couldn't drum up an ounce of regret.

Across the table, Jace chuckled into his coffee. "That's a first. Ryan Hamilton's pretty face completely ignored in favor of Brett's grunts and grumbles. Poppy must have put out the word that the other women around town better not even glance at you."

Ryan, looking like the movie star he'd been, settled back in his chair and eyed the still-smirking Jace. "I'm going to tell Shay you're dying to discuss the flower arrangements for your wedding."

Jace winced. "Ouch. That's pretty harsh, brother."

"Could be worse. You don't watch it I'll tell her you have an opinion on her Big Day hairstyle."

The other man groaned. "Don't. I beg you."

Brett shook his head at the other two. "I tried to tell you both. I counseled you, even. You shouldn't have popped the question. There's no need for a wedding, or a marriage even. My sisters would stick with you guys without all that hoopla."

Jace placed his coffee on the table and turned to Brett. "I want to make promises to your sister," he said, his voice low. "And I want her to make them to me. Publicly."

Ryan nodded, looking equally serious.

What Brett wanted was to scoff. Call them fools. But that seemed too damn rude, even for him, and he really did wish the best for the two couples. He didn't think Poppy or Shay would ever do a number on the hearts of these two men.

Too bad his choice of female companions hadn't always been so stellar.

Looking around the room instead of looking at them, his gaze snagged on the TV. As if to underscore his condemnation of his own lousy instincts, Lorraine Kushi's face appeared on the screen. She'd worked for years at an LA news affiliate, and when she came on he always switched the channel to avoid the sight of her sharp beauty and the memories it dredged up. He stood now, bent on doing just that, when a name flashed on the screen. Ralph Rodriguez.

Ralph Rodriguez was the name of Angelica's father.

Brett sank back in his seat as Lorraine reported the latest financial scandal. Angelica's father had stolen millions of his investors' dollars in a Ponzi scheme that had finally gone bust. The Feds had kept him in custody—for several days now—and the news had finally leaked.

His personal accounts and property had been frozen or put under the government's control. Rumor was he'd even robbed his own daughter while trying to cover up the crisis.

Angelica. Her father jailed. Her money gone…or at least inaccessible.

Did she know?

Of course she knew. It all made sense now. The darkened house. Her creeping around inside it. He'd suspected something was off. Then there was the job at Hallett Hardware.

In this very coffee shop, she'd told him she'd once wanted to work with her father but she hadn't been welcomed. *All for the best*, she'd said. *I'm not suited for that kind of risk.*

Not suited for the things her father did. Breaking the law. Cheating other people. Betraying family.

"Where are you going?"

He glanced at his companions, realizing he'd jumped up from his chair and was heading for the door. The two men were staring at him. "Where are you going?" Ryan repeated.

"I've got to go check on someone—I mean something." He needed to see her. To make sure that she was okay. While he cursed this drive to protect her, he couldn't deny it, either.

The morning air, as crisp as a pippin apple, didn't cool the heated urge. But as he unlocked his truck, he realized he had no idea where to find her. Where was she living now that the mansion on the lake was in government hands?

He slid inside, trying to think it through. Hallett Hardware. It was his best bet.

But a dumb idea, he realized, as he pulled into its small parking lot. The place was dark. It wouldn't open for another couple of hours. Frustrated, he banged on the steering wheel with the heel of his hands. Did she know the story was out?

If so, would she look for a new place to go?

Maybe she'd run from the mountains and he'd never see her again. She'd banish herself. That made sense, didn't it?

His hands thumped the steering wheel again. Then he cursed, because there was no reason for that idea to bother him so. It was what he wanted. Distance from gorgeous Angelica Rodriguez who fascinated him in a way he was sure would only lead to disaster.

A knock on the driver's side window caused him to jump. His head whipped around to see Vaughn Elliott, dressed in dark jeans and a wool coat. Brett had never warmed to the guy, but then again he had a knee-jerk distrust of Richie Rich types. Vaughn was certainly that. As far as Brett knew, he lived off family money and got off by playing cop. The sheriff's volunteer patrol car that he so often cruised around in was parked beside the truck.

Vaughn knocked again on the glass.

Brett unrolled the window. "Yeah?"

"Good morning."

"Uh-huh." Brett stared at a shiny piece of metal that was pinned to Vaughn's lapel. "You wear a badge now?"

The other man shifted on his feet and looked a little embarrassed. "The sheriff thought it was a good idea."

"Right." Wrong. Brett would bet this particular volunteer liked the—fake—authority the emblem conferred upon him. Everything about the arrogant jerk rubbed him the wrong way. "You here to arrest me?"

Vaughn looked back coolly. "Have you done something wrong?"

An image of Angelica popped into Brett's mind again. That kiss in the shadowy hallway at Mr. Frank's. What he'd been on the brink of doing. Sex in a public place was against the law, right? Shoving the idea of it out of his mind, he shrugged for Vaughn's benefit. "Nothing I'm willing to share," he said. "What's going on?"

"Thought I'd pass along the word about a burglary last night."

Brett straightened in his seat. "Another house was broken into?"

The other man's eyes narrowed. "You've heard?"

"Don Fleming clued me in a few days ago," he said.

"Ah." Vaughn nodded. "Well, this does seem part of the same string."

"What was taken?"

"I don't know all the particulars. It was the Smithfields' vacation home. There were some silver pieces missing for sure and an antique globe in a walnut stand."

Brett frowned. "Silver? An antique globe? That doesn't sound like the kind of loot kids would take."

"There was cash missing, too, I'm told. And, uh…" Vaughn seemed to think. "The medicine cabinets were rifled. A TV is gone."

"Hmm." It seemed to him an odd assortment of plunder, but Brett didn't know anything about what items could be fenced. Or the criminal mind.

The sheriff's volunteer patted the roof of the truck. "Keep vigilant."

Brett resisted rolling his eyes. "Will do," he said, and succumbed to the urge to mock salute.

The other man didn't appear to sense his irony and returned to his vehicle. Brett watched him roll slowly out of the parking lot and onto the highway.

As he did, he saw Angelica's vehicle drive past the hardware store. Most of her face was hidden behind a pair of celebrity-sized sunglasses. Without thinking, he pulled out after her. If she wasn't working at Hallett's today, where was she going?

More important, how was she faring?

At the next turnoff, an SUV took advantage of the gap he'd left between their vehicles and slid into place behind Angelica. Brett didn't mind. He could watch her just as well from here. Their short parade continued on for half a mile until her lights signaled and she hung a right into a parking lot bordering a rustic set of buildings that housed a branch of the county library, a gourmet market and a fancy day spa.

He followed at a sedate space, wondering about her destination.

Was she intending to massage her worries away?

His mind got busy again, picturing her naked on a table, a towel covering the delectable curve of her butt. Maybe he'd sneak in, pay off the real masseuse and help himself to the wealth of her golden skin.

He'd warm his hands by spreading coconut oil between his palms and then he'd stroke her shoulders, knead the tight muscles there. After long minutes he'd work his way down her back.

She'd moan.

At the thought of the sound of her pleasure, he had to shift on his seat and adjust the tight fit of his jeans. Damn, he thought, watching her exit her car as he idled behind a commercial-size Dumpster. Could he do it?

But instead of the spa, she approached the library and pushed some books through the mouth of the outside depository. Then she returned to her car, those big dark glasses still obscuring most of her face and all of her mood.

He'd go to her, he thought. Shove up the shades and look deep into her eyes. His hand went to the door handle. Then he'd tell her—

Just as a law enforcement vehicle whizzed by on the highway, the bar of lights on its roof flashing, and he caught himself. His hand jerked away from the door.

Maybe he *was* a criminal. Because it was criminally stupid to forget the promises he'd made to himself.

She wasn't for him.

She wasn't his concern.

This unfamiliar need to serve and protect would only cause him trouble.

CHAPTER FIVE

BRETT RETURNED HIS focus to the only places it should be: work and family. He spent long hours on other people's property, tiring himself out physically so that the only energy he had left was to grab take-out for dinner before heading to the remote cabin where he was living on the family property.

Though there was plenty of gourmet fare to be had in Blue Arrow Lake, he was grateful for the invitation to have a home-cooked meal with his siblings and their significant others at Poppy and Ryan's place a few days later. He arrived with a stack of fresh clothes and used one of the guest bathrooms at the expansive estate to clean up before joining the rest in the huge kitchen. Ryan handed him a beer and Poppy slid a plate of appetizers his way. He only took time to greet Mason, Poppy's son, and then he chugged half the beer and ate a handful of crackers and cheese.

"Good," he said around his last bite. "Thanks."

In a more mellow mood than he'd been in of late, he settled onto his stool at the granite island and listened to the family chatter. Mason was sharing something about the classroom hamster. London, Jace's teenage daughter, commented—kindly—without looking up from texting on her phone.

"Kid," Brett called, waving to get her attention.

She glanced at him, her expression open, her face devoid of the heavy black makeup she'd worn when she'd first arrived months back. "Yes?"

"High school going okay?"

"High school's going *great*. I'm on the homecoming committee and the yearbook staff, and my chemistry teacher wants me to wash the beakers and stuff during my free period. I'll even get paid."

"Yeah? Proud of you." Then he injected pitiful into his expression. "Too busy to help out with my files every once in a while?"

Her brows came together and her voice took on a scolding tone. "Uncle Brett."

He loved that she called him that, he'd admit it. She was a great kid and that she feel comfortable in the family was a goal of every Walker. "I know, I know," he said, hanging his head.

"You've let the paperwork get away from you again, haven't you?"

He thought of the sheets swirling in the wind and Angelica and he racing around to retrieve them. Her pink cheeks, upturned ass, cold hands. His very basic urge to warm her in every way possible. "You can say that again."

London sighed. "I'll see what I can do," she said, returning her attention to her cell, "my next free Saturday morning."

"Thank you," he said humbly. "I sure appreciate it."

His sister Mac dropped onto the stool beside his and spoke into his ear. "You big con."

"I don't know what you mean," he said, all innocence.

"Making London feel sorry for you. She's not onto you yet, but any minute now..."

"Shh," Brett said. "I'm milking it for as long as I can. And it's true I need her help. You know how lousy I am with the invoices and billing."

Mac shook her head. "Anyway…you hear the news?"

"Uh…" He'd been avoiding all media, not wanting to get sucked into any drama involving the duplicitous Ralph Rodriguez. "No. And I'm liking keeping my head clear of such stuff, thank you very much."

"There was another break-in."

The relief that she wasn't talking about anything Angelica related was short-lived as the new information sunk in. He groaned. "I don't like this."

Poppy nodded. "Me neither. I'm worried about you out at the cabins by yourself when there's criminal activity going on in the area."

Ryan slid his arm around her shoulders and kissed the top of her head. "Sweetheart, your brother could scare the crap out of a grizzly bear if he had a mind to."

Brett appreciated the vote of confidence, but all he said was, "Hmm." Then he tapped his chin. "Should we abandon the property again then, Pop?"

"No," she said quickly. After a second her eyes narrowed. "You're teasing."

The idea of refurbishing the cabins at the abandoned property and turning them into a revenue stream for the Walker family was her baby. Somehow, though legend said the land was cursed, the siblings had been persuaded to get behind the idea. After a fire in the most secluded cabin in the woods occurred a few months back, Brett had even moved into another of the bungalows, partly as security and partly to make it more convenient for him to do his share working on the buildings in his—admittedly limited—free time.

"I'm teasing," he admitted.

Jace strolled up, beer in hand. "Sorry I haven't been much use out there recently."

"Hey, I understand," Brett said. "You've got to get your home base established here." Glancing over at London, he wagged a thumb in her direction. "Somebody else seems to be getting established just fine."

The other man smiled at his daughter. "I'm a lucky guy." He reached over to snag Shay's hand and draw her to his side. "Even mountain fires have been blessings for me."

"When the days get shorter, I'll be able to work on the interiors of the cabins in the evening," Brett said. "You and Shay have most of the exterior repairs done, so we're ready for harsher weather."

"I just wish we knew what was going on with the break-ins," Mac said.

They all nodded. Poppy looked worried again. "I don't know that I like you cleaning houses alone, Mac."

"She could scare a grizzly, too," Brett said, elbowing her ribs. "Look at that mean face she makes."

"I'm serious," Poppy said. "You should have a partner."

"I do need some help," Mac conceded. "Haven't found the right candidate yet."

"I can do Tuesdays and Thursdays," Poppy offered.

Ryan opened his mouth, then closed it. Smart man, Brett decided. Poppy, as Ryan's wife, didn't need to lift a finger. But that wasn't the Walker way. They came from hard-working people.

"I'll meet you at the Maids by Mac office Tuesday at 8:00 a.m."

Brett took another swig of his beer, unwinding a crucial bit more at the idea that the two sisters would be working together.

"Speaking of the office reminds me of other news," Mac started. "Angelica Rodriguez."

Shay straightened. "You know Angelica?"

Mac slid a gaze at Brett. "She came by the business. Seems she knows our big bro."

"Mmm." Shay had a speculative gleam in her eye. "He doesn't like her."

"She's all right," Brett heard himself say in a defensive tone.

His youngest sister stared. "Oh, really? That's a change of tune."

"Who is Angelica and what does she have to do with Brett?" Poppy demanded.

Mac was watching him, too. "Beautiful, stacked—"

"Say no more." Poppy waved to end the conversation. "Brett has a pile of beautiful and stacked ladies he's left behind."

"Hey," he protested. "I'm right here, you know."

His sisters ignored him. "This one's different," Mac insisted. "Get this. She's a rich flatlander who also worked on that big auction event for the historical society you and Ryan went to last summer. Glory Hallett recruited her."

"She also works at Hallett Hardware," Brett heard himself interject again.

"Interesting," Mac said, sparing him a glance. "And if you kept up with the financial news—"

"I don't," Poppy and Shay admitted together.

"—you'd know that her father was a megapowerful hedge-fund manager who just swindled a boatload of people out of their life savings. It's been reported he took his only daughter's money before he was arrested."

Poppy, with her tender heart, looked stricken. "Oh, no. Those poor people. And poor Angelica, too."

"You don't even know her," Brett growled.

Poppy's big gray eyes fastened on his face. "Well? Did she deserve it?"

"No," he said, though it felt as if the word was pulled out of him. "I suppose not."

And there she was, front and center in his head again. The rest of the meal he heard the family talking and laughing around him, and he didn't join in, aware he was brooding but unable to yank himself out of the dark place.

See? She was bad for him in so many ways.

On the way home, he turned left instead of right, deciding to take a cruise through town before heading for the highway. He wasn't ready for the isolation of the cabins just yet. Maybe he'd stop off for a beer at Mr. Frank's. On a whim, he slowed as he passed Hallett Hardware. It was closed for the night, of course—

But there was Angelica's flashy convertible parked in the lot beside it.

Slowing, he could see her figure in the driver's seat. *Move along*, he told himself.

His feet and hands didn't listen and he pulled into the spot beside hers. In the dim light from an overhead streetlamp, her face was a pale blur. When he approached her window, she rolled it down.

An inch.

"Can I help you?" she asked.

"That was my line."

"I'm great, thanks."

Before she could push the button that would move the window back into place, he curled his fingers around the edge. The glass was cold against his palm and his fingers registered that the interior of the car wasn't much warmer. "What are you doing out here?"

"Communing with nature, not that it's any if your business."

The nose of her convertible was pointing directly at a battered Dumpster. "Lovely view," he said.

"I like it."

He bit back a smile. This was new, this prickly snideness, and some piece of him liked it. Liked her. Of course, that had always been the problem. How much he wanted to like her. How much he wanted her.

How soft—well, and hard—that wanting might make him.

"Good night," she said.

How are you really doing? he wanted to ask. *What's going on with your father? Is there anything you need? How can I help you?*

Fuck, he thought. There it was again. The urge to serve and protect. Keep her warm. Feed her. Soothe her with kisses. Distract her from her woes with sex.

Okay, that last might be a more selfish wish. But God, you couldn't blame a guy. Even in the shadows her face could stop his heart. The thought of her kiss could make him stiff even when it was thirty-four degrees outside and he was in shirtsleeves.

"Stay away, Brett." Her whisper floated through the centimeters of space she'd left open between them.

He removed his fingers from around her window. Staying away had been his intention from the beginning. But when she insisted on it now, wouldn't you know that the perverse side of him no longer wanted to agree. Now it clamored to do the opposite.

All his common sense, all those hard lessons he'd learned, receded in the background. He ran a hand over his face and into his hair, feeling the scars beneath his callous palms. When Angelica was around, it was as if every bit of wisdom he'd gained fled.

"Go home, Brett."

"Your wish is my command, princess," he said. But he still didn't move.

As if sensing his internal struggle, she glanced at him. "Really. I'm not your problem."

But she seemed to be his concern, no matter how hard he tried to shake that fact. Not until she rolled up her window, effectively cutting off communication, did he return to his car and drive away.

KYLE SCOTT CARRIED over the threshold of Hallett Hardware a rotund deli bag and an unfamiliar sense of excitement. Inside, it smelled of a pleasing combination of WD-40 and a light feminine fragrance. Pausing a moment, he breathed it in.

His muscles, especially those in his arms and shoulders, were sore. That was unfamiliar, too. He was more accustomed to a stiff lower back and legs frozen from time spent at a desk or at a conference table. But this pain felt good and he flexed his free paint-speckled left hand.

Looking down at his flesh peppered with green dots made him frown. Maybe he should have done a complete cleanup before his impromptu visit to see Hardware Hottie, aka Glory Hallett. But the idea had come to him like the flash of a lightbulb and he obeyed his sudden inspirations as a general rule. Over the years, they'd fattened his bank account—though at the same time draining all the life out of the social side of his world.

Anyway, he thought Glory would forgive his disheveled state. She was aware he was painting a house. For now, that was all she had to know, right?

Maybe he should feel bad he'd encouraged her impression he was a mere handyman who hoped to stay in the mountains, but the freshness of a woman being interested in him without knowing his net worth was irresistible.

He could hear her voice at the rear of the store. Clearly she was helping someone in plumbing supplies. And wasn't that novel, too? He sure as hell didn't know anything about angle stops and wax gaskets and he only found it more intriguing that this young woman was obviously well versed in the steps required to change out a toilet.

His father would appreciate that trait, he was sure. As a gastro-intestinal surgeon he'd likely have a lot to talk about with her.

A lot more than his father, mother, sister or brother had to say to him. They were all in medicine: two surgeons and two orthopedists, and they considered Kyle the cuckoo that had been left in their well-feathered nest. It had shocked the hell out of them that he refused to take his place in medical school.

What he did after that had left them completely flummoxed.

But now he was at Blue Arrow Lake, painting a house and bringing a woman he barely knew lunch. The idea had come to him as he was using the roller on the porch ceiling.

Bring Hardware Hottie lunch, an inner voice urged.

Become better acquainted with her in the guise of Kyle Scott, home-maintenance dude. Feel out the way things are going with her and if it seems right, then hit her with the whole truth.

He was still standing just inside the hardware store's door when she came around the corner. Her feet stuttered at the sight of him and she reached out to clutch an endcap featuring various sizes and colors of duct tape to steady herself. Kyle drank her in.

She was small and built on a delicate scale. Her hair was nearly platinum and cut in way that curled around her ears and showcased her triangular face. Pink lips. Dusting of gold freckles. Big blue eyes—no, turquoise—that warmed with pleasure as she looked him over, too.

His hands itched to snatch her up and kiss her. Instead, his fingers tightened on the brown bag and the crinkling sound had them both redirecting their gazes to what he held. His arm lifted. "I brought us lunch."

"You did?" Her mouth curved and he didn't think he was wrong that it was delight that turned up the corners of those pretty lips.

"I did. I needed a break and thought maybe you could take a little time off, too."

She grimaced. "I don't have anyone to take my place."

"Oh." Ridiculous to feel so deflated. After all, he understood what it required to build a business and keep one going.

"But if you don't mind sitting with me by the register…" she started.

"Would love to," he said, and followed her lead to the glass-topped counter at the side of the store.

She dragged a stool toward him, the plastic seat advertising a waterproofing product. Hers was matching except it promoted an automatic sprinkler system. "What'd you bring?" she asked, glancing toward the bag.

He scratched at the whiskers on his jaw. "I hope you don't think this was cheating."

Her brows rose. "Oh?"

"I asked at the deli two doors down for your favorite sandwich." He reached into the bag. "Tuna salad on rye." With a flourish, he set the wax-paper-wrapped package before her.

She stared at it.

"I was trying to make a good impression." Had the clerk got it wrong entirely? Maybe Glory was allergic to fish. Maybe the seeds in the rye bread got stuck in her dentures.

Then she looked up at him, her smile dazzling, her teeth obviously all her own. "Nobody has put out that kind of effort to please me in…maybe never."

"Not never," he scoffed.

Her smile still digging a dimple into her now-pink cheek, she unwrapped the paper around her sandwich, neatly cut in the middle. "And two pickles!"

"You have to have two pickles, one for each half." He pulled out his own meal—avocado, turkey and Swiss on sourdough.

Glancing over, he saw Glory was staring at him. "Nobody gets the double pickle thing. Did they tell you I always order that way at the deli?"

"Nope. It's the way *I* always order at the deli."

Her eyes narrowed, suspicious. "Are you trying to pick me up again?"

"With double-dill breath? I don't think so." He crunched into the first sour gherkin.

With a little laugh, she applied herself again to her

meal. They ate a few bites in companionable silence until she broke it. "Still painting, I see."

He held out his speckled hands. "Yep. How about you? How's your day been going?"

"We received a shipment of red, white and blue bunting. I carry the decorations—but starting in May, not September. A frustrating phone call later, I think it's straightened out."

Kyle's sandwich was the best he'd ever eaten. Or maybe that was the company. He grinned at her. "I heard you talking quite knowledgeably about toilet repairs."

She shook her head. "Now that's an image a girl wants to put in a guy's head."

His grin widened. "No, no. I was quite impressed. How do you know that stuff?"

"My dad. I'm hopeless at keeping our back storeroom organized—or so says my friend Angelica who works here part-time—but I'm aces when it comes to advising on how to fix things. Reps come into the store and talk to me about products and I've gone to a seminar or two, but the best learning begins at home. Since I could walk, I've been helping my dad around the house."

"No 'girls play with dolls and boys with tools,' huh?"

She shook her head. "No boys in the family. I'm the lonely only."

Kyle tilted his head. "Are you? Lonely, that is."

Pursing her pretty lips, she shook her head. "I don't know how I could be. I've got customers coming in and out of the store all day long. Not to mention my retired—" she made air quotes around the word with her fingers "—dad popping in all the time to comment upon my business practices."

Kyle knew from experience a person could be lonely

anywhere: in a packed boardroom, among the tables of a bustling company cafeteria, pounding out miles on a treadmill in a busy state-of-the-art gym.

On a sigh, Glory touched a finger to the nearby revolving display rack from which hung floatable key rings. "Take this stand for example. In summer, two rows of the chains are fine, they're very popular. But now that winter's coming on, on the lower rung I added a selection of miniature flashlights that you can hook to your ring. Dad did not like it." She made a stern face and lowered her voice. "All the flashlights are situated in Aisle F and always have been."

Kyle could commiserate. His own parents hadn't liked change either, especially the changes he wanted to make to his life. He'd been on the Scott-beaten path to a medical career and then diverted to go his own way. He'd tried to explain his interests to them, but they thought their field was the only one of value, and at best they'd been bored by his shop talk.

Most women he'd tried dating hadn't understood about business, either. They'd been impressed by money but not the man. Of course, he'd not had a chance to meet them as Kyle Scott, house painter, but still, he thought this instant connection he felt with Glory was...special.

She reached over and plucked one of the spare pennies sitting in the ashtray next to the register. "For your thoughts," she said, sliding it close.

He put his hand over hers. At her jolt of reaction he almost lost his hold, but he curled his fingers under her palm and gently squeezed. "I'm thinking I like you, Glory Hallett."

She wrinkled her nose at him. "Are you sure, or are you just trying to butter me up?" she asked, her voice light. "Tell me the state of the toilet at that house you're painting."

"As far as I know, my ballcock is in prime working order."

Her face turned pink even as she laughed. "Do you even know what a ballcock is?"

"Sweetheart." He gave her a look of gentle reproof.

"Oh, you." Now her face went really red. "You're being so bad."

"Not in the slightest," he protested, enjoying himself to the utmost. "I didn't say a word when you asked about buttering you up."

She laughed out loud now. "And I thought the double dill had lifted my mood. I've got to admit it's in the stratosphere now."

"Yeah?" He smiled at her.

As if suddenly shy, Glory glanced down. Then her chin came up and her turquoise eyes were aimed right at his. "Yeah."

God, she enchanted the hell out of him. He let go of her hand so they could return to their lunch. But they continued to talk, him asking questions about the products he could see on the nearby shelves. She gestured with her pickle and munched on her tuna-and-rye and he watched her every gesture with an avid gaze.

Glory, Glory, his inner voice commented. *Hallelujah!*

Then a customer came in, interrupting their private bubble. With an apologetic look, she slid off her stool to help the older gentleman who wanted parts for his pond pump. Kyle finished up his sandwich and finally, reluctantly stood. The house wasn't going to paint itself.

Glory waved the customer out the door and looked over. "Time to get back to work?"

"Yeah."

She walked with him toward the entrance. They lingered there. He flattered himself that she didn't want to end their interlude any more than he did.

"I have something for you," she said. "A gift. A little payback for lunch—which I'll get next time."

"No—"

"Yes," she said firmly. "And after that we'll be splitting the checks."

Kyle stopped himself from saying any more. Her concern about his finances was so damn uncommon and so endearing…and the fact that she was talking about next times wasn't something he wanted to halt.

"Okay," he conceded, holding out his hand and wiggling his fingers. "Gimme my present."

From the front pocket of her butcher apron, she pulled out a soft cap of lightweight material. A painter's hat. "Here's a secret. You cover your head and you won't be combing Evergreen out of your hair every night."

"Thanks." He took it from her and put it on at a jaunty angle. "How do I look?"

She was smiling as she pretended to consider the question, but as her gaze roamed over him, he saw the smile die and her body still. In the air between them, sexual tension hummed like a happy bee.

Kyle leaned close and spoke in a low voice. "I have a secret, too, Glory."

"What?" she whispered back.

"I might need your help with my ball cock after all."

And when she began to laugh, he kissed the sound off her lips. At his first touch she went serious again, and he did, too, because it had never been like this for him before. This sense of excitement, of rightness, of connection.

When someone passed on the sidewalk beyond the front window, they broke apart, both breathing hard.

"This isn't the place, the time," he said.

"Yes," she agreed. "But come back soon? I'm really liking getting to know you, Kyle."

"The feeling's mutual," he said with a smile. Then he left, taking the spurt of guilt he felt with him. There was an important part of him that she didn't know and that he was intentionally keeping from her. It could have come out at the bar. It should have come out today.

But damn, everything was going so well. If he spoke the whole truth now, it might ruin what they were just beginning to build.

CHAPTER SIX

ANGELICA INHALED A long breath on the doorstep of the Maids by Mac offices. The help-wanted sign was still displayed and it called to her like a siren. After two nights sleeping in her car and showering at the gym—her membership had been paid up in advance, thank goodness—she'd decided to take a second chance at getting the job. Yes, it might mean Brett eventually found out—and that would still sting her pride—but her situation became more critical each passing day.

Her circumstances had to change. For the better.

Staying in the mountains continued to be the best plan and the best place from which to construct her own, new life. Not only did she have at least part-time work at the hardware store and the emotional support of Glory, her own attorney had given her the heads-up. The financial press had been in touch with him. They wanted to talk with Angelica.

What were the odds that they'd look for her here, where she was selling paint and cleaning houses?

She hoped to be cleaning houses, anyway, but standing outside of Mac Walker's office wasn't going to make that wish come true.

On another deep breath, she turned the knob and stepped inside.

Three pairs of female eyes immediately locked on her.

Angelica froze, taking in the tableau. Two of the women she recognized. Brunette Mac Walker sat perched on the desk on the other side of the front counter, a coffee in her hand. Auburn-haired Shay Walker leaned against the back door that led to the courtyard when open. She held a mug, too, with black block printing on white that read I'm Silently Judging You.

"Angelica?" she said.

A pretty blonde with Brett's same gray eyes was already smiling at her. "Hey!" she said in a friendly tone. She glanced at her sisters. "Our brother's Angelica?"

"Not at all—no, um, well, we've met, but…" Angelica babbled incoherently under their increasingly interested gazes. Her face went hot.

"You need coffee," the blonde said kindly, crossing to a pot. Without asking, she doctored it with cream and sugar.

Angelica realized she'd seen her before. She'd been in the booth at Mr. Frank's that night when Brett had kissed her.

"I'm Poppy," the small woman said, walking the cup to Angelica while wearing a second winning smile. "You know, Brett's *nice* sister."

Mac rolled her eyes. "Also known as the village idiot."

Shay smothered a laugh. "Mac, you're proving her right, you know."

Leaning toward Angelica confidentially, Poppy lowered her voice. "Mac has a thorny side. We think it's because…well, never mind. Just don't worry about it."

"What?" Mac straightened from the desk, outrage on her face. "I don't have a thorny side!"

Poppy paid her no mind. "She needs to get l-a-i-d."

"What?" Mac stared daggers at the other woman. "What did you say?"

"I said, you need to get laid," Poppy told her sister with a little shrug.

Taking a step back, Angelica considered a full retreat, not sure if the family dynamics were amusing or frightening. Mac did look as though she had sharp edges and the way the sweet-looking blonde talked about her sister getting laid—or not—was too much after a night trying to get comfortable in the convertible's cramped passenger seat.

As Mac continued to glare at the blonde, Angelica held out her coffee to the third woman, standing just outside the fray. "Um, maybe I should go."

Shay shook her head. "Relax. Not a single one of us really bites. Did you need something?"

The other two were distracted from their standoff and looked over, expressions now curious.

"Um…" But this was no time to be tentative. She took a bracing sip of her coffee to wet her mouth, then managed to get out the words. "Can I apply for a job?"

They didn't fall down in dead faints, so Angelica supposed they knew some of her financial situation. But she did see them taking notice of her designer handbag and luxury leather boots.

Mac returned to her place on the corner of the desk. "Unfortunately I don't need office help. The position I have to fill involves scrub brushes and vacuum cleaners."

"I can scrub. I can vacuum."

Mac's expression turned doubtful. "You don't want to do that."

Angelica set her coffee onto the counter and straightened her spine. "It's not a question of what I want to do," she said quietly. "I'm in a bit of a predicament, as I'm guessing you've heard."

Mac nodded. "Sure, but it can't be that bad—"

"It's that bad."

Mac tilted her head as if considering the veracity of the statement.

Memories of two cold nights in her car welled up. The darkness seemed to go on for hours and hours and hours and Angelica had started at every tiny sound, thinking some mad hunter might emerge from the woods and murder her in the hardware store parking lot. She could have slept on Glory's couch, but Angelica already knew the other woman was giving her more hours than she could afford.

Taking additional advantage was something she couldn't stomach.

Said stomach growled now, its emptiness exacerbated by that small taste of sweet and creamy coffee. She hoped Mac, Shay and Poppy hadn't heard.

"It's hard physical work," Mac said. "I only have three days a week to offer."

Angelica felt the first stirrings of excitement. She could give Glory back one of the hardware shifts and still be working five days a week.

"Then there's half mornings on Saturdays—"

"I'll take it."

Mac held up her hand. "Wait. I'm not sure I think—"

A roaring was in Angelica's ears. Desperation sounded like that. So did a meager thirteen dollars in her wallet. Weak hot tea and a Slim Jim from the convenience store as her only meal the day before. A breeze blew at her back, but she didn't let it divert her focus from the woman who had three-and-a-half days of work a week to offer.

"Please," she said, her voice a little husky with emotion. Her knees were mushy and she reached out to grasp the counter to steady herself. "I've been sleeping in my car. I've—"

"You *what*?" a male voice bellowed.

Angelica froze. Humiliation washed through her. It was one thing to admit her troubles to these women and quite another to air the details in front of a man. In front of Brett Walker.

She closed her eyes. "I think I'll just go now," she whispered to no one in particular.

"Brett," she heard Poppy warn. "You'd better grab hold of her. She looks as if she's going down."

Angelica's eyes popped open. "I'm fine. I've got to be somewhere—" But hard hands grabbed her shoulders and spun her around. A furious face got too close to hers.

He was still holding her and heat seeped deliciously into her cold skin. The silk sweater had been a bad idea. The autumn chill went right through it. Her eyes drifted closed again.

Brett shook her a little. "Damn it, Angelica. You're falling asleep on your feet."

No. Her head was just a trifle muzzy. She'd been so nervous coming here and then it hadn't gone the way she'd imagined. Especially not the part about Brett showing up. Then he had one hand behind her head and he tipped her so her forehead met his chest. "She needs coffee. Pop?"

The woman sounded very far away. "Right there on the counter, Brett. It has lots of cream and sugar."

He pulled Angelica back by a hand in her hair and brought the cup to her lips. "Drink," he ordered.

She tried pushing his hand away, and he pinned her with a ferocious stare. *"Drink."*

The only reason she sipped at the stuff was because she wanted to, she thought, perfectly aware she felt both peeved and petulant.

"Another."

He smelled good, she decided, her mind oddly drifting again. If you had to be held by a man and bossed around by him, he might as well be pleasing in an olfactory sense. Brett smelled clean, like soap, and brisk, like an autumn wind. Four inches from her face was his pale blue plaid flannel shirt and it carried the faint scent of laundry detergent.

She wanted to rub her nose against it.

That was such a terrible idea that it woke her from her weird stupor. She struggled in his hold and moved back. This time, he let her.

"Color's better," he commented, studying her.

"Well." She pulled the strap of her purse higher on her shoulder. "Thanks for the, um, aid." Not knowing where to look, she addressed the tips of her boots. "I'll be on my way now."

Mac spoke up, a note of caution in her voice. "Brett."

"Don't worry, I'm not letting her go anywhere." Then, without warning, he scooped Angelica up in his arms. He strode toward the swinging door in the counter, ignoring her spluttering protest. "You've got eats somewhere around here, right?"

The Walkers were efficient and deaf. Angelica knew this, because they didn't listen to her during the few minutes it took for them to ensconce her at Mac's desk and present her a selection of foods. Soon a bowl of steaming oatmeal was in front of her, along with a sliced apple, a handful of nuts and a fresh mug of hot coffee.

When they all stared at her with similar unyielding expressions, she could do nothing but pick up the spoon and begin to eat. Once it scraped the bottom of the dish, Mac gave a nod. "Color's even better now," she said.

"I'm sorry to cause such trouble," Angelica began, misery returning as her hunger was abating.

"Nonsense," the brunette said briskly. "My newest employee has to have enough sustenance to do a full day's work."

Angelica glanced at her, startled.

Mac held out her hand. "Welcome aboard."

Under the light from Poppy's delighted smile and aware there was a matching gleam in Shay's eyes, Angelica returned the gesture. "Are you sure?"

"She's sure," Brett answered for his sister, his voice brusque. Then he squatted down so that his gaze met hers. The gray was icy now. "What the *hell* did you think you were doing sleeping in your car?"

Poppy made a noise. "Brett, now's not the time."

"It sure as shit is the time," he said, not even sending his little sister a glance. "Now, answer."

Angelica squirmed on the seat, she couldn't help herself. "The Bluebird closed for the season. I couldn't find another place." She couldn't afford another place.

He frowned. "For God's sake. You were living at that dump?"

"It was perfectly fine," she protested, finding some spirit. Straightening in the chair, she crossed her arms over her chest. "Marv and Alice are wonderful hosts."

Brett rubbed his hand over the top of his head. "How about your car? Has that been pleasant?"

"Well, no. I admit I was a little afraid of the Insane Knife-Wielding Killer Clown."

"The what?" His lips twitched.

She waved her hand. "Just a little someone conjured by my overactive imagination."

He shook his head. "You should have come to me."

"No, Brett," she said.

"Well, it's 'yes, Brett' now," he answered, rising so that he loomed over her. "We'll find you some decent digs."

"I can't afford—"

"The cabins," Poppy put in. "Wouldn't that be perfect? She could stay in the one next door to you, Brett. You'll be close enough to keep her safe from the Insane Knife-Wielding Killer Clown."

"Wait," Angelica said. "What? No."

"We already decided it's all yeses from you from now on," the annoying man said, his tone implacable.

"I don't know…" she said, looking around at the faces of the gathered Walkers. There was amusement and something else on the female ones…speculation? They were all staring at their big brother.

"It's free," Shay added. "Think of that."

"No, I couldn't," Angelica protested. "I really couldn't."

"Yes, you could and you will," Brett said, in a tone that declared the matter was closed. "We'll figure out some way for you to work off your rent."

At the suggestion, she went hot all over. He hadn't meant it to come out the way it sounded, she told herself. It was her active imagination working overtime again.

But Poppy was sending a significant look at Shay, and Mac was actively smirking.

Brett didn't seem to notice their regard. "It's settled then," he said.

Angelica put her forehead in her hand. It seemed she had another job. A place to stay. Her most pressing needs satisfied.

So, yes, she'd changed her circumstances, all right… but what if she'd gone straight from hot water into the fire?

THERE COULD BE only one person responsible for the knock at his cabin door, Brett thought. For about three seconds he resisted answering, then he cursed under his breath and crossed to it.

It was his own fault Angelica Rodriguez was his new next-door neighbor.

But it should settle him some, shouldn't it? Since learning of her father's perfidy, he'd been uneasy. Distracted by wondering how she was feeling, how she was faring. As much as he told himself to forget about it, forget about *her*, he'd not managed to push her from his thoughts for more than a few moments at a time.

And he'd been right to worry, hadn't he?

Pulling open the door, he took in the sight of the woman on the doorstep. His belly tightened in lust even as relief coursed through him. She looked a hell of a lot better than she had that morning in Mac's office. Then, she'd been pale, her big eyes shadowed. When she'd nearly gone down to the floor he'd felt his heart lurch in his chest.

It had pissed him off then.

He was still pissed off now, he decided. "What do you want?" he growled.

There was a plate in her hands, and she lifted it in his direction. "I made you cookies."

Shoving his hands in his pockets, he scowled at her. "Why would you do that?"

"As a thank-you? While I was working my shift at the hardware store, someone stocked the cabin with groceries, including flour, sugar and butter. Chocolate chips."

"Must have been Poppy," he said. "Maybe Shay or Mac."

One of her dark brows arched. "Are you saying you don't want a taste?"

He nearly groaned. Of course he wanted a taste. He wanted a whole feast—of her. "Angelica…"

"Brett." Her mouth curved. The smile looked wan. "It's just cookies."

The husky note in her voice had him studying her more closely in the porch light. Yeah, she looked better than she had this morning, but there was a distinct weariness in her expression. She'd been sleeping in her car after all. And it had been beyond chilly the past few nights. He bet she had a scratchy throat.

He couldn't let her continue standing out there in the cold. "You should have a jacket on," he said, opening the door wider. "Come by the fire and get warm."

She stepped inside. Taking the plate of cookies from her, he pushed her toward the living area. On a braided rug that had come with the cabin sat his own saddle-colored leather couch. Angelica trailed one slender hand across the back of it and he worried he'd feel the phantom touch of it every time he sprawled on the cushions.

Near the hearth, she spread her fingers before the

flames. He saw the light of them leap, golden orange and red, between her digits as if they licked her flesh. Brett wanted to run his tongue along there, too, then suck each fingertip into his mouth. Her eyes would widen and then close, her head dropping back to reveal the tender curve of her neck. He'd bite that next.

Shit. Turning his back on her, he placed the cookies on the kitchen counter. The food prep and living areas were just one big space. A hallway teed off to the bedrooms and bathroom. The bungalow was a decent size, but with Angelica between its walls there wasn't anywhere for the pulsing sexual attraction he felt for her to go.

"Are these yours?" she asked.

He glanced around. She was studying the two framed drawings he'd hung over the fireplace. They were part of a landscape design he'd done in school. One was a plot plan that showed an overhead view of the project, including the structure and the layout of the surrounding greenery. Beside it was a hand-drawn rendering—an illustration—that showed the same project from a boots-on-the-ground perspective. Nestled in the landscaping features he'd envisioned was a large, lodge-like building.

"They're mine," he acknowledged.

Over her shoulder, her gaze found his. "What is it?"

He shrugged. "This. Well, not this. Just an idea we once had for something we could put on this land."

"I know a little about your property," she said, turning to face him. The firelight limned her delectable body, her curves covered in denim and a lightweight sweater. "From my work with the historical society. It was a ski resort once, right?"

"And before that, timberland," he said. "The Walkers came to the area one hundred fifty years ago with a wagon and oxen and bought up acres for logging. A century later, this was the last piece we owned and my grandfather and my father after him operated the mountain as a ski resort in winter. A fire burned everything but the cabins when we were kids. Our father died not long after that."

"I'm sorry," Angelica said, her expression going soft. She glanced back at the drawings. "You didn't portray it in winter, though."

He shrugged again. The rendering showed the vacation lodge in the glory of autumn, with aspens blazing yellow and the pines laden with cones.

"You did a good job with the building, too," she said. "It looks both majestic and welcoming."

"I had a roommate who was an architecture major. I picked up a lot from him."

She had turned back to study the drawings again. "When are you going to follow through with it?"

"The lodge?"

"Yes."

"This land is cursed," he said. It was the simplest explanation and one he almost believed to be true.

She whirled around, her brown eyes wide. "What? You don't believe that."

Maybe it was he who was cursed. How could he want her so damn bad when she was so damn bad for him? He was mountain born and bred, his life as deeply rooted here as the oldest evergreens, and when she recovered from this temporary financial setback he was certain she'd beat feet for some other high-class playground, never to return.

Surely Blue Arrow Lake would only hold lousy memories.

"Brett?"

"Why didn't you tell me?" he demanded, striding toward her.

Her arms crossed over her chest. "Tell you what?"

"That you were in trouble. Broke. No place to sleep."

She turned back to the fire. "Did you sample the cookies?"

Stopping a foot from her, he stared at her back, frustrated. She was a flatlander. Not above his touch; he didn't think she was better than him, of course, but her type only caused trouble. Still...

He drew one hand down her hair, from the crown of her head to where the ends tangled at the middle of her back. The stuff was so silky it caught on his working-man's calluses. That's what she'd do to him—snag him up, if he didn't find some way to deal with her.

"You should have told me," he insisted, twisting the strands around his fingers. "How bad is it?"

She sighed. "I don't really know. Lawyers are involved. I have my own. My accounts were not tied into my father's fund, but it appears he found some way to siphon off my monies just before he was arrested. My attorney thinks it's possible we could recover some of it in time."

He tugged at her hair. "See? That wasn't so hard."

"I'm...embarrassed. Mortified, really."

"Why? You didn't do anything wrong."

She shrugged. "I feel stupid for so badly wanting the approval of a man who could do something so dastardly."

"You should have come to me when you first found out."

Pulling free of his touch she stepped aside. Her brown eyes bored straight into his. "Why would I? We're not friends."

"Because we're…" Shit. He didn't have a good answer. "You hungry? Do you want a beer? Or wine? I think Shay left some here."

Without waiting for her reply, he found the chilled bottle in the fridge and poured. He took up a beer, twisted off the top and was slamming some down even as he delivered her the glass.

She studied him over the rim. "Your family seems really close."

He was about to make some disparaging remark about siblings, when she continued in a soft voice. "I envy that."

"You're an only child." He'd thought so.

"Yes. My mother refused to ruin her figure again after she had me. I gained a stepbrother and stepsisters on my father's side for about ten minutes—the marriage only lasted that long—but it was just as well because they despised me on sight."

"Threatened by your beauty, I suppose."

Her cheeks went pink. "I don't know about that."

"Haven't you read Cinderella?"

"Despite what you might think, my life's been no fairy tale," Angelica said, frowning down at her wine. Then she looked up. "Why did you do it?"

Fantasize about her night and day since they'd met? Take cold showers too many times to count? Used his own hand twice that many times imagining what they might be like together? His fingers tightened on his beer. "Do what?"

"Get me the job with your sister."

"I didn't—"

"I might have been a little woozy, but I could sense the silent messages being passed back and forth."

"Mac needs a worker. You need a job. No big deal." Not that his sister had required any prodding to take on a new employee. They'd met gazes over Angelica's dark head and the deed had been done.

"And why am I living here? Why did you make that happen, too?"

"What's with all the questions?" he said, glancing away.

"Because I want to understand what's going on here, Brett. What I owe. And to whom."

"Christ," he muttered. "Do I look like the kind of man who expects sex—or whatever the hell you're worrying about—in return for one small good deed?"

"All summer you looked like the kind of man who didn't want to be around me at all."

Because he'd been trying to save himself from getting close to someone who would ultimately leave! Because he'd been trying to save himself from this protective, nurturing urge that had been plaguing him since the first time he'd glimpsed her angel face. Because he'd been trying to save himself from this greedy need to kiss her mouth, caress her curves, possess her body.

Yes, he wanted to have sex with her, but not as payment. He wanted to have sex with her for pleasure. Their mutual pleasure.

"We should be friends," he suddenly said.

She gaped at him.

"What? Don't you know you can't have too many friends?"

"Let me get this straight." She sipped from her wine.

"After months of giving me the cold shoulder, you've now gone out of your way to make my life easier—"

"I wouldn't say that."

"To make my life easier," she repeated firmly. "Because you want us to be friends."

Did she have to make it sound so stupid? But there was only one answer to the question. "Yes."

She shook her head, released a little laugh and then toasted him with her glass. "Okay."

"See how much better things go when you agree with me?"

"I suppose," she said, without sounding a bit convinced. She crossed to the kitchen sink, rinsed her glass. "It's time for me to be on my way, *pal*."

"Sounds good, buddy." Setting his beer aside, he followed her to the front door.

He held it open for her. She paused on the threshold, then turned to face him. The porch light sprinkled gold in her hair. A small breeze blew her scent over him. "Good night, Brett."

Without thinking, he yanked her into his arms. Or maybe it was she who made the first move. In any case, in a millisecond she was on tiptoe and their mouths were fused. Tongues tangled, heads slanted, the intimacy was hot, deep, wet. His hands slid down her back to her ass. He tilted her hips against his hard cock and she crowded as close as could be.

Someone was moaning.

One of his hands slid around and then under the hem of her sweater. He felt the bare skin over her rib cage twitch as his fingertips stroked up toward her breast. His palm covered the soft mound and through the thin fabric of her bra her nipple pebbled into its center.

Every muscle in his body tightened and his heart slammed in his chest. She was going to kill him. *Oxygen*, his hazy mind thought. *We need to breathe.*

He tore his lips from hers.

They stared at each other, panting.

Common sense trickled in. *This way there be dragons.*

Feeling a heartbeat away from sliding off the edge of the world, Brett drew his hand from beneath her sweater. Her expression just as wary as he felt, Angelica stepped back.

"So…" Her gaze trained on his face, she rubbed her palms along the legs of her jeans. "Still friends?"

"Yeah," he said, his voice gruff. It had to be this way. "We just…we just sealed the deal with a kiss."

He watched her walk the short distance to her cabin. Not until she was safely inside did he shut his own door.

We just sealed the deal with a kiss.

Hell! It wasn't a deal…it was a devil's bargain.

CHAPTER SEVEN

ANGELICA LINGERED IN the offices of the Mountain Historical Society, tidying her desk, then scrubbing the coffeepot. She made up tasks for herself rather than hurrying to her Walker cabin. As a volunteer, no one expected her to finish out her shift if her work was accomplished, but as the only one in the offices at the moment, she felt compelled to stay until the closing hour of five o'clock.

Her cabin would still be waiting, thirty feet from the one that housed Brett.

Her friend.

Sighing, she grabbed up the pet brush that someone had brought in and began to stroke the bristles over their mascot, the good ol' grizzly named Piney that dominated the center of the foyer. "You're cheerier than my neighbor," she told the stuffed beast. "Maybe you and I should spend the night together."

For the past few days she'd run into Brett coming or going. He'd avoided her eyes and muttered some semblance of a greeting here and there. It was so obvious he wanted to evade her that she'd taken to peeking out the door before leaving her cabin.

He must be on the lookout for her, too, because he managed to refill the wood box in her living room and the log holder on the porch when she wasn't around to catch him. Maybe he feared she'd kiss him again.

It had been her that had gone after him that last time, right?

She wasn't sure. She'd turned, said good-night, and then it was a filings-to-magnet moment. Their bodies slammed together, their lips locked. He'd managed to pull away first. She thought. At the time, she'd been so into the moment, into him, that all her senses hadn't been working properly.

To her, the kiss had been heaven and hell entwined. Burning fire and delightful promise, all the things she'd read about, heard about when it came to intimacy and sex. All the things she'd wanted to experience but had backed away from before.

Until Brett.

Clearly, for him, it had been no big deal.

Thus, friends.

The distinctive creak of the society's front door sounded in the quiet. She looked up just as it shut behind the newcomer, the wooden blinds clacking against the half window. It was a male figure that came in, bundled in a coat and hat, and her heart leaped, until he pulled the cap from his hair.

"Hey, Vaughn," she said, returning to her grooming of the grizzly. Something about the man made her uneasy. Maybe it was because she'd met enough of his sort in her lifetime. Trust-fund types who thought their entitlement didn't come from luck but because they were inherently better than the other guy.

"Angelica." He nodded, a smile beaming out of his tan. His hair was dark blond, his chin chiseled, but she thought Brett was a hundred times more manly with his scarred visage and his hard-earned muscles. "How's it going?"

"Great. I'm about to head out." She glanced at the old-fashioned school clock mounted on the wall. "Did you need something?"

"Nah. Just thought I'd pop in for a chat."

"You knew I was here?"

He shrugged. "Saw your car...only one in the parking lot."

Her stomach jumped a bit and she scolded herself for being silly. She'd known Vaughn for months, and he'd never shown much interest in her. Maybe he was only being polite. Concerned that she was alone at the headquarters.

"Anything new to report about the historical society?" he asked.

She drew the brush along Piney's...did grizzlies have arms? "Not really. The last of the auction items have been turned over to the new owners, and we were able to cancel the rental of the storage locker."

Vaughn had paused in the act of unbuttoning his cashmere overcoat. "There was a storage locker?"

"Uh-huh. When your grandfather's house went up for sale, we had to put the items somewhere."

"I hadn't thought of that," he said, almost to himself.

"It was expensive, that unit, so we're glad to eliminate the monthly fee from our expenses."

"Stupid of me," Vaughn muttered, "not to think of that."

"Well, done with it now." She glanced again at the clock. "Time for me to go."

Setting the brush aside, she headed toward the rack in the corner of the offices where she'd hung her purse and coat. Vaughn followed her there, and took the long coat out of her hands.

"Oh, don't bother," she said, flustered as he held it out for her.

"Nonsense," he said, with another alligator smile. "I was raised to mind my manners."

There was nothing she could do but turn her back on him—and that made her nervous—in order to push her hands through the sleeves. She shoved them through as quickly as possible but before she was able to turn around again he was sliding his hands beneath her hair at the nape of her neck so he could pull the swathe of it from beneath her collar.

Her flesh crawled at the dry touch of his skin on hers.

Whirling around, she stepped back and her shoulders hit the wall with a muted thud. "Um, thanks," she said, trying to suppress her shudder. The last man who'd touched her hair, who'd touched her, had been Brett. With him, she'd felt shivery in an entirely different way.

"What's the matter?" Vaughn asked.

Not for anything did she want to admit to him she didn't feel comfortable flying solo in male company. "Not a thing," she said, ducking her head to apply her attention to her coat buttons.

In her peripheral vision she saw his shiny dress shoes shuffle closer. Ignoring that, she kept her gaze down and used mental telepathy to communicate her disinterest. *Go away, Vaughn. Give me room.*

"You know," he said, his voice low. "You're a very lovely woman."

"Thank you." She pulled her gloves out of her pocket and began to inch them on. "That's a nice thing to say."

"Oh, I'm not just being nice." He moved closer, into her personal zone and she started shouting at him in her mind. *Back off!*

Her skittishness around most men flustered her so that she'd never mastered the ability to make a quick getaway. Maybe it was due to how young she'd been when she'd had that ugly experience in a dark closet, or maybe she'd been a rabbit in an earlier life. Whatever the reason, her tendency was to freeze up and hope the predator would move past. So she was standing there, pretending a preoccupation with her gloves, when suddenly Vaughn was much, much too close, surrounding her. She leaned back, pressing into the wall, and his bent arm was propped against it, above her head.

His breath moved the hair at her temple. "I heard you've had some financial trouble," he said in a low voice. "You know, I could help you out—or maybe we could help out each other."

A trickle of sweat rolled down her back. "Um, Vaughn—"

"I happen to have a cold bottle of wine in my car. Some cheese and crackers."

She cursed her curvy behind. If she'd had a flatter butt, she could have put more inches between them.

"Why don't I bring them in," he continued, his tone of voice the kind you used to coax a cat from behind a bureau, "and we can enjoy them while we get to know each other?"

"I don't—"

The squeal of the front door cut into her next words. She'd never been so glad to hear the screechy noise.

Or see the man stepping into the building.

"Brett!" She was pretty sure she sounded almost as squeaky as the door. Vaughn didn't move as quickly as she would have liked, but now she finally managed to duck and squirm to gain freedom from his imprisoning body. "What are you doing here?" she continued in a breathless voice.

His gaze ran over her from head to toe, his expression giving nothing away. "How are you, Angelica?"

"It's great to see you," she said, trying her mental telegraphy again. *Don't leave me alone with Vaughn. Please don't leave me alone with him.*

Maybe it worked, because Brett stepped farther into the room and let the door snap shut behind him.

His gaze jumped from her to the man standing behind her. "I suppose you know Vaughn, right?" She threw a glance over her shoulder and tried pretending her pulse wasn't skipping about, first from nerves and then from… well, just being in her neighbor's presence. "Vaughn, I'm sure you need no introduction to my friend, Brett."

At the word *friend*, he sent her a dark look, then turned his attention back to the other man. "Elliott."

Vaughn mumbled some greeting and moved close to Angelica. She edged away and returned her gaze to Brett. "What brings you by?" she asked in a bright voice.

"Saw your car in the lot," he said.

"Funny, Vaughn stopped in for the same reason."

Brett's brows rose. "Did he tell you one of your rear tires is flat?"

She slid the other man a look. "No."

Vaughn lifted his hands in a "who knew" gesture. "It must have happened after I came inside. Or maybe I just didn't notice."

"I'm not sure what caused it," Brett said, his narrowed eyes on Vaughn's face. "I didn't see a nail."

"Well, don't you worry about it, Walker," Vaughn said. "Angelica will call the road service, and I'll stay right here until she's… I mean, it's as good as new."

She widened her eyes in Brett's direction, trying to sync her brain to his once more. *Don't leave me!*

He didn't even look at her. "No need to make a call and wait for the truck." His gaze cut to Angelica and she thought, just for a second, it softened. "You have a spare, sweetheart?"

"Um, yes." She moved to the coatrack and fished through her purse, still hanging there, on the hunt for her keys.

"'Sweetheart,' huh?" Vaughn murmured to Brett.

"Just slipped out," he said. "We're friends."

"Buddies," Angelica added, her key ring in hand. "Pals."

"Never can have too many friends," Vaughn said, his tone turning jovial.

"That's what I tell her," Brett said, taking the keys from her hand. "This won't take long."

"I have an idea," Vaughn said, turning to Angelica. "We leave Walker here and let him do his grease-monkey thing. The two of us will head out for a drink to pass the time." Now he leaned close and spoke in almost a whisper. "Remember, we have things to discuss."

Behind him, Brett's brows rose nearly to his hairline. "Yeah, Elliott, if you stick around you might get some dirt on your fancy overcoat." His gaze flicked to her. "Have fun, angel face."

She tried to overlook the insult. But, really? "I'm not going to leave when Brett's doing me a favor," she said. Was that the kind of woman he thought she was?

"What else are friends for?" Vaughn countered.

Angelica took a step toward the door. "Not for running off." She glanced at Brett. "Coming? You'll tell me what I can do to help."

As she sailed through the door she called over her shoulder. "Goodbye, Vaughn."

Her neighbor caught up with her as she was examining her flat tire in the waning light. Without another word to either of them, Vaughn sped past as he left the lot. Angelica's eyes rounded. "Was he giving us the finger?"

"I think he meant that for me," Brett said. "Looks like I messed with his plans for the evening."

She shrugged, just glad to see the other man's taillights in the distance. Then she frowned at the state of her tire. "Flat" didn't even cover how airless it seemed to be.

"I really appreciate your helping me out," she said. "I'll try to think of something to make it up to you. What can I do right now?"

"Just move back," Brett said after a moment, propelling her several feet away with his hands on her shoulders. "Keep your distance."

She sighed as she watched him roll up his sleeves to reveal powerful, ropy forearms. *Keep your distance.* He should tell that to her hormones or whatever you wanted to call this feeling that compelled her to want to climb his body, kiss him silly, do all the wild and horny things that women did to men. Things that required a closeness and trust that had always alarmed her before.

That she only experienced around Brett.

Her *friend.*

"You could have gone for that drink," he muttered, his back turned to her.

She didn't want to admit that Vaughn made her skin crawl. It seemed…gauche.

"He's your type," Brett added, a hard edge to his voice. "You two have a lot in common."

She strove for an airy note. "How come that sounds like you're jealous?"

He snorted. "In your dreams."

"Right," Angelica said, swallowing her sigh. It seemed as if her dreams were the only places she'd have the man.

KYLE SCOTT ENTERED Hallett Hardware to hear a frustrated female threaten in a loud voice, "If you don't stop, I'm calling Mom!"

Hmm. He deduced that his date was in the back room at the rear of the store and that she might not be in the best of moods. That afternoon they had plans to peruse the fall festival being celebrated on the main street of the village of Blue Arrow Lake, just a couple of blocks away. He hoped whatever was causing her to yell wouldn't get in the way of their plans.

"Can I help you?" another female voice asked.

He glanced around to see a dark-haired young woman approaching. She was taller than Glory with long wavy hair and brown eyes. *Angel* was printed in block letters on her butcher-style apron. He smiled at her even as he heard more dire mutterings coming from the back room. "I'm here for Glory."

"Oh." The brunette came forward, reaching out a friendly hand. "I'm Angelica. You're Kyle?"

He nodded, pleased that Glory must have spoken of him. "Kyle Scott. The two of us were supposed to go to the festival this afternoon—"

"Dad!" Glory's voice interrupted. "I know how to place a window order. I've been doing it since I was thirteen years old, for goodness' sake. Go home. Go do something with Mom. Isn't that why you retired?"

"—but now I'm not so sure," Kyle finished.

Angelica sent him a reassuring smile. "Don't worry. This is nothing unusual. From what she's said, ever since her dad handed over the keys six months ago, they've been locking horns. I only started working here in June when Glory needed some extra help, but I'm beginning to think they enjoy it."

"I do *not* enjoy it," Glory corrected, storming up a nearby aisle. "I'm going to hire a guard for the door with instructions not to let the man over the threshold." She pushed her fingers through her hair, disheveling the pretty blond stuff into a becoming disarray. Then she blew out a long breath and glanced over at Kyle.

"Hi," she said, her expression turning from wrathful to uncertain. "Do you now want to run away from me? I wouldn't blame you if there was an accompanying scream or two."

"How about if we run away together?"

Her expression changed again, and he couldn't say exactly all that this one communicated. "Just for the afternoon," he added, tapping her cute nose because he had to touch her. "Don't look so concerned."

"I'm not letting a thing worry me today, not after I walk out of the store." She had her jacket over her arm and, now donning it, she addressed Angelica. "He's back there, doing who knows what. I'm sorry—"

"Don't be. We get along very well."

Glory sighed. "I know. You're able to handle him while all he makes me want to do is kick and cry like a two-year-old."

"Save yourself a tantrum," Angelica advised, shooing

her toward the exit, "and have a great time." Her smile for Kyle was bright. "Nice meeting you."

"Feeling's mutual," he said, holding the door for Glory.

When it swung shut behind them, Glory pulled a striped cap with a pink pom-pom over her blond hair. Then glanced up at him. "You sure you haven't changed your mind?"

Kyle couldn't think of anything besides how adorable she was. Jeans clung to her legs and were stuffed into tall, rugged-looking Western-style boots. The puff of yarn on the top of her hat matched the color of her full lips and the flush that was infusing her cheeks. By contrast, her turquoise eyes looked even brighter.

"Why are you staring at me like that?" she asked, shoving her hands in her coat pockets in a self-conscious gesture.

He pulled one free and entwined his fingers with hers. "Because there's no place else I want to be today. There's no one else I'd rather be with in the world."

The smile she returned was a dazzler.

At the sight of it, guilt gave him a little pinch. When he'd dropped by the hardware store the day before to suggest this outing, she'd been busy with customers. He'd managed to grab her attention for the three seconds it took to get her enthusiastic yes, but there and then he'd decided that the next time they were together, first thing, he was going to confess exactly what the real Kyle Scott was all about.

It only seemed fair.

But now he was reluctant to start off their time together with revelations.

Later, he told himself, to quell his conscience. *I'll tell her just a little bit later.*

They set off on a stroll down the sidewalk. Kyle breathed in the clean autumn air and found himself swinging their linked arms as if they were teenagers. "I feel like I'm drunk," he told Glory. "The smell of the pines, the way the sun has turned the air to gold, the company of a beautiful woman…"

"I'm not beautiful. Cute, I'll grant you. I've been cute since I was six months old and won the 'Cutest Kewpie' contest sponsored by the local bakery. My mom framed the photo that ran on the front page of the *Mountain Messenger* and it still hangs in her kitchen."

Kyle shook his head. "Beautiful."

She rolled her eyes. "Cute. Ask anybody in town."

"They've known you too long to appreciate you then. They're remembering the Kewpie-contest winner and not seeing the grown woman you've become."

She stopped and he had to halt, too, or drag her along the cement. "What?" he asked.

"Thank you." She shook her head, a little smile quirking the corners of her lips. "Just…thanks."

They continued on, even as his conscience began clamoring again. But were his words to her any different coming from Kyle Scott, house painter, than from Kyle Scott, businessman with a net worth nearing the multimillion-dollar level? *He* didn't think so, but would she?

Later, he told himself again. When he could find the right, quiet time to tell all, he would.

Now was not a quiet time, he was certain of that as they drew closer to the two downtown blocks barricaded for the festival event. The upscale boutiques had wares displayed on tables and hung on racks on the sidewalk outside their doors. Restaurants were offering tastes of their specialties. Civic groups had booths set up on the blacktop from which they sold shiny apples, slices of pie, popcorn and gooey cinnamon rolls. For those who wanted "healthier" fare, there were also baked potatoes drizzled with butter and cheese and roasted turkey legs with brown, crispy skin.

The space was crowded and every eighteen inches or so they ran into someone Glory knew. She was greeted with affection and more than a few curious glances were cast his way. She introduced him each time, and the only thing he regretted about shaking hands was that it made him lose his hold on Glory.

"I'm getting what it's like to live in a small town," he murmured to her as they examined some paintings by local artists.

"You're originally from the big city?"

He nodded. "You seem to know everyone here."

"Oh, yeah." She grasped his elbow and half turned him to face the passing throng. "In the red sweater? That's my third-grade teacher. Over there is my high school principal. Doctor Joe retired a couple of years ago—he's in the Rotary Club booth—but he treated every cold and also scolded me when he found me riding my bike without a helmet. It was a rigid family rule, and I would have caught hell from my folks if they'd known, but Doctor Joe kept my secret."

"I'm surprised you can have any secrets at all around here." He glanced down at her face, thinking how the slight nip in the air had turned the tip of her nose the same shade as her kissable mouth. He swooped down to give her one, hot but quick.

When he straightened, her hand was over her heart and her eyes had widened. "Wow," she said.

"Maybe I should have waited for a different moment—"

"No." She tucked her hand in the crook of his elbow and leaned her head against the side of his arm. "I shouldn't tell you, but that was pretty darn perfect."

"You should tell me. You should tell me anything you feel like saying." His conscience started jumping up and down again in his head, and he opened his mouth to reveal more of himself, but a middle-aged woman bustled up and began telling Glory a story about her daughter and granddaughter. Glory was caught up in it, smiling and laughing on cue.

"I'll have to get over to see Jules," she said. "It's been a week or two. Little Becca grows so fast that if I blink she's an inch taller and has learned twenty more words."

"I know, I know," the older woman said. "We shouldn't miss a moment of it."

Kyle bent to murmur in Glory's ear. "Be back in a second, going to get us some cider."

She beamed him a smile and continued her conversation.

When he returned, two steaming paper cups in hand, the middle-aged woman had been replaced with a man, who looked like a local in his work boots, jeans and plaid shirt covered by a quilted vest.

He was smiling down at Glory in a familiar fashion that stirred something inside Kyle. A little of his pleasure in the day dimmed. Still, he schooled his expression to one of mild interest as he met the other man's gaze and put the drink in Glory's hand.

"Hi," he said. "Kyle Scott."

"Stu—Stuart Christianson."

They shook hands and neither grimaced though their grips were overdone. "You know Glory," Kyle said, stating the obvious.

"Since preschool," she said. "On the first day I kicked over his block tower."

The other man grinned. "I kissed her in retaliation."

Glory glanced up at Kyle, humor in her eyes. "Cooties were taken very seriously. Little boys were the carriers."

"The next time I kissed you, we were fifteen years old," Stu said. "Remember, Glory?"

"Sure. I had to wait twelve long years for another opportunity to catch something from you."

At that, the other man gave her a light punch on the arm, raising Kyle's hackles. Not because there was anything the least bit violent in the action—it was the exact opposite. The gesture spoke of closeness, ease, affection.

He hated it.

"Well, see you later, kid," Stu said to Glory.

"See you," she said.

He lifted his chin toward Kyle, seemingly on his way, then he paused, his gaze shifting back to Glory. "January's coming up, honey."

Kyle watched new color brighten her cheeks. "Oh, *you.*"

"It's been two years," he added.

"I can count." She seemed disgruntled now.

He shrugged. "Just saying…" His grin was cocky. "You need a date for New Year's, you know my number." Then he was gone, swallowed up by the crowd.

Glory turned back to the paintings and sipped as she seemed to study them. Kyle remained silent for about five seconds…then he couldn't stand it any longer. "What was that all about?"

She waved her free hand. "Stu," she said, as if that was the extent of the necessary explanation.

"Stu…what?"

"We used to date."

"When?" Okay, this was like pulling teeth.

"For a while, here and there."

"What's the significance of January?"

She slid him a look, went back to the paintings. "It's kind of a joke. It seems like we always got together during that month. It wouldn't last. Then time would go by and we'd start dating again…in January."

"How often did this happen?"

Her shoulders moved up and down in a shrug. "A few times. Three." Now she looked up at him and tugged on the sleeve of his jacket. "Can we please stop talking about the past? I'm here, you're here, we're together and it's a beautiful afternoon. Let's make the most of today."

"Yeah," he said softly, taken in by her beautiful eyes, the mouth that he just had to bend and kiss again. She looked dazed at the end of it and whatever had been dragging at his mood since the appearance of Stu vanished.

Let's make the most of today. He repeated those words to his conscience.

There was no need to mar today with anything as serious as who he was, what he did, where he lived. None of those things mattered. Now mattered. Their kisses, their clasped hands, whatever pleasure might come of their brief time together.

It was all they'd have.

Because it was completely clear to him that Glory

was seamlessly integrated into this town of hers. She wasn't leaving…and he wasn't staying. Come January, he'd be back in LA, working with his keyboard instead of a paint brush. Glory would be with Stu again. Probably this time it would stick.

Until then, she was on his arm and he hoped she'd be in his bed.

If he could help it, neither one of them would regret their time together.

CHAPTER EIGHT

ANGELICA WAS NOT nearly as reluctant to join Glory on a trip to Mr. Frank's the next time ladies' night came around. Not only was it clear that Glory needed cheering up, but Angelica would do just about anything to avoid the tension around the Walker cabins. It was ridiculous, sure, but the truth was, she could feel Brett breathing when she was in her bungalow and he was in his. If someone told her that their heartbeats were in sync, she'd not be surprised.

It added up to nerves stretched to the breaking point.

Glory paused with her hand on the door. "I don't know if I'm in the mood for this."

"That was my line last time," Angelica said, and reaching around her shorter friend, she pulled open the door herself. "We'll have fun. Forget about our troubles. I talked to my lawyer today. Nothing's changed in my situation so that was his advice."

Glory glanced over and grimaced. "Sorry to be such a whiner. Even though you're now living in one of the Walkers' cabins, your problems are still bigger than mine. I should be used to relationships not working out for me, anyway."

They slid into one of the two-person booths along the wall in the bar area. Once they'd ordered from the prompt server, Angelica patted Glory's hand. "What happened? When I saw Kyle last week, on that day you went to the fall festival, he couldn't keep his eyes off you."

"We had a great time." Her gaze lowered to the tabletop. "Or at least I did. He kissed me...lots of times, and, Angelica..."

"I recognize that moony expression," Angelica said. "So what happened at the end of the evening?"

She shrugged. "He walked me to my car in the parking lot of the hardware store. There was another kiss or two. Smoking-hot kisses."

"Then...?"

"Then I didn't invite him back to my place. You know I don't just hop into bed with men. And he's essentially a stranger."

"I get that."

"I know you do. You're cautious because of that creepy stepbrother of yours."

"*Ex*-stepbrother. But you'd think I'd be over it by now." Angelica had told Glory a little bit about him one quiet morning in the store.

"We never get over wanting to protect ourselves," Glory said. "But you know what? You should consider putting yourself out there on occasion. If somebody appeals to you...go for it instead of shying away."

Angelica thought of the kiss she'd shared with Brett, the one he'd claimed sealed their friendship pact. How she'd wanted more! "Wouldn't that be..."

"Shameless," Glory put in with a grin. "But a woman's got to be a little shameless sometimes." Then her smile died. "Maybe that's where I went wrong with Kyle."

"You don't want to be with some guy who's not willing to wait until you're ready for sex. That's Woman 101."

"I *was* ready," Glory admitted. "That's what held me back. I thought we'd connected, really had something going on from the very first. But I worried I couldn't trust it. Looks like I was right."

"Men suck," Angelica said.

The sound of laughter drew her attention away from her friend. Glancing past Glory, she saw a large crowd of people gathered around a couple of tables pushed together. As she watched, her gaze snagged on Brett. He held his beer aloft and made some comment that caused another roar of laughter from the men and women surrounding him.

Then the amused expression on his face died, and his own gaze arrowed between two people sitting opposite the table from him. Across the room, he found her.

Her body flashed hot. A sudden need to escape welled inside her and she grabbed for her purse, ready to run.

"Here are your drinks." The server placed white wine in front of both her and Glory.

Glory. Angelica couldn't just up and leave when her girlfriend needed support.

Swallowing a sigh, she drew her glass closer to her and told herself to ignore the smoldering stare of her next-door neighbor. "So, back to the subject, Glory. There were smoking kisses, no sex and then…"

"Then nothing."

"What do you mean?" She flicked a glance at Brett and then wanted to kick herself because he caught her looking. Redirecting her gaze, she addressed Glory again. "Did he tell you it was over?"

"Why would he?" the other woman asked, her expression miserable. "To be over you have to have started something. It was likely all in my mind."

"He didn't call—"

"He said he'd come by Hallett's—but hasn't. As far as I know he doesn't have my number. I don't have his."

"He could phone the hardware store," Angelica said.

Glory's mouth twisted. "Thanks for reminding me."

"Sorry."

"So the long and short of it is that he isn't interested enough to make further contact."

"You don't know that for sure. Perhaps you should have more faith in him—it's only been a few days after all. There could be a logical explanation. Maybe he…" Angelica tried to think.

"Broke both hands?" Glory suggested hopefully.

"It could be a disease. A temporarily disfiguring one." Through her lashes, she checked on Brett, who was leaning close to some bottle redhead. Too bad he wasn't the sufferer of such an illness, she thought. Maybe if he didn't possess that winning combination of features along with those intriguing, sexy scars she could forget all about him.

"What about marriage? Maybe he's got a wife and decided to go back to her." Glory put her forehead in her hand. "I attracted a cheating bastard with a short attention span."

"You don't know that," Angelica said. "He didn't seem married to me. More likely he has some condition that caused all his hair to fall out and he's waiting until it grows back before he sees you again."

"Hair wouldn't stop a guy," Glory grumbled. "Maybe his dick fell off."

Angelica snickered.

At the sound, her friend brightened a little. She lifted

her wine toward Angelica's. "To dickless, faithless phi-landerers!"

Their glasses clicked, but then Angelica frowned. "Wait—why are we toasting bad guys?"

Glory drained her wine, then put her fingers over her mouth as she gave a small, ladylike burp. She signaled the waitress for another round. "You're right," she said, sounding a bit tipsy. "To their dicks!"

Angelica swallowed the last of her first glass and picked up the second that had just appeared on the table. "No, to their dicklessness!" She and Glory beamed at each other.

"Ladies!" A man stood at their table, glancing be-tween their faces. "What's the joke?"

Glory giggled while Angelica tried to hold it to-gether. "Um…roosters?" *Dicks*, she tried telling the other woman silently. *Cocks. Roosters. Get it?*

Her friend laughed so hard she nearly fell off her seat. Then she fanned her face with her hands and got herself under control. "Sorry, Jeff. Inside joke. Do you know Angelica?"

"No, but I'd like to," he said, with a friendly smile. "Wanna dance?"

"Oh. Well." Angelica didn't often go to bars. She'd never danced with a man she'd met in one. Without thinking, she looked over to Brett's table and noticed him watching her, his arms crossed over his chest. He appeared…watchful.

As if he thought she needed a father.

Well, she'd had one of those, and he'd left her flat and drained her dry. She only had herself to rely on and she resented that expression of his that seemed to imply she required a keeper.

She had no use for one. But what she did need was some way to work out the tension that had been building for days. "Sure, I want to dance."

Not only was it ladies' night at Mr. Frank's, but apparently Mr. Frank had a penchant for country music. The DJ started a Blake Shelton tune. A howl came up from the crowd, and Jeff drew Angelica out of the booth.

She didn't know how to two-step, but the kind man took a few moments to teach her, and then they were moving with the others on the dance floor. If she stepped on his toes a time or two, he didn't complain. A line dance came up next, and she fumbled through that, finally catching on about three bars before the end of the song.

But it was breathless fun and for a few minutes she was only thinking about her feet and the correct direction to move them. A slow and sultry piece started playing and she began to return to her table when a different guy snagged her hand. He pulled her close and on beery breath he informed her he was Gordon. With a polite smile, she tried pulling free of his hold, but his grip was firm, and she didn't find real cause for alarm.

That was, until one of his hands wandered to her butt.

"Uh, Gordon." She tried wrapping her fingers around his wrist to redirect him, but he was dancing with his eyes closed and he seemed to be in his own little world.

Now she tried breaking free of him altogether, but he only squeezed her tighter. Her breath caught in her lungs and incipient panic only made it harder to suck in air. The roof of her mouth was as dry as her tongue, and they only made a dull clicking sound as she attempted a louder protest.

A memory stuck a claw in her. A dark room. Groping hands. The sound of a door being locked.

Suddenly, Gordon was gone. Her heart racing, she swayed on her feet as her lungs seemed to compress. Her vision diminished, darkening from the edges inward, and as the floor rushed up, from faraway she heard a muffled oath. Then Brett had his arms around her, steadying her. His embrace was loose and she leaned in, her brow touching his shoulder. His big palm cradled her head.

"Shh," he said against her temple. "Just breathe in. Breathe out."

She obeyed, deliberately taking in the air she so desperately needed.

As the song ended, so did her anxiety. Embarrassed by her overreaction, she stepped back, avoiding the gaze of her rescuer. "Thank you. He was kind of handsy and I was having trouble breaking away."

"Don't thank me. Just go home."

"What?" She frowned and stepped off the dance floor, heading toward her table.

Brett followed. "This is a locals hangout. There are more Gordons in this room. It's not for you."

She'd been having fun until Groping Gordon. "He wasn't *that* bad. I just had a moment of…nervousness."

"Listen. If you're on the hunt for a sugar daddy, you won't find him here."

Her feet halted and she rounded on him. *"What?"*

"The trust-fund crowd, where you'll find the likes of Vaughn Elliott, wouldn't be caught dead line dancing at Mr. Frank's on ladies' night."

Vaughn Elliott? She wasn't interested in the man. "That doesn't mean I can't enjoy myself here."

"Tell me if I'm wrong," Brett said, folding his arms over his chest. "You went to a finishing school."

She narrowed her eyes at him. "Boarding school."

He shrugged as if they were the same. "A fancy college."

She mimicked his pose, folding her arms, one on top of the other. "Yes. So?"

"You don't belong here."

Angelica wanted to say she didn't think she belonged anywhere, but that was beside the point the big jerk in front of her was attempting to make. "I'm no snob."

"Listen to me. I'm doing you a favor."

"I seem to be racking those up," she said in bitter tones. Her gaze swept the room, returned to his face. "You know what? This is making me crazy. *You're* making me crazy."

He ran his hand over his hair. "How?"

I don't want to be attracted to you. I don't want to be thinking of you night and day. But she couldn't say that, could she? He didn't seem affected by her in any profound way, unless you counted all the times he made it clear he thought she was spoiled or shallow. It hurt.

"Angelica?"

"I don't like this—" her hand gestured between the two of them "—indebted thing we have going on."

"I don't know what we can do about that." For a moment he looked as frustrated as she felt.

"Let me work for you," she threw out. "I'm free tomorrow—no Mac and no Hallett Hardware. At least I can erase some of that debt."

"That's not—" he started, then gusted out a sigh and muttered something to himself. "Shit. Fine. Be ready to go at 7:00 a.m."

It wasn't until she slid into the booth opposite Glory that the reality of what she'd arranged sunk in. For a person who wanted to forget about her troubles, she'd spent a good part of the evening wrestling with them. And tomorrow, working with Brett all day, likely wouldn't be any easier.

Likely. Hah.

It was a recipe for disaster.

BRETT'S PLAN FELL to pieces the minute he exited his cabin. He'd expected her to roll out of her place heavy eyed and hardly ready, but instead he found her standing beside his truck with bright eyes and shining hair. No fancy jeans and boots for her today. Sneakers were on her feet, ragged denim encased her long legs and an old, stretched-out sweatshirt reading "Blue Arrow Varsity Basketball" covered her from neck to thighs.

He narrowed his gaze. "Is that mine?"

Either embarrassment or the morning chill was responsible for her pink cheeks. "I don't know. Mac gave it to me."

"Huh." With a will of iron, he tossed away the idea of his cotton fleece covering her magnificent breasts.

But he couldn't ignore the fact that she was dressed for outdoor work when his intention had been to drop her off in his cramped office where she could go to town on his files and invoices. It wasn't as if she could make them any messier than they already were. His glance caught on the canvas tote bag she carried in one hand, stuffed with who-knew-what.

"This isn't a photo shoot," he said. "No need to bring along your makeup."

Her brows slammed together. "I made us lunch," she said, hefting the bag higher.

"Well, then," he muttered, feeling as clumsy as a bear in a mud field. About as good-humored, too. "Let's go."

Yeah, he should apologize. But the words stuck in his throat and every instinct told him it was safer to keep the barrier of his bad temper between them. If he continued acting like an SOB, then they'd both be better off.

Still, instead of dumping her in his cluttered, one-room office, he drove straight to his first job of the day. He told himself it was because the double lunch she'd packed shouldn't go to waste.

Last night, it had been on the tip of his tongue to refuse her help altogether. But he sympathized with her dislike of feeling indebted. He would have railed against that himself.

Sighing, he pulled down the long driveway of the Forster estate. Its sturdy gates had been left open for him by the security firm that would have unlocked the wooden structures during morning rounds. Sadly, the owners rarely visited the place—the matriarch and patriarch were now closing in on ninety, and their assorted progeny too scattered or too busy to come up the hill.

So he and Angelica would be alone. Great.

She slid off the passenger seat and jumped onto the interlocking pavers, her expectant gaze on his face. "What do you want me to do?"

Such a loaded question. Visions of knees, mouths, her head bent over him tried taking hold, but he ruthlessly pushed them away. Striding toward the rear of the vehicle, he considered how to keep her busy.

"First, you rake the pinecones from the front and back lawns. After, while I'm mowing and blowing, you can pull any weeds you find in the beds." Rummaging through a metal bin attached to the side of the truck bed, he unearthed a spare pair of leather gloves. He knocked them against his thigh to dislodge any dirt or nesting critters, then passed them over. "They may be a little big, but use them anyhow. We need to protect your skin."

Her hands swam in them. "I don't know…"

"I'm the boss, remember? Use them."

Then it was the rake for her and a pair of hedge clippers for him. She took hold of the wooden handle in an awkward grip, but he didn't comment. There was nothing to it but to do it. When she tired, which he expected wouldn't take long, she could return to the truck cab and play with her phone apps or something until he finished the work.

Leaving her in the front, he walked around to the back where he did some judicious pruning of the shrubbery. Breathing in the fresh air and reveling in the sun on his face and the beautiful vista of the doubloon-dappled lake, he achieved the Zen-like state that he often achieved by combining the outdoors and physical labor. His mind flatlined and even thoughts of his coworker didn't intrude. When a cloud passed over the sun, the shadow goosed him. He glanced around, remembering Angelica and realizing he had a powerful thirst.

A jug of water was strapped to the back of the truck. He headed that way, presuming he'd find her resting on the seats. But the cab was empty of everything but his own discarded junk-food wrappers, and he caught sight of her near the side property line where she was fishing pine needles from beneath the fencing.

Surprised by her diligence, he filled two tall cups with water and noted the piles of cones she'd left here and there. Then he crossed to her, making noise so he wouldn't startle her as he came up from behind.

"Wet your whistle," he said, holding out one of the waters.

"Thank you." She blotted her forehead with her wrist. Her hair was tied back in a high ponytail, and tendrils of it had worked free to brush against her flushed cheeks. As she drank down the liquid, he realized her nose was trending toward red, too.

"All right," he said, when she'd drained the cup. "Sunscreen break." Then he grabbed her arm and towed her toward the truck.

There he rummaged in the driver's door side pocket and withdrew a bottle of the stuff that he then handed over. Still gloved, she fumbled the lotion and it landed at her feet. They both reached for it, bumping heads, and when his fingers found the plastic, he straightened with a wince.

"Here," he said, holding it out again.

This time she got a grip on it, but when she stooped and twisted her neck to see her reflection in the side mirror, he grabbed it from her. "Oh, I'll do it," he said. "Stand straight and hold still."

First he rinsed his hands with the remainder of the water in his cup and dried them on the bandanna tucked in his back pocket. Next, he squirted a dollop in his palm.

She looked at the lotion, a dubious expression on her face. "I don't know…"

"This is the good stuff. It's cool going on and doesn't feel sticky afterward." He nudged her chin with his free hand. "Turn up your face and close your eyes."

When she wasn't looking at him, he found he could breathe easier. With two fingertips, he painted the stuff on her forehead. She flinched at first contact, but then kept obediently motionless. Brett covered every inch of her golden-tinged skin to her hairline and then he drew a line down the straight edge of her small nose. He rubbed a circle of lotion on her chin, then used his thumbs to wipe it over her cheeks.

His heartbeat slowed as he completely, slowly, covered her skin. When it came to following the line of her lips with his fingertips, he felt half-hypnotized. Her beauty was just that enthralling. He could caress her forever.

Glancing up, he saw her eyes were open now and trained on his face. He jolted back, his guard slamming up. "Done now," he said, spinning back to the truck to throw the bottle onto the seat. Imagining the stupid expression he'd been wearing, he cringed and wiped his chin for drool.

The woman bewitched him.

Damn her.

"Thanks," Angelica said. "You can actually be nice."

"I don't want to be nice," he muttered, then returned to his tasks, his earlier serene mood impossible to recapture.

When his stomach growled, he knew it was time to stop for food. Usually he took his lunch late midmorning. Exertion made a guy hungry, and again he had to pull Angelica away from work. They'd traded places, she in the back of the yard and he in the front, and he took the tote bag to her and headed toward the lake.

"We can sit on the platform," he said, pointing to the covered structure sitting over the water that included a ramp leading to the actual dock. A table and chairs sat on the wooden surface. He made a mental note to remind the Forsters via email that security should use their keys to unlock the dock box and fold the stuff into the locker for the winter.

For now, he and Angelica had a comfortable place for their meal. She'd included thick sandwiches, pasta salad, cut-up fruit and a large container of cookies. "Good," he said, after swallowing his first bite of roast beef and cheddar. "How'd you learn to cook?"

"Making lunch is not 'cooking,'" she said.

"Still, a woman like you—"

"That's it," she said, dropping her own sandwich to her paper-towel place mat. Irritation sparked in her eyes. "I'm so done with you making assumptions and judgments about me."

He couldn't deny it—and it had been his practice to keep her at arm's length. "I—"

"Something happened. Somebody sharpened your cynicism to a razor's edge."

"It's a mountain thing—"

"Bullshit." Her glare turned hotter. "Glory isn't like you. Her dad didn't mistrust me on sight. Your sisters think I'm okay."

"They have soft hearts," he muttered.

"Well, so do I," she said. "And the way you treat me hurts mine."

He shouldn't care. He should have left her with his files. He should have turned around and walked out the day he found her nearly fainting in Mac's place of business.

"The truth is…" He hesitated.

"Haven't I told you my secrets?" she demanded.

Not even close. Without wanting to, he suspected there were layers left to be unpeeled, mysteries that if he knew them would only further serve to fascinate him. Ensnare him. Leave him trapped.

Yet maybe his truth—part of it, anyway—would make her understand why he resisted her with all his might. She might even cooperate and stop looking so damn beautiful all the time. Maybe she'd decide to turn off all her damn sex appeal.

Fucking stupid idea, he knew it, but at this moment he was willing to try just about anything. "When I was eighteen, I had this girlfriend."

"Stop the presses." Her eyes shot heavenward.

It was his turn to glare. "Are you going to listen or what?"

She rolled her hand in a go-ahead gesture.

"Summer after senior year. I was going into the army in the fall, and I met this girl…even then I was making extra money by working on a local landscaper's crew. Her name was Gabby and she rocked a bikini."

"And you think *I'm* shallow."

He had to give her that and even smiled a little. "I fell for her like a stone in water. Her family was filthy rich, her father the commodore of the yacht club and her house the most ostentatious on the lake."

"The one with the flags and the battlements?"

"Uh-huh." Pausing a moment, he remembered how his buddies had congratulated him for scoring the hottest babe of the summer. As full of himself as he'd been then, he'd still managed to float on cloud nine until the end of August.

"Then her father had me arrested."

Angelica's eyes rounded. "For what?"

"Not what you're thinking…we were both eighteen."

"I wasn't—never mind. What *were* you arrested for?"

"Burglary. You see, some very valuable items had gone missing from Bikini Girl's household. I knew nothing about this at the time. But when her father asked her about the stuff, rather than confessing what she'd been up to—stealing for kicks and passing the stolen things off to an acquaintance to fence—she had the perfect fall guy...in me."

Angelica clutched the ribbed neckline of her—his—sweatshirt. "That's terrible."

"Jail was kind of terrible, too. I had two days and nights to lie on a cement bed and piss in a stainless-steel toilet and think about how she'd betrayed me. I thought I would lose my spot in the army...the whole future I had planned for myself."

"I'd like to scratch her eyes out."

He shrugged. "The experience sure pulled the blinders from mine."

"What happened to her?"

"I have no idea. I know what happened to me. I contacted an attorney—a local guy—and he went to bat for me against Daddy Big Bucks. Actually, the sheriff was on my side, too... He knew that kind of trouble was out of character for me. By the third day, they'd wrung a confession from Gabby, her father had withdrawn the charges and they'd put Ostentatious Manor up for sale."

"And you went on to the army and the rest of your life."

With a few more bumps and painful falls in between. "So you'll excuse me my knee-jerk distrust."

"No, I don't know that I will," she said, musingly. Maddeningly. "Surely you don't think I'm going to sic the law on you."

"No." He cleared his throat.

"What is it then?"

Hell. She wanted the truth? "I thought you were bored. This summer, I thought you wanted to add a little novelty to your life by going slumming with the guy who had dirt on his hands, sweat on his back and scars on his face."

Her cheeks flushed. "That wasn't…it wasn't the dirt or the sweat or the scars."

Then he said the five damning words. They weren't planned, but they came from the heart of him, that dark place beneath his hard soul as he thought of how he'd resented the temptation of Angelica all summer—of how resisting her was imperative because of the lessons another woman had taught him about trust and betrayal. "I don't like being used."

Her breath sucked in, an audible gasp. The flush on her face leeched away. "You think that's what I'm doing." It was a statement. "Using you."

"No. Not exactly that." He wanted to pound his head against the table. Someone else had taken advantage of him, and he'd been playing defense with Angelica because of it. "It's—"

"I'm going to pay you rent, I swear it. Soon. I have money coming in from Mac now, and from the hardware store."

Shit. Shit shit *shit*. "That's not what—"

"Don't concern yourself with what it is exactly." She jumped up from the table, her sandwich just a couple bites less than whole. "I'll get back to work now."

Brett let her go. Because for the first time he'd found the right—though wrong—thing that would keep her at bay.

CHAPTER NINE

AFTER HIS LONG HOURS with Angelica had ended, Brett couldn't settle. She'd gone silent after their lunch, no surprise, but he couldn't fault her work ethic. Without complaint, she'd followed his directions the entire day.

But the physical labor had exhausted her. He'd seen it in the slow way she'd climbed out of the truck. Her gait had been halting as she made her way into her own cabin.

So here he was, showered clean and tired himself, unable to do anything but stare through the windows to the place next door. He'd yet to eat, though the homemade chili on the stove was heated through.

There was enough for two.

He had the wherewithal not to tempt fate by bringing both their dinners to her door. Instead he ladled a generous but single serving into an oversize mug and tucked a sleeve of crackers in his sweatshirt pocket. He'd pass the food over the threshold and leave her alone just as soon as he made sure she hadn't done herself any lasting injury.

On her porch, he hesitated. She'd been bushed. Maybe the princess was already asleep.

Then he heard music. A voice. She was singing.

He grinned. She really shouldn't. It broke off when his knuckles rapped on the door.

"Yes?" Angelica called out.

"I'm from the TV show *The Voice*," he called. "Here to beg you not to audition."

The door swung open. *"The Voice?"* she repeated, one dark eyebrow winging up.

"Yes, darling, and you don't have one."

She pursed her lips as if she was trying not to laugh. "What are you doing here?" Her glance took in the steaming chili.

"I brought dinner in case you were too beat to make some for yourself."

Her big browns flared wide with surprise. "You brought me dinner."

He shrugged, uncomfortable. "The least I could do."

"You brought me dinner." She sounded pleased now.

"As an apology," Brett muttered. Then his gaze slid past her to see that the living room furniture had been pushed together and covered with an old sheet. A ladder stood in the middle of the room and there was paint, brushes and a roller arranged nearby. "What are you doing?"

"Poppy said I could," Angelica answered quickly.

He brushed past her to put the food he'd brought on the kitchen counter. "I'm not accusing you of anything." Then he crossed to the paint can and peered into it. The color was a pale, creamy gold, the color of the sunlight through the trees on an autumn afternoon. "I like that shade."

She hovered by the open door.

"Are you going to shut that?" He realized he should take the hint and head back out. But his curiosity was roused. A long day of manual labor and she was willingly embarking on yet another task? "Can't this wait until tomorrow…or the one after that? Your muscles must be sore."

I can massage the hurt out of them. Go in the bedroom, strip down and let me put my hands on you. He recalled the little fantasy he'd had the day he thought she was going to the spa.

"I've been looking forward to this all day," she said.

The surprising statement dragged his mind away from that dangerous direction. "Looking forward to *painting*?"

She shrugged. "I get a discount at the hardware store. I love looking at the color samples and I often daydream about what they'd look like on walls." Her gaze dropped to the floor. "Weird, huh?"

"Can't say it's the kind of visualizing I play around with myself, but I get it."

Her head came up and her eyes widened. "Yeah?"

"Sure. I design landscapes in my head all the time. When I'm working, I'll mentally replant shrubs, move boulders, add a water feature."

"You should build that lodge that you imagined here. It's fabulous."

He smiled a little, surprised she even recalled the drawings. "I'm not going to be merely mowing and blowing forever—I've got plans for the design part of my business. But some dreams don't come true, honey."

"I don't know about that," she said. "I'm painting walls."

Her enthusiasm bemused him. "So it's really an ambition of yours?"

"As long as I can remember."

His expression must have communicated his disbelief. "Truly. The homes I've lived in have been professionally—very expensively—decorated. I was never allowed to move a cushion, hang a poster, paper my own bedroom wall."

"Don't. Wallpaper's a bitch to remove, and you'll get tired of it, believe me."

Her smile had a surprising sweetness. "I'd like a chance to find that out."

"Talk to Shay about the bathroom she had sophomore year in college. It was in an old house and there were something like five layers, each more god-awful than the one before. I suggested just painting over the mess, but she wouldn't hear of it."

"So you got in there with a scraper, I presume."

"You guessed it. A scraper and a rented steamer." He shook his head. "What a sucker. I think I did all that work for a medium pepperoni pizza."

"You're no sucker, Brett," Angelica said.

Uh-oh. They were suddenly swerving into dangerous territory. The new warmth in her brown eyes was like heat on his skin. It tugged on his dick and ignited the burner beneath his lust. He wasn't here for this.

"Stop," he said harshly. "You know how I am."

"I think I'm finally beginning to." She glanced at the chili, then looked back at him. "You've been honest with me, so I should offer my own apology…"

"For what?"

Pink washed her beautiful face. "This past summer… I don't blame you for holding me off. I was sort of…well, there's no sort-of about it."

He frowned. "About what?"

She glanced away again. "I hate to admit it…"

"Spit it out, princess."

"I wasn't interested in 'slumming' like you said. It

wasn't because there was dirt on your hands or sweat on your back or because of your scars. But I was…"

"Well?"

"Objectifying you."

His brows rose.

"Now that I think about it, I'm not very proud of myself. I crushed on you from afar." Her voice lowered to a whisper. "I used to watch you from my bedroom window whenever you came to the house."

He remembered the tingle on the back of his neck every time he worked at her estate. "That's no crime."

"Could be that what I was thinking about was illegal."

"Really?" Drawing out the word, he tried not to laugh. God, she tickled his funny bone as well as his libido. "Do tell."

She peeked at him from beneath her lashes. He didn't think she knew how fucking appealing he found that.

Which meant he should go, he thought, sobering. Immediately. But his feet didn't obey his mental order.

"Truth time," she murmured, as if to herself. Then she cleared her throat. "You have a rock-hard body, as I'm sure you're aware."

Uh, yeah, he thought, thinking about the shaft rising beneath the placket of his jeans.

"And without a shirt…" She rolled her eyes as if savoring a special treat. "But I feel bad about my…uh, appreciation. I didn't know a thing about you."

"You thought I had a girlfriend. That I might be married."

"See?" she said. "And I still admired every one of your muscles at every opportunity."

"Shameless," he chided, teasing her.

"Shameless?" She blinked, and he thought she might be a little proud of the fact. "Huh. Me, shameless."

Her pleased tone made him grin. "Princess, I looked back at you, you know."

Her eyes rounded.

"There was this one time I caught you in a bathing suit. I made a note of it on my calendar."

"Well, we know you have this thing for bikinis," she said, a prim note to her voice.

He grinned. "Believe me. You have a special way when you're wearing one, princess."

Now her cheeks went rosy, and she lifted a hand to brush a tendril of hair away from one. Elastic bandages circled every finger.

Frowning, he crossed to her in three long strides. "What's this?" He took hold of both wrists to see more bandages on the other hand. "You're hurt?"

She'd gone still. "It's nothing." Her voice sounded croaky. "Blisters."

"You didn't wear the gloves the entire time?" he demanded, inspecting her skin.

"I did. But they slid around…" She didn't finish because he'd lifted first one palm, and then the other, to his mouth.

He kissed their centers.

It was as if he saw the action from afar. The cynical, hard-souled Brett Walker stood outside his body while the Brett who wanted to protect Angelica from everything—hurt, cold, loneliness—soothed her with his mouth.

This close, she smelled like a beautiful, expensive mistake, and he just couldn't give a shit about what would break in his inevitable fall.

Her arms lifted, and she cupped his face with her battered hands. Their eyes met. "Kiss me," she whispered. "Kiss me again."

There was no denying her. He bent his head, and placed his lips against hers. A sigh left her, her breath warm on his skin and then she opened her mouth and touched her tongue to his bottom lip.

His belly clenched. His cock went as hard as a fist.

He let her inside, let her sweet taste slide into him. His hands curled around her hips and her arms crossed behind his neck. It was a dance, of tongues, of desires, of want that had been building for weeks. Months.

Oh, yeah, objectify me, baby, he thought, as her touch began to roam over him. He stood still for her, letting her acquaint herself with his back, his abs. When the heel of her palm brushed one nipple, he broke free to grab hold of his sweatshirt and yank it over his head.

Her gaze ran over him now, as hot as a touch.

He ran a finger around the neckline of the plain T-shirt covering her. "You?" he asked, his voice husky.

She dropped her hands to the hem.

"Let me," he said, and drew the cotton away from her. Beneath it she wore a bra that was lacy and low cut. His breath caught in his chest as he took in the plump rise of flesh over the peach-colored cups. "This isn't fair," he muttered. "I'll never be able to look at you in clothes again without thinking of what's beneath them."

"I want…" she started, then licked her lips. "I want to feel you against me." Her arms went back and she unclasped the dangerous piece of lingerie. Then she shimmied her shoulders and the lace responded to gravity's pull and slid along her skin. One cup caught on her upstanding nipple and then it lost its hold, too.

Finesse beyond him now, Brett bent his head to pull the gathered peak into his mouth. His eyes closing, he sucked, reveling in the scent of her, the weight of her breast in his other palm, the little sounds she made while he played there. Her fingertips sank into his scalp, and he muttered praise as he moved to the other nipple. His thumb strummed the wet one, and her nails dug deeper.

Delicious.

Lifting his head, he went for her mouth again, and they traded burning kisses as they explored each other's bare flesh. He slid his fingers down the back of her jeans, delving beneath her panties to clutch one glorious cheek of her generous ass. "You're amazing," he whispered in her ear, pulling her into him.

She ground against his cock and pressed her nose to his pectoral muscle. Her tongue flickered against his nipple.

He groaned and he felt her answering smile. "I want you," she whispered, as if it was a secret he didn't already know.

"Good thing," he said. "Because I'm about to objectify the hell out of you."

She giggled and the sound sent Cynical Brett even further away. There was no wariness in him now as he continued kissing her while propelling her toward the bedroom. Their mouths ate at each other, greedy and urgent, as he swung her into the darkened room. There, he kicked shut the door and spun so Angelica's back was against the hard surface and he could lean into her, rubbing their naked torsos together as the kiss went on and on. Wet. Deep. Deeper.

There was a creamier scent in the air, the sweet and spicy scent of female arousal. It quickened his blood and he felt himself go impossibly harder. He pulled his hand from her pants and went after the front clasp, needing to explore the center of her. Needing to open her up to him.

The snap popped, the zipper gave way, he moved to cup her.

And she screamed.

The sound was muffled by their mating kiss, but there was no denying its distress. Or the sudden frozen stiffness in her body.

Brett yanked his head away, and tried seeing her features in the blackness of the room. "Did I hurt you?" He pulled his hand from her underwear. "Angelica? Princess? What's the matter?"

She was shaking, and not with lust.

Cursing silently, he fumbled for the light switch. When it blazed on overhead, she cried out again, throwing one arm over her eyes and the other over her bare breasts. "No! Turn it off!"

"Okay, okay," he soothed. "Just the lamp by the bed." It was only four steps away. He flipped on the dimmer bulb and then doused the brighter one on the ceiling.

She slid against the door to the floor and then crawled to where her robe was flung on the end of the mattress. She quickly shoved her hands in the sleeves, her gaze on the floor.

"Angelica. Sweetheart—"

"I'm sorry. I'm sorry." She dropped her head to her bandaged hands. "I'm sorry. You can hate me. Please do."

"Angelica…" He crouched down and tried to peel one palm away. She resisted as if her life depended on it.

"There are ugly words for what I just did to you," she said. "I know it. I just thought that…with you…" She swallowed a sob. "Please go away."

Brett shook his head, not feeling the least bit angry or frustrated, though he didn't think she'd believe that. Instead, there was only his protective instincts rising up, ready to build a barrier between her and the world. Between her and himself, if necessary. "Do you really want me to leave? Maybe we should talk about it."

"Not tonight," she whispered. "Please. I'm so embarrassed."

He weighed his options. Doing things her way seemed the best of them. "All right," he said slowly. "Will you be okay alone?"

She still wasn't looking at him. "I'll be better."

It killed him to hear those words. *Oh, baby.* Rising, he gave her one last assessing glance. She was still curled in on herself, knees up to her chest, hair and hands obscuring her face.

Those elastic bandages were nothing. Physically, he knew she was fine.

But emotionally…hell. He had no idea exactly what he was dealing with here, but one thing was certain. There were monsters he needed to slay and there was no sense denying his driving need to pick up the nearest weapon.

No matter how vulnerable that might make him in return.

ANGELICA HAD DECIDED she would never talk to Brett again. Never see him again either, if she could possibly help it. That seemed a tall order, given they lived next door in an isolated location, but she could sure as heck try. Instead of going home after her shift ended at the hardware store at 6:00 p.m., she decided to stop by the historical society's headquarters. The president had texted her earlier in the day. Somewhere in the offices,

he'd misplaced the hard copy list of some potential in-
vitees for next year's gala event that weren't yet entered
into the society's computer files.

Angelica was certain she could put her fingers on it
and the time it took would postpone the possibility of
running into Brett.

She was mortified by the drama she'd enacted the
night before.

It had been more than ten years since she'd been
pawed in a dark room, unable to cry out or get away.
Since then, she'd thought she'd managed to overcome
that first unpleasant exposure to sexual touch. In college
she'd occasionally dated, concocting elaborate safety
procedures with a friend involving texts and drive-by
check-ins.

When she was twenty-two, she'd taken the virginity
of the twenty-year-old, mild-mannered librarian's aide at
her college. It was her first time, too. They'd both been
grateful to each other.

Subsequent interludes with the young man had been
less than successful—the first had been no better for her,
but she'd been happy enough to get the deed done—and
they'd parted ways without hard feelings. A few weeks
before graduation she'd been studying late one night and
happened upon him and a dazzled-looking sophomore
between the stacks. Over the girl's naked shoulder they
exchanged looks.

He'd given her a thumbs-up.

It had appeared that one of them had gotten over his
shyness.

While she, on the other hand, had never completely
let go of her hang-ups. Or just never completely let go,
period.

In truth, nobody had made her want to, until Brett Walker. It had started with those weekly fantasy fests over the summer, when she'd watched him work in shorts and nothing else. Bronze skin over bulging muscles. Sweat beading on his shoulders and running in rivulets down his chest.

She'd owned up to the ogling and it had seemed to amuse him. What if she'd confessed to more? Would he find it funny that she had lain in bed at night, imagining him, touching herself like she'd ached for him to do?

Well, last night all she'd wanted was for him to do that touching she'd been dreaming about for so long.

And then she'd gone and ruined it. Maybe *she* was ruined.

Pulling into the historical society's parking lot, she blinked away gathering tears. Stupid to cry. Even stupider when the parking lot was dimly lit and filled with furrows and lumps she'd like to avoid to spare her convertible's undercarriage.

Her car door snicked as she closed it, a loud sound in the quiet of evening. The society's headquarters were a few blocks away from the center of the village of Blue Arrow Lake. For the first time, she noticed how isolated it could feel in the dark.

In summer, the light had lasted longer, of course. She'd never visited when it felt so much like…night.

At the front entry of the building, she paused, clutching the keys in her hand. Not all the volunteers had their own set, but she'd had to open up early a few times leading to their silent auction. And then—there was nothing overt she could point to—all of her went on high alert.

The keys bit into her flesh as she gripped them more tightly. Her hairline prickled. Alarm churned in her belly.

Tiptoeing, she moved away from the front door and retreated to the far side of her car. She exchanged the keys for her cell phone, making sure the former didn't jangle when they landed at the bottom of her purse. Without thinking, she hit one of the first contacts in her list.

"What's up?" Brett's voice. Brett. He'd programmed his number into her phone the day before when she'd crewed for him. *In case you need to get my attention when I'm wearing the hearing protectors. I'll have it on vibrate.*

"Angelica?" He said it sharply. "Is something the matter?"

"I don't know," she whispered into the phone. "I have a funny feeling."

"Where are you?"

Afraid his voice might carry into the night, she hunched her shoulders to huddle around the phone. "Outside the historical society."

"What? Why? Never mind." He sounded annoyed... maybe with himself. Maybe with her.

"Sorry to bother you," she said quickly. "I can handle it."

"Don't you dare. Get in your car, lock it. Call 9-1-1. I'm not far from you."

"The cabin is a long—"

"I'm at my office. I'll be there in no time." He ended the call.

Shivering, she opened the door and climbed into the passenger side, sliding low so that a casual eye might not notice the vehicle was occupied. Then she dialed the emergency number.

Brett made it to the parking lot first. He glided into

the spot beside her, his headlights off and his truck silent. As he turned into the lot he must have cut the ignition.

She crept out of her car as he exited his in near-silence. "You stay here," he said in a whisper as he passed.

Um, no. She dogged his footsteps as he approached the building. He glanced around, rolled his eyes. His forefinger pointed toward her car in insistent demand. She shook her head back and forth.

He touched her breastbone with the tip of his finger and then drew it along his throat. *I'll kill you.* Another poke in the direction of her vehicle. *Go back.*

She patted her chest, then drew up her arms in a running position, jerking them up and down to indicate speed. *I'm fast. I'll be okay.*

He gave another extravagant eye roll, then made a circle at his temple. She didn't know which of them he was trying to say was crazy, but he turned toward the building without further communication.

Shadowing him, she hooked his back belt loop with a finger. He didn't appear to notice.

Tethered like that, they mounted the steps. Pausing at the front door, she could tell he was listening hard, as was she. "Do you hear anything?" she breathed into his ear.

He waved her question away. Gripping the knob, he tried turning it. It didn't move.

"Locked," she whispered, an embarrassed flush rising up her neck. Her voice rose to near-normal volume. "I imagined it. Nothing's going on."

Then a clatter came from inside the building. An "eek." Footsteps.

Angelica heard voices inside say "Shh" and "Shit" and "Go, go, *go*!"

Brett cursed and tried the door again. "I have keys," she said, and began digging through the purse hanging over her shoulder.

The footsteps sounded like a stampede, and they weren't coming toward the front. "Rear door," Angelica said, and started to scurry around the side of the building.

"Damn it," Brett exclaimed, following at her heels. "Would you get the hell back?"

She stumbled over a coiled hose, he tripped on her and they both fell in a tangle of limbs. "Are you okay?" he asked in urgent tones, getting to his knees.

Winded, she couldn't speak, and then realized he couldn't see her nodding in the darkness. She clutched at his forearms, trying to express she was okay.

Instead of understanding, he sat and drew her into his arms. "Angelica." He gave her a tiny shake. "Angel face, are you all right?"

She coughed, trying to move oxygen through her lungs. "I'm fine," she manage to choke out. "Go ahead, I'll be okay."

His hold tightened. "You're more important than whatever's happening."

"I'm fine." She struggled out of his hold and managed to get to her feet. "I want to know who's sneaking around even if you don't."

Cursing under his breath, Brett grabbed her hand as she rushed toward the back exit. Now she registered the sound of muffled laughter, the slamming of a door, the kick of an engine starting up.

A narrow lane at the rear of the building led to a

lower street. As they rounded the corner they saw a truck rocking down the skinny slice of crumbling asphalt. Its bed was teeming with human figures…and one not so human.

"Piney!" Angelica cried. The stuffed bear bounced as the speeding vehicle took a sharp right. A male voice howled, a girl's shrieked, raucous laughter lit up the quiet.

She turned on Brett. "They stole Piney!"

He rubbed a hand over his mouth. "Looks like it." Then he mounted the back steps and peered in the half-open rear door. "You'll know better than me if anything else is missing."

She peered around his shoulder. A couple of lights, the ones they left burning overnight, illuminated the interior. It didn't seem as if anything was disturbed. "We don't even keep petty cash here. I guess they might have stolen some ground coffee. The stuff we stock is pretty good. We get it from Oscar's. I think I remember seeing a couple of beers in the minifridge."

"A bear and some brew," Brett said mildly. "Quite the haul."

Angelica felt like a fool. "I shouldn't have called you. I shouldn't have called the sheriff."

Even as she said it, the lights of a cruiser pierced the darkness. "Great," she said, now more miserable. "They're here."

"Let me handle it."

She trailed him back to the parking lot. The sheriff's car had stopped near the front door, and a man in a tan uniform was looking about. "Brett," he said, as they came around the corner. "Why are you here?"

Her next-door neighbor took Angelica's hand. "Helping out, is all. She called me and I told her to call you."

With Brett's grip warm and firm on hers, she remembered him asking, *Do you have someone to take care of you?* She'd lied then. She wanted to lie to herself now and pretend that he could be a shoulder to lean on.

"Hi, sir," she said, disentangling herself from Brett and stepping forward. "Let me tell you what happened."

The other man had switched on a powerful flashlight. Between that and the light bar on his vehicle, the lot was bright enough for them to see each other's expressions. The man glanced at Brett when she'd told her side of the story.

"I tried the front door," he said. "Then we went around to the back. We didn't touch anything, but we did see a stuffed bear head off into the great unknown."

The uniformed man's brows rose. "Huh?"

"A recent acquisition," Angelica explained. "He's been in a place of honor in the foyer."

"Blue Arrow High Grizzlies," Brett added. "Homecoming's coming up."

The other man chuckled. "High school prank?"

Brett lifted a shoulder. "My guess."

Though the law officer sighed, she could tell he didn't think it was the end of the world. "Ma'am," he said, addressing Angelica. "Mind calling the head of the society? We'll get him down here to verify if anything else has been stolen."

"Sure thing," she said, and dug once again for her phone.

As she did so, she noted that the officer and Brett took a stroll around the building, giving her a chance for escape.

She placed the call, then jogged to her car and drove it out of the lot. Not very gracious of her, she was aware. But better for all. It was time to let go of the fantasy. Of the man.

Sure, she was running away from everything she wanted, but she knew she couldn't have it anyway... because last night proved she could never give all of herself.

CHAPTER TEN

GLORY HALLETT SPRAYED cleaner on the glass countertop and used a page of newsprint to swipe it away, wishing she could remove the dullness from her mood just as easily. Her overcast state of mind didn't make any sense.

It was her favorite time of year.

Summer could get crazy at the store. In spring there'd be fewer tourists but lots of people coming in with plans to spruce up their gardens or finish housing projects that had gone stale. During the winter, the cold was abated by the heat from the pellet stove in the rear corner, a cozy welcome for everyone, but the days were so darn short.

In autumn, though, lovely autumn, the door would swing open as it did right now and it would usher in that nutty smell of drying grasses and turning leaves. By late afternoon, the slant of the sunlight would cause the front window to blaze golden like a promise.

What was wrong with her? Glory thought.

She had all the elements needed for a happy life.

Angelica bustled out of the back room, waving a printout and wearing one of her infectious smiles. "Bookkeeping all caught up. Looks like September will be quite the successful month."

With such an enthusiastic helper on the floor and at the computer, Glory should be congratulating herself on her good fortune. "Great to know," she said, faking a grin. "Shall I book that round-the-world cruise?" Didn't that sound irresistible? A chance to see foreign places and new faces and hear something besides the too-familiar ring of the bells on the door.

They chimed now, and her mother walked into the store. "Hey, Mom," Glory said, plastering on yet another smile. "What's up?"

Katie Hallett strolled up in a fetching yoga outfit, which explained where she'd been that morning. She'd started attending local classes every day since her husband retired. Deep breathing, she'd confided, was her way of dealing with a man constantly underfoot. "Do I have to find a reason to visit with my darling daughter?"

That added a little shine to Glory's day. Her mom was awesome. Fun, a great cook and willing to take her daughter's side during the inevitable arguments over the store with Hank.

"I bought you something," Katie said.

"Oh?" Glory set aside the bottle of glass cleaner and wiped her hands on the canvas of her apron. She eyed the bag her mother carried. "I could use chocolate."

"It's not food." Her mother waved the bag back and forth and Glory saw the logo of one of the upscale boutiques in the village. "Bon Nuit was having a sale."

"Nice," Glory said. The store carried all sorts of pretties, from expensive bath goods to elegant linens.

"I know how chilled you get on winter nights," her mother said, her hand diving into the bag. "So I bought you this." Flannel came out of the plastic, yards of it, more yards of it. White, sprigged with little lambs.

A granny nightgown. Ruffled at the throat and wrists. She was short, so the hemline would trail along the floor.

Glory could barely swallow her groan as she pictured herself wearing it—the Ghost of Woman Past Her Prime.

"Um, thanks, Mom," she said, taking the bulky garment into her arms. It could serve as a tent if she ever got stuck in a storm. Tears pricked at her eyes as she bundled up the fabric. "I'm sure I'll get a lot of use out of it."

Wasn't that a miserable thought? Still, her mother had meant well.

Angelica took the folded nightgown from her. "I'll put this in the back for you." As she passed, she murmured into Glory's ear. "At lunch, we'll do some shopping in the Victoria's Secret online catalog, how's that?"

Glory returned a grateful smile. See? She had not only a successful business and a thoughtful mother, but a great friend in Angelica, too. Her happy should be soaring.

Though it wasn't, she managed a pleasant conversation with her mom as she continued tidying the store. Katie was trying to get her husband to plan an extended vacation, but he was balking.

"Sorry, Mom," Glory said. "I know he thinks he needs to be looking over my shoulder."

"That's all right," Katie replied. "I've signed up for a watercolor class. I've joined a second book group."

Despite her need to keep busy so Hank wouldn't make her crazy hanging at home all the time, her mother appeared content. Why wasn't Glory?

She'd always loved the store. As a little girl she'd explored the items on the shelves, horribly fascinated by the sticky strips used to catch rodents and bugs, intrigued by the woodworking tools and the socket sets. Her dad had taught her how to run the register at ten years old.

Which meant she'd been making change for seventeen years.

Glory sighed as she waved her mom out the door.

What was that saying? Familiarity breeds contempt? But she didn't hate Hallett Hardware, did she?

The bells on the door rang out again. Another mom—this time her best friend's. She was happy to see the other woman. She'd dropped by Jules's house just the day before to pick up some adorable shots of little Becca that Jules wanted to share.

They'd oohed and awed, and Glory wondered what it would be like to trade places with her friend. She could be the wife and new mom who managed to do medical transcription on the side in order to dote on her daughter and welcome her firefighter husband home every night.

Jules could be the dedicated shopkeeper who felt shackled to the store. The one who couldn't think of a single thing she was looking forward to in life.

But of course Glory wouldn't wish that on anyone.

Jules's mom purchased the deck sealer product that Glory recommended and was almost on her way when she paused. Retracing her steps, there was a speculative gleam in her eye.

"I just can't go away without asking…okay, prying," she said with a grin. "What's up with you and that very handsome young man you had with you at the fall festival?"

The question seemed to crack her sternum. Glory took shallow breaths and tried ignoring the pain. "Oh, him? Just a guy who came into the store occasionally and wanted to experience our community event."

"He didn't look like 'just a guy' to me. He looked like a man who was bowled over by the lady at his side."

Glory thought she was getting better with the fake grins. "Ha-ha." She took the other woman's arm and led her toward the door.

"Just tell me you won't go back to Stu Christianson," Jules's mother said as Glory ushered her out. "He's too high school for you."

Look at all she had, she thought, as she watched the other woman move down the sidewalk through the front window. So many blessings. A business. Friends. Family. A community that cared about her.

Stu. *He's too high school for you.*

High school or not, he might be better than being alone. She continued staring unseeing out the glass. Maybe this go-round she'd discover the magic that made her feel she and Stu were meant to be together.

Then a figure came into view, crossing the street toward the store. Glory's heart slammed once against her still-aching sternum. Without thinking, she flew to the rear of the store and ducked into the back room.

Angelica looked up from her place at the computer. Her eyes rounded. "What's wrong?"

"Tell him I'm out for the day. No, the rest of the year."

"What? Who?"

"Kyle Scott," Glory hissed. "I think he's coming this way."

What if he wasn't? What if he was on some other errand and he didn't intend to pop in at all? *The jerk.*

Spinning on her heel, she decided she'd spy out the front window and find out just what he was up to since he had no interest in her anymore. Maybe he'd set his sights on Rosanne at the deli. Claudia at Feet & I who specialized in selling orthopedic shoes.

She hoped he had a broken tooth and was here to visit

Dr. Howard. She was pretty sure no one in town could reattach a dick.

With righteous indignation, she stomped toward the front of the store, reaching it as Kyle stepped inside. Their gazes clashed.

Her stomach rose toward her heart, her heart floated into her throat. She felt hot, cold, hot. "Hello," she said, congratulating herself on her businesslike tone. "Can I help you?"

"Glory." He walked forward and reached for her hands.

She evaded his hold and stepped back. "Is there something you need?"

His mouth twisted. "I guess now isn't the right time to say 'you.'"

"You'd guess right."

"I had an emergency." He shoved his hands in his pockets. "I had to go out of town."

An inkling of concern trickled through her. "Was someone ill?"

"No." He rubbed at his eyebrow. "It wasn't like that."

"Your wife call you home?"

"What?" He stared. "*No.* I'm not married. I was just… occupied."

"Hmm."

"Another project. I thought I'd finished it before I came up here, but there were some problems I needed to address." Both hands went through his shaggy hair. "I thought if I gave it all my attention I could get back here sooner. Get back to *you*."

She crossed her arms over her chest. "What makes you think I was here waiting around?"

"Crap. I told you I was lousy at this." He looked away, looked back. "Glory. Please. Can we start over?"

It was ridiculous to want to agree. Starting over meant setting herself up to be left once again. "I think it's better that we don't."

He studied her face, then closed his eyes. "I blew it."

Glory could not completely agree. "It's not only that. I have to watch out for my reputation."

"You think I'd harm it?" he asked.

"It's about being a business owner. I'm not just responsible to myself. You might not understand that, but I have employees. My mom and dad who are still investors. I can't do anything that might turn customers off of shopping here."

His eyes narrowed. "Having a man in your life isn't going to affect your P and L."

A house painter knew about profit-and-loss statements? She barely knew about them herself, thanks to the most excellent accountant who had been doing the heavy lifting in that area for years. "Well—"

"Is Stu back in your life?" Kyle stepped close and grabbed her chin.

This close, he was dangerous. This close, the thrill of his proximity overwhelmed her good sense and her normal caution. "There's no Stu." At the weak note in her voice, she wrenched back. "But there's no you, either."

"Glory—"

"I'm not at a place in my life for a brief affair. I've got responsibilities—this whole place around my neck…" She frowned, hearing herself. Was it really an albatross? No, it was Kyle, messing with her head. Stirring her heart in all the wrong ways.

"Go away," she said, wearily. "That would be best."

His gaze ranged over her face. Then he nodded. Once. Sharply.

"I can be patient."

"No—"

"Yes." He smiled at her, and it was full of charm and a hint of guile. "We don't know each other well—I see that. But I'm nothing if not tenacious. And to my detriment, often single-minded. This time I think that trait will come in handy."

"I don't want you to hurt me," she whispered.

"Ah, Glory." He came close enough to ghost his fingertips over her cheek. "It's not living if we don't risk that. Take it from me, I've been breathing for years, but I've only been existing. Until I looked into a pair of turquoise eyes…that's when I finally felt my heart move."

Then he was gone.

Glory rushed to the window to watch him leave. Seeing the back of him didn't ease her mind or lift her mood.

Glory Hallett had all the reasons in the world to be happy.

But watching Kyle Scott walk away from her—she really, really wasn't.

AT THE KNOCK ON her cabin door, Angelica gritted her teeth, then wiped her hands on a rag and climbed down the ladder, fully aware of who it must be on her porch. Really, she had no choice but to face Brett. It had been cowardly of her to drive off without even a goodbye at the historical society the night before.

So now he'd see her like this, she thought, glancing down at her paint-spattered clothes. It served her right.

Though she'd left the porch fixture off, enough light from the cabin's interior spilled out to illuminate him.

In jeans and a white, long-sleeved T-shirt, he smelled like soap and looked gorgeous. The expression on his face was what struck her most, though.

Concerned. Caring. He studied her, the gray of his eyes soft now and not their usual ice.

"Are you all right?" he asked, his voice gentle.

"Sure. And, uh, thanks for rushing to help. I should have said that before."

"You're welcome." His gaze didn't leave her face. "Certain you're okay? That had to be a little scary."

"I'm fine."

But his kindness made her weak. It made her want to throw herself in his arms and hold on, clinging to him like she'd clutch a rock in a storm. But, damn it, she needed to be strong. Though it would be a heck of a lot easier if he'd revert to his summer self—cold and distant.

"I'm fine," she said, already swinging the door closed. "Busy."

He used his foot to stop the action. His gaze shifted from her to the room behind her. "You started painting."

"Mmm. That's why I'm too busy to chat."

"Babe." He made a face. "Men don't chat. But I should inspect your work…as one of the property owners."

What could she say? Without bothering to hide her irritation, she let him inside. He kicked the door closed behind him.

Okay, he wasn't intending this to be a brief visit.

Fine. She'd go back to what she was doing. Stomping, she crossed to the ladder set up by the corner windows. A shop light illuminated the casing.

"Wow," Brett said, tipping back his head to inspect. "The walls are already done."

She'd done them two nights ago, when she'd been unable to sleep after he'd left.

"I'm doing the trim in a color a step darker than the walls. Too neutral?" She climbed the ladder, then picked up her brush.

"I like it." He watched her dip the bristles into the paint.

"Darn," she muttered when she got paint on the side of her right hand. Switching the handle to her left, she wiped it off on her already messy shirt. Then she stilled, sensing his amusement. Frowning, she glanced down. "What?"

"This really is your first time painting."

"I told you it was." Looking away from him, she stroked the wood with the newly loaded brush. "Am I doing something wrong?"

"You ever see a professional at work?"

"Maybe…no," she confessed.

"They get little, if any, paint on anything but the intended surface."

"Oh." She took in the smears on her shirt, her old pair of yoga pants, her hands.

Her forearms.

Her elbows.

"Mortifying," she muttered. She was always making a fool of herself around him.

"Don't dip so deeply," he advised. "You won't get too much paint on the brush and you'll be less likely to get it on yourself."

She decided against commenting on the suggestion. Maybe if she didn't talk, he'd go away.

And as if he heard her thoughts and was determined

not to cooperate, he dragged a stool from the kitchen closer to where she was working.

"You're giving me performance anxiety," she complained.

"You're doing fine. My first time I got more paint on Shay than on the fence my dad conned us all into covering." There was easy humor in his voice.

It was impossible to ignore. "Conned?"

"Think Tom Sawyer. He wanted to get some help with the chore. We wanted to play hide-and-seek or some such kids' thing. The man could make anything look like fun, though. When he told us we had to audition to be part of the painting crew, we fell all over ourselves attempting to do the best job. He kept giving us second and third and fourth 'tries' to get it right…until the whole damn thing was done."

Angelica could picture the Walker kids striving to outdo each other. "Sounds like he was a great dad."

"Sure…but he screwed up, too. Before the painting con, he left my mom with three little kids when financial problems made their marriage rocky. Took a mining job in South America with no end date. My mom had an affair with a wealthy guy from down the hill and she got pregnant with Shay."

Surprised—not as much by the information, but that he was opening up to her when he so seldom did—Angelica stopped painting midstroke and swiveled her head to look at Brett.

He nodded, as if she'd asked a question out loud. "We don't think of her as anything but fully Walker, and neither did Dad once he pulled his head out of his ass and came back."

Hmm. Was Brett making a point with this story? She

turned back to the window. "Are you saying that I should give my father a second chance?"

"I wouldn't presume to make that judgment." He paused. "What about your mother? Where is she in this?"

"Not involved. With the financial scheme—they've been divorced for years—nor with me." She glanced over her shoulder to see Brett frowning. "Her current husband is not that much older than me… I don't think she likes to remind him of her grown daughter."

He cursed beneath his breath and she felt heat burn at the back of her neck. In boarding school, they'd trotted out their dysfunctional families like badges of honor. *My sister's a kleptomaniac. My mother's been to rehab five times. My little brother made a bonfire out of all my stuffed animals.* But talking about the situation with Brett, whose domestic troubles appeared minor compared to the complete disasters that were her own, embarrassed her.

It was as if she'd done something to deserve the abandonment and duplicity. Not to mention that one episode of groping hands and rubbery lips that had apparently ruined sex for her.

Ruined her for someone as masculine and vital as Brett, anyway.

"Are you ready to talk now?" he asked, his voice quiet.

He was reading minds again! But she wasn't prepared to talk about *that*, which would only serve to make her feel damaged and…and *less*. Sneaking a glance over her shoulder, she could tell he wasn't going to be put off easily.

Sucking in a breath, she dipped her brush once again

in the paint. "Sure. I'd love to hear more about your growing-up years in the mountains."

He was silent a long moment. Then he whispered, "Okay. Your way, angel face. For now."

She ignored the ominous last two words. "What's your first memory?"

"Skiing," he said promptly. "We had—have, they're still around somewhere—a short pair with rubber bindings you slipped your snow boots into. I think I was two or three, and I was determined to make it down this slope in our rear yard without falling."

"Did you?"

"I don't remember. I recall my dad hauling me back to the house and my mom pulling me free from my outer gear before distracting me with hot chocolate and cookies. What about you?"

"You know I can be completely sidetracked by cocoa and sweets."

"First memory, princess. We're trading or not playing at all."

"Wearing my mother's shoes," she said, thinking back. "You know, fancy high heels. I was running down a marble hallway in them, I remember that, and I fell and bumped my head. My mother fired the nanny. I liked her."

"The nanny?"

"Well, not my mother." She shot a look at him. "Sorry. That sounded very poor little rich girl."

He shrugged. "Was that what you were?"

Instead of answering, she asked her own question. "Halloween costume? Your favorite. The holiday's coming up... Glory stocked a few things for the hardware store—miniature hard hats and tool belts—though her dad's going to have a fit when he sees them."

"Halloween costume…" He seemed to think it over.

"Don't tell me it was the time you went as a cheerleader," she teased. "I'll be very shocked to find you have a perky side beneath your surly exterior."

He snorted. "No. Somebody gave me a replica of an astronaut's jumpsuit, though. I think I wore that when I was six, and I thought I looked very cool. After that it was dumb rubber masks and plastic hatchets. I'd scare myself if I caught sight of my reflection in the mirror."

"An astronaut?" That intrigued Angelica. She tried imagining him in space, far above the earth he seemed so connected to. "An ambition?"

"Never," he said. "I'll always be here, feet on the ground, angel face. You understand that?"

It was a message. *I'm a mountain man, and you're likely not long for this part of the world.* It reminded Angelica of Glory's bone-deep distrust of flatlanders. The other woman had gotten over her suspicion of Angelica and welcomed a new friendship, but did that make her a real part of this place?

She'd never really belonged anywhere. To anyone.

"I once asked the housekeeper to help me with my costume. My mother had commissioned a Marilyn Monroe outfit from her dressmaker—the famous white dress, complete with wire in the hem so it appeared to be blowing up. And a platinum wig."

"Glamour girl," Brett said.

"But I didn't wear any of it, to my mother's fury. Our housekeeper was petite and I was tall for my age and I borrowed one of her uniforms. At my mother's party, I passed around canapés on a silver tray. She was mortified."

"Photos?"

"God, no. There was a professional photographer there, snapping shots of the 'beautiful people' who were Mother's best friends. He was given explicit instructions to keep me out of every one."

"Harsh."

"Not so much. I hated cameras even then. The only reason I did the modeling thing was to make my mother happy. It paid well, but I became horribly self-conscious. They began serving me a few mojitos beforehand to loosen me up."

He was silent so long she thought he might have left without her being aware of it. She glanced around. His expression appeared unreadable. Then he ran his palm over his hair. "You have a choice next," he said, his voice casual. "Share about a recurring nightmare or tell me all about your first kiss."

What if they were one and the same thing?

Suddenly, she recognized the question for the setup it certainly was. It was one thing to trade memories, yet another to be mined for the marrow in her bones. "Don't go there," she said, her voice sharp.

"I don't know what you mean."

"You're prying."

"We're talking childhood. Let me tell you about Nancy Earle. She puckered up for every boy in second grade. The day she came after me, I ran and hid in the teachers' restroom. That didn't stop her."

"I still don't want to talk about it."

"My nightmare—" He suddenly broke off. "You're right. Maybe we shouldn't talk about those."

Surprised, she pivoted on the ladder to stare at him. Her abrupt movement set the device rocking and Brett was there in a blink, steadying the thing…and her. His big hand was on the small of her back.

"I've got you, princess," he said.

The simple sentence made her heart quake. Did he get her? Did he know about the insecurities and the loneliness? If he could see inside her as if she were glass, didn't that mean she was just that fragile?

A terrible thought, when it was time to stand on her own and create a new life for herself.

His hand caressed her and it sent goose bumps racing up her spine. "What do you see in the dark, Angelica?"

Never tell. Never say. No one will believe you. They don't even want you here. Nobody wants you. Her insides lurched, but she ignored the sick sensation.

"What I *prefer* is privacy," she said, firming her jaw. "Peace. Quiet."

That icy cool came back into his eyes. "Me to go away," he said.

"Yes," she whispered. And she watched him go. Finally.

CHAPTER ELEVEN

GLANCING AT ANGELICA'S cabin in his rearview mirror, another surge of frustration rolled through Brett as he drove to his office for a morning of catching up on paperwork. He'd gotten exactly nowhere with her. A woman suddenly screams during a scorching kiss that until that moment had obviously been mutually pleasurable, and you'd think she'd be willing to explain herself.

He'd given her time before pressing her—twenty-four hours!—and everyone knew he wasn't a patient man. Still, she'd stonewalled him for a second time.

So maybe it was better to be done with the whole thing. With her. What was he thinking? *Of course* it was better to be done with her. When it came to women, getting too involved had never worked out for him. He touched the scars on his face, running a fingertip over the jagged lines.

For God's sake, he wore the reminders every day—and had been grateful for them.

Mac would be in her office this morning and he decided to make a visit. She'd remind him of his attitude toward ever-after. It was fine for other people, but not for either of them.

His sister's head came up as he breezed through the door. Her eyebrows rose, too. "'Sup?" she asked.

He'd stopped for coffees at Oscar's. She had a coffeemaker, but she notoriously forgot to count when she dumped in the grounds so it was usually either too weak or strong enough to bring a zombie back to life.

Bumping the swinging door with his hip to pass through the counter, he held out one of the paper cups. "Brought you something."

"Nice." She took it from him, but her pale blue eyes remained on his face. "What do you need?"

To remember who I am. To recall the lessons I've learned in life. "A little company," he said instead. "It's pretty quiet out on our mountain."

Mac leaned back in her chair. "I warned you about that when you decided to move there."

He shrugged and took a sip of his coffee. "After that fire this summer it was clear we needed a more-than-occasional presence out there to keep the riffraff away."

"Which reminds me—you have company in the cabins now. How's it working out with Angelica next door?"

He propped the small of his back against the counter that separated the small space into lobby and work area. "She's painting."

"A portrait? A still life with fruit and flowers?"

"The interior of her cabin. Poppy said she could. She gets a discount at the hardware store."

Mac blinked. "Okay. Does it look all right?"

"Looks great, actually. Classy colors. Neutral enough, but upscale to go with Poppy's plans." His sister wanted to create a secluded, rustic retreat, if rustic could include fancy sheets and a gourmet meal service.

"Shay's plan, too," Mac reminded him. "I think she's riding right beside Poppy in that particular train's engine. You, too."

He opened his mouth to deny it, but she stopped him

with a pointed finger. "Why else would you be living at the cabins, Brett?"

You should build that lodge that you imagined here. Poppy had her vision for the cabins. He supposed he'd not entirely let go of what he thought might be erected on the top of the mountain.

It was on old dream…something grander than a ramshackle though beloved set of ski runs. Instead, it would be more like what was known today as a boutique hotel… a small and stylish destination for snow sports. A peaceful retreat for hikers and bike riders in other months.

Rolling his shoulders, he shook thoughts of it away. There were several reasons it couldn't happen, not the least of which was their father having made a financial deal that precluded further development. Maybe if the cabins took off in a big way, they could consider trying to buy out…

But he wasn't holding on to that as a possibility either. As a realist, about life, about romance, he didn't set himself up for disappointment.

"You're like me, Mac, right?" he said aloud.

"I don't know, bro," she said with a smirk. "I managed to shave today."

He palmed the grit on his chin. "I mean we're not falling in with all this white lace and promises crap like our sisters, despite Poppy finding Ryan and Shay getting 'be-ringed' by Jace."

Mac knocked back a swallow of her coffee. "Prince Charming is not coming by with the glass slipper," she affirmed, propping the soles of her heavy boots on the edge of her beat-up desk.

Brett narrowed his eyes. Did she look a little sad about that?

The door opened behind him and he swung around to see the local mail carrier, Lewis, come bustling in. He grinned at them both and handed a rubber-band-wrapped bundle of envelopes and advertisements to Brett. "Walkers," he said, by way of greeting.

"How are you, Lewis?" The older man's children had been in school with the Walker siblings. "Dinah? Your kids?"

"Good, good." Wild hairs grew out of the centers of his gray eyebrows, giving him a puckish appearance. "Hannah was asking about you just the other day."

"Huh." Hannah had been in the same grade as Brett in school, and she'd married before she turned twenty-one. "How's her husband… Clyde?"

"Ex-husband. He's a loser, just like I told her on her wedding day. She's moved back home and wouldn't mind getting out for a drink now and then."

Brett considered it. Acting as rebound man was no hardship when he didn't plan on sticking with any woman for the long term. "Tell her to give me a call when she feels up to it."

As the mail carrier signaled a will-do and left, Brett decided his visit could be considered a success. A new woman in the offing—already he felt more like himself.

"Back on the prowl," Mac said, toasting him with her coffee.

He tried frowning at her, but what the hell? It wasn't that he was a merciless player—every woman he went out with understood the score—and he wasn't looking to fill the family Bible with another name in the tree, either. Setting down his coffee, he snapped the band off the mail before handing it over to his sister.

A postcard fluttered free as he tossed her the stack.

She made a grab for it, but it sailed out of her reach and landed near his foot. He bent for it, glanced at the photo of the Golden Gate Bridge and flipped it over to see who it was from. He ignored his sister's bleat of protest. Come on, it's not as if postcards were confidential correspondence.

Then he did a double take. Only a single symbol was written in the white space intended for a message. Three lines assembled to make a bold *Z*.

He switched his gaze from the letter to his sister's face. "Zan? Mac, Zan is sending you postcards?" Alexander "Zan" Elliott, Brett's one-time best friend and the boy that Poppy claimed had ruined her sister for all other males.

She wouldn't meet his eyes. Instead, she half rose to snatch the card from his hand. With another quick movement, she opened the bottom drawer of her desk and flipped it inside.

Brett felt the whites of his eyes drying out, they'd gone so round. "What the hell, Mac?" There'd been a heap of postcards in the drawer. "You've been writing to Zan and nobody knows about it?"

It pissed him off, thinking that the other man had been corresponding with Brett's sister and not with him, the best friend who had considered him as close as a brother.

Zan had left at twenty-one, never to be heard from again—or so he'd thought—causing his reputation to morph from Blue Arrow Lake bad boy to the most interesting man in the world. Outrageous rumors circulated every few months or so. That he was the true founder of Bitcoin. A European circus starred him in a high-wire act. He'd been adopted by an indigenous tribe in Antarctica. Brett had snorted at that one, informing the person who repeated this nonsense that unless Zan called a penguin Mom or Pop, this was pure, stinking bullshit.

Mac slammed her arms over her chest. "I'm *not* writing to Zan." Two spots of color flagged her cheeks. "He sends me the occasional card."

Ignoring her sputters, he strode over to yank open that drawer and grab a handful of colorful missives from the pile. "Those are private!" Mac protested.

He held them over his head to avoid her reaching fingers. Being the big brother had its occasional perks. Torturing younger sisters being one of them. The cards captured scenes from all over the world. Australia. Sweden. South Africa.

His puzzled gaze sought out his sister's. "What's with this? There's nothing written on any of them but his initial."

Mac collapsed back in her chair. "Yeah." She shrugged, indicating indifference.

"The one that just came from San Francisco is no different."

Her spine snapped straight. "San Francisco?"

He found it, tossed it atop the desk.

Mac watched it as though it was a coiled snake ready to strike. "That's the closest he's been," she murmured, as if to herself. "How many miles away is that?"

"Four hundred fifty, give or take a mile or two." But Mac wasn't listening. She'd gone somewhere in her head and it unnerved him. He'd come here to return to his regular skin. He'd looked forward to being resettled like a phonograph needle finding a comfortable, vinyl groove.

Brett Walker, dedicated, enthusiastic bachelor.

But even though he'd been contemplating meeting the postman's daughter for drinks…

Mac suddenly didn't look like Mac.

Which somehow threatened his grasp on his usual, cynical self.

Zan had been writing to Mac for, what, years?

His sister apparently wasn't going to explain any more about that, so after a few minutes Brett escaped. Still hoping to return to his former, comfortable identity, though—the one that didn't worry about secretive women and mysterious missives—he dropped by the house his youngest sister shared with her fiancé and his daughter. As he pulled up to the massive modern structure, he saw London hop into a light truck and take off in the opposite direction.

"Car pool," Shay explained, when she let him in the door. "I'm afternoons this week…or Jace is afternoons, if he gets back from LA in time."

The other man ran a worldwide construction business. Because he loved Brett's sister and the daughter he was just becoming reacquainted with, he was reorganizing his company so that he could spend the majority of his time in the mountains.

Shay led him to her enormous kitchen and he pulled up a stool to her stainless-steel island. Though he was risking a caffeine overload, he didn't say no to a mug of coffee.

"What brings you by?" she asked.

Poppy was soft, Mac was flinty, and he'd always considered Shay to be a balance of the two. His littlest sister had also suffered from unfounded guilt over their father's early death. In trying to help her with that over the years, he'd revealed some of his own interior landscape.

Studying her over his coffee, he took a sip. She had elegant bones and an air of complete serenity. Damn, Jace was good for her. "How are your nightmares?" he asked, knowing they must hardly bother her any longer.

Her gaze narrowed on him, turned shrewd. "How are yours?"

That wasn't exactly what he'd term them, since they didn't happen during sleep. They were actually flash-backs to a string of black events that had put increasing pressure on his heart, squeezing down until it was dense and inflexible. Coal.

Instead of answering, he deflected. "I wish you'd talk to Angelica," he said.

Shay's fingertips touched her chest. "Me?"

"You're a good listener. Something bothers her. She has secrets."

"Everybody knows about her swindling father."

He glanced down at the gleaming countertop. His re-flection was discernible, yet hazy. The outline of himself was there, but it showed him as he'd felt since meeting Angelica...as if his hard edges were becoming blurred.

"This is not about her father," he said. "It's something else that I think is hard for her to share." Something sex-ual, that was clear. A prior bad experience that had left her skittish. No, scared.

"Try taking her into your confidence," his sister ad-vised. "Tell her about the things you can't let go of."

He looked up, alarmed. "Why would I put what's in my head in hers?"

"Because that's how you build trust, Brett."

"Shay—"

"Listen to me." She leaned across the countertop, her gaze boring into his. "If you want to lessen her load, you're going to have to show her some of what you're carrying yourself."

His hand went to the top of his hair and he rubbed it there, over and over, as if he could wipe free from his skin what never seemed to wash away. He yanked at his short hair as if he could yank from the roots the memories that had lodged inside his head.

Whop whop whop. They always started with that sound. Ended with the wash of red, the feel of it, the coppery smell. He didn't want to tell anyone about that. About life dying out of a pair of pain-filled eyes.

If you want to lessen her load, you're going to have to show her some of what you're carrying.

It would be unthinkable, except that at the moment he didn't know how else to get beneath Angelica's defenses. If Shay was right, it was his way to reach those shadowy places in Angelica. And, God help him, he wanted into those. He wanted to shed light there, in order to flush out her demons.

Damn his protective streak.

Somehow she'd exposed it. And though he cursed her for that, it didn't make him any more able to ignore it.

ANGELICA HEARD A KEY turn in the lock of her cottage's front door and realized that this time Brett hadn't bothered with knocking. From her place on the drop cloth covering the living room floor, she glared as he came in.

"I could have been taking a nap."

"Saw you through the window," he said, without a ripple in his neutral expression.

Once again, he appeared just out of the shower. His hair was damp, and the clean scent of soap carried through the air, reaching her even over the odor emanating from the open cans of paint and the carton of ice cream she'd set on a card table she'd found in a closet and covered with newspaper.

Brett approached, his eyes on the experiment she was conducting.

Planting her feet on the floor, she continued her offense. "Well, you still could have indicated your interest in chatting in the normal manner. Knuckles to wood—you recall that, right? It's called knocking."

"Told you, babe, men don't 'chat.'" He stopped on the other side of the square table and his gaze roamed over the containers. "What's all this?"

"Returned paint." Using a clean wooden stirrer, she indicated the cans that Glory had given her for free. "I'm mixing them to make my own custom color. Well, I'm trying it out, anyway."

In a plastic bowl, she'd combined a couple of colors. Now she gave the concoction a stir.

Brett rubbed his hand over his chin. He hadn't shaved, and she could hear the scratch of the bristles as he brushed his callous palm over them. The small of her back prickled as she imagined that work-roughened hand touching her there.

Then she had to swallow, hard, thinking of the whiskers surrounding his lips ghosting down her neck.

"I guess I have to ask about the ice cream."

"I left out a half gallon of Neapolitan ice cream once and it melted. When I stirred it, the color was a dawn-tinged shade of light cocoa brown. If I can match it with real paint, it might look nice in the bedroom." Reaching over, she gave the wooden spoon poking out of the carton a twist, folding the liquidy milk-and-sugar concoction.

He was shaking his head and fighting a smile. "You're something."

She lifted her chin. "You can take inspiration from anywhere." Then she cleared her throat, anxious to return to her color-combining without his distracting presence. "Can I help you with something?"

"You trying to get rid of me, angel face?"

Duh. Because being around Brett was increasingly a trial. Kissing him hadn't made him any less appealing. Reacting to his touch like a frightened fool didn't mean he'd lost an ounce of attraction.

But it was torture that she couldn't follow through with the desires he kindled inside her.

At the thought, she returned to stirring the paint, moving it around with such vigor that it slopped over the side, sloshing liquid on her wrist. Though she knew it wasn't a disaster, hot pressure built at the back of her eyes. "I'll never get this right," she muttered, abandoning the stick in frustration.

"Relax, sweetheart."

That's what she couldn't manage, no matter how much she wanted to be at ease in his arms, lose herself in his kiss, open herself to his touch. Setting her jaw, she directed her attention to the melting ice cream once more, grasping the wooden spoon to work at the soupy mass.

It didn't look right to her now either, and she cursed it under her breath.

"Wow," Brett said. "I've never seen you in such a temper."

The warning look she sent him should burn. "It's fiery."

His lips twitched.

YOUR PARTICIPATION IS REQUESTED!

Dear Reader,

Since you are a lover of our books – we would like to get to know you!

Inside you will find a short Reader's Survey. Sharing your answers with us will help our editorial staff understand who you are and what activities you enjoy.

To thank you for your participation, we would like to send you 2 books and 2 gifts – **ABSOLUTELY FREE!**

Enjoy your gifts with our appreciation,

Pam Powers

**SEE INSIDE
FOR READER'S
SURVEY**

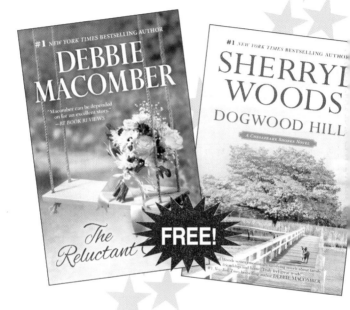

YOUR READER'S SURVEY
"THANK YOU" FREE GIFTS INCLUDE:
▶ 2 FREE books

▶ 2 lovely surprise gifts

PLEASE FILL IN THE CIRCLES COMPLETELY TO RESPOND

1) What type of fiction books do you enjoy reading? (Check all that apply)
- ○ Suspense/Thrillers
- ○ Action/Adventure
- ○ Modern-day Romances
- ○ Historical Romance
- ○ Humour
- ○ Paranormal Romance

2) What attracted you most to the last fiction book you purchased on impulse?
- ○ The Title
- ○ The Cover
- ○ The Author
- ○ The Story

3) What is usually the greatest influencer when you <u>plan</u> to buy a book?
- ○ Advertising
- ○ Referral
- ○ Book Review

4) How often do you access the internet?
- ○ Daily ○ Weekly ○ Monthly ○ Rarely or never.

5) How many NEW paperback fiction novels have you purchased in the past 3 months?
- ○ 0 - 2
- ○ 3 - 6
- ○ 7 or more

YES! I have completed the Reader's Survey. Please send me the 2 FREE books and 2 FREE gifts (gifts are worth about $10) for which I qualify. I understand that I am under no obligation to purchase any books, as explained on the back of this card.

194/394 MDL GH6X

FIRST NAME	LAST NAME

ADDRESS

APT.#	CITY

STATE/PROV.	ZIP/POSTAL CODE

If offer card is missing write to: Harlequin Reader Service, P.O. Box 1867, Buffalo, NY 14240-1867 or visit www.ReaderService.com

BUSINESS REPLY MAIL
FIRST-CLASS MAIL   PERMIT NO. 717   BUFFALO, NY

POSTAGE WILL BE PAID BY ADDRESSEE

HARLEQUIN READER SERVICE
PO BOX 1867
BUFFALO NY 14240-9952

NO POSTAGE
NECESSARY
IF MAILED
IN THE
UNITED STATES

Aggravation leaped. The light in his gray eyes had turned them to silver and with amusement written all over his handsome face he appeared years younger. "Are you laughing at me?" she demanded.

He shook his head. "Laughing *with* you?" he asked, fakely hopeful.

"Nothing's funny," she hissed, and when he actually tried to cover a chuckle with a cough…it happened.

Yanking the spoon from the thawed ice cream, she flicked it toward his face, like a spasmodic witch casting a spell with her wand. Droplets of pinky-beige liquid landed on his forehead, his nose, his chin.

"Uh-oh," he said.

Uh-oh, she thought. He glanced down at the table and she swiped up the carton, holding it close to her chest.

"I'm in a mood," she said. "Go away," she added, pointing toward the door with her spoon. Another spray of ice cream landed on his shirt. *Oops.*

He glanced down at it, then took a step forward. "Angelica…" His tongue made a tsking sound.

Shuffling back, she dipped her spoon in the carton. "I'm armed," she said, swirling the wooden handle as if reloading it. "You don't want to mess with me."

He took another step, rounding the table between them. "I have three younger sisters. I don't scare easily."

Her heart was pounding too fast and her blood was rushing through her veins, sweet and bubbly like soda pop. Without a first thought, let alone a second, she flung a spoonful of the viscous liquid in his direction. It landed in his hair and she gasped, then scurried in reverse even as a wild giggle climbed her throat.

Brett kept coming. She managed one more sloppy sling of ice cream before he wrenched the carton from her curled arm and the spoon from her hand. For an instant, she froze, then she darted forward to reclaim the utensil, getting her fingers around the sticky tip.

Her move must have surprised him, because one tug and it was hers. Dancing back, she crowed in triumph.

"Sweetheart," he said, a smile playing at his mouth as he weighed the carton in one big palm. "You forget, I have the ammo." He dipped a hand inside and his fingers came out, covered with ice cream ooze. Without hesitation, he flicked them. Drops landed on her face and in her hair.

She gasped.

"Play with fire, gonna get burned." His hand returned to the carton.

With a squeal, she prepared to run. On a lunge, he snagged her with his hand, his sticky fingers curling around her biceps.

"We're just starting to have fun," he said, drawing her close.

He was smiling and she was breathing hard, her gaze following the carton as he lifted it over her head. "You wouldn't dare," she said, between pants.

"If it keeps you from thinking so hard, I very much would," he said. He tipped it so the runny ice cream drew dangerously close to the rim.

"Really, you wouldn't," she said, staring at the foamy liquid, then at him.

His eyes laughed. "What'll you give me if I don't?"

And because she needed to take back control of the moment, she popped onto her tiptoes and pressed her mouth to his.

He accepted the kiss, his grip only slightly tightening

around her arm. When she landed on her heels, it was to notice the carton still hung over her head…

Like her inability to have a normal sexual encounter with him.

"You're thinking again," he warned. The carton tilted deeper. On instinct, she leaped for it, but he was faster, lifting it higher. Then he pressed his body into hers, moving her backward until her shoulder blades thumped into the wall and she was pinned, the two of them torso to torso.

"Brett," she protested, not sure what his manhandling was leading to. "I'm sticky. There's ice cream on my face. I think we're fair and square."

"Not even close," he said. And with both hands now free, his fingers went back in the carton. Two came out, covered with melted cream.

She shrank back. "No."

He smiled. "Yes," he said, and he drew them along her eyebrows, then down her nose. Then he bent his head. "Sweet," he murmured, his mouth following the sugary path. "So sweet."

This time, when she trembled, it wasn't a response to an ugly past incident. It was a reaction to Brett's lips on her skin. She closed her eyes, relishing the sensation, maybe more so because she worried that at any second the old memory would grab her like a mugger in a dark alley.

"Stay with me, babe," he murmured against her cheek. Then he lifted his mouth so he could watch himself dip into the ice cream once again and paint her lips with the liquid. When his mouth found hers, the tackiness of the sweetness glued them together, until he used his tongue to lick it all away.

Her head swam, and she let it rest on the wall behind her as he nipped at her jawline. His lips trailed down her neck, his whiskers scratching delicately. Her nipples beaded, their tightness almost painful. She wasn't wearing a bra, and for an embarrassed instant she wondered if he could tell.

Then she didn't have to ponder any longer because he'd palmed her breast. As she squirmed, caught between the wall and his heavy body, he groaned, and bit her shoulder.

Face burning, body quivering, she glanced down at his hand, the thumb pressing the beaded tip she could clearly see beneath the old, paint-smeared T-shirt. "You're getting ice cream on my clothes," she told him, as if dressed in silk.

He glanced up and caught her eyes, one brow winging high. "'Spose we should take them off then."

She shrugged, as if adrenaline wasn't making her feel as if she'd inhaled helium. Her toes curled as if she was standing on a cliff and about to dive. "'Spose."

His grin flashed. "Go, girl."

The brief praise added an additional layer of warmth to already-heated skin. Her belly twitched as he found the hem of her shirt and yanked upward. It was gone in an instant, and she froze, her pretend insouciance gone.

If he realized her mood change, he ignored it. "Hold this," he said, thrusting the melted ice cream into her hands. Then he drew off his own shirt.

Oh, God. It was his second baring for her. For *her.* She'd ogled him shirtless many times before, but this was for her pleasure. And it did, it pleased her, as she ran her gaze over the strong column of his neck, across his collarbone and heavy shoulders, down the slight mounds of his pecs and the rippled muscles of his abs. His body hair was light, blond, but there was a dark brown sprinkling of it below his belly button, leading to territory hidden by his jeans.

She could look forever.

Slowly, he held his arms away from his body. "You want to play?"

Her gaze flew to his. *Play?*

"Nothing wrong with fun and messy," he said, a gleam in his eyes.

"No?" But the look on his face was giving her permission for anything. Everything. Excitement surged through her veins, more bubbly and sweet.

"You like to paint?" He nodded at the ice cream carton. "Paint me."

Her hand clenched, denting the soft sides of the cardboard. Inside, the mixture was completely thawed. Warm, even. Warm enough not to pucker his nipple if she touched it with a dab.

It contracted before she even brushed it with her forefinger.

He drew in air, a sharp, audible sound that set another match to her blood. Then she made contact with the hard point, bathing it in sticky liquid.

Leaning in, she tongued it away.

His body tensed, and he felt bigger than before…and, strangely, less scary. She affected him.

Like he affected her.

Glancing up, she took another finger of melted cream and dabbed it on his other nipple, then drew a line down the center of his rib cage to his belly button. His fingers curled into fists.

"Relax," she whispered, feeling whole and wicked and

womanly. Then she sucked his nipple into her mouth, swirling her tongue around the hard point until his fingers dug into her hair. Moving her mouth, she tasted his skin, licking away the line of cream until she was half-bent and she'd reached denim.

His hand jumped free of her hair as she curled her fingertips into the waistband of his jeans. She smiled to herself. He'd never insist on anything she didn't want to give.

So take, she directed herself, popping the button.

"Angel face," he whispered.

"Hold this," she ordered, pushing the carton against his belly. "Both hands."

Then she dropped to her knees. Angelica could hardly believe herself. But this was *play* and *fun*, he'd said that, and though the ice cream was sticky and crazy, the only real mess would be the one that disrupted her exploration if she thought of things besides Brett's sculpted body, his iron control, his...

She stared at the column of flesh she'd revealed by parting the denim and pushing it down along with a pair of navy blue boxers.

"Angel face—" he started.

His words ended abruptly when she sucked the head into her mouth.

The carton hit the ground with a squelch and a splash.

Angelica licked the heavy tip of his penis. Her fingers gripped the denim-covered muscles of his thighs and for a moment she thought of the techniques taught by boarding-school dorm mates who spoke in stupid terms of lollipops and carrots. Then she closed her eyes and learned all she didn't know by tactile means—touch, taste, scent.

So male.

One moment she was running her cheek against the thick shaft and the next she was tumbled to the ground. His mouth caught hers and their next kiss was hot and frantic.

Maybe he was as scared as she was. It must be hell to be with a woman who went from wanton to weird in the space of a moment.

"Here," he murmured against her lips. "You're right here with me."

Angelica stayed sure of that by keeping her eyes open and it added another sensual edge to each moment. She saw the gold tips of his hair as he dipped his head once again to her breasts. Rubbing her chin against the soft brush of it, she watched her hand trail across the powerful breadth of his shoulders.

When he drew her nipple into his mouth, she arched up, pushing more of her flesh into the pleasure and heat. His gaze shot toward hers, the gray now silver fire.

He was crouched over her as he moved between her breasts. She thought hazily that he was leery of putting too much of his weight on her. The consideration pierced her heart and she felt a hot tear trail from the corner of her eye to her temple.

"Baby," he whispered, lifting his head.

But she didn't want to stop, so she pushed on his shoulders and took him to the ground. Then she was over him, the kisser, the aggressor, the dominant position giving her the confidence she needed to proceed.

He grunted when she, flying high on lust, bit his pectoral muscle. She almost apologized, until she glanced up and saw the look on his face—the skin pulled taught over his sharp features as he struggled for control—and when her knee bent and brushed the heavy bulge of his sex, he sucked in a sharp breath.

His hand clutched the back of her head. "If you're wondering, you can bite me all you want."

Be shameless! she thought, recalling Glory's advice.

Angelica grinned at Brett, a gleeful smile because she finally felt free to be exactly that—and *do* all she wanted.

She suspected it was going to better than painting walls the color of her own choosing.

Instead of biting again, though, she moved up to baby kiss his bottom lip, and then the edge of his cheekbone. Her tongue followed his facial scars, sliding across the bridge of his nose and then tracing the jagged line that went through his eyebrow and into his hair.

"Frankenstein's monster," he murmured.

Surprised, she kneeled up to look into his eyes. "No monster," she said. "Those only make you more…man."

One corner of his mouth kicked up and his hand reached up to caress her breast. He held it in the cup of his palm and his thumb gently brushed the tip. Her belly tightened; between her legs she felt heated and swollen. She squirmed, automatically trying to ease the pressure by moving against the denim of her jeans.

Brett smiled a smile that was slow and lazy. Her breathing stuttered in her lungs as his hand moved from her breast to her belly button. One rough fingertip drew circles there. "You need something?"

Her face burned and she was keenly aware of her naked torso—and the rest of her that was covered. She sneaked a look at his lap, where he was still fully erect, his penis framed by the open edges of his jeans.

She redirected her gaze to his face to see the laziness

was gone. He was breathing hard, his beautiful chest rising and falling and when their eyes met, his loitering finger drew down the millimeters to the button of her jeans. His fingernail bumped over its upraised design as he toyed there.

She felt weak with desire, hungry, hollowed out. A vessel that was empty and needed affection, touch, *him* to feel full. Longing came to the surface of her skin in the guise of chill bumps, spreading everywhere.

"You're cold," he said, softly.

There was the click of the heater automatically turning on again, the renewed warmth nothing compared to the fire that was consuming her from the inside. "I'm not cold at all," she whispered.

"What do we do next, Angelica?" He was studying her with a seriousness she did not like.

"I want to play." *Nothing wrong with fun and messy.* And with those words echoing in her head, she reached for the discarded carton of melted ice cream. With a loony smile stretching her mouth, she dumped the remaining contents onto his chest.

His eyes widened and he jackknifed, sitting straight. "Why you—"

Angelica didn't hear the rest of it because she ran. Giggles rose in her throat like hiccups as she fled toward her room, intention unformed. But he caught her before she reached the safe haven and when he pulled her around she was laughing and breathless.

Then he was kissing her again, his tongue in her mouth, their torsos fused by sticky ice cream. She writhed, and one of his big hands clamped on her bottom.

The pressure of his fingers made her wiggle back and she moaned, caught between his hold and his hard body.

God, she thought, head reeling. *This is so good.* There was promise in each kiss, another step toward splendor that she'd never reached with any man.

He lifted his head, his gaze lazy, his expression aroused. "I need a shower," he murmured.

"Oh." So much for splendor. Hopes dashed, she looked away.

"You need a shower," he continued, and tugged her in the direction of the bathroom.

"Brett—"

"If you liked ice cream, wait until you see what I can do with soap," he said, and suddenly she was giddy again, thinking of him naked and wet. With his palm on her bottom, he urged her into the small tiled room.

He turned on the water and as the ensuing steam heated up the room, he undressed her, crouching low to push her jeans and panties from her legs. Any embarrassment she felt fled when he pressed a string of kisses between her hip bones. Then he helped her into the enclosure and followed in moments.

They washed the ice cream residue from each other's body with slow, slick hands. The experience was so new to her...sharing a shower, trading touches, kissing under the spray like kissing in the rain, that there was no way the ugliness from her past could find an opening in the novelty and intrude.

When a slippery hand brushed between her thighs, her legs quivered. She let him explore there, holding tight to his shoulders as he open her furled flesh. It parted for him easily, already swollen and slick with its own moisture. He made a satisfied noise of discovery, and she almost released another giddy laugh.

But then his finger slid inside and she could only

shudder and press her cheek to his shoulder. His thumb brushed her clitoris, swirling and nudging and then caressing with short, tender strokes. She gasped and her muscles clenched around the delicious intrusion of a second finger.

He groaned and tucked his head close to hers. His other hand drifted from her bottom, to her ribs, to her breast and she jerked as his fingers plucked at her nipple.

Pressure was building. She knew what this was, but no man had ever given this to her and she tightened her hold on him, as if to make sure the pleasure wouldn't slip away. Her hips tilted as his hand moved.

"Angelica," he said.

She looked up. Then his mouth was on hers and his tongue surged inside with the same rhythm of his fingers. It was possessive and the spray rained down with enough force on her supersensitized skin that it added tiny pricks of almost-pain that only served to keenly edge the pleasure that grew and grew and grew...

Until it burst, rippling through her body in wave after wave of sharp, bright joy. It almost hurt, the goodness was so deeply sweet. Her fingers tightened on him as he stroked every bit of bliss from her. Then his hand slowed and gentled, drawing out the last twitch.

As the thrill abated, awkwardness closed in. Shy, she tried shuffling back, but he slid his arms around her, his shaft hard and heavy at the hollow where her hip met her belly.

It was his turn, she thought, suddenly anxious. She wasn't any more practiced in satisfying a man than she was in being satisfied by one. But Brett had allayed her fears and made her feel glorious. How could she stop short of returning the favor?

But she wondered about doing that for a man like Brett, who was both virile and experienced. Maybe she would be all groping hands and rubbery lips to *him*. Her body stiffened and the nervous beat of her heart seemed to echo off the tiled walls. Maybe—

"Angel face." Brett rubbed his rough-skinned palms up and down her back. "What's the matter?"

She shook her head. Then, desperate to do the right thing, she turned up her mouth to press it against his throat. His pulse beat wildly beneath her lips, boosting her confidence. Her hands tugged on his head, drawing it down, and she threw herself into the kiss.

She felt his big body shake against hers. "Just a second," he said, amusement in his voice as he eased away. "The water's turning cold."

The faucet squeaked as he reached behind and turned it off. It sounded as rusty as her sexual skills and she felt stupid and clumsy all over again. Hopping out of the enclosure, she wrapped a bath towel around herself. Brett threw another over her wet head, gave it an affectionate rub, then wrapped a third length of fabric around his hips.

He strode from the room.

Angelica had no idea what to do now. His clothes were strewn at her feet, but he could very well head back to his cabin without them. It wasn't as if anyone would see.

As a matter of fact, if he left now, maybe *she* could pretend the whole event had never happened. That might be good. That there was still residual throbbing in intimate places…it would abate by morning.

Surely.

Then she wouldn't have to remember that it had been

a one-sided performance that had ended in a cold shower for him. She put her face in her hands. *Oh, God.* How humiliating.

She stood on the bath mat for a long time. Then, resigned, she finished squeezing water from her hair, hung up that towel and dragged a comb through her tangles. Stuck in her misery, she didn't notice any sounds or activity in her bungalow until she heard Brett call her name.

She froze. He was still here? It had been less than ten minutes since she'd presumed he'd left, but was he back now? Or if not, what had he been doing?

Wary, she padded down the hall in her bare feet, her towel still wrapped closely around her, covering her from her armpits to her knees. What he wanted from her, she couldn't imagine.

What she found…well, she could never have imagined that either.

Flames were crackling in the living room fireplace. Still in his own towel, Brett appeared to have created a double bed–sized pallet before it. Blankets were stacked. A couple of extralarge beach towels were spread over the padding.

There was wicked mischief in his eyes again as he held out his hand to her. She responded as she always did to him. As if her body was designed to be as close to his as possible. Moving forward, she felt another surge of lust…or was it longing? Just moments ago she'd felt abandoned and alone, her feet on the cold tile.

Now she was walking toward heat and promise.

As she drew nearer, she noted the foil packets stacked by the makeshift bed. Then her gaze caught on the squeeze bottle warming on the hearth. Its contents glinted gold in the firelight. Her glance shifted back to Brett.

He smiled. "This time it's caramel sauce," he said. "Ready for more play?"

CHAPTER TWELVE

BRETT WOKE UP before first light, as he always did. He lay in Angelica's warm bed with his eyes closed, gathering himself for what needed to be done first thing: make clear to her they'd shared nothing more than a one-night stand.

He was no good for her.

Well, he'd been good *to* her—to her body, at least. But nothing they'd done the night before had addressed her issues as his sister Shay had suggested he do. And Angelica had issues—with trust, men, sex or some combination of the three—yet instead of talking with her, learning what was going on inside that beautiful head of hers, he'd ducked all the complicated stuff. Using distraction and that carnal combustibility between them, he'd led her into sexual games.

Fun times.

But not what she needed. He wasn't the kind of man she needed. That guy would be willing to delve into her heart and soul. Unlike Brett, he'd have his own generous heart and a willing soul he'd be happy to lay bare to her.

Bracing himself to tackle the situation immediately, he opened his eyes, directing his gaze to the other pillow.

It was empty.

Frowning, he glanced through the open bedroom door

to the bathroom across the hall. It was unoccupied. So where was she?

He was the earliest riser he knew.

It took only moments to draw on his clothes—grimacing at the dried ice cream stains. On stocking feet, he moved toward the front of the house. He found her in the kitchen, staring at the contents of her open refrigerator.

For a moment he allowed himself to merely gaze upon her. It was a hardware-store day, he decided, judging by the nice jeans she was wearing with boots. The denim hugged her generous ass, the one he'd resisted biting the night before, though the temptation had been great.

Aware that he'd spooked her before by taking the dominant position, he'd decided his best course lay in avoiding darkness, the bedroom, him on top. She'd responded with enthusiasm to firelight and caramel sauce and his encouragement to take the lead. With her on her knees over him, he'd had a delightful view of her bouncing breasts. His hands had been free to roam, his caresses nudging her toward nirvana.

He'd followed right after—and it had nearly blown his mind.

Perhaps she heard his thoughts because she whirled now, her hand going to her throat. That killer face of hers, lush of lips and lash, nearly arrested his heart.

What a beauty.

A smile turned up the corners of her mouth. "Good morning! How are you? Did you sleep well?" Then her mouth turned down and she gave him an apologetic look. "I've been told I'm too terribly cheerful first thing in the morning."

Good God, she was, not that he'd say so. "Who the hell would tell you that?"

She shrugged. "Dorm mates. My dad."

"Screw 'em," he said, stepping forward. "And a good morning back at you." His steps halted, as he recalled what he'd promised to do. Set the boundaries. Draw the lines. Make a box around the hours of their entwined bodies. Explain that last night was last night and today they were moving on…separately.

Probably a "good morning" was a bad entrée into that discussion.

He opened his mouth to begin again, but she beat him to it. "I don't have anything here for breakfast," she said. "I'm out of everything."

"No problem." He didn't want to stay for a meal. His intent was to spit out what needed to be said and then head next door to dress for the rest of his day.

She yanked on the hem of the sweater she was wearing. It was the same warm, peachy-gold as the flesh of her belly. The nervous gesture pulled the knit fabric closer to her breasts and he remembered her response as he caressed them, tongued them, pinched them. He sucked in a harsh breath, his cock starting to harden.

"What about you?" she asked.

"Me…what?" He crossed his arms over his chest in hopes her innocent gaze would stop there.

"Do you have breakfast stuff at your place?"

"I—" No. He could not have her over there, bustling in his kitchen so they'd bump elbows and brush hips while making a meal together. And he couldn't leave her flat, without the most important meal of the day, right after telling her she'd been a fine lay but now that he'd had her he was done.

Making it clear their interlude was over was the right thing to do, but he couldn't do it—the moment felt wrong.

Not here, where she might cry or something. Not here, when she didn't even have a piece of toast to throw at his head.

"Get ready," he said, his voice gruff. "I'll follow you into town in fifteen minutes. Buy you breakfast at Oscar's."

Walking to his place in the crisp morning air, he cursed himself for not getting right to it. *Shit.* But he'd never been one for kicking kittens.

Thirty minutes later, he decided that a field trip to Oscar's hadn't been a better move. The place was packed. He stood in line for their coffees and breakfast sandwiches, while she found two seats across from each other in the center of one of the long picnic tables in the place.

Anything he had to say would not be private.

As he strolled up to her, beverages in hand, she glanced up. Her face had a becoming flush—as if she needed any further enhancement to her looks—that he suddenly realized might very well be residual beard burn.

The marks he'd left shouldn't send a surge of satisfaction through him.

She smiled as she took her latte and indicated the couple sitting beside her. "You know George and Nan, right?"

Of course he knew George and Nan. He'd known them his entire life. The only question was, how did she know George and Nan? Angelica was quite familiar with the pair, that was clear, because she chattered to them about everything under the sun in between sips of her drink. They gazed on her with indulgent expressions and sent a couple of meaningful glances his way.

"You know," Nan told Angelica when she paused for a breath. "We never thought Brett would settle down."

"Umm." Angelica slid him a sideways look.

"What a busy tyke he was. Never a wild boy, you know, but not one to keep still. Then he went into the army and received a medal on his very first day in Afghanistan—it was all over the local paper. We were so proud of him."

Aware Angelica's eyes were on him again, Brett signaled the server who came with their breakfast trays and pretended he didn't hear Nan's prattle. He'd return the fucking medal if it would allow him to expel the memory of that day from his brain.

"He's always had a different girl on his arm, that's for sure." Nan sent him a look. "But still such a good man— and even playboys settle down, you know."

That's when he caught on. Straightening in his seat, he stared at the older woman. Mountain people were supposed to be suspicious of rich flatlanders like Angelica. The locals here weren't impressed with big city wealth and big city baubles. Christ, the bodacious brunette sitting across from him still drove the ridiculous convertible that would be sure to strand her when winter arrived in a few short weeks.

But Nan was trying to sell Angelica on him!

"Then there was the hurricane relief effort…" Nan started.

Oh, no. He wasn't going to sit still for this, Brett thought. He'd get up, walk back to his truck, get on with his day.

Without getting things straight with his night-before lover.

Shit!

Still, he was not going to listen to anyone making him out to be a hero while describing the time in his life that had proved him to be a total fool. He shoved up from the bench, preparing to vault to his feet.

At the same time, George leaned forward. Under the cover of his wife's continuing natter he said, "There was another break-in last night."

Brett froze. Then he brushed a hand over his hair. "Not again."

"Yep. Don't know any details, but heard about it at the gas station. What do you think is going on?"

Uneasy, Brett shifted in his seat. "I don't know."

"Someone told me they thought it could be Lewis."

"Lewis our postman?" Brett frowned, glancing about the room. Any number of people could potentially be the culprit, actually. There was the president of the historical society having coffee with the principal of the high school. It could be either of them, right? "It's not Lewis."

"Yeah, I believe you, Brett." George lowered his voice. "But what about that Harris boy? The one that was dealing drugs last spring."

Brett rubbed his temple. "I don't like all this doubting of our community members. That was just a rumor about Ian Harris."

"In any case, we gotta do something about the situation," George said. "See what you can find out, will you, Brett?" Then he glanced at his wife. "C'mon, Nan. You can talk to Angelica another time. The grandkids are expecting a ride to school."

As the older couple headed for the exit, Brett framed

his coffee with his elbows and scraped his face with his hands. He didn't like trouble in his town, in his beloved mountains.

"What's the matter?"

"What?" He glanced up, taking in the line of concern between Angelica's brows. "Oh. Nothing."

"Not nothing. Did I hear George say there was another robbery?"

"It's true," a male voice put in.

They both looked up to see Vaughn Elliott standing nearby, holding his own to-go cup.

"Separate from the incident at the historical society?" Angelica asked. "Did you know about that, Vaughn?"

"An email from the society president landed in my inbox. But nothing was stolen besides Piney."

"Poor Piney," Angelica said, sighing.

"He'll probably be returned to the front doorstep once Homecoming weekend is over." Brett glanced back to the other man. "What do you know, Vaughn?"

"You're aware I'm a sheriff's department volunteer—"

"Yes," Brett and Angelica said together.

He huffed. "The consensus is that the heist of Piney is completely separate from the other goings-on. Just kids bent on a prank."

Brett frowned. "They scared Angelica…so not that funny."

"But you're okay now, doll, right?" He propped one expensive boot on the bench beside Angelica.

He likely checked his reflection hourly in the buffed leather, Brett thought sourly. "She's fine," he said, his tone cool.

"She's even still got her tongue," Angelica added, with pseudobrightness.

He shot her a look. In response, she arched an eyebrow, and silent messages transferred between them.

Brett: *He's a jerk.*

Angelica: *I know that, but I can speak for myself.*

Shrugging, he looked away, regretting the moment of personal communication. He was supposed to be cutting ties with her, not encouraging further intimacy. "Thanks for the intel, Vaughn," he said to hurry the man on. Once rid of him, Brett would launch into his speech. It would be some blend of "It's me, not you" and "I don't do strings."

Or maybe, simpler, cleaner, would be the truth.

Whatever the hell that was.

His head throbbed, and he glanced again at the sheriff's volunteer who seemed to be lingering. "Is there something else?"

Vaughn leaned over his bent knee. "I think you should know the word that's going around."

Brett rubbed at his temple again. More fruit from the mountain grapevine. It was a flourishing, powerful thing, which was why he'd been so alarmed at Nan trying to talk him up to Angelica. Fifteen more minutes in her presence and there'd be rumors they were already Vegas-married with triplets on the way. "What word is that?"

Vaughn lowered his voice. "Maybe the person responsible is that guy," he said, nodding toward a solo man sitting a few tables away. "The newcomer."

Brett didn't have a clue. "I've never seen him before."

"He's come into the hardware store a couple of times," Angelica said, sliding a look his way. "Then he disappeared for a while and now he's back again—fiercely pursuing Glory."

The man was in work clothes that were well-worn and spattered with stains. "It's not a crime to come and go," Brett said. "Or to be a new arrival."

Though, again, it wasn't uncommon for the mountain people to mistrust the new guy. As a matter of fact, the only person who seemed to have been adopted into the region in a quick and easy fashion was Angelica, with her two local jobs, her local friends, and her place on the local historical committee.

Since the summer, even before her financial disaster, she'd been weaving herself into their fabric, he realized. An uncomfortable thought because it meant he might be dodging her beyond the first snow—though not unless she replaced that impractical vehicle of hers. Ultimately, however, he was convinced she'd go.

"There's another theory floating around, as well," Vaughn said.

"Yeah? What's that?"

"Mac."

Brett went cold, even as he saw Angelica bristle. Without thinking, he reached over and placed his hand over hers. "What about Mac?" he asked Vaughn, his voice careful.

"You know." Vaughn shrugged. "Local girl, knows all the back routes and every shortcut. Aware of who's in town and who isn't. Nobody looks twice at a Maids by Mac car cruising around."

"Cruising around?"

"Casing joints," Vaughn clarified.

Brett glanced at Angelica. *Did he say* casing joints?

her big brown eyes asked. Squeezing her fingers, he returned his attention to Vaughn.

"Well, I hope no one repeats that suspicion in front of me," he said, his tone mild. But deadly.

Vaughn flinched. "I'm not repeating it, Brett."

"You just did—" Angelica started.

Brett sent her a warning look. "Anything else, Vaughn?"

"Well…" The other man took his time taking a swallow of his coffee. Then he straightened, both feet square on the ground. His gaze held a challenge. "Same story…"

"But a different Walker," Brett finished for him.

"Have a nice day, Brett," Vaughn said with a thin smile. He saluted Angelica with his cup. "You, too, doll."

The minute the door closed on his back, Angelica turned her gaze on him, outrage written all over her face. "I can't believe—"

"There are suspicions about everyone," he said, realizing their hands were still joined and her fingers clutched his. "Take it easy."

"I can't. Mac's almost a friend—will be, when we get to know each other better, I'm sure. I'm incensed for her."

"It'll be okay."

"And then to mention you—"

"I've been accused before. Remember, I do have a history. And memories are long here."

Her jaw dropped. Then she closed her eyes, tight, and seemed to be concentrating on something. Was it a wish?

"What are you doing?"

She looked at him, eyes still narrowed. "My great-grandmother was reputedly a *bruja*—a witch. In case I have my own latent powers I just wished ill on that girl who lied about you. If I have my way, she now has a furry tongue, scaly skin and a car with a wonky starter motor."

He stared at her, fascinated. "A car with a wonky starter motor?"

"I had one of those once, and it took forever to get it properly diagnosed. Think how many times she'll be late to work or to meet a date."

His lips twitched. "You'd do that for me?"

"We're friends, right? At least I hope that our one-time event hasn't changed the friendship we've established. So as my pal, that means…"

As she continued on in a furious whisper, he continued watching her mouth move and her eyes flash without taking in a single sentence. *We're friends. One-time event.* Her words.

Relief should be rolling through him. She'd done it, without him initiating the conversation. She'd put them, and all that had happened the night before when their limbs were entangled and their skin was fused by sugar and sweat, into her very own box.

The buddy box.

Terrific. Great.

He couldn't be happier.

GLORY STOOD BACK from the metal stand she and Angelica had just moved to the southwest corner of the store to examine the new placement. "No, not here," she said.

Her friend's brows rose. "We've moved it five times."

"Yes, yes, but the pressed wood fire logs are big sellers and also impulse buys…so I need to have them in the exact right place."

"Your dad will tell you they should be located near

the fireplace tools—where they've always been," Angelica warned.

"I know. But now the business is mine and I want to make it feel like my own."

"How about a compromise? We put the log holder where regular customers will expect to find it. Then we put a smaller stack near the register for the impulse buyers to discover."

Glory stared at her friend. "Brilliant!" She grabbed her end of the stand. "Let's do it."

Angelica didn't complain as they returned the contraption to its original location. She'd been fabulous that way, not pointing out that Glory had been in a frenzy since Kyle Scott had made his return. Not pointing out that Glory had been moving things around all over the store as if that might cure her malaise.

She still held hope that it would.

"What do you think about that display of rodent eradication products?"

"I try not to think of rodent eradication at all, Glory."

"Ha-ha." The sound of the front door's bells chiming made her start. "Go see who that is, would you? Just in case…"

Just in case Kyle had bribed yet another local. First, it had been a skateboarding preteen with a pumpkin under his arm. Carved into its skin was a message: "Go out with me. —Kyle."

She'd tossed it into the Dumpster out back.

The next day, a toddler had arrived, one hand held by his mother, the other clutching a steaming blueberry muffin. A paper flag attached to a toothpick was stuck in the center. "Please go out with me. —Kyle."

She'd pitched the toothpick into the trash. After a

moment's consideration, she'd eaten the muffin in two big bites.

As Angelica headed off to the front of the store now, Glory called after her. "Beware of strangers bearing gifts!"

But it was no stranger who accompanied the brunette on her return trip. Glory's oldest friend, Jules, came down the aisle, pushing a stroller that contained a snoozing two-year-old Becca under a kitten-print quilt.

Still, Glory cast a suspicious look at them both. "Is there anything hiding under that blanket? Did a tall, dark and handsome man ask you to bring something inside?"

Jules appeared confused. "Huh?"

Angelica answered. "Glory has an admirer."

"Stu?" Jules guessed.

"Not Stu." Glory frowned. Why did everyone think of her and then think of Stu? It was the rut, she decided, the rut she'd always been in.

Angelica was admiring the sleeping little girl. "How adorable she is."

"I know," Jules said, beaming. "Sometimes I pinch myself in the morning. I could have missed all this."

"Missed it how?" Angelica asked.

"Jules was a famous actress in Hollywood," Glory explained.

"Please." The famous actress snorted. "I was in commercials for a local flooring chain."

"Don't forget you played the girl in the diamond store in that movie."

"None of us can remember the name of 'that movie,'" Jules pointed out.

"Still…" Glory remembered fantasizing about her and Jules trading places. Glory as wife and mother, Jules as the head of the hardware store. Now she played another little game in her mind. Glory in Hollywood—or anywhere besides Blue Arrow Lake, really—following a different dream...

"You're sorry about your adventure?" Angelica asked Jules now.

"Not at all." The young mother bent down to adjust the blanket around her daughter. "If I hadn't gone down the hill, it would have been built up in my mind as 'that thing I didn't do.' So I went, experimented, found it wasn't for me and returned, happy to move on with my life here."

"I read that the average person will have something like eleven jobs over their lifetime," Angelica said.

Glory stared at her. "Really?"

"Well, not you," her friend said cheerfully. "You have your lifetime job right here, right now."

Of course she did. Glory was telling herself to be grateful for that, when the sound of distant snare drums caught her attention. All three women looked at each other, and then headed to the front of the store.

"What the heck?" Outside the store, the high school marching band was arranging itself on the street. Thirty of them assembled in rows, not counting a five-member squad of white-gloved, kicky-skirted girls at the front. When the band started playing "Call Me Maybe," the young ladies in front danced under the mellow-yellow afternoon sun.

Glory stepped out the door and onto the sidewalk, one of the many spectators to gather and watch. Angelica spoke in her ear. "I wonder who had this idea?"

Telling herself not to do so, she glanced around the crowd to see if Kyle was among them. But there was no tall and rangy house painter in sight. Homecoming was approaching. Maybe the band was out for an impromptu practice. But the kids all seemed to be staring at her.

Prickles rose on the back of her neck. The people on the sidewalk were staring at her, too, as if they'd never seen her before. She glanced down. Was something wrong with her clothes? But she was in her same-old, same-old work uniform: khaki jeans, a long-sleeved T-shirt, her butcher-style apron. Self-conscious, she fluffed her short hair and bit at her lips to give them color. Had she worn lipstick today?

"You look great," Angelica whispered in her ear.

Glory steeled her spine. She didn't care how she looked. She didn't care that other people were looking at her. To them, she'd always be Cutest Kewpie anyway.

The band was winding down. Soon, they'd be moving along, she supposed, continuing along the street or back to school. This unexpected, out-of-the-ordinary moment would be gone from her life...just like Kyle Scott.

Angelica had been pressuring her to give him another chance. Just because he'd done one disappearing act didn't mean he couldn't be trusted not to leave again, she'd said. But Glory couldn't shake her unease, though perhaps that was due less to the man and more because of the strength of the attraction she felt for him.

It was unprecedented...so how could she trust it to last?

At the final crescendo, cymbals clashed and the dancing girls swept down in graceful arcs. Glory realized there were pieces of cardboard lying facedown at their feet, and they plucked them up, to hold them chest-high. Each was a letter, and spelled out Beautiful Glory, Go Out with Me.

Marching again to the single beat of a snare drum, the band split in two and fanned to each side, so that beyond the girls she could see the lone man seated on the bench across the street.

Kyle's elbows were on his knees and he was studying her with that single-mindedness he'd warned her about. His dark eyes bored into hers.

A yearning spread inside her chest, but it seemed to empty her out, too, making her ache. Afraid of the feeling, afraid of everything but the familiar—her rut seemed so safe—Glory swung around and fled into the store. Behind her, the trombones let out a low, mournful call.

It echoed in her heart.

She immediately began tugging on a heavy cardboard bin of hoses. Aware that Angelica had come inside, she pitched her voice to her friend. "Let's put these by the rakes and brooms." It made no particular sense to relocate them. Nothing was making any sense.

"Glory—"

"I told you I need to make the store my own," she said through her teeth, not looking over. "Can't you understand that?"

"I'm not fighting you."

"I'm sorry." She straightened and put her face in her hands. "I'm sorry."

"I think you're fighting yourself."

A dozen thoughts were whirling through Glory's head. The business; her father's continued intrusions into it; the rut that was her life; Stu, standing in the offing until the calendar turned to January.

Kyle, who she'd rejected again.

Her feet acted of their own free will. One minute she

was standing in the store, the next she was racing out of it, flinging open the door to call out, "Don't go!" She looked wildly about, searching the sidewalk in both directions, trying to find him. To the right, no sign of him. To the left, the same.

"I'm not going anywhere," he called out, from his seat on the bench directly across the street.

He hadn't left.

Her pulse skidded to a stop like a galloping horse suddenly encountering a cliff. She rubbed her damp palms along the crisp fabric of her apron. "Why?"

"You know why."

Because he wanted to be with her. She stared at him, trying to comprehend it. Like troubling to find out her favorite sandwich, he was willing to take the time to win her over. He thought she was beautiful, when everyone knew she was cute as a button.

Nobody had ever thought differently. No one had ever gone out of their way to be with her. Not even Stu, whom she'd been with—if you added it all up—longer than anyone. He just took for granted she'd be there at the store, willing to date again when the right January rolled around.

He'd never worked to have her. To please her.

"This is probably a bad idea," she said.

Kyle came to his feet. Cars were going slowly between them. Gossip would be all over the mountains in an hour. "Are you still worried about people talking?"

They already were, Glory thought. They'd know Kyle had referred to her as "beautiful." Her face flushed. "Maybe."

"We can take a street survey, right here, right now.

Find out if people will still stop in for their dowels and doorknobs if you let me take you on a date."

"Only if she reports on the details," a white-haired woman said as she emerged from the beauty salon next door.

"She doesn't have to tell me nothin'," the passing postal carrier said, bustling by with an armful of mail. "In my job, I see way more interesting things than details of your dates. You wouldn't believe what people write on the backs of postcards."

"Gee, thanks, Lewis," Glory groused, but she could hardly hide her grin.

Kyle had crossed the street now. He hadn't climbed to the sidewalk, though, so she didn't have to look up quite as far to see into his face. "What do you say, gorgeous?" he asked.

Gorgeous. That was him, in another pair of broken-in jeans, a plain white T-shirt and a denim jacket for warmth. It was Christmas morning she was feeling now, that warm and excited sense of good things about to be unwrapped.

She glanced around, noticing a woman standing nearby, just a little younger than herself. Megan Newsome, who'd had her heart broken a few weeks ago when the guy she'd fallen for in June had gone back to his real life in Boston at the end of summer. They'd all seen it coming, and tried to warn her against getting in too deep with a vacation romance. The local girls knew never to fall for one of what they called the Summer Beaus.

But Kyle wasn't going to be a mistake, Glory decided. She wasn't even going to see him as one of the temporary summer guys who so often showed up in the mountains to make hay with the mountain girls while the sun shone. It was autumn, after all.

Instead, Kyle was going to be her Hollywood.

She was too smart and too cautious to expect anything between them to last forever. But she wasn't going to let him become her own "that thing I didn't do." Her recent malaise made it clear she needed to shake up her life a little. He'd do that for her. He'd be the ten other jobs she was never going to have.

She'd date him for the short term, an adventure of sorts, and when it ended, she'd return to being Cutest Kewpie, behind the register in Hallett Hardware, happy to move on with her life there.

CHAPTER THIRTEEN

"You're tougher than you look," Mac said to Angelica. They were taking a break from cleaning the palatial, lakeside Whitmore home to savor coffee they'd brought in a thermos.

Grinning, Angelica pushed up the short sleeve of her T-shirt and flexed her biceps. "Tougher than you thought I'd be, you mean."

The other woman made a face. "Okay, you got me."

Angelica wasn't sure that she did. Even with the small amount of interaction she'd had with Poppy and Shay, she felt she understood them. Both were friendly, curious and openhearted. They loved the men in their lives and were racing forward, clear-eyed and optimistic, into their futures.

Mac, on the other hand...

She was more like her brother. Guarded. Private.

They sat companionably enough, though, perched on stools drawn to the kitchen island. They both looked out the expansive set of windows to the lake. It was a deep, sparkling blue and the dark green of the pines that ringed the shoreline were broken up here and there with the yellow flame of an aspen.

"Will you miss it?" Mac said.

Angelica glanced over. "Miss...?"

She gestured with her cup. "Your house. It was right on the water, too, right?"

"Oh." She thought of her summer, rattling around the lonely rooms, when the only thing she'd had to look forward to was the weekly arrival of the buff landscaper. "Not so much as you'd think."

"You like the cabin, then? Being on the Walker mountain with my brother?"

Angelica promised herself to dance away from the second half of that question. After that night with Brett by the fire—well, after breakfast the next morning when he'd barely looked at her—she'd admonished herself to not expect a repeat performance. It had been a one-night stand, and she wasn't going to whine about that, considering she'd had an excellent time with a considerate man. She knew he'd gone out of his way to make it…easy for her.

So Angelica had vowed that when working with Mac she wasn't going to probe, pry or pump his sister for more information about him. There wasn't any point to it.

"The cabin is great. I so appreciate the use of it. I'll be talking to Poppy about paying rent."

"I heard you've painted the place. That's contributing right there."

Warmth bloomed in Angelica's chest. "I hope… I hope you all like what I've done."

Mac's eyes were blue, a color paler than the lake, and cool. They went well with her finely etched features but added to her air of reserve. It only made her smile more unexpected. "Brett says it looks classy."

Angelica couldn't hold back an answering smile. "He

said that?" *Don't sound so delighted*, she scolded herself, and hastily took a sip of her coffee. "That was kind."

Mac snorted. "Brett doesn't hand over compliments out of kindness."

It was another opening. Angelica could very well ask why that was, couldn't she? Brett had explained some of his attitude—the rich girl who had once had him arrested—but she suspected there was more to his extensive set of sharp, defensive thorns than that. Still... she'd made that promise to herself.

"I should get back behind the vacuum," she said, crossing to pour the rest of her cup into the sink.

Mac sighed. "I suppose we both should get back to it." Standing, she glanced around the large room, with its custom range, copper pots and dual stainless-steel refrigerators. "I was here two weeks ago. Cleaned it top to bottom then. Now I'm back, and nobody's been here in the meantime."

"It's too bad the family hasn't been able to enjoy an autumn at the lake in all its glory."

Mac turned her head to study Angelica, her gaze sharp. "You really like it up in the mountains, don't you?"

Angelica nodded. "I've lived a lot of my life in places where it was easy to feel anonymous. Or maybe it was me, not feeling as if I belonged in any of them. But here I encounter people all the time that I know from the hardware store or the historical society or from the coffee line at Oscar's."

"Now that's the business I should have gone into," Mac said, pulling on her long rubber gloves. "We'll break again about one—we should be done by then."

They went into town for lunch, as their afternoon

would be occupied by cleaning two condos near the village. They split a deli sandwich, sitting at a shady table on the sidewalk, tucked away from the passersby. A raucous group came into view, a multigenerational party that included gray grandparents, skipping little kids and trailing teens. Everyone carried ice cream that was melting quickly in the sunshine that at midday still held a bit of summer heat.

"Oh, look at that," Angelica said. "It's the Dorseys. They have a house near my old one on the lake. It looks like a reunion."

"It's Walt Dorsey's eightieth birthday this weekend. The whole family managed to get away for it early," Mac said, then answered Angelica's unspoken question. "I clean their place, too."

Angelica watched the group pass, wincing when a toddler took a tumble. But the towhead was quickly scooped up and its wail cut off by a spoonful of ice cream. "Cute kids. You want any?"

"I have my nephew, Mason, and now we have London. I suppose Poppy and Shay will add more to the Walker ranks at some point." Mac crunched on a chip from the bag they were sharing.

"None for yourself?"

"I'd want to be married, and Brett and I think our family's happy-ever-after odds are already stretched far enough by Poppy and Shay. Isn't it like fifty percent of marriages that end in divorce?"

"I don't know exactly. But I've got reality to point to, as well. Between them, my parents have been divorced six times."

"Mine almost broke up, too." Mac folded her napkin, then folded it again. "I was young when things were at their worst—and they were happy once they got back together—but I still remember the slamming doors and tense silences."

"You think those memories weigh heavily on Brett, too?" Then, hearing herself, she hastily waved both hands, as if wiping a surface. "Forget I asked that."

Mac gave her an arch look. "I don't know, Angelica. So you're aware, we're a very nosy set of siblings."

"How lucky all of you are to have each other," she said, desperate to change the conversational path. "I'm envious of how you watch out for one another, support one another—"

"And never fail to point out one another's faults," Mac finished, grinning. "Speaking of which, we should probably contract you to work some paint magic in my brother's cabin. Who knows what his slobbiness has wrought."

"Oh, I don't think he's slobby at all."

Mac's smile was sly. "Ah, so you've been inside? I'm aware he checked out your…paint job, but I didn't know the neighborliness between you two extended so far as him letting you into *his* space."

Angelica hoped her flushed face was at least partially disguised by the shade. "I brought him cookies on the first night I was there. The interior of his cabin looked just fine. Homelike, even."

"Really?" She frowned. "I haven't visited since he moved in."

"There are things hung on the walls. His two lodge drawings are over the fireplace. I loved them."

Mac froze, her gaze still on her napkin, which she'd folded into a one-inch square. "Lodge drawings?"

The careful question pinged a warning in Angelica's

mind. But she didn't know how to get out of answering. "Um, one was from overhead and you could see the shapes of the structure and landscaping elements."

"A plot plan."

Angelica shrugged. "The other was an illustration of the same building and surrounding plantings. How it would look when complete."

"It's a lodge—you're sure?"

"He said it is. An idea he'd once had for your land. Your mountain."

"It wasn't his idea," Mac said, her voice tight. "Not his alone, anyway."

"Oh, well." Angelica decided she'd really stepped in it. "I'm sure—"

"It was *our* idea." Mac looked off, as if seeing something besides the cars and stores and people strolling along the sidewalk. "Brett and me and Zan."

"Who's Zan?"

Mac was still lost in the past, it appeared, her gaze still unfocused. "My brother's best friend," she murmured. "*My* best friend. Alexander Elliott. Zan."

"I don't think I've met him," Angelica said. "Though I'm familiar with that last name."

"Zan isn't around," Mac said. "He left years ago, eager to shake off the dust of the old hometown." Her voice lowered. "Shake *me* off."

"Oh." Angelica swallowed, unsure what to say next, but unable to pretend she didn't hear the other woman's deep hurt. "That can't be the case."

Mac shook herself, then met Angelica's gaze. "It doesn't matter. Those old dreams don't matter. I'm just surprised Brett still remembers all that. We must have been...I don't know...I was probably around twelve and the boys fourteen when we first started talking about it. Before the fire, even."

"It's beautiful—the lodge. You should consider making the dream come true."

Mac smiled, but it didn't warm her eyes. "I was twelve. A lifetime ago. I'm over it now."

"Twelve can be just yesterday." A dark room, a sense of powerlessness, a memory that lasted for years and years.

Her tone must have said more to Mac, because the other woman gave her a sharp glance. "Angelica—"

"I have to tell you how jealous I am," she said, moving on in haste. "A brother, a best friend who was a boy. You must have all the male mysteries completely figured out."

"No one with two X chromosomes will understand their ability to memorize baseball box scores." Mac grinned. "And my brother…he came home from the army as murky as a mountain lake churned up by a winter storm."

Why? Angelica wanted to ask. But she held herself back. "And Zan?"

"Zan…" Mac's lashes swept down, hiding the expression in her eyes. "Zan was a deep pond, as clear as glass. *Zan* was clear as glass. Even though we'd lie about in the sunburned grasses, building mountain lodges in the sky, he was always up front about what he wanted for his future."

"He was your first love," Angelica guessed.

Mac gave her a quick glance, grimaced. "My first everything. First kiss, first love, first goodbye."

"What did Zan want for his future?"

"To explore the world. To never feel leashed to this place."

"Is that how you feel…your brother and sisters, too? Does your family feel trapped by the mountains? Leashed? Restrained?"

"We've been here for one hundred fifty years. It's a legacy…and the place we love." Mac shrugged. "Shay's got Jace digging his roots deep now. Ryan has work down the hill, but he plans to spend most of his time in the mountains and teleconference or commute for the occasional meeting. I think we Walkers plan to be right where we are for a very long time."

A certainty that was just something else for Angelica to envy. Given her circumstances, she might be forced out of the mountains by financial reasons…or emotional ones. She couldn't live next door to Brett Walker on the family land forever…and how would she handle it when she was forced to witness her summer crush ushering some snow bunny through his front door in winter?

Mac suddenly straightened in her seat, her gaze focused on something across the street. "I wonder what the hell she wants," she murmured.

Angelica followed the direction of her gaze. A woman was strolling toward Oscar's. She wore a red suit, city sleek and completely out of place in the mountains where, even for flatlanders, fall "fancy" ran to expensive boots and silk T-shirts. The stranger glanced over her shoulder and her sleek black hair swung out. Her face was beautiful—perfect angles and almond eyes— as well as familiar.

"Who is that?"

"Lorraine Kushi," Mac said, still on alert.

"Oh, right." She recognized her as a reporter for an

LA television network affiliate. "She did that big charity exposé, right? The one that showed how little cash from that sports star's foundation was being spent on actual people."

Mac nodded. "The bitch."

Angelica's eyes rounded. "Um, don't you think that was a good thing?"

Mac flicked her a glance. "I don't mean about that. I'm talking about what she did to my brother."

"What she did to Brett?" Angelica couldn't fake nonchalance now. She stared at the reporter as she disappeared into the coffee shop, then transferred her gaze to Mac. "What was that?"

"I don't know all the details," the other woman said. "But I'm sure she broke my brother's heart."

TIRED AFTER A long day of physical work, yet mentally made alert by the new nugget of information about Brett—his heart had been broken?—Angelica left her car outside Mac's offices and decided to take a stroll in the direction of the historical society headquarters. It was on the other side of the village, and she shoved her hands in her jacket pockets as a chill had come on with the dusk.

The village shops and boutiques were dressed for the season with pumpkin and scarecrows on display and yellow-and-orange fairy lights lining the windows. She breathed in the clean air, edged with the faintest scent of a hearth fire, and remembered how her inner voice, on the day she'd learned about her father's imprisonment and the state of her own personal accounts, had told her to see the situation as an opportunity.

It had untethered her from her misplaced sense of

responsibility to her father. Yet, being unmoored was a little scary. More than a little. Still, she had employment and shelter and people who knew her, at least a little.

And a person she wanted to know a lot more about.

Of course, all afternoon as she'd scrubbed and vacuumed, she'd thought of Brett and how that reporter had broken his heart. Mac hadn't said more—Angelica wasn't sure she knew more anyway—but it had been like a puzzle piece she'd examined for hours. How did it fit with all she knew of him?

And then she'd remembered something else. Nan and George at Oscar's. The older woman leaning close. *He received a medal on his very first day in Afghanistan—it was all over the local paper.*

It was something she could investigate without opening herself up. No one would have to know how everything about him fascinated her. That could continue to be her secret even as she delved into this aspect of his life.

It was all over the local paper.

That had to refer to the *Mountain Messenger*. The local newspaper had ceased publication a few years back, but Angelica happened to know they had twenty years of its issues archived on the computers in the historical society offices. She had the key to the front door in her purse.

She had an easy excuse for being there, if anyone even happened to ask. A couple of times a week she stopped by to sift through the incoming mail. Junk to the trash. Bills in the treasurer's box. Other correspondence was destined for the president. It was a little chore she'd assigned herself, else the letters that were shoved through the slot in the door would pile up and then be scattered or worse when one of the board members finally ventured in.

There was still some daylight when she reached the headquarters. The porch light was already on, however, triggered by the shadows of the towering trees, and she didn't feel nervous as she let herself inside.

"Miss you, Piney," she said aloud, noting his empty place in the foyer. She hoped Brett was right and the bear would be returned after the high school's homecoming.

Then she bent to gather up the armful of mail. She dumped it onto the nearest desk. Before starting to sort, she flipped on the computer. It wasn't a quick starter.

With the correspondence divided into appropriate stacks, she dropped the circulars into the round file and seated herself in front of the now-humming computer. A rattling sound at the door sent her heart to her throat. Spinning on the seat, she saw a figure through the half-open blinds covering the door.

Vaughn.

He waved and gestured her toward him.

Damn. She glanced back at the computer screen, still a solid blue. With slow footsteps, she approached the door. "Can I help you?" she asked, pitching her voice so he could hear her through the closed door.

"Open up," he said. "I have to get some materials for the newsletter."

"Now?" But it was only a perfunctory protest, because she remembered an email that had reached her yesterday. Vaughn had volunteered to take over the society's newsletter, the most thankless task of every organization Angelica had ever been involved with. The woman who'd had the job before him had been doing it for four years and begged at every meeting for a replacement.

He smiled as she let him in. If he made a move again, she decided, she'd go straight for his balls.

But he beelined for the wooden inboxes where information for the board and committee members was routed. The one labeled Newsletter was stuffed full. "What are you working on?" he asked Angelica, as he began pulling out papers and assembling them into a neater stack.

"What? Oh, a few odds and ends." She found the mail she'd meant to put in the newsletter box and walked it over. "It's good that you're taking on this job," she said. "Janice was more than ready to hand it over."

"I'm looking forward to it," Vaughn said. "My first issue is going to be all about the auction and the pieces we sold and where they ended up."

"You've taken quite an interest," she said, then frowned. "But we can't announce who won the items, remember? That's confidential."

"Mmm. Right." Vaughn didn't look up. "I'm still hoping I can sweet-talk our president into relaxing that rule. Unless you…"

She shook her head. "I don't have access." Or she wasn't supposed to have access.

Vaughn shrugged. "I can make a good start with simple word of mouth. Rumor flies around these mountains, as I'm sure you've noticed."

He received a medal on his very first day in Afghanistan.

She broke my brother's heart.

"I've noticed." Then a new thought struck her. "Hey, Vaughn…"

He glanced over his shoulder.

"Are you related to Zan Elliott?" she asked. "Alexander Elliott?"

"He's my cousin." Vaughn's eyes narrowed. "How do you know Zan?"

"I don't. I just heard his name come up."

"Because he inherited our grandfather's estate, I suppose."

"I didn't know that," Angelica said.

"Well, it's true. Grandpop had two beneficiaries, Zan and the historical society." One of the papers in his hand crumpled in his sudden fist. "Everything. The house, the cash, the stocks, the bonds."

"Oh. Well." There was a new, bad vibe in the room and Angelica decided to leave. Immediately. Trying to appear casual, she strolled to the computer, turned it off and picked up her purse. "Can you make sure the door locks when you let yourself out?"

He was muttering something as he shuffled more papers.

She took it as a yes and, tense and suddenly tired, slipped through the front door. Though her legs ached from her day spent cleaning, she jogged toward the village, slowing only when she reached the main street. A couple of blocks more and she'd be at her car. Though she still felt a little skittish, she forced slow breaths as she continued onward.

Several of the boutiques were open late. A cute wine bar was doing a booming business, and a German polka sounded from the beer garden across the street. It wasn't nearly as crowded as a summer night—when you had to dodge and weave to make it from one establishment to another—but apparently this was a popular destination on a fall Friday night.

Now that she was away from Vaughn, she cursed her nerves. If she'd just waited him out, she could be satisfying her curiosity about now. *He received a medal on his very first day in Afghanistan.*

She supposed she should feel guilty for wanting to dig into Brett's secrets. When not a drip of shame trickled through her, she decided it was his fault. *Don't look like that, don't touch like that, don't kiss like that*, she'd tell him if he'd ask. *Then I wouldn't want to know everything about you.*

Up ahead, a woman slipped out of Bon Nuit, the sweet boutique that sold expensive nightwear, soaps and fragrances. A small bag hung from her hand. Angelica's gaze sharpened.

Lorraine Kushi.

A wild impulse overtook Angelica. Maybe from too many Nancy Drew books, an early love for *Harriet the Spy*, a onetime obsession with *Veronica Mars*. Keeping her distance, Angelica began to trail the other woman. Was she here to make another play for Brett?

Lorraine's high heels clicked on the sidewalk. In her sneakers, Angelica was silent on the cement. When Lorraine fished through her purse and brought her cell to her ear, Angelica hurried to get closer. To eavesdrop.

"No luck yet," the reporter groused into her phone. "I'm staying in a B and B for the night."

The woman glanced over her shoulder and Angelica ducked behind a seven-foot carving of a bear climbing a pine. When Lorraine continued without pausing, Angelica drew her hood over her hair and returned to her surveillance. A little grin tugged at her mouth. This was kind of fun!

Then a hard hand closed around her arm. She yelped,

and a palm was put across her mouth as she was yanked into a recessed, darkened doorway. "What the hell do you think you're doing?" a man's voice hissed in her ear.

She already knew it was Brett. That soapy scent, that hard body, was impossible to mistake.

There was no way to answer with his hand clamped over her mouth. She considered biting him, then decided good manners dictated she wait for him to figure out her silence for himself. On a curse, he let her go, then got his face so close to hers that even in the dim light she could read the fury in his eyes. "Well?"

"I was merely enjoying the evening—"

"And I'm Kriss Kringle."

"You need to fatten up, Kriss," she said, patting his flat belly. He placed his hand over hers, holding it against the basket weave of his long-sleeved, long-underwear-style shirt. Beneath it he was furnace hot.

A little shiver tripped down her spine. If she went on tiptoe, she could put her mouth to his throat. She could lick the strong column of his neck, find the place where smooth skin turned to sandpaper whiskers. If she ran her tongue over his bottom lip, would his anger melt? Would he let her in?

"Angelica…" It came out low and drawn out, like a groan.

Her fingers curled beneath his, her nails digging through the fabric of his shirt, wanting a more intimate touch. Skin.

Then he shook his head and ripped her hand away from his body. "We've got to get out of here." Once again wrapping his fingers around her arm, he towed her in the opposite direction to that Lorraine Kushi had been moving.

"Wait—" she started, then clamped her mouth shut. She could hardly tell him she wanted to return to trailing his ex-lover. That would be weird, though short of kissing him again, that's what she wanted to do most. Call her curious, but she was wildly interested in learning more about the former object of his affections.

"Wait what?" he asked, without slowing.

"My car's in the other direction," she said, feeling a bit triumphant. "I left it in front of Mac's office."

"No duh," he said, continuing his long strides. "How do you think I knew where to start looking for you?"

"Oh." Tired of being pulled along like a toddler, she lengthened her steps. "You wanted me?"

He sent her a scathing glance. "Don't ask stupid questions."

She bristled. "Hey!" Planting her feet, she was gratified when he was forced to turn and face her. "My car. The other way."

"I'll be driving you home tonight. That candy-ass thing you call a vehicle shouts your name in neon letters."

"Another useless piece of fluff, huh?"

"I'm not going there with you," he muttered, and started towing her again.

"Your truck says your name on the side of it," she pointed out, though not entirely sure what this focus on anonymity was all about.

"I have my SUV. There are hundreds of black SUVs in the mountains."

"Oh." Still, none of this was making sense. Not his tension, not the way he'd tracked her down after avoiding her so studiously since their night together. At his car, he unlocked the passenger side and practically threw her inside.

Then he was behind the wheel and gunning out of town. "Buckle your seat belt."

Obeying, she glanced over. "I assume there's a reason we're being all Bonnie and Clyde."

"That may be more apt than you know," he muttered. "There's a manhunt going on."

She frowned. "What?"

He muttered again, then said, "Lorraine Kushi."

"The reporter?" Angelica said, as if she didn't know. As if she didn't know he'd once been lovers with the woman. "What's she got to do with, um, us?"

Okay, that didn't come out right.

"With you," Brett said.

"With *me*?" Did she want to beat up Angelica for sleeping with her ex?

"Think, darling. She's an investigative journalist and she's on the prowl for an exclusive interview subject."

Angelica's chest tightened and she wrapped her hands around the shoulder strap as if it could keep her safe from everything. How dumb of her! She'd been so focused on finding out about the woman who'd broken Brett's heart, she'd not considered that a story might have brought the reporter to town. "Me?"

"You."

CHAPTER FOURTEEN

ANGELICA HAD GONE screamingly silent.

Brett glanced over, trying to get a bead on her expression in the meager light of the dashboard. It revealed nothing.

Fingers tightening on the steering wheel, he cursed silently. Lorraine, himself, Angelica's vulnerable state. "Are you all right?" he asked, his voice gruff.

He didn't want to care if she was all right. He didn't want to be drawn into any drama between the woman who'd once fucked him over and the woman he was dying to fuck all over again.

"I'm all right," Angelica said, the strain in her voice evident. "How do you know she wants an interview?"

"Because she tracked me down." And wasn't that pleasant. He'd been stowing his tools in his truck when he'd felt a warning tickle at the base of his spine. He'd looked up to see Lorraine's cold and beautiful face. The scars on his had instantly begun to throb. "She wanted me to point her in your direction. Knowing how small our little world here is, she thought I might know how to find you."

"You didn't tell her."

"Hell, no. I wouldn't send a wolf on the trail of a rabbit."

"I can take care of myself."

He snorted. "Do you want me to make an introduction, then?"

"No, thank you."

So effing polite. He squeezed the steering wheel again, wishing he could throttle down all his emotion. But he hated the idea of the razor-edged reporter getting within an arm's length of Angelica, who didn't have what it took to protect herself from a bristly bush, let alone a predator like Lorraine. It made his skin itch and his mood smoke like a poorly banked fire.

The princess needed a shield. A knight. A protector.

And, for the moment, she only had him. "We need to think of a place you can go. Have you reached your mother?"

"We haven't spoken." She hesitated. "And I feel good here. I—I don't want to leave just yet."

Of course she didn't. That would make things too simple for him. Since she'd shown up last summer, everything about her had been a challenge. Her warm brown eyes, her dangerous curves, her tender mouth.

How she made him feel…as if he couldn't control himself.

His car started climbing the steep drive that led to the cabins. Once she was stowed away in her place for the night, he'd breathe more easily. And maybe think more clearly. There had to be some way of keeping her safe from Lorraine, who would tell Angelica's story with a minimum of sympathy and a maximum of scandalmongering.

The first thing he noticed was that the porch lights over both their entry doors were off. "Shit," he said, glancing over as she straightened on her seat. "Looks like the bulbs went out."

"Both at the same time?"

He parked between their cabins, leaving the head-lights on. "Stay here," he said, but wasn't surprised when she followed him out. The lack of light didn't set off any warning bells. Squirrels could have been trying to nest in the light covers and broken or loosened the bulbs. It had happened before.

"Give me your keys," he said, and she placed them in his hands.

The switches just inside the entry weren't working ei-ther, though the gas heater must be, because the interior was pleasantly warm. "Hell," he muttered. "Electricity's out. We're going to have to head back to the village."

"And do what?"

"Bunk with Poppy or Shay for the night," he said, glancing down at his phone. "Cell coverage is crap as usual. We'll have to surprise one of them."

"I'll get a couple of things from my room."

It was pitch-black down the hallway, but he figured she'd lived there long enough to know her way. He lin-gered by the front door, remembering that time he'd spooked her in the dark.

Listening hard, he traced her footsteps along the braided runner. Then there was a thump, a cry, a louder thump. His heart slammed against his ribs, and his pounding footsteps mimicked the noise of it in his head.

He caught himself on the bedroom's doorjamb, the dark so impenetrable that he worried he might slam into her if he moved farther inside. "Angel face?"

"I'm okay," she said in a small voice. He sensed rather than saw her rise off the ground. "I tripped."

"This way," he said, hoping to guide her with his voice.

She seemed to move closer, then she let out another surprised sound and pitched into his body.

His arms closed around her. Tripped again, he thought, his hands running over her body to make sure she wasn't hurt.

She trembled against him, and she released another strangled cry of distress.

Shit. He leaped away. "Sorry, sorry. Are you all right?"

"Yes. No." Her voice sounded thick with shame or tears.

"Let's get you to the car. Light. People other than me."

"You know it's not you." She inhaled a shaky breath. "I don't even mind the dark as a general rule."

"Let's get you out of here, anyway." To Shay, to Poppy. Someone who had the power to comfort and soothe.

"This is horrible." She was hauling in breaths, but still sounded strained. "You must think I'm some nutcase."

He closed his eyes. "I don't. But we should go."

"Let me...let me explain. You deserve that."

"Believe me, baby, you won't find anyone less deserving of anything." Didn't he want to get gone at this very moment? Hand her over to a sister? But he couldn't seem to move. Her voice kept his feet glued to the floor.

"My father didn't want to believe it happened."

Oh, shit. Brett reached out to brace his hand on a wall. "We can talk about this later. We'll get to where there's lights and—"

"It'll be easier to say when I can't see you."

What the hell was he supposed to do now? He couldn't drag her from the cabin. He couldn't risk touching her.

"Remember those stepsisters I told you about?"

"Yeah," he muttered. "Yeah, I do."

"I wanted them to like me so much. I thought I was going to have a real family for the first time. They were a bit older than me, high school age. Their brother was fifteen."

"Tell me he didn't—"

"Not quite."

Still, his stomach roiled. "How old were you?"

"I had just turned twelve." More air stuttered into her lungs. "The girls hated me on sight. I don't know if they put him up to it or if he was just a…"

"Perv. Creep." *Someone whose neck I'd like to wring.*

"My dad and his new wife took us all on their honeymoon. We had rented a villa in Cancun, and one night… one night…"

"Don't—"

"His sisters locked the two of us in the walk-in closet in the bedroom the girls shared. Then he…he went after me."

"Bastard."

"I'd never been kissed. I'd never *wanted* to be kissed. I was tall and had started to develop, but I wasn't yet, you know, curious."

"What happened?" he asked, through his teeth.

"He groped me. Kissed me. Though I was trying to push him away, he kept coming, pulling at my shirt, trying to undo my bra. Then I hit him across the mouth."

"Good for you. You should have gone for his balls."

"I did," she said, the hint of a smile in her voice. "But not before he ripped my clothes and scratched me and… bit me. If I didn't have those teeth marks, I wonder if my father would have been able to pretend I was just making up the story."

Brett closed his eyes. "I'm sorry."

"The experience…stunted me, I guess. Stunted my sexual growth. It took me a long time before thinking of being touched in that way didn't make me want to throw up."

He wanted to throw something. "Understandable."

"I seduced a library aide when I was twenty-two and he was twenty."

"Okay."

"That was the first time I had sex. We did it a couple of times after that. He seemed to like it."

He seemed to like it. Oh, Angelica. "What about you?"

"To tell the truth, I decided to give up on the activity altogether." There was a long pause, and he could imagine her biting that full bottom lip that drove him mad. "Then I…I saw you."

Heat raced over his skin. He didn't know what to say.

She cleared her throat. "Let me clarify. I'd decided to give up on the activity as an, um, doubles event."

His lips twitched, despite everything. "Why, Angelica. Whatever do you mean?"

"So. Anyway. I was messed up and now…now I think I'm less so. Thank you." Air stirred as she came nearer. Her hand touched his shoulder. Her lips brushed his cheek.

His mouth turned toward hers.

Maybe he meant the kiss to be avuncular. Brotherly.

He didn't intend to slip his tongue inside her mouth. But it went there, and her fingers tightened on him.

Still, Brett refrained from touching her, except with his mouth. "We should go," he murmured against her lips.

"Or we could stay," she suggested. "Give me a new

memory of the darkness. Of touch during darkness. I…I think I'd like that. I think I can handle it now."

Lifting his head, he wished for supervision. "If I can't see you," he said, drawing the backs of his knuckles down her warm cheek. Nothing grasping. Not insistent. "How do I know if you're with me?"

"Are *you* with *me*?" she asked.

He dropped both arms to his sides. "Check it out."

Her hand reached toward his waist. She traced a fingertip over his belt. Her touch found his cock, thrusting against the confining denim of his jeans. He drew in air but gritted his teeth, willing himself not to grab, direct, control. Her palm cupped him and he panted, determined not to grind against her.

"You'd do this for me?" she asked.

"It's a real hardship," he said, swallowing a groan. "But I'll make the sacrifice."

"What will you get out of it?"

"You're not that naive, angel face." He sifted his fingers through the hair at her temple and then drew them along the silky stuff. The more gently he handled her, the harder he felt…everywhere.

She stroked him with her hand.

His cock twitched and she made a little sound. "I can't see you, either," she said. "Does that mean you liked that?"

"It means I liked that." With another woman, he might have pressed his hand to hers to show her what he really liked, but he didn't dare force anything on Angelica. "It means I want you to do it again."

He groaned when she attacked his belt. The clink of metal and then the low grind of his zipper releasing made him sweat. Then her small hand was inside his boxers, her touch so sweet he had to grit his back teeth together or go off immediately.

"Kiss me," she whispered.

He bent his head, angled it, finding her soft mouth and playing there, sucking on her bottom lip, then her top. She was so distracted by the kiss that her hand didn't move on his cock, but feeling her possessing him there, wrapped in her five fingers, he couldn't complain.

When he ended the kiss they were both breathing hard. "Do we get to make dark memories on the bed?"

Her fingers squeezed on him. "That sounds..."

"Entertaining?"

"Not exactly..."

"Enticing?" Please, God.

"Shameless." It came out as a throaty whisper. "Empowering."

Yeah, baby, he thought. "Take all the power you need."

She drew him toward the bed, kicking the shoes she'd tripped on out of the way first. Then he was on his back. At her mercy.

A happy, happy sacrifice.

He allowed her to undress them both. His touches were fleeting. A thumb to her nipple, a palm shaping her hip. As reward, he got her hair trailing along his torso, her tongue dabbing at the notch of his throat, her soft mouth at his ear.

"I want you," she breathed into it, the tone thrilled, as if he'd given her a gift. "Have since the first time I saw you."

"Objectifying me again?" he said, though there was little humor in the question because she was cupping his balls now, exploring there with curious fingers.

She kissed the tip of him, then licked off the seeping liquid. "You want me, too."

He groaned and clutched at the bedcovers. "You're killing me, baby."

"Come inside," she whispered.

He'd tossed a condom to the mattress during the disrobing process. He felt for it now, fumbling to put on the protection with hands that were shaking with want. Need. And a desire not to frighten her in any way.

She was on her side, facing him, and he drew her nearer, scooting her hips closer and then moving her leg atop his thigh. "Will you like it like this?" he wondered aloud. "Tell me if I do something wrong."

His fingers—gentle, gentle—wandered low to open her for him. Her arousal drenched him, but he felt her stiffen slightly and he stilled, two of his fingers just inside the heated cove of her. Her muscles clamped down on him, a vise that didn't allow him to move.

"Shh, shh," he said, soothing her with a kiss to her brow, her nose, the hot shell of her ear.

If you want to lessen her load, you're going to have to show her some of what you're carrying yourself.

"You make me afraid, too, Angelica," he murmured, his fingertips moving just enough to massage her inner walls. "I'm with you—I feel exposed."

A rush of wetness bathed his fingers. They slid deeper. "That's right, baby. Let me in."

One of her hands curled around his head to bring their mouths together. "Let me in, too," she whispered.

And fool that he was, he did. With gentle forays of mouth and fingers, he opened her for him and in turn felt himself bared to her. Her undulating body seemed to rub away his hard shell and he gasped as he pierced her with his cock because he felt it in his heart.

Her trust, breaking him open.

In the morning, he could only hope his scar tissue would have covered over the wound.

ANGELICA FOLLOWED MAC into her office to retrieve her purse. They'd worked that morning together, cleaning the local women's club and then a quick spiff of the historical society's headquarters. Saturday afternoon stretched ahead and she had Sunday completely free.

"Big plans?" Mac asked.

"Not a one," she answered. "Keeping a low profile in case Lorraine Kushi is around town, but that's all." First thing that morning, she'd confided in the other woman and told her about the reason the reporter was in the area. Mac had promised that Angelica's whereabouts wouldn't come from her.

"Good of Brett to give you an early warning," his sister said now, glancing over.

Good of Brett for everything he'd given her, Angelica corrected, turning away in case her blush might tell more than she cared to share. The night before he'd been a thorough, generous, gentle lover. In the morning, they'd shared a shower before he'd taken her to Mac's for work. His job for the day was to figure out why their electricity was out.

She'd been stern with herself about not expecting anything more than what they'd already had. *Live in the moment!*

As she scooped through her purse for her car keys, the office door swung open. Angelica's belly jumped and her face flashed hot…before she saw the newcomer was Glory, dressed in scruffy jeans and an old flannel shirt, the sleeves ripped away.

There was something a little wild about her bright blue eyes.

"Is anything wrong?" Angelica asked.

The blonde shook her head. "Mom kicked me out of the store. She's called Dad in to finish out the rest of the day with her. I was snapping at the customers."

Angelica's brows rose. Glory had been testy of late. "What can I do?"

"Go on a hike with me?" She examined Angelica's jeans, T-shirt and sneakers. "You're dressed for it."

"Okay." For friendship alone she would have agreed, but it also seemed an excellent way to prevent her brain from taking dangerous turns toward what-ifs and maybe-nows. Daydreams were not allowed.

Mac popped in from the courtyard where she'd been watering plants. Glory gave her a smile. "You should come, too."

Mac narrowed her eyes. "Come to where?"

"A hike. When was the last time you enjoyed our natural wonders?"

The brunette considered. "I have another offer, but since that involves a stack of bridal magazines and two overly sentimental sisters…yours is the better option."

"Excellent," Glory said. "I have lunch in my car. Enough for three."

They shared the food at a picnic table located in a clearing close to the trailhead. Angelica idly listened to the other two chatting, catching up on people they knew and gossip they'd heard. None of it penetrated. In the dappled shade, she raised her face to take in the pines towering above her. She breathed in the smell of dirt and evergreen and drying grasses. During the summer she'd driven the mountain roads and been on the beach beside the lake, but she realized she hadn't actually made any forays into the surrounding national forest.

"Before you totally space out," Glory said, "we should get moving."

Angelica was the first to her feet. Her friend had promised an easy hike that included a creek and a waterfall. "It's like the Nature Channel," she said, as they started, taking in the oaks and dogwood, the scattered pinecones and the dramatic mountain vistas in the distance.

"City girl," Glory teased. "Keep your eyes peeled for bears."

Alarmed, Angelica glanced around. "Really?"

"Not to mention mountain lions and coyotes."

A queasy feeling settled in her stomach. "Tell me you're kidding."

Mac snorted. "Don't let Glory scare you. We're more likely to run across a wild burro than any of the others."

They continued walking, but Angelica made a point of staying abreast with her two friends.

"Speaking of jackasses," Glory said, idly, "what's this I hear about Zan coming back to town?"

"Word of Zan's return bubbles up every few months," Mac answered, lengthening her strides. "Nothing ever comes of it."

Behind her back, Glory gave Angelica big eyes. "So cute," she mouthed. Then she pointed toward Mac and whispered, "Still gone for him. Totally."

"Shut up, Glory," Mac called out. "Stop dwelling in the long-gone past and enjoy the day."

Unrepentant, Glory swooped down for a pinecone

and threw it at the other woman's butt. Mac retaliated, and soon they were in a full-fledged fight, laughing like loons and running ahead of each other for the choicest specimens. Angelica hung back, Mac's words reverberating. *Enjoy the day.*

Her friends lost interest in flinging pinecones in a few minutes and they walked forward together again, the powdery dirt clinging to their shoes and the hem of their jeans. Blue jays scolded them from the branches of the evergreens and squirrels raced up their trunks.

They came around a bend, and an incredible view was spread before them. At their feet was a lake, impossibly blue. On its far side, nut-brown, grassy hillsides gave way to craggier mountains covered with dark green conifers. Even taller shapes were etched against the sky beyond that, a wilderness where Angelica imagined there were still some places that no human being had ever wandered.

For a moment she experienced a thrilling exhilaration. Against the great expanse and natural beauty, her problems diminished to the size of a pebble. A seed.

But following on the heels of that thought was another—against the landscape she felt that she was smaller, too. With her father in prison, her mother unreachable, she was alone in a world that was much, much bigger than the slice of it she was gazing upon now.

Glory goosed her with an elbow. "No sad faces."

"What am I doing, Glory? What am I *going* to do?"

"Whatever you want. You don't need to please anyone but yourself anymore. It's your chance to find your bliss."

Angelica grimaced. "Are you sure you're not really

my inner voice? The one that tells me losing just about everything is really an amazing opportunity?"

"You know it's true," Glory said.

Mac came to stand closer. "Think of the choices," she said. "You have all the choices in the world."

Angelica lifted her arms. "It's so...so vast."

"And beautiful," Mac said, with a sweeping hand encompassing the trees, the lake, the sky, the mountain-tops.

"So beautiful," Angelica agreed.

"Come on," Glory said, tugging on her elbow. "We'll look for a sign to tell us what we should do."

"Us?"

"Yeah. Us." Glory moved forward on the path that returned them to the shady forest. "You need to figure out your next life steps. I need to decide whether I want to sleep with Kyle. Mac has to find a way to admit to herself that she's not over Zan."

At that, Mac shrieked, scaring three birds from the brush. Another pinecone fight ensued, until they encountered a creek, the water providing a soothing trickle of sound that grew louder as they paced alongside it.

"The waterfall?" Angelica asked, and then it was in front of them, the mountainside dropping off in a series of wide, staggered steps. The first platform was the width of a car, and at its center the water had worn a hole in a recognizable shape. As the pool filled, it overflowed and the liquid ran along the rocky surface, then fell to the next tier. "It's a heart."

"Is that your sign?" Mac asked Angelica, her voice sly.

Angelica lifted her gaze from the waterfall, distracted by a loud chattering from above. Bushy-tailed squirrels looked down in disapproval, then continued on with the business of stuffing their cheeks with food for winter.

"They might be," she said, pointing upward at the critters. "It won't be sunshine forever, will it? I'm going to have to replace my convertible with something sturdier."

"If you decide to stay here," Glory agreed.

They were quiet after that, each seemingly wrapped in their own thoughts as they trekked back to the trailhead. Angelica mulled over really trying to make a go of it in the mountains. She had that finance degree...though nothing seemed as attractive to her as a day spent in Blue Arrow Lake, helping customers at the hardware store.

Once in the car, on their return trip to the village, Glory turned into one of the highway's designated overlooks. This one presented a view very different than what had caught Angelica's breath before. Below them, "down the hill," was the vast urban sprawl of the towns and cities of Southern California. One could even imagine that the smudge on the western horizon was the ocean.

Would Angelica's bliss be easier to discover in a high rise or at the beach?

"More than eleven jobs to be found down there," Glory murmured.

Angelica shot her a look. "Glory?"

"Never mind," her friend said, pulling back onto the road. "My future's already set in stone."

They reached Mac's offices as the sun dipped beneath the pines. Warmth still lingered in the air, but it felt almost sentimental to Angelica. A summer memory quickly fading.

Climbing out of the car, she decided to take that as her sign. This was no time to be floating along, aimless.

She had to think beyond tonight's meal and tomorrow's schedule. She smiled to herself. *Winter is coming.* Hah!

Still, it meant she had to start getting serious about her life. Take charge. Make a plan.

Make that future she'd been wanting. The future that was built on *her* choices.

Once again, she followed Mac inside her office to retrieve her purse. When she emerged, it was to see a black SUV slide in at the curb, right behind her small car. Brett unfolded himself from the driver's seat, a thunderous expression on his face.

"Where the hell have you been?" he demanded, hands going to his waist. His jeans were black, the shirt he wore was white, vaguely Western-style and rolled up on his powerful forearms. If she swooned, she'd fall at his feet, shod in a pair of plain black cowboy boots. He looked masculine, vital and a tiny bit dangerous.

She felt disheveled and dusty and noticed that one of her shoelaces had come undone. Maybe she could run inside to wash her face and comb her hair. Surely there was a lipstick at the bottom of her purse.

As she stepped back, Mac and Glory crowded onto the doorstep, preventing her escape. Her belly fluttered.

"Well?" he said.

"Um…"

"You worked a half day with my sister." He sent an annoyed look over her shoulder to Mac. "Then you disappeared."

"Uh—"

"Neither of you answered your cells."

"Coverage is shit, you know that," Mac said, though there was no heat in her voice. She glanced over at Angelica, then back to Brett. "Cool your jets, big bro."

He wasn't paying attention to her. His brows slammed together over his nose, and he stalked toward Angelica. "You're sunburned."

Suddenly her mind flipped to a different day. Another time with Brett, his attention focused on her then, too. *Stand straight and hold still. Turn up your face and close your eyes.* His fingers, cool with lotion, stroking over her skin to protect her from the sun. To protect her.

"Mountain roses," Glory put in.

Distracted, Brett looked to her friend. "What?"

Glory shrugged. "That's what my mom calls the color that comes from a hike in our beautiful outdoors. Angelica has mountain roses in her cheeks. Don't they look pretty?"

He pinched her chin between two fingers and lifted it higher. His gaze ran over her features, as if cataloging each one separately.

Angelica forced herself not to jump away, though her pulse stuttered and her heart pounded as he studied her. "We didn't see any bears. Or mountain lions. Not a coyote. Not even a wild burro," she heard herself say. The way his hands touched her was making her babble. "That was disappointing. Glory and Mac had a pinecone fight, though. And we found a heart."

A sign.

The true, real sign.

"You guys went to the falls. It's a beautiful place," he said, his voice soft. Gentle, like last night when he'd made her feel safe in the dark. When he'd made her feel…cherished.

And now here he was, worried about her.

Concerned about her well-being, like no one had been for a long time.

Forever.

His thumb traced her bottom lip. Angelica wanted to close her eyes and fall into him. Resting against his strong body, maybe the making of future plans would be easier.

Within the circle of his arms, maybe she could figure out how to deal with the fact that she'd fallen in love with Brett Walker.

CHAPTER FIFTEEN

BRETT DECIDED HE should have made some excuse to avoid a Walker family dinner at Poppy and Ryan's. Hours alone would have suited him better. The women in his life were making him mad.

He brooded from his place on the oversize couch in their oversize family room. Tipping back his beer, he stared at the flames in the fireplace and wished it was summer. Then he could have hung out by the grill on the terrace, doing manly things with a pair of tongs and a metal spatula, far from the chatter of the females.

His nephew, Mason, came skipping into the room and threw himself on the cushion beside Brett. He clutched a paper in his hand, something he'd drawn.

They sat in a chummy enough silence, the boy studying his illustration, Brett contemplating the inside of his eyelids. If he fell asleep, then maybe no one would bother waking him and he could snooze the entire evening away.

"She's pretty," Mason said. "Grimm likes her."

"Grimm likes anyone who drops him morsels from the vegetable tray." He looked down at his nephew. "Who's pretty?"

Mason shot him a sly side eye. "You know who. You saw her feeding my dog carrots."

Brett frowned. "How old are you again? Forty-two?"

"Five."

"Nuh-uh." Brett shook his head. "You're too smart for five."

"Duke says I'm the smartest boy in the mountains," Mason boasted.

Brett glanced up as "Duke"—Mason's name for his stepfather-to-be, Ryan Hamilton—strolled into the room. The other man toasted him with his own bottle of craft beer, then his gaze shifted to the little boy, a warm expression overtaking his face. "Mace, you want to help me bring in some more wood for the fire?"

"Sure." The boy slid off the couch and ran toward the other man. His hand slipped naturally into Ryan's.

Brett watched them walk off together, ignoring the painful twinge in his chest. They were going to be a great father-son team. Already were. That he'd been the man in Mason's life for the first five years...well, a kid couldn't have too many people to love him.

At the thought, his gaze shot toward the kitchen, where the women were gathered, stirring, chopping, chattering. Usually he would join them and do his part for the dinner prep—the Walker ladies didn't buy into strict divisions of labor and he didn't blame them—but today he was steering very clear.

Because Angelica had joined their ranks.

He only had himself to blame. He'd worried when she hadn't arrived back at the cabins that afternoon, imagining a run-in with Lorraine, car trouble, any number of small and major disasters. Once he'd tracked her down at Mac's office, the invitation—more like order—for her to join them all at Poppy's had just tripped out of his mouth.

She'd tried to demur, which had only served to piss him off.

Yeah, he wasn't being reasonable, he acknowledged, tipping back his head to swallow more beer. Like he said, the women in his life were making him mad.

A muted footstep on the thick rug made him glance around. Jace. Phew. Male company was the only kind he was fit for at the moment. Big brown eyes and flushed cheeks were just too appealing. Mountain roses.

For a moment, with her dusty shoes and flushed face, Angelica had looked like a mountain girl. As if she belonged.

"Why are you in here all by yourself?" Jace asked. During the past summer, while Brett had been drooling over a brunette beauty and dodging her overtures, the other man had reconnected with his teenage daughter and fallen for Brett's youngest sister, Shay.

"I'm working on some way to elicit London's sympathy," he lied. "My paperwork is still a mess."

Jace dropped into a chair and stretched out his legs. Like Brett, he'd worked with his hands his entire life and now ran an international construction firm. He'd come to Blue Arrow with the intention of leaving as soon as possible, but now he was willing to stay anywhere London and Shay wanted.

Brett was happy for his youngest sister, but God, as a man it was more than a little disconcerting to witness how both his future brothers-in-law were besotted. But the Walker women were handfuls, so he supposed he was happy to have some help in keeping them reined in.

Not that he could ever say such a thing. They'd flay him.

"She wants the wedding at the cabins," Jace said.

"Late spring, then. Or summer."

Jace frowned. "I don't want to wait that long."

"Your ring's on her finger. What's the big deal?"

The other man shook his head. "I don't want to wait that long."

There was a term for a man displaying this kind of ardent devotion, but Brett wasn't going to utter it. Still, the devotion was mutual, so he had a suggestion. "Tell Shay, then. With exactly that same stubborn inflection. I know my sister. She'll melt."

"Dispensing romantic advice, huh?" Mac perched on the arm of Jace's chair. "You're full of all sorts of surprises today, bro."

He was going to retort something about how people holding their own secrets shouldn't jab—Zan had been sending her postcards!—but then Angelica made her way into the room, distracting him. Their gazes met, and silent communication ensued.

Okay?

Good.

Sure?

Smiling, she nodded and sipped wine the same burgundy color as the sweater she wore with jeans and boots. Though he knew Poppy would be fine if Angelica had arrived just as she was after her hike, she'd insisted on a quick trip back to her cabin for a shower and a change of clothes.

He'd waited in her living room and when she'd walked toward him, smelling of a light perfume, he'd read the misgiving on her face. They'd communicated without words then, too.

His eyes had narrowed. *Yes. You're not getting out of it.*

Now he didn't know why he'd been so insistent. One of them should have stayed away. Him. Because Mac said something to her and she turned to the other woman, laughing, those damn mountain roses blooming even brighter.

Making her even more beautiful, as if that were possible.

Then the rest of the crowd gathered in the room. Ryan strode over the threshold holding a giggling Mason by the ankles. Shay glided in next, to perch on the other arm of Jace's chair. He instantly pulled her into his lap, making his daughter mock shudder and roll her eyes as she arrived with Grimm, the Lab/Shepherd mix at her heels, a tray of appetizers in her hands.

Poppy appeared last, a package under her arm, beaming at everyone like the sweetheart she was. The combined noise of the party filled the room, and Brett relaxed on the cushions, taking it all in. At times like this—not that he'd admit it to anyone—he'd feel the presence of his parents. *Keeping it together, Mom and Dad*, he thought.

Warmth and that tantalizing perfume settled next to him. He glanced over at Angelica, who was watching the interaction around her, her lips curved. "Pretty wonderful...all of you."

"I was just thinking that."

She smiled at him and he felt it like a blow. This morning, he'd awoken beside her but felt a surge of relief to find his defenses securely back in place. Then she'd gone AWOL, and now he realized that the hours of worry had cracked his walls.

He had work to do if he was going to get through this unscathed.

But he couldn't make a move now, drag her home so that they could retreat to their separate corners because she looked so damn pleased to be in the midst of the chatter and laughter. Grimm trotted over to gaze at her adoringly and she leaned close to rub her cheek on top of his big head.

As if the simple creature comfort of touch was something she treasured.

Without thinking, he reached for her hand.

Before their fingers met, Poppy called his name. He started, cursing himself. His sister practically ran over to him, the package she'd brought into the room held out toward him.

He gazed at it, suspicious. It was flatter than a shoe box and wrapped in brown paper. "It's not my birthday."

She thrust it closer. "It's a thank-you."

"I should pass it to Ryan, for taking you off my hands."

A rumbling came from all three of his sisters, their displeasure at his joke that their care had to be passed to a lowly *man* evident. He glanced over at Angelica, and saw the sparkle in her eyes and the curve to her lips.

I know you're teasing, her laughing expression said.

"Just take the present," Mac advised.

As Poppy put it in his hands, he studied her face. She looked one part uncertain and three parts excited. "Featherhead?" he said, the word came out as fondly as he felt toward her. "Are you okay, hon?"

"Walkmedowntheaisle," she blurted out.

"Huh?"

Her fingers tangled at her waist. "I know you're not sentimental. I know you think I'm sappy. But I want to be on your arm."

Brett glanced around, still not catching on. It was Angelica who took pity on his confusion. "Walk her down the aisle," she whispered, "on her wedding day."

He stared at her, then back at his sister's anxious face. "I don't know that I really want to give you away, Pop," he said honestly.

Of course that made her cry. Tears made her gray eyes shine like crystals. Ryan crossed to her, pulling her back against his chest. "He's teasing, sweetheart."

She shook her head and smiled even as two of those tears trailed down her cheeks. "No, he's not. But the good news is, I'm not leaving this family or anything close to it." Her head twisted to look at her fiancé. "We're just pulling *you* in."

Ryan mock groaned. "Maybe I do deserve the present."

They all laughed, and Poppy wiped her face while Brett peeled the wrapping from the parcel. Beneath the brown paper was a heavy, old-fashioned-looking pair of binoculars. "Pop, these are incredible. Where—"

"The historical society's silent auction. I saw them and they just screamed you. They come from the estate of Walter Elliott. I was going to wait for Christmas, but…"

"You couldn't keep a secret that long." Brett stood and yanked his sister into a hug. She'd never lost her sense of wonder, her honest delight in everything, her belief that the world would smile back if she kept on beaming at it, full power. Once upon a time he'd worried over that. Now he thought she might have finally found her reward for all that cockeyed optimism.

Over Poppy's head, he looked at Angelica, who was staring down at her lap as if to allow the family a private moment. It bothered him, that impulse she had to distance herself. Again, he was struck by the certainty that she was another Poppy at her very core, buoyant and bright, but that ugly circumstances and parental indifference had tarnished her sunny side.

It was a damn shame.

So for the rest of the evening he stopped thinking about himself and worked on integrating her into the group. He passed her crackers he spread with cheese himself. When Mason wanted to play a card game, he insisted Angelica be his partner. After the meal, when London brought out the stack of wedding magazines, he didn't bitch like he normally would and absent himself from the scene. Instead, like his two brothers-in-law-to-be, he sat back, sipping a final beer and enjoying the hell out of watching all the females bond over finding the most atrocious gown design. Mason fell asleep, his feet in Brett's lap, his head on Ryan's.

Jace fondled Grimm's ears as he smiled at Shay and London from an easy chair. "Good times, guys," he murmured, glancing at the other men.

Brett found he couldn't disagree.

Finally, they bundled up and headed out the door. Maybe the aisle thing had *him* feeling sentimental because he hugged each sister for a long moment and gave Ryan and Jace slaps on the back along with a handshake before leaving.

"Made her day, man," Ryan said, nodding toward his bride-to-be. Poppy was humming to herself as she danced about the room, picking up stray glasses.

"I've never seen her so happy," Brett said. "That's you."

Not long after, when he pulled up to the cabins, he recalled his sister's dreamy expression. Angelica had a similar distant look in her eyes as he walked her to her door, though it wasn't soft like Poppy's. Again, the remoteness didn't sit well with him.

"Angelica," he said.

"Hmm?" She had her keys in hand and turned to face him as if suddenly realizing he was beside her.

That rankled.

"Are you going to be all right?"

"Of course." Her smile was perfunctory. "I'll be fine."

Alone, she meant. Without him now. Without him in her future.

He caught her shoulders, the madness once again descending. Blast every damn female on the earth, but he couldn't let her walk in there by herself. For now, for whatever reason, he needed her close. He thought she needed to be close to him. "Stay with me," he murmured.

She tilted her head.

Stay with me? He eased the panic bubbling inside by clarifying. "Come to bed with me." With slow backward steps, he pulled her in the direction of his cabin. "My mattress is bigger."

Her footsteps only dragged, so he added a kiss as persuasion. When he lifted his head, she was no longer resisting. As he unlocked the door to his cabin, she did manage to make one last protest. "Really, Brett. You know I'll be fine."

He nodded as he guided her inside instead of expressing the sudden worry that he might not be. He might not be fine ever again.

ANGELICA PULLED A plastic-wrapped staple gun from the cardboard packing box and handed it up to Glory, standing on a stepladder. "I'm still not sleeping with Kyle," her friend said.

"That's your prerogative." Angelica passed on another package.

"I want to," Glory said. "But I'm being cautious."

"He told you he wasn't married. You believe him, right?"

"Yes." Glory frowned as she took the last package. "But I still think he's holding something back."

Angelica frowned, too, as she broke down the now-empty box. She'd been sleeping with Brett. Three nights in a row now. And though he was thorough and slow, every time, she could feel his restraint.

Maybe she should have some herself. But she'd gone willingly to his bed. So willingly.

Now she had to admit their relationship, such as it was, was going to end soon.

In the past couple of days, though she might wake up warm and sated, she'd also become more clear eyed. Despite her great attachment to the mountains, as the temperatures grew colder, she saw it was time to be a realist. Her sojourn here was drawing to a close, maybe even before Brett had the chance to tell her it was over between them.

Every night, she'd held out hope he'd share more of himself. A couple of times she'd brought up Lorraine Kushi, thinking he might reveal what had gone on with her…and then what had gone wrong. But instead he'd taken her to bed to terminate the questioning.

He wasn't opening up to her.

Common sense reared its head each morning when she started her car and her vehicle's engine protested the cold. By the first heavy rain, she'd need another way to get around. Without more hours or another job, replacing her convertible was an impossibility. Just yesterday, her lawyer had said her funds were still lost to her.

Maybe if she could believe in a future with Brett, she could find a way to stay in Blue Arrow, but that wasn't the case.

So her life would have to restart down the hill. Soon.

She carried the flattened cardboard out the rear exit and stacked it in the recycle bin. Back inside the shop, she saw that Glory was on the phone. A supplier, probably, because she wore that pained expression that came with an order mix-up. Gesturing Angelica over, her friend passed her cash and a note. The last read "Coffee! Please!"

Figuring she could use a midafternoon pickup herself, Angelica headed out to the village center. The air smelled like the lake and the breeze held a distinct chill. She'd borrowed Glory's heavy sweatshirt on her way out the door and she zipped it now, even going so far as to pull up the hood to cover her hair.

She nodded to a couple of acquaintances and staved off a growing melancholy by pausing to admire the florist's front window. The only practical solution was to leave Blue Arrow and the mountains. Even if she managed some way to make staying financially feasible, it would hurt too much to be here once Brett moved on.

Because he *would* move on…right?

Biting her bottom lip, she stared at a cornucopia-shaped basket filled with mums and roses, seeing none of it. Instead, she remember the night before—the crackling fire, being stretched out on the couch with Brett over her, his big body kindling more flames.

He bent his head to kiss her neck, her mouth, her temple. "Give it to me," he'd whispered.

"What?"

"That little noise you make in the back of your throat when you get wet."

"Brett!"

"Or are you wet already?"

She'd glanced away, embarrassed.

"Such an easy girl," he'd teased. "So easy for me." His hand had slid down her twitching belly and into her jeans. He'd teased her over her panties until she squirmed. "So easy," he'd murmured again.

So easy to love was what she'd longed to hear.

Shaking off the memory, she started up the sidewalk again. *Be a realist*, she reminded herself.

A man came out of the shop ahead and she realized it was Jace Jennings. He stopped short upon seeing her. "You're the answer to a prayer!" he said, looking relieved.

"Um...happy to be?"

"I'm not kidding," he said, taking her arm and dragging her back into the store he'd just exited. It was one of her favorites—a boutique stocked with unique women's clothing in California surfer/mountain style, as well as a selection of boots and shoes. "I need something," he said, with a vague wave at the shelves and racks.

"Okay." Her lips twitched and she pretended to look him over. "What's your size?"

He blinked, then grinned. "Funny. It's for London."

"Shay—"

"Informed me I had to pick out the gift myself. I'm new to this dad thing and she believes I need to practice."

"So isn't appealing to me kind of...cheating?"

"Yes," he said, looking pleased with himself. "But nobody has to know about that but you and me."

He was irresistible, she decided. Handsome and all-guy, but so anxious to select something just right for his daughter. They settled on a multicolored sweater with a vaguely Tibetan air to it as well as a pair of boots that had a matching woolen design woven into the brown leather.

His kiss to her cheek was exuberant as they parted ways. "You'll keep my secret?"

"Of course," she said, grinning.

He tapped her on the nose. "I hope Brett knows what a jewel he has."

She thought she should protest. *He doesn't have me! We don't have each other!* But instead she held close the warmth of Jace's regard. She didn't realize she and Brett had even revealed their attraction that night at Poppy and Ryan's, but apparently the family had guessed.

Or they could read Brett better than she and thought he was truly into her.

Her heart gave a little skip.

Maybe he *was* truly into her. Maybe…

Reaching Oscar's, she swung open the door. There was a line at the counter, as usual. People crowded the tables inside, and there was even a man and woman seated at one of the bistro sets on the patio.

She glanced at them, then her gaze swiveled back. The couple was none other than TV reporter Lorraine Kushi and Angelica's own man-next-door, Brett Walker. If body language could be believed, he was pissed. His arms were crossed over his chest. Lorraine leaned forward as Angelica watched, putting a placating hand on his shirtsleeve.

He shifted away from it.

"Can I help you?"

Angelica started, realizing her turn was up. She quickly gave her order, then shuffled to the side to wait for the drinks. After a moment's resistance, she peeked around the side of her hood to take in the drama on the patio.

Though she wasn't trying to touch Brett again, Lorraine had scooted her chair closer to his. His expression had gone from angry to frozen and the look in his icy eyes made Angelica shiver a little.

When her drinks were up, she tore her gaze away and retrieved the two cups. Then she hesitated. Out the front door was the right thing to do. But there was another exit, at the side, that would take her to the alley behind the patio. She'd be hidden by the arbor at the back.

But she might be able to hear something.

Would a jury of her lovelorn peers find her eavesdropping unsympathetic? What if it was because she wanted to better understand the man she cared for… and who had been so kind to her? Her war with herself lasted two seconds. Then she was out the side door and just a couple of feet away from the pair.

Lorraine's voice was low. "I know it was unforgivable of me—"

"Then why are you asking for forgiveness?"

"I'm aware I hurt you—"

"The memory of it greets me every morning, babe."

Angelica blinked, surprised his pride didn't dictate a denial. Mac had said the other woman broke his heart, and now she had confirmation from the horse's mouth. Her chest hurt as the knowledge settled there, as chilling as the autumn breeze.

"Please," Lorraine tried again. "Brett—"

"It greets me every morning…and I prize the lesson." The scrape of chair legs accompanied the angry words.

"Don't leave," Lorraine begged.

"I'm out." Heavy footsteps receded in the distance.

Angelica hesitated half a second this time. Then she scurried down the alley, in the same direction as the man who'd slept with his arms around her the night before. She wanted to… She needed to…

It seemed imperative for her to get a clearer understanding of his mood. Maybe she was overreacting to the overheard conversation. Everybody knew eavesdropping could lead to misconstrued clues.

She didn't want to believe he'd once cared so much for someone else, especially when he couldn't have that same depth of feeling for her.

Popping onto the village's main street, she saw he was half a block ahead of her. Again channeling her inner private investigator, she followed at a discreet distance. Once she thought he felt her presence, because he paused. She slowed her steps, but then he rubbed the back of his neck and kept on going.

At the next corner, he turned right. When she reached it, she hesitated.

Fingers pinched the thick fabric of her sweatshirt and yanked her onto the narrow side street. Brett stared down at her, his face still set in grim lines. "What are you up to?"

"Coffee," she said, holding up the cups. "For me and Glory."

"The hardware store's in the opposite direction."

"Oh." She tried on an innocent expression as she glanced about. "You're right. I got turned around."

"You're a terrible liar."

True. She took a breath, trying to come up with a

better one, then shrugged. "I saw you stomp away from Oscar's, and I was…worried about you."

He leaned one strong shoulder against the building behind him and crossed his arms over his chest. "Worried."

He was in his surly mood from the summer. "I just… I don't know—"

"Spill it, angel face."

"I saw you with Lorraine Kushi." The words tumbled out.

He could start a second career as an interrogator. When he merely continued staring, she wanted to spill every secret.

Last summer, I used to think of you at night in my bed and touch myself.

I once wrote "Angelica Walker" in the condensation on my shower door.

I'm in love with you.

What came out was the *L* word, all right, but turned on its head. "You loved her, didn't you?" she said.

Brett's expression froze over. "What does this have to do with you?"

Nothing. Everything. She sucked in a breath. "I…I just want to help. You've been my friend—"

"Oh, fucking stop the friend stuff." He grabbed a hold of her sweatshirt at the throat and yanked her to her toes. "I've sucked your nipples and bitten your neck. You've taken my cock in your pussy and in your mouth. None of that happened because we're friends." He released her and she fell back to her heels.

Her face was hot. She cleared her throat. "Well, that was frank."

"You want frank? Here's frank. Lorraine Kushi is a

snake. We had a thing…years ago when I got back from Afghanistan and was almost immediately sent to Florida for a hurricane relief effort. I wanted a woman and she wanted access. Fair enough, I suppose, until she dumped me for a superior officer with superior access." He ran a finger over his scars.

"Um—"

"I got the breakup text while I was waiting to show her into a restricted area full of damaged homes for her latest story. While I was standing there gnashing my teeth, I heard something from inside one of the houses. Without thinking—because that was how I'd been operating of late—I went inside. In moments, the place fell down around me." He pointed to his face. "Cuts here, broken bones elsewhere. I was alone for the next twelve hours, trapped in the dark."

"Oh, Brett."

"Don't. Don't pity me about that. Because here's the frankest of the frank, princess. I'm glad I had that time to think…to see things clearly. It was just long enough for me to realize I can be an idiot."

"You're not an idiot," she protested.

"Oh, I am," he said. "I have lousy judgment when it comes to women."

Angelica reared back.

It gave Brett the space he needed to stride off.

I have lousy judgment when it comes to women.

Stinging from the verbal slap, she watched him go. Okay, she thought, blowing out a breath.

Answers given. Situation clarified. She'd wanted real…and that's just what she'd received.

CHAPTER SIXTEEN

GLORY'S HEAD SWUNG around at the jingle of the bells on the door. Brett Walker stood at the front of the store, his wide shoulders tense and his expression carved from granite. A plastic bag dangled from one of his fists.

Uh-oh.

Angelica had returned from her trip for coffee thirty minutes before, her usual glow gone. Glory had sent her to the storeroom to handle paperwork because her sad face would have upset the customers—she was that much a favorite.

Smiling as if she couldn't sense his mood, she approached. "Hey, there! How are you?"

"Where is she?"

Oh, yeah. Here was the source of her friend's low state. Angelica had hinted that things between her and Brett had become…friendly, and here was evidence that all wasn't so warm now.

"Glory, where is she?" he repeated.

"Hi, Glory," she said in overly cheery tones. "I'm peachy. Yourself?"

"I need to talk to Angelica."

He'd completely missed the point. "No social niceties?"

"I'm not feeling very nice at the moment."

If he'd already bitten off Angelica's head, and now

thought to take another piece of her, he had another think coming. "Then why don't you toddle out to the deli and pick up a soda or something? Maybe it will sweeten you up."

Instead of answering, he raised his voice. "Angelica!" With long strides, he ate up the linoleum floor in the direction of the back room. "Angelica!"

At a run, Glory managed to get herself in front of Brett. Cutting him off, she put her hand on his chest to halt his forward movement. He glanced down at her fingers. "What the hell? What's gotten into you, Glory?"

Panic. Fear. An unreasonable—maybe—concern about the state of her pal's heart. It was projection, possibly. Probably. Yes.

But she and Angelica were connected, sisters of the soul, and it suddenly seemed important to save her friend from heartache. That way, she could have hope she'd avoid her own.

"Angelica's not here," she said.

He plucked her palm away. "You're as bad a liar as she is. Her car's in the parking lot."

"I sent her out…to…to…" Before she could drum up a bullshit errand, Angelica emerged from the back room carrying a clipboard. She glanced over, hesitated for a second when she saw Brett, then she continued on to the stock ladder currently set up in the aisle of cleaning supplies. As if the man had ceased to exist for her, Angelica climbed up and began ticking off items with a pen.

Good for you, Glory silently cheered.

Then she took a peek at Brett's face. *Oh*, she thought. *Oh.* The hard expression on his face had softened. He was staring at Angelica, his free hand flexing as if preparing to snatch her off the ladder and throw her over his shoulder.

He was a caveman itching to claim his woman.

But there was hesitance there, too, as if he feared he'd break something important by making a wrong move.

Having observed Brett and his casual, serial dating ways for years, she could see his feelings for Angelica were different. The phrase *highly engaged* came to mind. But the spine of his object of attention was ramrod straight, and her head was bent over the clipboard, the fall of her wavy hair masking her face. She appeared completed absorbed by her work and as if she was alone in the room.

In the world.

Blinking against the hot pressure behind her eyes, Glory rubbed her aching chest. Suddenly, she was struck by it all: Angelica's fundamental loneliness; the naked want on Brett's face and the way he seemed unable to move toward her; Glory's own uncertainty about reaching for the only man in years who made her excited about life.

Brett took a step forward, the sound of sole to floor as loud as a shot.

Angelica flinched, proving she was not so immune to his presence.

He hesitated again, and Glory finally was spurred to action. She gave a solid shove to Brett's back.

He glanced over his shoulder, as surprised by her romantic whim as she was. In for a penny… Glory thought, and shooed him toward her friend.

Brett took a step and then another and another, until he was standing at the base of the stepladder. "Climb down," he said.

Glory winced. Really, Brett, *really*? This was no time for gruff orders. To prove her right, Angelica didn't even flick him a glance.

"No," she said.

"How else can I apologize for being a big dick?"

"I can hear you just fine from here."

Ooh, Glory thought with admiration. Nice royal coat of frost, there.

"I'm sorry for being a big dick."

"Mmm." Her pen made another tick on the paper.

Brett stared up at the ceiling, blew out a breath, then took in another, the picture of a man seeking patience. "Are you going to come down the ladder now? Look at me?"

"Why?"

"I brought you a present." He held up the bag.

She glanced at him now, suspicious. "What is it?"

From the plastic, he drew out a package of hot dogs. "Franks. To throw at my head."

It might get a *huh?* from Glory, but at the sight of them Angelica's lips twitched. Then she was smiling, the bright one that had won the heart of every male that came looking for tape measures or tool boxes. "You think you're funny," she said, clearly trying to turn her mouth down in a frown.

"I think I'm groveling." Brett looked astonished at his own admission.

It surprised the hell out of Glory, too, because Brett Walker wasn't a humble kind of man.

His voice softened and he ran his hand over Angelica's calf, clad in dark indigo skinny jeans. "I snapped at you, angel face. That was wrong of me."

Glory didn't think her friend could hold out for another minute, not when the big, handsome mountain man was speaking in such gentle tones. And when she was right, when Angelica started down the ladder and Brett pulled her free of it, Glory's eyes stung again.

Franks, pen, clipboard fell to the floor as Brett slid Angelica down his tall body until her toes touched the floor. He held her close, one arm banded around her waist, the other sifting through her hair. His mouth close to her ear, he whispered something that had her pushing her forehead into the hollow of his shoulder.

Glory couldn't look away.

But she did, finally, when their mouths met. She busied herself behind the register, sorting through the detritus that gathered in the space beneath the cash drawer. A few minutes passed, then the bells over the door rang out again, and she saw Brett's back as he exited.

Angelica stood by the front window, her hand on the glass, watching him cross the street.

"You okay?" Glory called.

Angelica glanced over her shoulder, a small smile on her face. "I'm better than I was an hour ago."

"That Brett Walker can sure work an 'I'm sorry,'" she observed.

"Yeah." Angelica straightened her shoulders and tugged at her sweater as if returning to work mode. "He can."

"Do you trust it?" Glory asked. What she really wanted to know was if Angelica could trust Brett. No, if Glory could trust Kyle.

Her friend bent to retrieve the fallen items: clipboard, pen, hot dogs. She crossed the floor to put the package of food on the counter. "Winter's on its way, but I still see sunshine. I guess I'm enjoying it while I can."

I STILL SEE SUNSHINE. I guess I'm enjoying it while I can.

Those words played in Glory's head as the afternoon waned. She thought she knew what Angelica meant by them. The other woman wasn't counting on forever or fretting over change or a season that might turn hearts in a different direction. The now was good, this moment, and her friend was embracing it. Standing in the sun and accepting its benevolent rays.

While Glory was still hiding in the shadows, worrying about what-ifs.

In her mind's eye, she saw Brett and Angelica's embrace: the beauty of the yin and yang of it, the muscled man, the soft woman. His face as she took the first step toward him.

The beauty of that was what Glory had been denying herself.

On impulse, she picked up her phone. Kyle answered his after two short rings. "Hey," he said. "I was just thinking of you."

Her stomach fell toward her knees. It had to be a good omen. "I can say the same."

"Good," he said. "That's good."

"Where are you?" Suddenly, she wanted to see him. Had to see him.

"On a picnic table at Lake Arthur."

"I love Lake Arthur!" Another omen. Surely. "Stay right there, will you?"

"I'm wherever you want me to be, Glory."

Ending the call, she looked over at Angelica and committed family sacrilege. "We're closing early."

Her drive to the lake was short. Dusk was just beginning to add its purple filter to the air when she arrived at the almost-empty parking lot near the public beach.

Kyle's beat-up truck occupied one of the spaces. In the distance, she could see him sitting atop one of the picnic tables near the sand.

He'd turned his head when she pulled into the lot and he continued watching her now as she climbed from her little SUV and made her way toward him. Her heart was galloping, but her strides were more cautious.

Was she being a fool?

Then she was within an arm's reach and could take in his handsome features, his sexily disheveled hair, the dark shadow on his jaw. They'd traded kisses the few times they'd been out, but she'd been careful then, too. Always so damn careful. Constrained in her box of caution just as she was physically bound by the walls of the hardware store.

He reached out to her, a lean hand asking for hers. *Break out.*

She touched just the tips of her fingers to the cup of his palm, taking in his warmth, feeling it travel through every digit toward her heart. He tugged her closer. "It's getting colder."

Winter's on its way.

But she pushed that from her mind and climbed up to snuggle beside him, hip-to-hip. They both wore heavy jackets over their jeans. She had a scarf that she tied close to her throat now. Her mother had made it for her in knitting class and it featured a pattern of jumping frogs. Cute.

But Kyle was looking at her as though he saw beauty.

"Why are you here?" she asked, gesturing toward the beach and lake with her hand. It was nothing near as big as Blue Arrow Lake and was a county recreational area, not a private body of water surrounded by posh homes and estates. There was the wide sandy beach and a hiking trail all the way around. In the summer, you could rent paddle boats or rowboats or kayaks or paddleboards. During that season a massive, snaking water slide was open for the brave to make a splash.

"Appreciating," Kyle said. "I still can't get over all the natural wonder the mountains have to offer."

Glory opened her mouth, closed it.

But he must have sensed something because he sent her a sharp glance. "What?"

"Well…" She cleared her throat. "I hate to break this to you, but this isn't natural in the least. The land was owned by Samson Arthur, who put up a sawmill here to make crates for the citrus fruit he grew down the hill. When the trees were gone, he talked the federal government into damming two forks of a creek that ran through here via a WPA grant in the 1930s."

"Oh." Kyle appeared deflated.

"Mother Nature still had a hand in it, though. The story goes that they estimated it would take three years for the lake to fill. But that season the rains came big and they came early and it was filled in three *days*."

"Must have been quite a winter storm."

That season was hovering. Glory shivered.

"Cold, honey?" He curled his arm around her and drew her closer to his side. "Shall we go somewhere else?"

The sun still lingered, though low, in the sky. "Just a few more minutes," she said, then rested her head on his shoulder. It felt solid. Good. Her gaze took in the quiet waters. "I used to love this place. And that slide. My favorite. I haven't been on it in years."

He ghosted his mouth over her hair. "Why not?"

"Summers are so busy at the store. I'm always working."

"We've got to fix that," Kyle said, jumping off the table and pulling her with him.

"What?" She tried resisting, but he was towing her toward the slide. "It's closed, it's cold, we...we can't!"

He glanced down at her. "But honey, isn't this what it's all about? We *can*."

That's when she realized that her call had been riskier than she first thought.

THE COLD TOOK Kyle's breath. When the water closed over his head, the shock to his system also stopped his heart. Jesus. He was too young to die. But then he remembered Glory was right behind him and he kicked, straining for the surface.

He had to stop her.

His head broke the surface and he was already yelling. "No! Don't!" But she was whizzing down the plastic tube, an unholy grin on her face. Despite that, he hoped she was praying, because this stupid idea of his might be the death of her.

Dog-paddling to keep his muscles moving, he watched her fly off the end of the slide. At her touchdown splash, he stroked in her direction, running through all the lifesaving procedures he'd absorbed from a lifetime of living in a household of doctors.

Seeing movement beneath the water, he reached down and found something of her and pulled. She emerged, sputtering, and he realized he'd fished her up with her ridiculous frog scarf. "Are you okay?" he yelled at her, as if she was deaf instead of likely frozen.

She threw her head back and let out a howl. Then she

grinned at him. "H-h-hypothermia is setting in." Her teeth began chattering.

Clearly, the cold had gotten to her brain.

Instead of stopping to investigate that fact, he urged her toward shore. "We'll get you warmed up." His mouth was numb, as was most of the rest of him.

They stumbled onto the shore and water sluiced from their bodies and onto the sand as he grabbed her hand and moved them as quickly as he could to his truck, stopping to grab his keys and wallet he'd left on the picnic table. At the passenger side, he stripped her out of her dripping coat and tossed it in the bed before lifting her into the seat. His jacket went the same way, then he climbed behind the wheel. The key made it into the ignition on the fifth try and he nudged the heater to the highest position.

"Okay," he said when he could feel his tongue again. "Dumb idea."

"Great idea!"

Startled, he glanced over. She was grinning again. "Honey—"

"I feel alive," she said, flinging out her arms. Her hand caught him in the side of the face, but he figured he deserved it—and he was too cold to feel much of the slap anyway. "Don't you feel alive?"

He laughed, her exuberance catching. "Maybe. But more soggy and cold than anything else."

"I *never* do anything wrong. We climbed over the chains that were supposed to keep people out."

"Such a rule-breaker," Kyle teased.

"You can't imagine how good it feels."

Yet he did. He fiddled with the vents so more of the heat blasted in her direction. With his undergrad degree behind him, the Scott family rules said he'd go to med school. The idea of it had felt like an anchor tied to him. He'd known he'd drown.

But when he'd partnered up with his roommate to go into business together, he'd finally felt as if his feet were on the right path.

Then he'd dropped into the work, determined to prove to his parents he could be a success on his own terms, and had become an all-work, no-play dull Jack. Not until he met Glory had he understood what he'd given up.

She was unwinding that silly scarf from around her neck. "I guess we should go," she said, sending him a quick glance. There was something in it, something he couldn't read in the gathering dark.

"Cold?"

"Getting warmer."

"Let see what I can do to hurry that along." Leaning close, he cupped her cheek and took her mouth in a kiss.

A hot kiss. They'd been sticking to public spaces before now. Meeting at local restaurants. So he'd only managed to go lip-to-lip in locations populated by people she knew. Which was virtually everyone in a thirty-mile radius.

This time he let his tongue plunge. Beneath his clammy clothes, there was suddenly so much heat he expected steam. Lifting his head, he drew in a gasp of breath. "Glory—"

"Again," she demanded, her fingers sifting through his wet hair.

She tasted like fresh lake water and heaven. He nuzzled her throat while pulling air into his lungs and the coolness of her skin registered. "We need to get you warmer," he said, as he felt her shiver.

But she turned her head to capture his lips again, the kiss urgent and edged with a desperation he found contagious. His hands found the sodden hem of her long-sleeved shirt and he drew it up, allowing the heat to hit her bare skin. She moaned into his mouth and then he broke from her again to drag the fabric over her head.

It was full dark now, the truck their private space that was warming by the second. He reached around for the clasp of her bra.

Her hands covered its cups as the closure released. "I've never done this, either. In a car, I mean."

"Okay." He kissed her eyebrow. Her ear. "Is it time to live a little or do you want to leave?"

"Live," she whispered, and then her hands dropped. The bra fell to her lap and she whisked it away to her feet.

Kyle fought his own shirt and sent it flying over the back of his seat. Then her hands were on his chest and he groaned, giving himself up to her exploration. But his will only lasted so long before he had to have her naked breasts at his mercy.

He slammed up the arm of her bucket seat and leaned over the console, bending to touch her with his tongue, finding her pebbled nipple in the dark. Sucking it into his mouth, he reveled in her moan. Her skin was still cool and he warmed it by taking as much as he could into his mouth.

His hand plucked at the other hard tip and he felt the cab's temperature rise another dozen degrees. His jeans were drying in the heat, strangling his cock in a grip that might do damage if he didn't release it soon.

Afraid to move too quickly for her, he groaned against the flesh of her breast and lashed the nipple. Her hand dug into his shoulder—sweet pain—and going slow was impossible. Sliding his mouth across her skin, his hand went to the fastening of her jeans. Her belly hollowed out as he fumbled with the snap. She was breathing roughly and her hips lifted as he yanked on her zipper.

"How are we going to do this?" she asked, breathless.

"Do you want to?"

"Oh, God." She groaned as he managed to insinuate two fingers beneath her panties. "I want everything."

Vehicle sex was awkward. But Glory was a good sport, or maybe it was that he was doing a good job keeping her on the edge, dropping kisses to bare skin, caressing her as he worked at her jeans, praising her in rough whispers as she followed his instructions. *Lift up, good girl. Gorgeous, move here. Give me your mouth while you hold on to this.*

Then he was bare-assed on her seat and she was kneeling over him as he took the foil-wrapped condom from her and rolled it over his pulsing cock. He gritted his teeth, then took her bottom in one palm and her hip in the other and drew her lower.

Her wetness brushed his tip and he leaned forward to take a nipple into his mouth. He gave it the tiniest bite and she jerked in his hold and then sank down on him. They both groaned.

He pressed his mouth to her throat.

"What is this?" she asked, wonder in her voice.

"It's me," he said. "It's us."

That last word echoed in his brain as she began to rock on him. *Us...us...us.* He crooned to her, more praise, and her movements sped up, taking his control with it.

"Glory," he said, gripping her hips to slow down the rushing onslaught of pleasure. Sex wasn't supposed to be like this. Before, it had been a function. Textbook stuff. The physical expression of the dry explanation of hormones and responses that his father had given him—complete with diagrams like something he'd draw on the paper covering of an examining room table—when he was ten.

Instead, this was more than his reaction to the female form. More than his biological response. This was about Glory, too, her small body enslaving his, her tight pussy sheathing him in an impossibly good vise. Not only did he want her to get off, he wanted her happy. He wanted her exhilarated and free, wearing that grin she'd given him after breaking all her rules and jumping into a ridiculously cold body of water.

It had taken his breath. Now *she* was taking it.

The little sounds she made now were aroused and almost a little anxious. He couldn't read her expression in the dark, but he knew it was time to soothe her by sending her flying a little higher. He brought his hand to his mouth, wetting his fingers. Then they traveled down the center of her body to trace the place where they were joined. He shuddered, feeling his shaft being engulfed by the soft heat of her body.

His fingertips found the knot of nerves at the apex of her wet folds and he began stroking her there, short strokes and tight circles. She gasped, held up, and then she ground down on him. Harder. Filthier. Better than anything.

His other hand caressed her belly, then moved upward to brush her breasts, her straining nipples. He closed his eyes as she moved more quickly and he followed her lead, strumming her clit.

Her internal muscles were clamping down on him and

he was dangerously close—so close—when she grabbed his free hand and brought it to her mouth. She took two fingers into her mouth, sucking on them as she ground down a final time. Rocking there, he felt the orgasm overtake her and it slammed into him, too, the release surging through muscles and sinew and blood.

Glory collapsed against him. He petted her, trying to take her down easy, even though he felt as if he'd expired in those final moments.

A definite ending.

When he returned to LA, work was never going to be enough again. No down-the-hill woman would ever be enough either, not after having this woman—Glory Hallett, mountain to her bones.

CHAPTER SEVENTEEN

ANGELICA HAD DISCOVERED that while Brett was an early riser, he wasn't a morning person. Not as much as she was, anyway. While she moved about his kitchen with quick steps, humming, he sat sprawled on a stool, staring at the surface of his coffee as if it was a television screen.

With a tiny shake of her head, she swiped up the carafe and topped off his mug. As she made to move away, he shot out his hand and arrested her movement by hooking a finger in the back waistband of her jeans. "Thanks."

"He speaks!" she exclaimed, in exaggerated surprise.

"Ha," he said, then freed his hand to lightly smack her on the butt. "Maybe you wore me out last night."

Rolling her eyes, she headed back to the countertop to replace the coffee on the warmer. There was no way she'd worn him out…not when it was clear he was holding back. Yes, they'd had sex and he'd been solicitous, very careful to please her. Maybe because he still worried she was damaged. Maybe because he felt guilty for their scrap—*I have lousy judgment when it comes to women*—but she was beginning to believe it more likely that caution was a way to keep himself separate from her.

To not allow her close to him, the real Brett Walker. Despite being aware of the ticktock of the clock running down on her time left in the mountains, she couldn't fight the urge to shake things up.

Shake him up.

She buttered toast for herself, aware he wouldn't eat until his second cup of coffee was gone. Though her days didn't usually start as early as his, this morning she was heading into the hardware store hours before opening. There was some paperwork she could accomplish for Glory, a task she hadn't completed because they'd closed early the day before.

Glancing over, she saw Brett was still in that zone where he was half asleep and half awake. "I had a text from Shay this morning."

He grunted.

"I'm invited to a marathon viewing of one of those wedding dress shows. Jace is out of town for a couple of days, Ryan's going to do something manly with Mason. A girls' night with all the trimmings—wine, cheese and crackers, a gooey dessert."

He didn't seem to think it was weird that she'd been asked over for something chummy with his sisters. Or maybe he was mentally still snoozing under the covers.

"Shay said I should spend the night."

Straightening, he opened his mouth, but then he subsided again, his eyes back to their study of his coffee. "You'll have fun."

Had he wanted to protest her being absent from his bed?

It gave her morning mood a little happy jolt. "I do enjoy all the nuptial hoopla. Shay and Poppy are so excited about their upcoming weddings. London, too."

"Mmm," he said, bringing his mug to his mouth. Then he set it down on the counter and looked at her with narrowed eyes. "I thought you weren't a bridal enthusiast. You said you didn't believe in happy-ever-afters."

She shrugged. "I said I didn't believe my *parents'* marriages would ever last. As for my attitude toward weddings themselves…it's pretty hard to be scornful when your sisters are spinning with delight over the idea of getting hitched to their men."

"Jace is the same," Brett said. "Shay was thinking of a spring or summer wedding and he's unwilling to wait that long."

"Poppy said Ryan's threatening to kidnap her for an elopement. He wants to be her husband *now*."

Brett took a swallow of his coffee. "That's kind of nauseating."

"Oh, you!"

"Has anyone told you you're a brilliant conversationalist in the morning?"

Well, he'd sure woken up. Angelica crossed her arms over her chest. "Admit this. You were thrilled to be asked to walk Poppy down the aisle."

"I'm the oldest. Mom taught me I had to let the younger ones get their way once in a while."

"You're just being a curmudgeon to maintain your rep."

"What rep is that?"

Angelica grabbed her purse from the counter and sorted through the items inside. Keys, wallet, phone. Glancing over at the clock, she realized she only had a few more spare minutes.

"Angelica? What rep is that?"

"Dyed-in-the-wool bachelor. Guy stubbornly clinging to the idea that a single life is best."

"I am a dyed-in-the-wool bachelor—which by the

way sounds like someone wearing a Mr. Rogers sweater. And while I wouldn't say I'm stubbornly clinging, I do think the single life is best."

"Knee-jerk," she said with a dismissive wave.

"What's that supposed to mean?" he said, now sounding not only awake, but grouchy.

"Blanket statements about how being single is best are ridiculous. They're knee-jerk remarks from the bachelor sans a sweater."

"Okay," he said, eyes narrowed. "I'll qualify it. The single life is best for *me*."

He was looking increasingly peeved and she was feeling a bit irritated herself. "How can you say that? Maybe you just haven't found the right woman yet." *Oops*. That sounded a bit too plaintive. "What I mean is, there are your sisters, with two of the best men on the planet panting to be their partners. Don't you think they'll be happy together?"

"I hope they'll be happy together."

His unconvinced tone got on her last nerve. "Honestly, you're taking this whole skeptical thing just too far."

He shrugged. "So I'm not sentimental."

Okay, she had yet another last nerve. Digging through her purse, she found her phone, held it out. "You should call Mason."

He eyed her warily. "Why?"

"So you can tell him there's no Santa. Blow up his fantasy about the Easter Bunny, too. While you're at it, tell him there's no Tooth Fairy either."

"And I'd do that because…"

"No sense letting the boy believe in anything, I don't know, *sentimental*."

"Angelica—"

"I bet it was you who told your sisters that nobody really came down the chimney."

A ruddy flush edged his cheekbones. "I'm not convinced Poppy knows there's no Santa to this day," he muttered. "I bet she *still* believes."

"Even more reason for you to break the news to your nephew that his mommy and his Duke will never be in love. Oh, and maybe you can get London in on the call, as well, and tell her that her father and her stepmother-to-be don't have anything real either—"

He shoved himself up. "Angelica—"

"—no matter how that might shake Mason's belief that *he* is loved or undermine London's confidence that *she* is cherished."

"Angelica."

Ignoring the dark note in his voice, she raised her arms, let them fall. "Seriously. What does it take for you to acknowledge love when it's staring you in the face?"

He leaped to come toe-to-toe with her, his stool toppling to the floor in the process. "And you're an expert?"

"I know what I know. I trust my eyes."

"Trust." He spit out the word. "What the hell do you know about trust? The very people who you should have been able to rely on—your parents—have only abandoned or betrayed you."

There was a high whine in her ears as she stared into his eyes—so icy cold they burned as they ran over her from head to toe and back to her face.

"As for love…who has ever given that to you, princess? How do you know anything about it?"

"Brett—"

"Tell me. Tell me who the hell has ever loved you?"

Her mouth opened, but words couldn't make it past the sudden constriction in her throat. *Who the hell has ever loved you?* The heat on her skin chilled and, snatching up her purse, she ran. Away.

"Fuck. Shit. Wait. I lost my temper. I didn't mean it to come out like that. Angel face…"

She was too fast for him. Or he didn't follow after all. Because nothing and nobody stopped her from jumping into her car and pointing it in the direction of the village. She was breathing hard, and her hands trembled as she gripped the steering wheel.

The person shaken was herself.

Still feeling unsteady as she approached the back entrance of the hardware store, Angelica fished for the employee keys from her purse. The scent of cigarette smoke alerted her first, then she jolted back as a woman stepped forward.

Lorraine Kushi. The woman wore a black wool coat loosely belted over a gray dress. Her knee-high boots were gleaming black leather in a severe style that matched the dark wedge of her hair.

Pretend you don't know her, Angelica admonished herself. She tried donning a polite expression. But Brett's attack had made her numb on the outside even though she was still a mass of raw emotion on the inside. For all she knew, she was wearing a scary, serial-killer grin.

Looking at it, the reporter took a quick, nervous drag from her cigarette.

Be cool, Angelica thought. "Can I help you?"

"Are you Angelica Rodriguez?"

"This is Hallett Hardware," she said, then immediately thought, *fail*. "I've got to get to my job."

"I thought we could talk."

"No time, sorry."

"It's a shame how the internet makes anyone recognizable."

Angelica swallowed. The jig was up. "What is it you want?"

"We have a lot in common, you know."

She tilted her head. "How's that?"

"Brett Walker."

"I don't have anything to say about him."

"Your father, then. Your circumstances. I can help you get your side of the story out into the world."

Angelica's fingers tightened on the ring of keys. "Why would the world care about my 'side'?" Though of course her attorney had warned her of this very circumstance from the first.

Lorraine dropped her cigarette to the asphalt and ground it out with the toe of her dominatrix boot. "Don't be naive. It's human nature to be interested in the only offspring of a now-infamous fraudster. People want to know if you're innocent or complicit."

Innocent or complicit. Angelica felt her face flame. "I have nothing to do with my father's business." Or his Ponzi scheme. "That's already been reported."

"I'm aware of that. And he siphoned off cash from your own accounts, hoping, it seems clear, to make it to another day when he could recoup his losses. It was way too far gone for that, though."

Angelica shrugged.

"But you acted as his hostess on occasion. Many times that was how he met new investors."

In the first year after college she had arranged several parties at the Beverly Hills house. But he'd stopped socializing at home after that, preferring to take friends and clients to dinners at LA restaurants or the country club. She'd really noticed the change when he'd decided against his annual Christmas party. He'd given her no reason, and still hoping she could please him, she hadn't pressed.

"It was those new investors that propped up the operation," Lorraine continued. "As long as new money poured in, he could make payments to those who wanted their money out. When an imbalance occurred, more money being demanded than was coming in, the whole scam collapsed."

"I have a degree in finance. I understand the fundamentals."

"Which is yet another reason why the public wonders if you actually didn't know…or if you should have figured it out."

Tension wrapped Angelica's neck like a strangling hand. *Should* she have known? Her father had been so secretive the past couple of years. Then, at the very end of spring, he'd insisted she take up residence at the lake house. There'd been renovations he'd ordered her to oversee during the summer months.

And she, still trying to win his approval—*who the hell has ever loved you?*—had driven up the hill.

"I won't be the last journalist to find you," Lorraine said. "For now, the press has been easy on you because you look blameless. But to keep smelling sweet and clean, you should get ahead of this."

Angelica hesitated. The lawyer had mentioned that idea, too.

Lorraine stepped closer, as if sensing her waffling. "I'm your best bet. I asked around town and heard you're buddies with the Walkers—working for one of the sisters, I believe? Brett and I are good friends, you know, and the two of us…we could be good friends, too, Angelica. I won't lie to you, getting you in front of my camera would be a coup. But I'll treat you right."

Like she'd treated Brett right? Angelica's roiling thoughts calmed. Lorraine Kushi, as Brett had remarked, was a snake, and Angelica certainly wasn't going to reward her reptilian ethics. There was no way she'd believe the other woman would go out of her way to treat her fairly. Her priority would be gaining viewers, not reporting the truth.

"So…" She pretended to be mulling over the reporter's proposal. "We should do this soon?"

"Today," the other woman snapped out. "Word is there's going to be a presser regarding your father's case this afternoon… He'll be all over the news tonight."

While she'd be watching a wedding-gown marathon, please God.

"You think…you think you'd be the best to interview me?"

"If not…well, this is an interesting town. Without you, I might end up reporting on that string of burglaries I've been hearing about." She hesitated. "And the rumors that the Walkers might be responsible."

Angelica went cold to her bones. This was how the woman was Brett's "friend"? But she kept her expression free of the disdain she felt for Lorraine. "I see. But there're other stations—"

"Channel Six barely beats us in ratings. Their financial reporter, Sean Marks—he's an asshole."

Sean Marks. Channel Six. Angelica made mental note, then met Lorraine's eyes. "Let me think about it, talk to my attorney."

"An interview is the way to go. You need to start thinking about yourself."

"Yes." Angelica nodded. She did need to start thinking about herself. And *for* herself. With a new certainty of purpose, she headed for the hardware store's back door. No longer was she going to let circumstances bat her about.

It was time to take real charge of her life.

KEEP CALM, GLORY admonished herself, even as she did a little jig while pulling food from the refrigerator. *You're only having a man over for dinner.* No reason to feel so… uncontained, even though she'd had wild sex the night before in the cab of a truck.

Even though the man coming to dinner was the man she'd had wild sex with. Even though he was the man she'd fallen in love with.

At the sudden thought, Glory nearly dropped the head of lettuce in her hands, and she had to juggle it along with the tomato and the cucumber. When she managed to control them, she shut the fridge with her hip while trying to calm her skipping heartbeat.

She was in love?

She couldn't be in love.

Her acquaintance with Kyle Scott only went back a few weeks, and during one of those he'd been gone. A person didn't fall in such a short time—didn't that go against the laws of nature or something?

But then she had a mental picture of the two of them on that table the day before. Herself telling Kyle that the lake had been expected to take three years to fill and instead had taken three days.

The world could work that way.

Dropping the produce on the countertop, she placed her hand over her stomach, which was doing flips and turns like a kid hopped-up on sugar. All of her felt that way, revved and just a little bit nauseous.

"Get a grip, Glory," she said out loud.

But still, she nearly jumped out of her shoes when she heard the knock on her front door. She had only a few steps to gain some kind of composure—her bungalow was just that small—and she supposed she might still look a little bit green because he gave her a quizzical glance when she opened the door.

"Okay?"

"Mmm. Yeah," she said, bright as a button. "Come in."

And he did, walking right to her and yanking her close for a kiss, bending her over his arm and laying it on, hot and intense. She stumbled back, blinking, when he let her go.

"Is that a smirk?" she demanded, straightening her shirt and trying to look annoyed, even though she was considering dragging him straight to the bedroom.

"I think it's my smug look," he said. "I can't help it. God, you're beautiful."

Swoon!

Then he glanced around, taking in the living room and kitchen and tiny dining area that were really all one space. "Nice."

She waved a hand. "Some people call it open concept. I, on the other hand, realize it's merely small. There's a bathroom and one bedroom down the hall."

He glanced that way, then gave her a little smile. Smug smile. "Maybe you'll give me a tour later."

"Maybe," she countered, trying to sound airy and unconcerned and not at all like a woman who was *in love*!

"You live here long?" he asked, following her the short distance to the kitchen area.

"About a year. The people who had it before me used it as a weekend and vacation place. They lived—"

"Down the hill," he finished for her.

She nodded. "Then they got too busy with work to come up very often and I got the chance to have it. I love how it's nestled in the big pines and that there's a creek out front." You had to cross a footbridge to reach the front door, which gave it a fairy-tale quality to Glory.

With her very own lover within its walls, it seemed even more fantastical. She pulled a beer from the refrigerator for him and sipped at her glass of wine as she began chopping vegetables. "What about you? I just realized I don't know where you've been living."

So cautious, she'd avoided most things personal, worrying she'd become too invested in him. But now she wanted to know everything.

"The house I'm working on…the owner's letting me stay there."

"Oh. That's great." It made her worry a little, though. Money must be tight. "You shouldn't have been paying for those dinners out we've had."

"Glory—"

"I know I said we'd trade picking up the restaurant tabs." She punished the cucumber because she couldn't stab herself for her inconsideration.

"You're making dinner for me tonight," he pointed out.

She glanced up. Smiled. Because making dinner for him meant now she felt safe having him in her home. Her heart was no longer at risk. It was already lost.

She allowed herself a moment to study him, her gaze tracing him with a lover's intensity. His hair was longer than it had been when they'd first met and wavy at the ends. His lean features were handsome and masculine, and his dark eyes were more black than brown.

If they had children, would there be blue-eyed brunettes and dark-eyed blonds? She thought the combination of their DNA would create strong and smart mountain kids…who would ultimately be roped to the hardware store like she was.

Roped…?

"Glory? What is it?"

She shook herself, refusing to let her mind delve into that random, uncomfortable thought. "I'm okay," she said, throwing the vegetables into the salad bowl on top of the torn lettuce. "So…which do you like? Cats or dogs?"

"I'm an equal opportunity pet person. Except for tarantulas. And iguanas." He cast his eyes to the ceiling. "Fish are okay, but watching them as a screensaver is simpler than aquarium care."

"You spend a lot of time on a computer?" she asked, trying to see him bellied up to a keyboard. It was easier to imagine him with a hammer or a paintbrush. "Do you actually type or do you do the two-fingered hunt-and-peck?"

"Uh…" He looked away. "I like to watch those videos of kittens scared by paper coming out of printers just like everyone else."

The oven dinged and Glory pulled out the chicken casserole she'd made from her mom's "company" recipe—one that harked back to her childhood. It was really nothing special, Glory realized as she'd grown older. Cans of soup and stuffing mix. Her mother was into more complicated dishes now that she'd taken those cooking classes at the gourmet chef's shop in the village.

"Do you have family?" she asked, as she dished out plates.

He carried them both to the table she'd set for two. "Oh, yeah. Parents. And I have a brother and a sister. You're a lonely only, though."

That's right. She'd told him that once. "I envy you siblings."

"Because you weren't tortured enough as a child? My sister let her friends put makeup on me when I was four and then they took pictures. They blackmailed me with those for the next ten years."

She had to grin. "And your brother?"

Kyle took a bite of the chicken, made an appreciative noise. "So good. The food—not my brother. Once when my parents were gone he locked me out on the upstairs balcony so he didn't have to let me have a turn at the video game."

"I'm guessing you were the youngest."

He nodded, but there was enough of a smile showing that she figured it hadn't all been painful. "Not an enviable position."

"Still…" Glory sampled the food and was happy to note it tasted fine to her, too. "As my parents age, I realize it's going to be up to me alone to take care of them."

"Don't they have a lot of good years left?"

"Sure." She waved her fork. "They're in excellent health and all that. But my dad's retired and I swear, if he doesn't find a hobby, my mom might just murder him. Then I'll have the sole responsibility for visiting her in the clink."

"The clink." He grinned at her.

The smile made her stomach jitter again. She wanted it beaming her way, morning, noon and night.

"You know," he went on. "If you have someone in your life…a man at your side, you won't be alone. There won't be such a thing as a 'sole responsibility.'"

God, Glory thought. Even the burden of Hallett Hardware could be shared. That notion exploded like a beautiful dream in her head. Technicolor with stereo sound. Clasped hands. Twined bodies. Merged lives.

Glory + Kyle 4-ever.

The idea continued to surge inside her, filling empty spaces that had been there for so long. For too long, she'd felt so solitary.

How weird, that isolation. She lived in a small town where everyone had known her from birth. Each day, people came into her hardware store with greetings and news, and yet she still felt like her own island in the mountains. Maybe because her community was so certain they knew her, from heart to soul. They expected her dream was the life she was living behind the cash register at Hallett's.

There won't be such a thing as a "sole responsibility."

Her head came up and her voice was full of wonder. "How do you know to say these things to me?"

He shrugged, his gaze trained on her face. "I just… talk to you. I told you I was rusty and I am, or was, anyway. I wasn't out there dating and practicing pickup lines these past few years. But conversation with you… it seems easy."

"You made a few mistakes at first," she reminded him.

"But you cut me some slack. How come?"

Because I fell in love with you. I think I fell in love with you at first sight. At least over that first beer. That day you brought me double dill pickles for sure.

When she stayed silent, he set down his fork and wiped his mouth on the cloth napkin. "Glory... What's going to happen in January?"

She blinked. "I put the Christmas lights on sale. Any leftover tree stands I stow away to sell next year."

Laughing a little, he reached out to grab her hand. "I wasn't talking about the store. I was talking about Stu."

"Stu?" She stared at their laced fingers, thrilled by Kyle's touch. Thrilled by the symbolism. The two of them, joined. "There's not going to be any Stu."

Kyle brought their hands to his mouth and kissed her knuckles. "That's my girl."

"Because that's exactly what I am," Glory whispered. "Your girl." The words could no longer be held inside because she was no longer fettered, the bubbling essence of her breaking free. "I'm in love with you."

Horror came on the heels of the admission. How could she have spilled that? It was too soon, not safe, stupid. Stupid. *Stupid!*

Pulling her hand free of Kyle's she leaped to her feet. "Don't say anything. Don't do anything." Panic flooded her bloodstream, icy, like the water of Lake Arthur in autumn.

"Glory—"

"I have to...to..." She looked around wildly, her gaze dropping on the package she'd brought home from the hardware store. Racing to it, she called over her shoulder. "Something came in for you today. Angelica said you ordered an address plaque?"

Walking back, she began tearing at the brown wrapping so she didn't have to see his face. "We always check them before handing them over to the customer, but this arrived right before closing."

"Glory—"

"Sometimes the company gets the numbers or letters wrong…" Her words trailed away as she stared at the square stone, address and name carved deeply and painted white so it stood out cleanly against the black background.

"1493 Cedar Summit," she read aloud. "I know where that is." One of the fanciest streets in the most exclusive of the mountain enclaves. There was no home there worth less than five million dollars. It wasn't the address or the likely worth of the place he was working on that gave her pause, that made her feel as if something was about to drop on her from overhead. She went so far as to glance upward. Then she shifted her gaze back to Kyle. "It says 'Scott' on this plaque."

He stood from his chair. "About that…"

"Is the house…your house?"

"No. Well, yes. I bought it, but it's not my house. I bought it for my parents." He shoved his hands through his hair. "I meant to tell you before. I meant to tell you long ago."

"You bought the house. You bought a house on Cedar Summit for your parents." A housepainter didn't do that. Not a handyman, either. She'd told him he could put a flyer on the bulletin board at Hallett's. Offered to recommend him to potential clients. Said he shouldn't be buying her dinner, when he'd actually purchased a piece of prime mountain real estate.

The back of her neck and her face burned. "What is it you really do?"

"Right now I'm taking some time off. I'm fixing up the house like I said."

"Time off from what?"

He sighed. "I'm in business. Big data. I have a company I run with my old college roommate."

Glory had only a vague idea of "big data," but the way he said it gave her the impression his company was important. "You're well-off?"

"I…" He sighed again. "Yes."

"You have a life down the hill that you have to get back to." Her face felt hot, but the muscles beneath felt cold and stiff, like modeling clay. "You're not staying."

"I can't, Glory. I've been a workaholic for the past seven years, and I would like to change that, but the truth is my business, my life, is down the hill."

"My business, my life, is up here," Glory said. "You knew that and yet you still…you still…" There would be no tears! She had more pride than that. She felt trampled on. Flattened. "I think it's time you go."

"Glory. I can't leave right now. I can't leave things between us like this."

He looked upset, but who knew what to believe when it came to him? A businessman. A rich businessman, who'd toyed with her affections and had a life far away from Hallett Hardware. It was everything she'd always protected herself from. The sting of tears had her turning away from him. "Go. Please."

"God, Glory. You just said you loved me."

"I didn't know who the hell you were when I said that." She crossed to the front door and pulled it open. "Goodbye. Goodbye, stranger."

CHAPTER EIGHTEEN

BRETT HAD A hangover when he walked into Oscar's for morning coffee with his brothers-in-law-to-be. The pounding between his ears was all for the best, he decided, because it didn't leave a lot of room for regrets and self-recrimination.

The night before, the one Angelica had spent at Shay's, Brett had devoted to quality time spent with the cold beers in his refrigerator. Until he'd passed out on the couch in front of the TV, he'd told himself and his best girl Stella Artois that his unfeeling remarks to the princess had actually been beneficial.

Now she knew what kind of bastard he was.

Now she'd keep her distance—finally!—aware he wasn't good enough for her to kick, let alone kiss. He *wasn't* sentimental. Any soft feelings he'd had were hardened by experience...and by the very fact he'd worked to banish them. Like Poppy, Angelica needed someone who would nurture her heart, not someone who would smother it with clumsy words and a lousy temper.

Who the hell has ever loved you? Shit. He'd actually said that.

He wasn't the right man for her, and to prove it, he wasn't even going to apologize.

Though the subject hadn't been tackled directly, he supposed she wasn't long for these parts anyhow. She'd dropped hints about leaving recently, and as the temperatures continued to drop, he'd always figured her interest in mountain life would, too. From the beginning he'd known she'd be going down the hill sooner than later.

If he'd pushed her in that direction...well, it had been inevitable anyhow.

Jace and Ryan were already at their usual corner table. Jace had driven up from LA that morning, but it didn't look as if the commute had worn him down any. Brett couldn't see Ryan's face because he had a ball cap pulled low over his eyes—his habitual effort to camouflage his famous movie-star features. Though this time of year, midweek among the locals, he didn't draw special attention unless someone acquainted with Poppy wanted the word on the upcoming wedding.

Once his coffee was in hand, he tossed his coat over the empty chair and dropped onto the seat. According to the TV, an arm's reach away, the weather was predicted to be warm and sunny by the beaches. Angelica was made for such moderate climes, with her warm-toned skin and bright smile. She'd be happy there.

"What's the scowl all about?" Ryan asked. "And by the way, good morning."

"Keep your jolly down," he groused. Then he remembered Angelica calling him out on his negative attitude. Shit. Guilt added a backbeat to his pounding headache. "Sorry. I have a hangover."

"You might not be the only Walker feeling the effects this morning," Jace said. "The call I had from Shay last night was accompanied by the roar of the blender. They were arguing about how much tequila goes into a margarita. By the sound of their voices, I think they decided on 'a lot.'"

"Mmm." Cursing himself, Brett shifted his gaze from his coffee to the other man. "Do you happen to know... was Angelica there?"

"Oh, yeah." Jace nodded. "She was singing."

Brett winced. "She really shouldn't."

"I have to agree with you there," Ryan put in. "She was still at it when we called, so Mace could wish his mom good-night. But she's enthusiastic, I'll give her that."

And apparently she wasn't broken up over the words they'd traded in the morning. Well, good, he thought. That was just great.

Jace drew back. "Take it easy, fella. Those bared teeth look lethal."

Instead of answering, Brett's attention turned to the television. Usually the nearby big-city stations didn't cover much about the mountains except for fire and snowfall, but during a roundup of local news, the burglaries in the Blue Arrow Lake region were mentioned. It made sense when some of the missing items were described. Beyond the usual cash and computers, items once belonging to the recently deceased philanthropist Walter Elliott were gone: a pair of dueling pistols, an antique sets of golf clubs, some Native American artifacts.

"Your binoculars are safe, right?" a voice asked.

Brett glanced up to see Vaughn hovering near their table. "My binoculars?" He just remembered that he'd left them at Poppy's and he would have to retrieve them. "How'd you know about that?"

"Poppy. I ran into her the other night. She told me she bought the pair and gave them to you. Remember, Ryan?"

Ryan grunted and drew the free chair at their table

closer with his foot. Apparently the volunteer sheriff got on his nerves, too. But Poppy, chatterbox and bubbly with happiness these days, likely told everyone she met all her business and that of everyone else she knew. It was both the plus and the minus of life in the mountains.

It was the community that he was embedded in, hip-deep. He'd never wanted a life outside it.

Vaughn wandered off. Ryan rubbed the back of his neck with his hand. "I can't take that guy."

"It's the fake badge," Brett said, then he shoved up from his chair as Lorraine Kushi came onto the camera. "Time for a channel change."

Switching to a different station would make him feel better. *Out of sight, out of mind.* Except then he went cold all over.

"What the…?"

"You didn't see it last night?"

He glanced over at Jace who was leaning back in his chair, his gaze on Brett, a little smile curving his mouth.

His attention returned to the screen. Angelica sat on a chair—in Jace's house, maybe?—and was speaking to a slick character in a dark suit. "I didn't watch any TV last night."

"She granted the interview because—"

"Shh!" God, she looked so beautiful, Brett thought. Dressed casually in her usual autumn uniform of sweater, jeans and boots, her long hair wavy and gleaming under the lights. If she was nervous it didn't show in her big brown eyes. Her tender, lush mouth didn't tremble.

The reporter gave a rundown of the charges against her father, and that's when Brett learned the man had pleaded guilty to half of them, while the other half had been dropped. Speculation was that his sentence would be over fifty years.

"You might never see him outside of prison again," the man said to Angelica.

She sucked in a quick breath. "That's true. I can only hope that this plea bargain in some way helps the victims and that it means at least some of their losses might be quickly recouped."

"Your own money was lost, as well."

"Not through investing it with my father," she said quickly.

"It was lost when he stole it from you to pay his investors."

"I don't know his motives."

The journalist leaned closer. "You haven't spoken with him, then."

"No."

"Your mother, his first wife, is remarried now. What's her take on this?"

Brett saw that Angelica's hands, folded in her lap, clutched each other a little tighter. But she was all cool princess when she answered. "I haven't had a conversation with her, either."

The pounding in Brett's head redoubled. It killed him, killed him, that she was so alone. *Who the hell has ever loved you?*

"Angelica, tell me this. Do you think the reason your father kept you out of his business was to spare you?"

She blinked. "I—I don't know."

God, hearts would be breaking all over Southern California at the sweet hesitance in her voice.

"If you had found out what he was doing before his arrest, would you have turned your father in?"

"Oh, fuck," Brett exclaimed, wanting to punch the asshole through the TV screen. "What kind of question is that?"

Angelica tackled it anyway. "I believe I'm a good person…so I also believe I would have done so. It would have been difficult, but I don't run away from difficult things."

No, she didn't, Brett thought. She took on as many jobs as she could and she put up with his surly attitude and attempts to push her away. Despite her fears about intimacy, she pushed past them to be the sweetest fuck of his life. And how had he rewarded her? *Who the hell has ever loved you?*

"Last question, Angelica." The journalist was clearly won over by her. There was warmth in his gaze and he leaned in again. "What's next for you?"

"Living my life." A faint smile curved her mouth. "Striving to build a good one."

"Best of luck."

Best of luck? That's all the asshole had to say after filleting her open and exposing her tender soul?

"God." Brett rubbed the top of his head with his palm, over and over. How had she made it through that with such grace? His eyes narrowed on Ryan. "This was first aired last night?"

He nodded.

"How did that guy find her?"

Ryan grinned. "Oh, she called him."

"Huh?"

"Lorraine Kushi ambushed her at the hardware store."

"Oh, hell. This is all my fault."

Ryan was still grinning. "Don't flatter yourself. After

speaking to her, it was Angelica who decided to contact Lorraine's biggest rival."

His eyes rounded. "Really?"

"Oh, yeah. Beautiful *and* clever." He hesitated. "And maybe just a little bit vengeful toward Lorraine for trapping her, which I personally find kind of hot."

"Jesus." Brett glared. "You're engaged to my sister and Angelica is…"

Ryan tilted the brim of his hat. "Angelica is…?"

"Stop poking at me."

"Will it hurt if I tell you she was feeling happy after that interview? She knew she had come out all right, hence the loud renditions of 'Here Comes the Sun.'"

Though reluctant, Brett couldn't help but smile. "I'm so glad I didn't hear that."

He also couldn't help but be glad she was doing well now that the cameras were off. At least she was last night. But how about now? His arms actually began aching along with the throbbing beat of his head, he wanted to hold her so much.

But shit, wasn't that impulse wrong? He had no forever in him.

WITH SHAY'S CAR idling outside her cabin, Angelica turned to her. "Thank you for the ride."

"No problem. My day for the car pool run, anyway."

"My convertible—"

"Jace will take a look at it when he gets home. If it's something he can't easily fix, we'll call."

"Okay. I have an auto service…" Or she thought she did. Was she paid up?

Shay reached over to pat her leg. "Stop worrying. Everything will work out."

Angelica gave her a smile. "I'll hold you to that. And thanks for last night, too. I had a great time if we don't count the little headache pulsing about right here." She touched her fingertips to a spot between her eyebrows.

"It was great, wasn't it? And in celebrating your television debut—"

"First *and* last appearance, I hope."

"—we even got Mac loosened up. Who knew that Zan has been corresponding with her all these years?"

"Does it count as correspondence if he never gave her an address where she could write back?" Angelica wondered.

"Probably not." Shay grimaced. "But I think he still managed to keep her heart shackled to him anyway. It explains a lot about Mac's attitude the past few years… and it means I might punch Zan in the face if he ever shows up again."

Shackled hearts were not a topic Angelica wanted to pursue right now. "Well, I should let you get on with your day." She wrapped her fingers around the door handle and thought of Shay returning to the house she shared with her fiancé and the engaging, amusing teenager London. "You're really lucky, you know that?"

Shay beamed. "Luckier once Jace gets home," she said, adding a quick wink.

At that, Angelica exited the SUV. Glancing right, she noticed that all was quiet at Brett's place. He was already on a job, she supposed, while she actually had a whole day free. Considering the stress of the TV interview and the long night over margaritas, she could use a nap. That her lawyer considered the televised Q and A a success, as well, only gave her more reason for untroubled sleep.

It was cold inside her cabin. She played with the thermostat, then walked into the bedroom and undressed. In flannel pajama pants and a tee, she climbed between the sheets and closed her eyes.

Hours later, she awoke, groggy from daytime sleep and her head still filled with a dream in which her mother was insisting Angelica bake a cake with a file in it to send to her father in prison. It was so weird—and yet so real—that she even checked her cell phone.

Not only was there no missed call, text or voice mail, she also had no service. It was like that often at the cabins. The bars would fluctuate, it seemed, on the whim of the breeze. Maybe the same squirrels that Brett discovered to have interrupted their electrical lines had done something to the nearest cell tower.

When she moved down the hill, at least those kinds of problems wouldn't plague her.

Sitting up, she rubbed at the last of her lingering headache. Fresh air would get rid of it completely, she decided. A walk would give her a chance to explore the woods around the cabins, something she'd yet to do. It would be another item she could tick off her goodbye checklist.

She'd been creating a mental one, ever since coming to grips with reality a couple of days ago. Her new life would have to begin elsewhere. As far as her heart was concerned, she'd have to get out of the mountains. But her car was also impractical for the climate, and she could find cheaper living as a flatlander as well as more employment opportunities.

Though it was sunny outside, she dressed in layers that included a hat and scarf. Her sneakers weren't hiking boots, but she'd been fine on the walk to the falls and didn't think this trek would be much different.

Slipping her cell phone in her pocket out of habit, she set off into the woods. Besides the cabins in the clearing, Mac had told her there were others nestled among the trees. Angelica could discern a faint path, and she followed it, her footsteps muffled by the fallen pine needles. The air smelled like shaded green and damp earth and it seemed to Angelica that Mother Nature might be some kind of *bruja* in her own right because it felt as if she was under a spell.

Her fingers trailed rough bark and feathery cedar boughs. She stooped to gather a handful of powdery dirt that she rubbed between her fingers, then let it sift to the ground like sand through an hourglass. At a granite boulder just off the path, she took a seat to unlace her shoe and dump out a troublesome pebble. Task done, on impulse she bent down to sniff the stone.

It was cool on the tip of her nose and smelled salty. She touched her tongue to its rough surface. It tasted… clean. Fresh, like water. Then she glanced around, wondering what someone might think to see her licking local rocks. Brett would likely tell her it was past time she left the high elevation. It was making her *loco*.

She continued on, discovering each of the other Walker cabins. They were quiet surprises around bends or tucked into a stand of sheltering trees. Poppy wanted to renovate them all in a style she called "rustic chic." There would be seclusion, but with luxuries, including the option of delivered gourmet food and beverages.

No internet. No TV. Just the lovely woods and delicious things to eat and drink.

"Maybe someday I'll come back and stay here," she said aloud, testing out the sound of the idea.

The only answer was the wind rustling high in the trees.

On a sigh, Angelica kept walking until she encountered the burned shell of another bungalow. This was the last cabin, she knew, the one destroyed in the summer. Instead of turning back, however, she glanced around and saw another path leading upward.

She didn't have the directional sense God gave a GPS, but she suspected it would take her up the mountain that had been the location of the ski runs. The place of Brett's dream—the one that he and Zan and Mac used to envision as kids.

Angelica began trudging upward.

The trail soon took her out of the thick trees. She walked up what must have been the bunny slopes, because the angle wasn't steep. Her breath felt just a little labored and there was only the hint of dampness around her hairline. She'd become accustomed to the thinner air, she thought.

No longer such a city girl.

Would there be some adjustment when she returned to sea level? Certainly an emotional one. She'd miss Glory and Mac and Shay and Poppy and the other Blue Arrow people she'd come to know. She should have found a group of friends when she lived in LA. But the women she'd met through her father had been older. Stupid of her not to have joined a Pilates studio or found some yoga classes to regularly attend. Then she'd have acquaintances to call, girlfriends she could tell about her sojourn in the mountains.

I fell for a rugged, complicated man.
I fell for the mountains where he lives.

Would there be a physical cost for leaving such beauty, as well?

For leaving Brett?

What did a broken heart feel like?

Pausing, she turned in a slow circle. From here she could see just the tip of the rooflines of the cabins in the clearing below. Wanting to press a memory of them in her mind, she scrabbled sideways along the dry grasses to get a better view. She slipped on the slick, hay-colored shoots and fell to her butt, hard.

Lucky for her, she had plenty of padding, and she slid on her denim jeans a little way before she could dig her heels into the mountainside and halt her movement. Folding her forearms on her upraised knees, she rested her chin on them and gazed upon the place where she'd spend her last days in the mountains.

The breeze caught the ends of her hair, sending them over her eyes and cheeks. When she drew them away, she glanced at Brett's cabin. Neither of his vehicles was in evidence. So, he wasn't home yet. Late afternoon was sucking the light out of the sky, but he might not be home for hours...if at all.

Her gaze sharpened. From this angle she could see the windows of his bedroom at the back of the cabin. Was that movement? A figure? Had he returned after all?

She shot to her feet, thinking she wanted to go to him. But why? It seemed to her they'd already said some sort of goodbye.

Who the hell has ever loved you?

As his voice, those words, echoed in her head, she closed her eyes. It was definitely time to move on. Pulling her phone free of her pocket, she checked for messages and then for cell coverage. Maybe Shay would tell her she had a working car with which she could make her escape.

But there were no texts and not even a single bar.

She glanced back at Brett's cabin and froze.

A figure was standing on the back porch, which was just an A-line overhang sheltering a postage-size doorstep. From here, she couldn't make out much about the person, just legs and feet, but those legs and feet did not belong to Brett Walker.

Maybe Jace, she thought. Maybe Ryan.

But wouldn't either of the men have come in a vehicle? She should be able to see one.

And because she didn't…she remembered the burglaries.

"Crap," she whispered, staring down again at her phone. Still no way to make a call. She began scrambling downhill, and not because she wanted to head into danger. It was her best bet to find a signal to call for help.

At first she stayed clear of the tree line. But it felt as though the mountains surrounding her had eyes, so she slipped between the trunks and weaved around them, hoping she could trust her sense of direction. Squirrels ran along the limbs above her, scolding, but she ignored their complaints.

Rodents didn't worry her—at least not right now. She thought of bears and mountain lions and wild burros, but it was a human danger that seemed more threatening. Not that anyone had been harmed by the thieves, but who knew what would happen if there were a confrontation? Still, she couldn't sit back and do nothing. At least she might be able to get a description to give to law enforcement.

The journey back to the cabins seemed a lot longer

on the return. She kept her phone in hand, checking for decent signal strength every few minutes. Once, when her gaze was on the screen, her toe caught a root that sent her sprawling. To protect her device, she kept one arm in the air and landed awkwardly onto her side and other elbow.

Breathing hard, she took stock. Her phone was fine, the parts of her that had met the ground stung. After a minute she sat up, noticing the rip in her sweatshirt sleeve and the bloody skin beneath. Her knee felt bruised, but the denim was intact.

She plucked pine needles from the knot of her knitted scarf. Then she got to her feet and continued onward, though more slowly. A little rattled now, her heartbeat was loud in her ears. She picked up the pace, glancing around because she had the distinct sense of being watched again.

A shiver rolled down her spine. Her footsteps thudded against the ground and oxygen was harder to pull into her lungs.

Someone was watching.

Someone was following.

Panic dried her mouth. Her gaze flicked to the screen of her cell once again. *Please. Bars! Please.*

Another root snatched at her shoe. Her stomach jolted and she felt her body flung toward the ground once more, an almost violent pitch.

Then arms locked around her.

She was pulled upright and yanked against a tall, muscled body.

Angelica screamed.

CHAPTER NINETEEN

"OH GOD, OH GOD." Brett's voice was hoarse and filled with harsh terror. "Are you all right?"

"I'm okay." She struggled in his hold, alarmed by his tone, but he only tightened his arms.

"Give me a minute." His heart was pounding much too hard against her back. "Oh, God."

"Brett." This time she forced herself around. She was still enclosed by him, his clutch still too constricting, but one look at his face and she froze. He was staring at her, the lines of his face harsh, his eyes glassy.

"I smell blood," he said, shoving her away with his hands at her shoulders. His gaze jerked from her head to her toes and back again. "Where is it? You're bleeding. You're hurt."

He wasn't in his right mind.

His head swung up toward the trees. "Are those the choppers?"

She only heard the wind, rustling through branches high above. "It's nothing. It's the breeze."

His gaze shifted to her again. "All the blood."

"No," she said, starting to really worry. She lifted her elbow to show him the tear in her sweatshirt and the scraped skin beneath. "See? Just a scratch."

For a long moment, he stared at the abraded flesh, then he let go of her to sink to the ground. "Shit," he said. "Sorry. Shit." His knees were drawn up and he buried his head in his hands. "I'll be all right in a second."

She dropped to the soft pine needles and placed her hand on his shoulder. With gentle strokes, she rubbed there, feeling the tension in both muscle and bone.

After several long moments, he lifted his head on a sigh but didn't look at her. "What are you doing out here?"

"I went for a walk."

He gave a quick nod. "Okay." His voice was still hoarse, as if he had to force each syllable through constricted vocal chords. "When you weren't at either cabin…"

New alarm had her fingers tightening on him. "You just came from the cabins? Did you see anyone there?"

"Not you, obviously." He glanced over and his eyes narrowed with a new alertness. "What is it?"

"I saw someone. I hiked up the mountain a ways and I could see your cabin. I thought I saw a man in there. There was definitely one on your back porch."

"Was it me?"

"No. I could see where you park and there wasn't any vehicle."

Brett frowned. "And I didn't go out the back door. Shay had told me about your car, so I wanted to give you a report. When I didn't find you, I came into the woods."

"You must have arrived after the intruder left." Angelica jumped to her feet. "Did you see anything missing from your cabin?"

"Like what? There's nothing there to steal but flannel shirts and a boring selection of canned soup."

"Someone was there."

"Okay, okay." Brett rose. "Let's check it out."

He led, she followed. While she was wild to know what had set off his temporary outburst, the first priority was the intruder she'd spotted from above. At the edge of the clearing, they paused. Brett pressed a big palm to her middle, pushing her back a step. "Stay here while I check things out."

She opened her mouth. "Brett…"

He turned, put his hands to her shoulders and his forehead against hers. "Angel face, listen to me this time," he said, his voice low. "This might not be kids after Piney."

"I know, that's why—"

"Please. I can't bear the thought of anything happening to you. Right now I'm not in a good place and I need to know you're safe." He drew her close and she felt a shudder run through him. "Give me this, okay?"

"Okay," she whispered. And as his arms pulled her even nearer, she pressed her cheek to his chest. It was impossible to deny him, not now when he seemed vulnerable.

When it seemed like he might care about her in a way that went beyond the casual. More than friends.

From behind a tree, she watched him approach the cabins. He stooped to grab a hefty log from the woodpile, then he climbed the steps to her place. He used his keys to enter and came out moments later. He shook his head at her, then strode to the bungalow next door.

Her fingers dug into the bark of the tree and air didn't seem to make it to her lungs. She couldn't bear the thought of anything happening to him, either.

But then he was back on the porch. He tossed down the log and beckoned to her. "All clear," he called, but the expression on his face was grim.

Angelica scampered across the clearing and up the steps. "What?"

"Nothing's been taken," he said. "But it doesn't feel right."

"We need to call the sheriff's office. Do you have a signal?" she asked, pulling out her phone and frowning at the screen. "I've got nothing."

"Me neither," Brett said, and took her hand to tug her into the house. "But with the only evidence a bad feeling, the deputies aren't going to come out anyhow."

"I saw someone!" Angelica protested, as Brett towed her to the bathroom.

"We'll go into town and report that. But first let's get you cleaned up."

"Cleaned up? I—" The rest was muffled as he yanked her sweatshirt over her head. Underneath she wore a tank top and goose bumps broke over her skin as Brett grabbed her bare arm.

"You're cold," he said. "Let me get this cleaned and then we'll warm you up."

"It's just a scrape."

But he pushed her onto the closed toilet lid and bent her arm, pressing her hand to her shoulder. She winced as the movement stretched the injured skin.

"Ouch," he said, his voice sympathetic. He ran a knuckle along her cheek, the action gentle. Tender.

Angelica could only be glad she was seated, because his warm gaze and soft touch were taking the starch out of her knees. This wasn't the way a man looked at someone he hardly cared about, was it?

Who the hell has ever loved you?

He was right about that, but it didn't mean her instincts were wrong.

Maybe there was hope for them…

"I have a message for you from Shay," he said, as he tended to the wounds.

"That's right, my car." She sucked in a breath as he dabbed on some antiseptic. "It wouldn't start this morning."

"Jace checked it out when he got home. Corroded battery cables. That's all. He cleaned 'em up and you're good to go."

Good to go. That had been her intention, to go as soon as possible—when she wouldn't be leaving Glory and Mac in a lurch. Maybe as soon as the end of the week. But if there was a chance that Brett…

Heaving in a breath as he turned to grab a couple of elastic bandages, she decided to test the waters. "Great about my car… I'm planning on leaving soon."

His gaze down, he stilled in the process of ripping the paper covering away. "Leaving?"

"I've mentioned it before. My car won't make it through a mountain winter…so I guess that means I should head for other climes before the temperatures cool even more."

He tossed the wrapping into the trash after applying the bandage. "I guess you should."

Disappointment dropped like a stone in her belly. Why was she such a fool? It was time to stop this silly hoping. She fluttered her lashes to blink away the tears forming in her eyes.

He glanced up. "Oh, sweetheart. I'm sorry it hurts." His palm cradled her cheek and he brushed away an errant drop with his thumb. "But it's clean now. Want some pain relievers?"

She shook her head. "They won't help." They wouldn't stop the shrouding ache of sadness.

"I owe you a couple of things," he said, his attention focused on the first-aid supplies he was packing back into their case. "First, an apology."

"It's all right—"

"Let me finish." He stowed the plastic box into a drawer in the vanity. "I shouldn't have said no one has ever loved you."

She gave a shrug. "But it's true."

"I saw the interview you gave."

Her eyes widened. "You did?"

"This morning." He dropped to the edge of the tub, pushing the shower curtain away so they were seated knees to knees. "I was very impressed."

Not even the hem of that shroud lifted. Still, she pasted on a smile. "Thanks."

"And you know what I thought at the end of it?"

She shook her head.

"That you for damn sure should love yourself, Angelica Rodriguez." He nudged her leg with his. "You're a beautiful person, inside and out."

You for damn sure should love yourself. Staring at him, the words echoed again and again in her head. *You for damn sure should love yourself.*

Her spine straightened. Even though her heart remained heavy, a new vigor infused her. She should love herself. Of course she should. She did.

Wow.

"Thank you, Brett." She found his hand, gave it a quick squeeze. "That might be the nicest thing anyone has ever said to me."

It was his turn to shrug. "And speaking of truth…"

He shifted his gaze to his knees. "I think I'd better explain what happened out there."

"You don't—"

"I think I do if I don't want you approaching my sisters about their crazy brother, Brett."

"I don't believe you're crazy." But she did want to know what had made him so anxious. Though he wasn't trying to hold her back from leaving Blue Arrow, that didn't cut off her feelings about him. Her loving him.

He still sat, eyes downcast. "Brett?" she prompted.

He ran his palm over the top of his head then seemed to force his hand away. "I had a bad experience in Afghanistan. Well, Afghanistan was a series of bad experiences, but my deployment didn't begin well."

Reaching out, she grasped his hand again.

"Shay knows a little about this," he continued, absently beginning to play with Angelica's fingers. "But the other girls are not aware of anything beyond the basic details."

Did he mean not only Mac and Poppy, but every other woman he'd ever let into his life? It was another wow moment to imagine that big bad Brett Walker was going to let Angelica in on something private.

"Not until then did I fully appreciate how things can go bad, so very bad, and so very fast. You'd think, after a swift-moving fire destroyed the ski resort and how quickly my father's health deteriorated following that, I would have already learned the lesson."

Ah. The roots of his distrust.

"The choppers dropped us off in the mountains...a remote-as-shit place. The bad guys always like to give the new guys a little welcome party. We had to sprint from the helicopters to the gates of the forward operating base as mortar rounds were dropping around us."

"Oh, God." Angelica put her free hand to her mouth, remembering how he'd been distressed and worried about blood in the woods. "Were you hurt?"

He shook his head. "Not me. Some villagers were heading into the base at the same time that we landed. Just…bad luck on their part. A woman went down right in front of me."

She could see that he'd squeezed his eyes shut.

"It was instinct. I…I scooped her up in my arms and kept running. But I knew it was bad. I could smell the blood. Feel it running down my arms, feel my uniform soaking it up. When I got her to the triage area…" He shrugged.

"I'm so sorry," she whispered. "On your very first day."

"I saw her die," he said. "She was looking up at me, moaning. I told her to hang on. I *willed* her to hang on. But it was no use."

He stood up, turning so she only had his back. "I can't forget the life leaving her eyes. The smell of blood. I was trying to wipe it off my hands."

One hand went to his head, and she realized now what was behind his habitual gesture…Brett trying to clean his hands, likely on the only place free of someone else's blood. Angelica moved, coming up behind him and putting her palm against his back. He didn't seem to register her touch.

What irony, she thought, that this was coming out in here, a room where a person went to be washed.

"I closed off after that," he spoke as if it was something he'd come to terms with long before. "The only way to survive was to build defenses around your emotions. Shut down anything soft."

"You had feelings for Lorraine."

"My one attempt after I returned. That experience shored up any chinks in my guard I might have had left, believe me. Now...I'm hardened through and through."

Glancing to the side, Angelica found her reflection in the mirror over the sink. Her face was pale, her eyes dark pools of trouble. "You had to protect your heart."

He glanced over his shoulder at her, his mouth turned in a frown. "That's what I'm trying to tell you, honey. I don't have one anymore."

Oh, Brett, she thought, further dismayed. Of course he had a heart. There was evidence of it everywhere in how much he cared about his family, his town, his mountains. In how he'd been devastated by a stranger's death and stung so deeply by a later betrayal.

But that certainty didn't bring her any relief from sorrow. He was so intent upon keeping his heart armored, it was, actually, the same thing as having no heart at all.

THIRTY MINUTES BEFORE opening time. Glory was moving the coiled straw wattles from the bin she'd dragged to Aisle B back to their original bin in Aisle P one at a time. The scratchy fibers bothered her hands and wrists, but she took it as fitting punishment.

She kept screwing up.

First, she'd fallen for a lying—though not dickless—bounder from down the hill. She didn't exactly know what a bounder was—

"Hey, Angelica," she called to her friend who was working on a laptop at the counter beside the register. "What's a bounder?"

"A cad," Angelica called back.

Glory grunted. Yep, she'd formed a stupid attachment with a bounder from down the hill, just like some silly mountain nineteen-year-old falling for a filthy rich university dude bro summering on the Blue Arrow Lake beaches.

Except it was autumn and that was supposed to have saved her.

"You need help, honey?" Her mother stood at the end of the aisle in jeans and a smock, since this was her morning for watercolor class.

"Thanks, but no, Mom." *I like being miserable all by myself.*

Her mother didn't seem to sense her mood, because she smiled at Glory. "I love the email newsletter idea Angelica came up with for the store. I'm going to sign up for a computer course at the community center so I can learn to do one myself."

"Fabuloso, Mom." She pitched the wattle toward the bin from seven feet away.

Missed.

Her footsteps clattered on the linoleum as she stomped over to retrieve it.

"Would you like me to bring you back a coffee from Oscar's? I'm meeting Dad to show him some cruise brochures I picked up."

Glory straightened, squeezing the wattle between her fingers. "Mom, you know he's not going to take a vacation."

"Well…"

"He doesn't feel comfortable leaving me in sole charge of the store. He doesn't trust me to make the decisions." Not that she'd been making *any* good ones lately. The wattles were a case in point. The construction guys who came in for them pulled their trucks around back as a loading point. When she'd moved their location, it had made that process longer and less convenient.

"I still believe," her mother declared, turning toward the front exit. "And if not, there's always Temari!"

When the bells announced her mom had left, Glory called once again to Angelica. "What the hell is Temari?"

There was a moment's silence during which Glory figured the other woman was putting her search-engine chops to use. "Japanese thread balls."

Huh? "Do you eat them?"

"It looks like you make them. An ornament of some kind."

Glory pushed at her hair, felt pieces of straw stuck in the strands and tried picking them out without the aid of a mirror. Knowing her mom, she'd make Temari into some kind of mountain cottage industry and next week Glory would be selling Japanese thread balls alongside the portable heaters and masking tape.

Her life sucked.

"You know what?" she yelled to her friend. "I used to love playing with steel wool and sandpaper. How sick is that?" Sicker still was that it held no allure for her anymore.

"I never liked dissecting earthworms and frogs," a voice said.

Male voice. *His* voice.

She looked up, glaring. "We're not open."

"Just turned nine," Kyle Scott said.

Today, he wasn't bothering to be fake housepainter/ home repairman. But he didn't look any less delicious in a pair of dark gray dressy jeans and a pale blue dress shirt, tails out. Expensive leather boots on his feet. Big-data-dude chic, she supposed.

"Go away. Go home."

Kyle sighed. "I've got a few things still to do at the house." He pulled a list from his pocket. "I need some door hardware and a couple of insulating strips."

"Get them at Murphy's."

"All right. Fine. I came to see you."

"I'm too busy to talk." She stomped to the wattle bin and snatched up another two. He followed as she walked them to the correct aisle.

"What's this all about?" he asked, eyeing the violent manner in which she slam-dunked the coils.

"Me, giving up on my dumb notions."

"Don't do that," Kyle said, catching her arm as she marched past.

She tried shaking off his hold. But he was stubborn, just like the grip he had on her heart. This close, she could smell him, an expensive smell she should have realized right away was out of her league.

"Glory, don't give up on your own ideas."

"You don't know what I'm up against," she muttered, staring at his shirt pocket. In thread the same exact shade as the cloth, was a tiny monogram. An *S* with a *K* and *J* cuddled close.

God. The only thing guys she knew had monogrammed were their beer cozies. Out. Of. Her. League.

"I know you have to follow your heart," Kyle said now.

Oh, no. Hers had made a very stupid choice.

"Particularly about work," he continued. Then he hesitated.

She frowned up at him. "Does this have something to do with the dissection you mentioned?"

He glanced around. "Is there someplace we could talk privately?"

Glory opened her mouth to tell him no. But before she could get that out, Angelica called from her spot by the cash register. "The back room is free."

Grr. "Oh, fine," she conceded with ill grace, slipping her arm from his loosened grasp to lead the way. As she passed her friend, she shot her a sidelong look. "We have a male-bashing date at Mr. Frank's tonight," she muttered.

Angelica's gaze flicked from Glory to Kyle and back. "If you're free."

The cramped back room smelled like sawdust, WD-40 and now Kyle's expensive cologne. Hell, she had to admit it was miles better than the body spray of the last guy she'd dated. Stu had always used Ivory soap, which might explain why being with him always made her feel as if she were fifteen.

So high school.

While Kyle made her feel like a woman. *No.* Upset. No! Angry.

She slammed her arms over her chest. "Say what you have to say."

He winced. "I screwed up."

"I think we covered that."

"Shit," he muttered.

His hand shoved through his hair, disheveling it in that way she found so sexy. Glory sucked in a quick breath. "Honestly, spit it out. I don't have all day."

"My parents are doctors," he said. "As are my brother and my sister."

"Okay…" He'd said he didn't like dissecting. "And you didn't want that for yourself."

"Exactly. It didn't go over well with the family."

"But you're a successful businessman, right?"

He nodded. "We hit the marketplace at the right time. My partner is a genius."

"So aren't your parents proud of you now?"

"Doctors…or at least my family of doctors…" He forked his hair again. "Healing, working with your hands to do good for people, that's what they put supreme value on."

"But not everyone can do that."

"I could have. I got into med school. I just…didn't want to go."

"Oh." She grimaced. "Did they disown you or something?"

"No." He shook his head. "They just…disapproved. Silently. So when I had the chance to buy the house, I thought it would be a nice idea to show them my hands could still be used for good."

"And you needed a break."

"And I needed a break."

"Okay… I get that." Glory glanced down and saw her Hallett's butcher apron was dotted with pieces of straw. She started brushing at them. "Why didn't you tell me this right away?"

A smile flitted across his face. "Don't hit me, but it was because you were so sweet. Open. Kind. You offered to buy me a drink and help me get work."

Glory's face heated. When the rich guy didn't need anything she had to offer. "I feel foolish," she muttered.

"No!" He shoved his hands in his pockets. "I told you I haven't had a lot of time to date and when I do it's been some sort of fix up where the woman knew the score."

"Hot, desk-bound businessman desperately seeking female companionship."

"Ugh. More like, guy with his head lost in data dragged by his friends to some event or other. I'm sure they were very nice. But it always felt so contrived. Me and you…we came to the table with just a couple of smiles." The one he gave her now was rueful. "And we discovered chemistry I don't have the analytics to measure."

Damn him for making his reticence seem reasonable! And wasn't "chemistry I don't have the analytics to measure" pretty much geeky but also…great?

Then she hardened herself against him. Why be soft when this was going nowhere? She had to be as tough as her pioneer ancestors, as hard as the mountains. Granite to the core. "Okay. Explanation shared. You're absolved. Go forth…and data away, or whatever."

"You could go forth with me."

"What?" Her eyes went wide.

"Come down the hill. Be in my world. Try it for a while, at least."

She still stared.

"I have to get back. I'm determined not to be that guy who works a hundred hours a week, but I still have to check in with my people. Put in a normal day at my desk." He swiped a hand over his mouth. "We employ eight hundred. I say that not to boast but so you'll understand I have responsibilities that go beyond myself."

"Kyle…"

He leaned closer to pluck a piece of straw from her hair. "I'd say more, ask more, give more, but that's probably not fair to you."

"Not fair at all, because I have responsibilities, too,"

Glory said, commanding herself not to cry. "Hallett Hardware, the family business. The mountains, my home."

"I don't want a long-distance romance, Glory."

"I don't want a long-distance romance, either." She turned away, staring sightlessly at shelves stacked with no-parking signs and steel padlocks and heavy-gauge extension cords. "You've ruined everything!" she said, the words dragged straight from her soul. "You were supposed to be my reward for running the cash register for the past seventeen years!"

She sniffed and felt the burn behind her eyes. "You were supposed to be my belief in love!"

"Glory…"

Now she whirled on him, getting toe-to-toe. "Did you know that people have an average of eleven occupations in their lifetime?"

Bemused expression on his face, he shook his head.

Emotion roiled inside her: disappointment, resignation, anger, loss. It made her voice ragged and rough. "You were supposed to be my ten other jobs!"

Instead of responding to that, he trailed a finger over one of her eyebrows. She tried not to shiver. "What have I done to squelch your belief in love?" he asked, his voice soft.

Hers was nothing of the kind. "You could have said you loved me back!" Then, aghast, she slapped her palm over his mouth. "No, don't! You lied, and that's answer enough."

His fingers wrapped her wrist and he pulled her hand away. "I'm in love with you." She tried yanking free, but he held firm. "I want you to come down the hill with me. Try life there."

Then he hauled her into his arms and they were kissing the kisses of the desperate. Of those hopelessly in love. Oh, God, Glory thought. Hopeless love.

She tore her mouth away from his. "That isn't helping."

"How about persuading? Is it helping with that?" he asked. "I want you. I want you to come live with me."

"How can I?"

"You get in a car and point it downhill, darling. I'll even do the driving." He pressed his mouth to her forehead, her cheeks, her nose. "Come live with me and be my love."

She narrowed her eyes at him. "I might be from the mountains, but I'm no hick. I recognize poetry when I hear it."

He grinned. "Christopher Marlowe. 'Come live with me and be my love, / And we will all the pleasures prove / That Valleys, groves, hills, and fields, / Woods, or steepy mountain yields.'"

Glory thought, *A man is quoting poetry to me! He thinks I'm beautiful and he's quoting poetry! Still...* "I'm not sure what it means, exactly."

"I can't know for certain what Marlowe intended, but for me it means I believe we can find this magic we have in the mountains anywhere we go. Anywhere we go together."

"Say it again," Glory whispered.

He framed her face with his hands. "Come live with me and be my love."

"What's going on here?" a blustering voice demanded.

Glory tried to spring away, but Kyle didn't let her get far. Holding her hand, he turned them both toward the back room's doorway, now filled by her father and mother.

"Don't be like that, Hank," her mother said. "Ask her about the ten other jobs."

Glory blanched. "You heard that?"

"And everything else this snake-oil salesman of a young man said," her father added.

"Hank." Her mother tugged at his sleeve. "Really."

Her father stepped farther into the room, her mother at his elbow. "I'll ask again. What's going on?"

Suddenly the back room was a metaphor for her life. It was cramped and too familiar and filled with some things she loved and some she didn't... Hello? Who cared about aphid dust? Her parents stood, guarding the exit point. Loving guards, but guards all the same.

Doubts crowded in, too, but then she looked over at Kyle and made a decision. Glory Hallett, mountain girl and tough tomboy who knew how to fix toilets and mend fences, was acutely aware she was about to fracture a relationship. Then her emotional pipe burst, tears overflowing as she ended one life and began another.

CHAPTER TWENTY

ANGELICA STEPPED ABOARD the Arrow Ferry, a tour boat that gave tourists hour-long rides about Blue Arrow Lake. It offered a great vantage point from which to view the luxurious mansions and gated estates that the general public wouldn't have access to otherwise. But Angelica wouldn't be scouting out fancy homes to ogle.

Once again, she was looking for a sign.

Seating herself on one of the vinyl cushions, she peered out a long window. *Should I stay or should I go?*

She had the means to stay in the mountains now. Or, at least, an offer that would lead to the means.

"Hey," a male voice said. Friendly, like a puppy. "How are you? Angel, right?"

She looked up, smiling at Stu Christianson. "Angelica."

"Oh, yeah." His sweatshirt was embroidered with the ferry logo and beneath it was his name and "Captain."

"This is yours?" Angelica asked, gesturing at the boat's interior. It was filled with less than a dozen people.

"Family thing," he said. "As soon as the snows come, we shut this down and go to work higher up the mountains at one of the ski resorts."

Winter's on its way.

The sound of the engines shifting gears had Stu pressing two fingers to his forehead in a farewell salute. "Give Glory my best," he said with another attractive grin.

She wondered if Stu would still be smiling when he heard the news. Glory was going down the hill with Kyle Scott. Angelica's mouth curved as she thought of the scene she'd left behind at Hallett Hardware. Upon meeting Kyle and hearing Glory's stated intention, Hank had looked ready to blow, and Katie had appeared concerned about the sudden decision, too.

But then their daughter had calmed them both.

She'd reminded her mother how man-made Lake Arthur had filled in three days instead of the expected three years—whatever that meant.

And she'd told her father it was past time he gave up all this retirement baloney and busied himself with what he loved best—running the hardware store.

Then Hank and Katie had put their heads together. The thing was, Katie had her heart set on taking some trips now and then. And Hank enjoyed his newfound opportunity to play a round of golf or two on occasion. What they needed, they decided, was a store manager, who would do all the day-to-day activities but still with Hallett input on a regular basis.

They'd offered Angelica the position.

The pay wasn't a fortune, but she wasn't looking for riches. She was looking for a place to stay. A place to call her own. And she loved the mountains and the community here. She loved working in the shop, of all things, because it required organization, and financial skills, and the ability to connect with people. Rolled them together into one job and she'd found her bliss.

Though the ferry rocked a bit as it churned through the water, Angelica braved the unsteady movement to cross the aisle and take a different seat for a different view. The boat swung into one of the lake's many bays and Angelica recognized the house where she'd spent the summer, mostly alone. Almost useless. Always mooning after the landscaper.

The place looked empty and idle, just as she'd been during those months.

Her gaze moved from the house to the mountains above, rising in uneven, ever-steepening tiers that went from bristling with green to naked gray granite. There was solidity and strength, both things she'd gained once she'd decided to forge her own path.

You for damn sure should love yourself, Angelica Rodriguez.

"So, what brings you out for a ride?"

Stu again. Angelica glanced up at him. "Part of my checklist," she told him. Maybe her goodbye checklist… or maybe not now. "Things I want to do while I'm here."

"I thought from the way you were staring out to the shore you were seeking signs of our local burglary ring."

Angelica grimaced. She and Brett had reported the activity at the cabins, but it hadn't seemed to impress law enforcement much. "Maybe the problems will die down with the colder weather."

"More stuff went missing last night," Stu said. "My uncle works for the sheriff's department. I got a rundown on what was taken…though we won't know for certain until he gets an inventory from the owners who are in Europe. But some drawers were rifled, so likely just cash and jewelry."

"That's too bad." But maybe now the cabins were safe, at least, considering the bad guy or guys would also have discovered that there was nothing to be had out there but clothes and canned food.

"Good news, though," Stu said, smiling again. "That stuffed bear is back. Found tied to the flagpole at the high school."

"Piney!" Angelica's spirits lifted. "Our Piney from the historical society?"

"The one and only." Someone called his name and Stu glanced around, muttered a "gotta go" and strode off.

Piney, home safe and sound. Was this her sign?

But it didn't feel quite right, so Angelica was still in a quandary as she debarked, waving at Stu as she returned to land. Should she stay or should she go?

She strolled the main street of the village as she returned to her car. Dusk was cooling the air and she pushed her hands into the kangaroo pouch of her wool sweater. Passing the elegant boutique, Bon Nuit, she was startled by the sound of knocking on the plate glass. Her head jerked and she saw Mac Walker inside, gesturing for Angelica to join her.

Why not? she decided. Maybe she could find a going-away gift for Glory. Something slinky to make up for the flannel gown her mother had given her.

Mac offered her a wide smile when she walked inside. "I heard the news," she said. "Congratulations."

Angelica's brows lifted. "News?"

"Hallett Hardware's new manager," she said, lifting her hands toward Angelica as if she were presenting a celebrity.

"Oh." She grimaced. "It's not official…or even decided."

"I stopped in to see Glory and it seemed pretty decided

to me. She is gaga over that guy. Going down the hill for him." She grimaced.

"The guy is Kyle Scott." She had to smile at Mac. "But 'going down the hill' is not exactly like going to the other side of the world."

"We'll make sure she gets her malaria shots anyway," Mac said, laughing. Then she sobered. "I guess Maids by Mac will be short a maid again."

"One way or another," Angelica agreed. She began perusing a rack of racy lingerie.

"Who's that for?" Mac asked, her voice sly.

"Glory."

"Oh, come on." The other woman nudged her with an elbow. "You and Brett…"

Angelica put her hand to her head as it started to pound. This was the issue. There was no Angelica and Brett. He didn't want to be anyone's "and." Even if she could accept that, what would it be like to live in the same area, running into him at the hardware store or at Mr. Frank's? It might not be so bad over the counter when he came in for fertilizer, but what about seeing him on the dance floor, snuggled up with some siren from down the hill?

"Hey, hey," Mac said, patting her shoulder. "You look like you lost your last friend."

"And Glory's leaving," Angelica whispered, the truth of that piercing deep. She looked at Mac. "That's going to be hard."

"I know it," Mac said. "But when you need a girl for… well, whatever you need, I'll be around."

Angelica sniffed. "You're nice."

"I am not!" Mac countered. "I'm prickly. I cultivate that, you know."

"I do." Angelica pressed the back of her hand to her nose. "It's not working that well right now."

"Huh." Mac looked about, then spotted a man just coming into the store. "Jimmy!"

He looked over. "Hey, Mac."

She sidled close to him, shooting a mischievous glance Angelica's way. "How are you?"

"Good?" He went wide-eyed as she began playing with his tie. "Jimmy, this is Angelica. Angelica, this is Jimmy Sheets. He works at the bank."

"Nice to meet you," he said, barely lifting his gaze away from Mac's hand, which he watched as if it was a live snake crawling up his chest.

"Would you like to go out with me sometime, Jimmy?" Mac asked in a sweet voice. She looked sweet, too, Angelica decided, unaccustomed to seeing her wearing anything other than her housekeeping uniform of jeans and sweatshirt. Now she had on black pants, black high-heeled boots and a fuzzy sweater the same pale blue as her eyes.

Poppy Walker was a daisy. Shay an elegant orchid. But Angelica realized that Mac was some other kind of beautiful hothouse flower…one that might just eat you alive.

"Go out?" Jimmy echoed, his voice rising an octave at the end.

"Yeah. We could have fun."

"Fun?"

Mac shot Angelica another wicked glance. "Unless you're afraid of me…"

"Hell, no," Jimmy said, frowning. "I'm not afraid of you, Mac. I'm scared as hell of Zan Elliott. I heard the warning he gave as he drove out of town, and I heed it to this day."

Mac froze. Then her hand fell away from Jimmy. *"What?"*

Now the man looked truly alarmed. "I gotta be on my way, Mac. See you!" Then he was gone.

"Are you all right?" Angelica asked. Mac remained in place, her color waning by the moment.

"That bastard," she said, then pink washed up from her neck to her cheeks as her temper clearly kindled. "That ugly, smelly, conniving, rat bastard."

She whirled toward Angelica. "I hate men. Do you hate men?"

Angelica tried valiantly to hold back her smile. "I sometimes want to hate men," she said helpfully.

"That's good enough for me," Mac declared. "You and I...we're going to own cats together."

"I think I'm allergic," Angelica lied, just to see what the other woman would do.

Mac's blue eyes went icy as she narrowed them. "Are you laughing at me?"

"A little bit? But I sure appreciate the mood lifter." She hesitated, then leaped into the fray. Mac had been a helping hand when she needed one. "What's this about Zan and a warning?"

"It's about him getting six feet under if he ever dares step foot in the mountains again," Mac said grimly.

"Do you think he told the other guys you were...out of bounds?"

"That's exactly what I think." She sucked in air. "And he apparently also believed I would wait around like... like... Who was the chump who was married to Odysseus?"

"That would be Penelope."

Mac's hands curled into fists. "I have to go. I have a stack of postcards to burn." Then it was her turn to exit the boutique.

Angelica had lost her taste for shopping and followed after her. She stood on the sidewalk, watching Mac stride off, anger in every step.

Maybe that was her sign. The frustration and the pain of Mac's infatuation with Zan—because really, her feelings could be in no doubt—were evidence that Angelica should cut her losses when it came to Brett.

In his mind, she was already put in the "past and done" pile. They'd had sex a few times, but that was over and he'd moved on—she knew this, because though he'd slept on her couch after the intruder incident, he hadn't touched her. Which meant the answer to the "should she stay or should she go" question was a simple, unequivocal *go*.

In her car, she drove slowly toward the cabins. Mac already expected her to be leaving Maids by Mac, so that was essentially a done deal. As for Hallett's, tomorrow she'd let the family know her decision was to leave. She wasn't expected until noon, but she'd go in earlier and explain in person. Hank had already voiced his intention to return to working regular shifts while a manager got up to speed, so there wouldn't be an interruption in customer service.

They'd find someone to take her place.

Here she wasn't indispensable to anyone.

Well, she wasn't indispensable anywhere, but she could change that. She'd made an almost-place here and it was her choice to leave her job, her volunteer work at the historical society, the friends she was making.

You sure as hell should love yourself, Angelica Rodriguez.

Remembering that, she could make her way and make herself a home somewhere else.

Brett's vehicle wasn't in its usual parking place and his cabin was dark except for the single porch light. She refused to allow her imagination to conjure up what he might be doing and with whom. Instead, she parked her car and got out, breathing in the bracing mountain air. Strengthened by it, she marched up her steps and turned her key.

As the door swung open, she realized she wasn't alone.

Her eyes widened. There was a table in front of the fireplace. It was covered by a cloth and set for two. Wax tapers flickered in candlesticks and embers glowed on the hearth. Brett Walker was standing nearby, a half smile on his face and a full bottle of champagne in his hand.

Over his head was a banner. It read Congratulations, New Mountaineer!

As he came forward, she couldn't take her eyes off it. Even as he bent to kiss her cheek, she continued staring.

Was *this* the sign she'd been waiting for?

ANGELICA'S AWESTRUCK SURPRISE evaporated any embarrassment Brett might feel over the cheesy banner. Still, he jabbed a thumb toward it and said, "London's idea."

Big brown eyes shifted to his face. "Really?"

Angelica still appeared gobsmacked. It pleased him but also made him want to kick his own ass. Why hadn't he thought to do something nice for her before? Christ, she'd shared her body with him while he hadn't even bothered taking her out for a decent meal in the village.

"What is all this?" she asked, indicating the table, the fire, the champagne.

Which reminded him. He poured two glasses, handed her one. "To you," he said, and the flutes rang out as the crystal kissed.

She took a sip, looked at the platter of cheese and crackers, then cast a glance toward the kitchen. "I smell something good."

"We'll get to that later." He put a slice of cheese—the fancy stuff from the fancy cheese place—on a cracker and handed it to her. It made him pause a moment. His mother had always done that...served his father the first appetizer. He'd forgotten that.

Angelica put the small morsel into her mouth and closed her eyes in appreciation as she chewed. Brett stared at the dark fan of her lashes, fascinated as he'd always been by the little, perfect details of her.

The tiny dot of a beauty mark high on one cheekbone.

The delicacy of her wrists.

The fragile frame of her collarbone.

The lushness of her lower lip.

Blood rushed south, his cock beginning to harden. When she opened her eyes, he half turned to study the flames, hoping she wouldn't notice the heavy bulge in his jeans, and rebuked himself for being a randy jackass. This evening was supposed to be about giving her a gift of sorts. Doing something for her. Not *doing* her.

Those three words didn't help, damn it. In his mind's eye he saw her naked limbs, her golden skin washed by the light from the fire. He could taste her in his mouth, the sweetness of her kiss, and he wanted to sample her everywhere. Burying his mouth between her legs would be his first stop.

"Brett?"

He threw the entire glass of champagne down his throat, then cleared it. "Yeah?"

"I didn't see your car."

"Oh. That." This was kind of embarrassing, too, come to think of it. "I wanted to surprise you...so I parked it down the road a ways instead of up here."

"You went to a lot of trouble."

"I had help," he admitted, turning back to grab the champagne. He refilled his, and then topped off her glass. But he'd taken it, the help, the moment the inspiration had struck. "It was Poppy who gave me the news about the manager position."

"Poppy?"

"Sweetheart, surely you understand the speed of the mountain grapevine by now." He told her about rendezvousing with his sister to get the binoculars. London and Mace had been along for the ride. They'd all been standing on the sidewalk in the village when she'd dropped the info.

It was only a small leap from him audibly mulling over providing some kind of celebration and his sister recommending a local caterer to put together dinner. An hour and two stops later—to said caterer and then to the print shop—and he'd been all set.

"Are you hungry? The beef stroganoff is ready whenever you are."

She hesitated. "Would you...would you mind if I change first?" She glanced down at her jeans and sweater. "I've been in this all day."

"Sure," he said, biting off the urge to ask if she needed help undressing. "Take your time."

Champagne glass in hand, she headed toward the hall, then paused. "Speaking of the grapevine...did you hear there was another burglary last night?"

He nodded, almost struck dumb by the picture she made, the low light giving her skin an angelic glow. "Yeah. Ran into Vaughn on the street when I was with Poppy. He just loves being the bearer of bad news. A fancy edition of *The Call of the Wild* was taken."

She turned back toward her bedroom and he stewed about the spree of robberies while she was gone. While he couldn't fathom why anyone would want to burgle the cabins in the first place, let alone make a second attempt, he'd insisted on sleeping on Angelica's couch.

Of course, he'd tossed and turned the entire time, thinking of her lying on a bed just a few feet away. But he'd accepted the misery, choosing that over risking more attachment.

There was going to be a reprise of that same suffering this evening, he reminded himself. Until the bad guys were caught, he was sticking close, no matter how that tempted his control.

Then she walked back into the room and he thought, *Oh, fuck.*

"I thought a fancy meal needed a fancier set of clothes," she said.

Fuck, fuck, *fuck*! A merlot-colored dress wrapped her spectacular body. It had long sleeves but dipped deeply between her breasts. Its hem swished somewhere above her knees, revealing her incredible legs. High heels only served to draw his eyes to her magnificent ass as she once again approached the table.

"I don't deserve this," he said honestly. He was supposed to be gifting her, not the other way around.

She must have realized it was a compliment. "Thanks," she said, with a little smile.

He pulled himself out of his sex stupor to head to the kitchen. "You need to eat. You've lost weight."

"What?"

"Let me just say I know every inch of every one of your curves." He glanced at her, saw her head was tilted and she was regarding him with a bemused gaze. "Yeah, I'm a dog like that."

She laughed, seeming to take no insult.

In minutes he had the food dished up. Remembering his mother again, he held out her chair. As she sat, he leaned close to take in a breath of her faint, exotic perfume and the scent tugged at his dick.

Yeah, a dog.

He tried to keep his baser impulses to himself as they began to eat. "So when do you move into the big corner office?" he asked, knowing very well there was no such thing at Hallett Hardware.

She hesitated. "Can we talk about something other than work?"

"Sure." Maybe she was a bit nervous about taking on the new responsibility. "Like what?"

Her fork toyed with the field greens of the salad. "Tell me about the seasons I've missed. I saw summer, now it's autumn." Her voice lowered. "Tell me about winter."

Brett eyed her with some concern. The request sounded strained. As though she wasn't interested in idle chitchat. He shrugged off the niggle of concern. "We have rain first. When it gets cold enough, snow."

She smiled a little. "I think I have that concept down. What's it like here?"

"At the cabins?"

She nodded.

"This will be the first winter I've been here since the fire. Ryan wants to get some snow shoes to explore the woods. I've promised Mace and London that we'll go sledding." It pleased him to think of that. Sometimes he allowed himself to get too busy to enjoy all the area had to offer. "We'll find a good run up on the mountain."

Her gaze on her plate, she nodded again, as if painting a picture of it in her mind.

"In spring, there's daffodils."

"What?" Her head came up, her eyes wide.

"It's a community project. Bulbs have been planted all along the highway and alongside plenty of the byways, too. In April, they bloom, a bright yellow surprise."

"I was here one weekend in March. They weren't up yet. I'd sure like to see them," she murmured.

Thinking of how she'd appreciate the sight made him anticipate their appearance, too. He caught her hand, squeezed. "You will."

She stilled, staring at their entwined fingers, and heat rushed up his skin like a flame finding favored tinder. The atmosphere in the room changed that quickly. Like the strike of a match.

From across the table he could feel her blood coursing beneath her skin. Her face was flushed, even her lips looked swollen, their color a darker pink.

Like her other lips would be, when he moved down her naked body to slide his tongue between them.

They were both breathing unevenly.

"I have a checklist," she suddenly said, her gaze still focused downward.

He was staring at her breasts, rising and falling against the thin fabric of her dress. Beneath it, beneath the bra he could faintly see the outlines of her nipples, and they were hard.

Ready for his mouth.

What had she said? "Checklist?" He sounded stupid. Or a little drunk. But this intoxication didn't come from the two glasses of champagne he'd downed.

"I want to have sex with you."

"You have," he pointed out, then wanted to bang his brain against the table. If she wanted to go another round...but they shouldn't, he remembered. It sent the wrong message.

Tonight was supposed to be a gift to her, not another opportunity to screw.

"I want to have sex with you your way."

Her eyes were on him now, those big brown eyes with the feathery lashes that had made him burn from the first day he'd looked up to find them on him. The sun had been bright that day and he'd just taken off his shirt. A tingle had run down his spine and he'd looked about to discover the curvaceous brunette staring at him. His abs had contracted. His cock had gone instantly hard.

She'd looked like expensive, high-class trouble.

And he'd wanted to push her into the soft soil he was tilling and drill her like the unrefined laborer he was. For months, he'd thought of holding her down with his dirty hands and availing himself of her body in every manner possible.

He sucked in a sharp breath. "I don't have a way."

Her look might have held some pity. "Brett."

"What?" He should release her hand. Get up. Take their plates to the sink. Call one of his sisters to babysit the brunette beauty while he went back to his cabin—no, it would have to be a drive to the village where he would get too drunk to climb back into his car. A buddy would give him a sofa or a patch of floor, far from Angelica's lure.

Instead of him rising from his seat, she did. He was forced to let her go. Her hand moved to the side of her dress at her waist. One tug, and Brett's jaw dropped.

Just like the dress, when she shimmied her shoulders.

His brain flatlined. Beneath the garment, she wore a panty and bra set of sheer black net that included incongruously innocent pale pink bows: one between the cups of the bra, one at each hip.

Lust poured into him, making every muscle taut. He came to his feet. "What is it you want?"

"I told you." She toyed with the ribbon between her breasts. "I want Brett Walker in bed, not some stifled gentleman."

"Stifled?" If she was trying to goad him, it just might be working. "Gentleman?"

"Don't treat me like I might break," Angelica said then. "I'm sturdy, you've got to know that by now."

She wanted him to prove it. "Oh, angel face." His feet knew where the rest of him wanted to be. Standing in front of her, he cradled her cheek in his palm. Her skin was warm, her dark eyes trained on him. Every inch of her telegraphed tight nerves.

Was this the gift he could give? His belief in her strength?

His gaze fell from her sweet mouth down to her body.

"That's some dangerous lingerie, sweetheart. But what's with the prissy ribbons?"

She seemed to relax at his teasing tone. "Comes with the territory. You should know. You have three sisters."

"I've never looked at their underwear!"

At his faux outrage, she giggled. And he bent to bite the sound right off her lower lip.

She gasped and her body bowed into his. His arm snaked around her waist and he palmed the plane of her lower back, his pinkie finger trailing beneath her panties to stroke the curve of her plump ass.

Her body trembled under this new touch and her mouth opened to his. His tongue plunged inside and hers tangled with it, eager to play. He kissed her until neither of them could breathe, then he tore his mouth away, looking at her again.

Her lips were swollen, her expression dazed. He supposed his tongue lolled from his mouth as he took her in—heaving breasts, decadent little-nothings, those high heels. His control was officially shot. His reluctance up in smoke.

"No matter what, the shoes stay on," he ordered.

Another tremor racked her body. He smiled at her, but there was nothing tender in it. It was hot and a little mean, because he was going to take from her what that uncivilized laborer had wanted all summer.

He wasn't going to ask permission; he was going to extract every sigh, cry, shiver he could get from her.

Pointing to the couch, he directed her silently. Angelica gave him a look that was all pleading arousal. "You asked for it, beautiful girl. You're going to get it…slow."

A little moan escaped her lips as she walked away

from him. Her high heels made her hips sway…and made Brett sweat.

He stripped off his shirt. Toed off his shoes and peeled of his socks. She'd reached the designated destination and was staring at him, all big eyes. Something moved in his chest. "Angelica…" he said in a soft voice.

Her eyes flared wider. "Don't you dare. I want… I want *everything*."

And so did he, God. So did he.

Striding to where she stood in front of the couch, he didn't give any warning, but just reached around to unlatch the bra. It dropped into his hand and he tossed it aside without looking where it landed. Her breasts presented themselves in all their bountiful glory.

Enough fragrant female flesh to take a man to his knees.

But he stiffened his, and bent at the waist to slide his tongue over one tightly gathered nipple. She made a sound, desperate and lovely. He moved to the other, wetting it, then sucking it deep in his mouth. Her hands reached out to clutch his shoulders. Grabbing her wrists, he forced them to her sides again. "No touching until I tell you," he said in a harsh voice.

Another lovely little moan.

He moved back and forth between her breasts, toying with them with his lips and tongue, but not touching her anywhere else. Her perfume was rising from her skin, a dizzying scent, and he lifted his head before he fell prostrate at her feet.

Looking down, he drank the sight of her in: her flushed face, her swollen breasts and their slick wet tips, her thighs, pressed tightly together as if she was trying to relieve a certain ache between them. Her eyes drank him in, as well, and something he saw in them made his belly clutch.

And made his next action rough. With hands on her shoulders, he pushed her onto the couch. She sat abruptly, her breasts bouncing.

Shit. "All right?"

Her glare was molten. "Brett, I'm fine."

Then that became his goal. To "not fine" the princess. He wanted her so revved up that when he asked if she was fine she'd just say, "Fuck me, please fuck me."

He wanted her so not-fine that she wouldn't even know his name.

So he did drop to his knees in front of her. Then he manacled her ankles with tight fingers and propped her high heels onto the edge of the cushions. Her breath was raw in the room—or was that his?—as he reached up to grab the elastic of her panties. He yanked the fabric down without finesse, until stopped by the shoes. Then he pressed on her inner knees and opened her to him, butterfly-style.

God. So pink. So pretty. So wet she was glistening in the firelight.

If he died right now—and it was possible—he'd face-plant right into her lovely, beckoning pussy.

Glancing up, he saw her gaze was as fascinated as his. "Yeah, baby," he whispered, his voice husky. "You're beautiful, there and everywhere."

Then, bracing his palms on her legs to keep them flat and open on the cushions, he leaned in to trace her folds with just the tip of his tongue. Instantly, her hips tried to jolt upward, but he held her down, one hand moving to her shoulder now, his other forearm across her knees.

His next foray wasn't any less delicate.

She moaned.

He didn't let the sound spur him. Instead, he continued at a slow pace, tracing her with the faintest of strokes. Her fingers touched his hair, but it only took a look for her to drop her hand. "Good," he said against her wet flesh.

Then he rewarded her with the flat of his tongue. Her hips tried to rise again, but he held her down, made her his captive. The castle's gardener finally getting his taste of the treasures inside. Getting his taste of princess.

She was delicious. Her flavor, her responses, the way she moaned, breathy and low.

He pushed deeper into the soft layers of her, getting his nose and cheeks and chin wet with her juices, not worrying about his raunchy urges, not trying to hide the crudest, rawest part of his nature. Taking what he wanted from her.

She'd asked for it. And revealing his animal side was revving *him*, his lust building as he explored the hot center of her. He speared her with his tongue, feeling her muscles clamp down on him and he almost lost it inside his jeans.

Her body was trembling, all of her strung tight. The hand at her shoulder drifted to her breast and he tweaked and toyed at her nipple again, noting it was tighter and harder than ever.

"Please," she said. "Oh, please."

Music to his ears. He glanced up, saw that her eyes were at half-mast, her bright pink cheeks shadowed by her spiky lashes. Her teeth sucked in her puffy lower lip. Stunned by the absolute splendor of her, his belly clutched again. His tongue wiggled up the cleft of her sex and he pierced her channel with two fingers just as his lips latched on to her clit with a firm pressure.

She gasped, every muscle shuddered like an earthquake, and then she was coming, each pulse of pleasure communicated through the clench and release on his fingers.

When she quieted, he gentled his mouth and slowly withdrew his fingers from her. Sitting back on his heels, he saw she didn't move from her open pose, even though he no longer held her in that position. "So pretty," he said. *So trusting*, he thought.

She blinked, her eyelids moving up and down like a sleepy cat. "Is that all you've got?" she asked, her words slurring as though she was half-drunk.

And that killed him. He'd just gone down and dirty on her and she was still challenging him, still standing up for herself.

Still trusting.

Shit, he thought. He rose to his feet, palming his stiff cock through his jeans. Her gaze followed the movement. "I want that," she said pointing at the bulge.

And for some reason, his temper spiked. He didn't know why that was—offense, defense, a resentment fostered during all those weeks when she'd seemed so far above his reach—but it fed a mean streak that was part of his pessimistic temperament.

Without warning, he grabbed her elbow and hauled her off the cushions. She rocked on her high heels, and reached down to pull her panties up in a hasty movement.

"Don't bother," he said in his scariest voice, though he allowed her to complete the action.

His hand still on her arm, he hauled her to the end of the couch and bent her over the padded arm and fished a condom from his wallet. Then he used his bare foot to push her legs apart. His hands stripped those panties back down as far they would go, to the tops of her knees.

His heart knocking against his chest, he tore open his jeans and shoved aside his boxers to release his cock. Angelica trembled at the sound. *Good*, he thought. *Now you know who has the upper hand here.*

His own hand shook as he palmed one ass cheek. She made a sound. He told himself he would be gentle if she asked, but there was blood rushing in his ears, lust firing it hot like gasoline.

Then Angelica glanced over her shoulder at him. Not afraid. But lusting. And so full of trust.

"Fuck," he muttered, took the moment to sheath himself in the condom, and then he fitted himself to her, sliding inside her pussy to do just that. She took him easily, her hips tilting to accept the deep thrust.

His body pistoned and she pushed back on every drive, taking him in. Taking him as he was.

Taking.

He knew what it meant, even as he knew her excitement was growing, as well. Bracing with one hand on the small of her back, he kept lunging inside of her, telling himself this was his turn, reminding himself that he didn't need to be tender or gentle or even care if she got off on this round.

Hadn't she asked for him to be who he was?

Hard, wary of attachment, insulated from feeling.

But even as he thought that, he was curling over her back, pressing his cheek to hers, kissing her ear, her temple, the corner of her mouth. Her head twisted and they were lip-to-lip, the kiss tender, even as he was pounding into her body.

It was a dichotomy, a contradiction, every perverse and perverted urge she brought out in him.

The climax rose from his toes and coiled in his belly, a whirlwind of pleasure that was gathering, gathering. His hand slid around her hip and along her belly until he once again found her clit. She jolted back at his touch, taking him another inch, and then he was coming…and then so was she.

In the aftermath, he lay heavily on her body, panting. She was quiet.

When he could, he stood and pulled free from her, unsurprised she didn't stand herself. He zipped his pants, then managed to lift her into his arms. Her head fell heavy to his shoulder as he carried her to the bedroom.

That's when she gave him the final gift of the night. "I love you," she murmured against his throat.

He sucked in a long breath, an action that put more pressure on his already-aching chest. "I know," he said. "I know it."

CHAPTER TWENTY-ONE

THE NEXT MORNING, Angelica learned they were going to pretend she'd never spoken those three words. That was fine with her. She hadn't meant to let them loose, of course. Trailing in Brett's footsteps, following the flashlight he was using to light the way in the darkness just before dawn, she hunched her shoulders for warmth.

It would have been better to awaken alone. But instead, it was obvious he'd spent the night once again on her couch after tucking her into her bed. She'd smelled coffee and so she'd decided to get up and face the music—which turned out to be silent—so that afterward she could tick off another of the items on her goodbye checklist.

Seeing the sun rise from the Walkers' mountain.

When she'd mentioned her goal to Brett while they were sipping coffee and she couldn't stand the quiet in the cabin, he'd grunted then told her he'd lead the way.

Her pride had demanded she didn't make some excuse or refuse his company.

She loved him. He knew. Big whoop. The world was full of sad stories like hers. But she'd survive. She knew that now, thanks to her time in Blue Arrow. She had bootstraps and she knew how to pull them up.

People didn't die of broken hearts.

Though thinking of never seeing Brett again made it hard for her to breathe.

Ahead, he halted as he crested a knoll. She joined him, following his pointed finger toward the east. Another, taller range of mountains stood there, looking as if it was torn from dark construction paper, then pasted against the silvering sky.

"Keep your eyes on that saddle," Brent said, indicating a low dip. "The sun will rise right there."

She could see the barest glimmer of it, an edge of gold warming the black-and-gray predawn. It washed the underside of the flat-bottomed clouds, making them glow like she thought an angel's wings might.

Change came rapidly after that, pale gold giving way to a deeper orange that washed the sky in tones from petal pink to the full red of robust passion. It was what had happened to her, she thought. At first there had been that golden promise of her fascination with Brett. Then it had risen, expanded and ultimately changed her entire interior landscape.

"Look there," he said now, in hushed tones. "Below."

A small lake in the cleft between two jagged peaks had caught the light. An unexpected gold coin, waiting to be plucked by a giant hand. Angelica's breath caught, awed by the beauty and the poignancy of this moment.

This goodbye. Because if he didn't return her feelings, couldn't return her feelings, she had to leave.

Brett lifted the binoculars he'd hung around his neck—the antique pair Poppy had given him. His strong hands framed them, but his touch was delicate as he made the proper adjustments. Then he passed them to her.

She had to crowd close because of the leather strap still circling his neck. Once again following his direction, she aimed them downward, and caught sight of a deer picking its way through the dried grasses.

"So pretty," she whispered, supremely aware of the warmth of him at her side and back. "How very beautiful this all is."

"Yes," he said. "Even more so through your eyes."

Stepping away, she returned the binoculars. He brought them to his face to scan the surroundings.

"You should put your lodge right here," she said.

His brows rose as he let the device drop. "As a matter of fact, this was the very place we planned to build it."

"Then do it. Really put down roots."

He glanced over, letting the device drop. "Really put down roots? I'm a landscaper. I do that every day."

"No." She shook her head. "You tend things, not create them. Didn't you tell me you rearrange gardens all the time in your head?"

"Those gardens belong to other people. I do what they want."

"This could be what *you* want," she said, indicating their surroundings with a circling hand.

"Too risky."

Angelica was feeling anxious and brave and excited, all three at once. "Take a chance," she urged. "Put your dream on the line."

His expression let her know he was closing down. Her pulse began racing and she thought, *You should put your dream on the line, too.* She obeyed the sudden impulse. "Tell me to stay, Brett."

He frowned. "What?"

"Tell me to stay. Tell me you want me to stay."

His gaze shifted away from her.

"When I drove back to the cabins yesterday evening,

I'd decided not to take the job. I'd decided to go down the hill."

Though the atmosphere between them was suddenly charged with tension, he didn't break his silence.

"You really want me to go?" She tried to keep her voice even. "Then say that."

"I…" He shook his head. "Angelica…"

"I'm in love with you," she declared.

He winced. "That's because last night was…good."

"Don't dismiss my feelings as pillow talk." *Take the risk*, her inner voice urged. She glanced around at the grandeur of the mountains and the sky and that still-glowing golden lake and took strength from it. "Brett…"

"What do you want?" he asked, his voice edged with impatience.

"I want you to love me." She hauled in a breath. "Do that. Love me back."

His whole body flinched as if she'd slapped him. Then he spun away from her, presenting her with the rigid line of his spine and the stiff set of his shoulders. "I told you. I can't. I won't."

"Brett…" It sounded like a plea.

"Don't you listen?" he asked harshly. "I don't have it in me."

And at the bitter finality of his words, her heart seemed to tumble out of her chest. But she guessed that made sense, as she rubbed at the aching emptiness there. Because she was leaving it behind.

"Goodbye, Brett," she whispered.

Then she turned, and left Brett behind, too.

WITHIN TWENTY MINUTES Angelica was driving away from the cabins, heading for her flatland life. It was still early when she neared the village, and the parking lot at Hallett Hardware was empty. Once Hank or Glory arrived, she'd go inside and tender her resignation. She was sure they'd understand.

For a moment she allowed herself to think of what Brett was doing. Had he continued hiking on the mountain? Was he back at the cabins and now aware she was truly gone? Angelica could see in her mind's eye his big hands cradling the binoculars just like they'd once cradled her face, with both power and gentleness.

An aching loneliness tried descending, and she pushed it away by thinking of other things…and yet her mind circled back around to Blue Arrow. So much she would likely never know about the people there.

Would the Walker weddings happen without a hitch? She thought so.

How about Mac? Would she find resolution for her feelings for Zan Elliott?

And the cabins…would Poppy make a go of them?

Then there was the mystery of who was behind the burglaries. She mused over the items that had been taken, feeling a little more melancholy. Via the silent auction, she'd helped many unique articles find good homes and now they'd gone missing. Stu had told her the last theft had likely only involved cash and some jewelry.

Vaughn, however, had reported to Brett that a first edition of *The Call of the Wild*, which Angelica knew was from the Elliott estate, had also been stolen. She frowned. Was it weird that Vaughn had more information?

At least Brett hadn't lost his binoculars—they hadn't

been at his cabin when the intruder or intruders had been in his place.

Full circle, Angelica thought on a sigh. Brett.

He was so closed off. Could she blame him? Burned by the girl who once had him arrested, wounded by his war experience, betrayed by a lover in a way that left him scarred.

It didn't leave a woman with any choice but to walk away from him.

That's what the bikini girl had done. Lorraine Kushi.

Angelica Rodriguez.

Damn. She slapped the steering wheel, and then stared out the windshield, unseeing. Leaving him made her like the others.

And if she was so willing to give up after round one, then she was unworthy of him. Unworthy of her new resolve to take charge of her own life. To go after what she wanted instead of waiting around for someone else's approval.

Hands shaking, Angelica turned the key in the ignition and turned the car in the direction of the Walker cabins.

BRETT GRAPPLED WITH the intruder, battling a red-hot rage and a deep sense of urgency. In a rush to get his keys so he could stop Angelica from leaving the mountains, he'd been completely surprised when a man had jumped on his back when he'd entered his cabin. The guy had him in a grisly hold.

But he had to get to the girl. The thought of missing her, of her slipping out of his town and out of his reach, galvanized him.

With a grunt, he broke the guy's grip by throwing

open his arms. The interloper fell back, and Brett whirled around to confront him, fists up.

Only to see it was Vaughn Elliott who leaped to his feet, his face red and his blond hair disheveled and sweaty looking. Brett gaped. "What the hell—"

The door swung open. Angelica stepped inside.

Being closer, Vaughn was able to reach out and grab her. He yanked the startled woman in front of him.

Holding his hands at chest level, Brett gave Angelica a quick assessing glance, then focused on the other man. "What's going on, Vaughn?" There was a light in the asshole's eyes that didn't look altogether right.

"There's been a mistake," the man said, panting.

"We can fix mistakes," Brett said, in a calm voice. "Why don't you let Angelica go, and you and I will find a solution."

Vaughn glanced at the woman he held in a tight grip. "Angelica," he said, as if noticing it was her for the first time. "I can trade her for the list."

"The list?" Would Vaughn have a weapon? Brett thought, trying to decide. As a sheriff's department volunteer he wasn't issued one, but it would be no surprise if he owned a gun.

"The list of people who bought items from the Elliott estate at the silent auction." Angelica said. She sounded calm, too.

"Those things should have gone to me." Vaughn's tone was belligerent. "My grandfather left the money and the house to Zan. I should at least have been willed the contents of the place."

"That seems fair," Angelica mused.

Fair? Brett telegraphed orders to her. *Keep quiet. Don't attract his attention.*

As usual, they could communicate with a look. *I'm okay*, she said back. *Follow my lead.*

Then her mouth moved and he could read her lips. "Trust me."

"Here's what we can do, Vaughn," she continued. "I happen to have just learned the password to the historical society database."

"I thought you didn't know it," he said, frowning down at her.

"And I didn't. But Ruth needed me to do something new with the members section and gave it to me." Her expression was guileless. "Yesterday."

"So…" Vaughn drew out the word.

"So you and I could—"

"No!" Brett interjected, his body going cold.

Angelica shot him a quelling look and continued as if he hadn't spoken. "You and I could take a drive to the headquarters and I can print out the list for you there. I have the keys to the front door."

"Why would you do that?" the other man asked, suspicious.

"She wouldn't," Brett said.

Angelica rolled her eyes at him. Yeah, yeah, his remarks were agitating Vaughn, but there was no way he was going to let her leave with him. "Listen, Elliott," he said. "That's the love of my life you're holding there, and it's making me twitchy."

Vaughn seemed surprised by the bald announcement. His head jerked back. "Brett Walker, finally settling down?"

"Absolutely. So let go of the girl."

"She's got to do something for me first," Vaughn insisted. "The list."

"It won't take a lot of time," Angelica put in brightly. "I'll do this little favor for Vaughn and then we'll continue on with our plans for the day—"

"Vegas. We're getting married in Vegas this afternoon."

Angelica's eyes rounded. "Um—"

"You remember, honey—you don't want to be stuck wearing something itchy or ugly. In Vegas you can get married in sweatpants."

"Sweatpants!" There was outrage in her voice. "I'm not getting married in sweatpants."

The conversation was clearly confusing Vaughn, who somewhere along the line had gone round the bend from arrogant asshole to irrational idiot. But his hold on Angelica was still strong and there was the niggling question of concealed weapons.

"No sweatpants, then. I don't care what you wear as long as you're my wife by the end of the day, angel face."

Her smile looked more strained now. "Sure. Anything you say, sweetums. Let me do this with Vaughn first, though."

Sweetums. She was going to pay for that later. Brett pasted a put-upon expression on his face and let out a long sigh. "Well, all right. You can run this errand if it's not going to take very long."

"Good," Vaughn said.

Keeping his pose relaxed, Brett sidled over to put himself between the pair and the door. "A quick trip now."

Vaughn shot him an impatient look and stepped forward, still holding Angelica. "Let's go."

As if he'd let that happen. Brett shot out his hand and

wrenched her from the other man's grip at the same time his fist came up with an uppercut to Vaughn's jaw. The man stumbled back, and Brett shoved her behind him and moved in on the dazed would-be robber.

It was over in seconds.

Brett and Angelica stood over the moaning figure. Brett had fished a gun from the back of the guy's waistband. It looked to be an antique. She glanced at it and then up at him. "Is this where I say 'my hero'?"

"You were the one directing the show. I followed your lead."

"Not at first. Not at the last, either."

"Did you think I would really let you walk out of here and drive into town with that SOB?"

"I don't know what I was thinking exactly."

He ran a hand down the back of her hair. "Had you figured out he was the burglar?"

"I was just putting it together this morning. When I saw him…I knew I was right."

"He was here for my binoculars, I'm guessing," Brett said, moving to retrieve them from the floor, where they'd gotten lost in the scuffle. "They fell from my hands when he jumped me."

"What do we do now?" Angelica asked. "Tie him up and drive him to the sheriff? We don't have any cell coverage to make a call."

"Tie him up here, then call the sheriff from the road, once we have some reception."

Clearly puzzled, Angelica studied his face. "The road? Are we going for coffee? I could use some Oscar's caffeine."

"We're going for happy-ever-after," Brett said, pulling her into his arms. "I wasn't kidding about that Vegas wedding this afternoon."

She went still, her brown eyes bigger than ever.

He pressed his forehead to hers. "I'm not letting you get away from me. When you left me on the mountain... God, I couldn't imagine what I was going to do without you. At the idea of it, I felt like the sun and the moon and the stars had left the sky. The lakes were drained dry. I'm in love with you, Angelica."

"I thought... I thought..."

"You should think I'm an idiot because I've resisted you for too damn long."

"You didn't want to love me," she said, the slightest tremble in her voice.

"Because I thought I would lose you," he said. "But now I've figured out that I just need to hold on—and then you'll hold me back."

Her whole body trembled now. "You trust me."

"And you trust me."

In a flurry of movement, she stepped near and pressed her face into the cup of his shoulder, where she fit as if she were made for him. "I wasn't giving up on you," she told his flannel shirt.

Sliding his arms beneath her perfect ass, he boosted her up so they were face-to-face. "I promise to never make you contemplate the thought again."

She gave him that sunny smile of hers and it struck him like a blow, shattering any remnants of the guard around her heart. He could feel the organ pounding in his chest, sending the blood rushing through his body, bringing him to life, filling him with elation and a new vision of the future.

Making him soft, but he didn't worry about that, because it made him worthy of this warm, beautiful woman and the happiness they'd find together.

Who was the cockeyed optimist in the Walker family now?

"Angelica Walker," he whispered. "What do you think about that…and what do you think about a Vegas wedding?"

There were tears in her eyes. "Not in sweatpants."

"But this afternoon."

"Really?" She swallowed. "How will we get your family—"

"Just you and me," he said. "We can do something else later, if you'd like."

"They're going to be mad," she warned.

"No, they won't," he said. "Because they'll be so happy we all get you."

ANGELICA WAS UNSURPRISED that her new husband had underestimated the peevishness of Poppy, Shay and Mac. But he shrugged off their complaints and she attempted to distract them with their other big news: upon leaving the wedding chapel at their chosen casino, he'd stuck a dollar in a slot machine—*I'm feeling lucky*, he'd said—and won nearly one hundred thousand dollars.

He'd already promised to use it to grow his business. And she thought someday that business—with her help on the organizational side—might build his dream lodge on the Walker mountain.

But they both knew there was no greater fortune than the two of them cuddled in bed at his cabin. A harvest moon was shining through the bedroom window, as fat and happy as her heart.

"I have a place," she whispered, not sure he was still awake.

His arm tightened on her, proving he was. "Always." He pressed a kiss to the top of her head. "On our mountain. In our family. By my side."

* * * * *

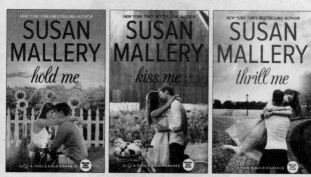

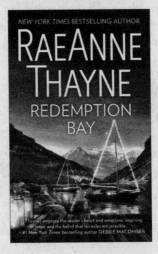

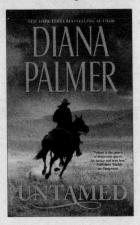

Come to a small town in Oregon with
USA TODAY bestselling author

MAISEY YATES

for her sexy, heartfelt new
Copper Ridge series!

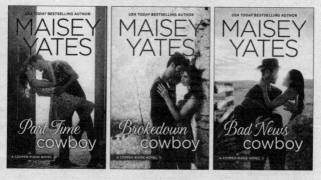

Available now!   Available now!   Coming July 28, 2015!

Can these cowboys find the love they
didn't know they needed?

Pick up your copies today!

www.HQNBooks.com

CHRISTIE RIDGWAY

77832	MAKE ME LOSE CONTROL	___ $7.99 U.S.	___ $8.99 CAN.
77740	BEACH HOUSE NO. 9	___ $7.99 U.S.	___ $9.99 CAN.
77715	THE LOVE SHACK	___ $7.99 U.S.	___ $9.99 CAN.

(limited quantities available)

TOTAL AMOUNT	$ _____
POSTAGE & HANDLING	$ _____
($1.00 FOR 1 BOOK, 50¢ for each additional)	
APPLICABLE TAXES*	$ _____
TOTAL PAYABLE	$ _____

(check or money order—please do not send cash)

To order, complete this form and send it, along with a check or money order for the total above, payable to HQN Books, to: **In the U.S.:** 3010 Walden Avenue, P.O. Box 9077, Buffalo, NY 14269-9077; **In Canada:** P.O. Box 636, Fort Erie, Ontario, L2A 5X3.

Name: _____
Address: _____ City: _____
State/Prov.: _____ Zip/Postal Code: _____
Account Number (if applicable): _____

075 CSAS

*New York residents remit applicable sales taxes.
*Canadian residents remit applicable GST and provincial taxes.

HQN™

www.HQNBooks.com

PHCR0715BLR